About the auth

The author was born in Scotland and, after serving in the Army, embarked on a career in industry.

He has worked in several different sectors in senior roles and was latterly CEO of a large international data capture company.

He retired for the first time in 1995 to take on a consultancy designed to help new businesses become established.

In 2018, he finally retired from business life to become a full-time author.

John lives in Scotland and Portugal with his wife and they have two grown-up sons.

THE DISCIPLES
The third DCI Burt murder mystery

JOHN REID

THE DISCIPLES
The third DCI Burt murder mystery

Vanguard Press

A CIP catalogue record for this title is
available from the British Library.

ISBN 978 1 80016 315 7

*Vanguard Press is an imprint of
Pegasus Elliot MacKenzie Publishers Ltd*
www.pegasuspublishers.com

First Published in 2021

**Vanguard Press
Sheraton House, Castle Park
Cambridge England**

Printed & Bound in Great Britain

Dedication

To my wife, for her unflinching support, and also to Guy, Jim and
Mike for their ongoing encouragement.

Also from the DCI Steve Burt Series by John Reid

The Forgotten Gun
The Auction

Coming soon in the same series

The Watchers
The Voice
The Norwich Murders
The Abduction

Acknowledgements

Thanks go to our son Richard for allowing us to use his marketing and technical skills and also to our son and daughter-in-law David and Rosie for their continued help in assisting us navigate our way through the high-tech world we find ourselves in.

Chapter One

Mr Percy Wilson was taking his dog Tigger for his early morning walk, on the 24th of January. Percy liked to walk early come hail or shine. Tigger was equally enthusiastic. He was a multi-cross with more terrier than any other breed and found more things to investigate and dig up in the mornings. His afternoon and evening walks weren't as interesting. There were more people around later in the day and he couldn't explore as he could in the morning.

As was his usual practice, Percy's route took him into Green Forest Country Park just outside Southend. He'd been taking Tigger on the same route through the park for years. This particular morning Tigger was as happy as Percy had seen him. He was frolicking about retrieving the ball Percy constantly threw for him.

Percy gave the ball a great heave and Tigger set off. But instead of collecting the ball, he carried on running deep into the woods. Percy knew Tigger was obedient and when he failed to return, despite Percy's calls, the dog owner reluctantly and with some annoyance set of after his dog. Percy usually walked on the footpaths in the park and didn't normally wear heavy shoes. He could see the path Tigger had taken was muddy, and he feared Mrs Wilson wouldn't be happy if he spread mud all over the kitchen floor on his return.

"Tigger," the dog's owner shouted. "Come here you silly dog. Where are you?"

Percy could hear his dog barking so had an idea of the direction to walk in. He followed the sound until he saw Tigger standing over what looked like a dress shop mannequin abandoned on the ground. The dog was clearly excited and took no notice of his master's instruction to come away. The dog's barking sounded extra loud within the confines of the wood. Percy removed the dog's lead from his pocket, intending to re-attach it to his collar as a means of getting Tigger away from his latest plaything.

As Percy approached, holding the clip end of the lead in his hand, he suddenly stopped, horrified to see the manikin wasn't a manikin but what looked like a young girl, and she appeared to be dead. Percy swiftly attached Tigger's lead and took a look at the body. He concluded she must be dead but on closer examination saw that her clothes had been cut open to her waist and what looked like intestine was showing from a deep cut to her chest and stomach.

Percy dragged Tigger away and was violently sick yards from the body. It took him several minutes to gather himself and assemble his now jumbled thoughts into some order. He'd have to call the police but didn't have a mobile phone. He'd often said at his late stage in life he didn't need to be contacted everywhere he went. Today he wished he'd listened to his wife and bought one. Instead, he ran as quickly as his seventy-five-year-old legs would carry him back, to his house with Tigger running ahead on the full extent of his lead.

Mr Wilson didn't say anything to Mrs Wilson when he opened the back door of their bungalow and ignoring the mud on his shoes went straight for their telephone in the hallway.

He dialled 999. "I want to report a murder."

Chapter Two

Richard Meadows finished his night shift at Stanstead airport where he worked as an aircraft engineer. It was the 14th of February. He liked working nights and particularly enjoyed his bicycle ride home. He was approaching his thirty-fourth birthday and told himself the five-mile bike ride to his home in Great Dunmow was good exercise and kept him fit. His wife, looking at his shape, disagreed. She constantly told him cycling was a good way to keep fit, but not if you drank as much beer as he did.

Richard followed the same route home each morning taking the old backroads so as to avoid the new dual carriageways that had sprung up with Stanstead Airport's development.

On this particular morning with the sun just beginning to show he detoured through Dunmow common. It was a flat piece of common land with a pretty duck pond at its centre. When asked later why he took this route he had no answer other than it was a nice morning.

There was a path through the common and Richard stuck to this. Towards the end of the path just as it exited the common, he spotted a bundle lying beside a park bench. He thought to himself, *Must be a homeless guy*. Richard was a good neighbour when his wife allowed him to be, so he stopped and laid his bike on the ground. He approached the bundle while pulling out his wallet intent on giving this unfortunate person money for a hot meal.

As he drew nearer, he noticed the bundle was smaller than he might have expected and that the rough sleeper was a woman with long blond hair. He was unsure whether he should offer money and was about to turn back when he noticed a bare foot sticking out from under the cover. He looked at the cover in more detail and realised it was a multi-coloured cover from a bed. He lifted the corner nearest the foot and saw the other foot but neither foot had any shoes. He took a pace to the other end where the blonde hair was showing and lifted the corner. It was clearly a young girl, and, at first glance, she didn't appear to be alive.

Richard pulled the cover further back and saw it was indeed a girl. He staggered back at what he saw next. His meals over the last twelve hours rushed up to his throat and he threw up. He almost fainted at the sight of the young girl's stomach. He was no doctor but even he could see someone had opened her up and left her entrails hanging out. He sat down a few yards from the body gasping for air. His thoughts were scrambled and almost on pure instinct he reached for his mobile phone, dialled 999 and reported finding a body.

This was exactly fourteen days after Mr Percy Wilson and Tigger had discovered their corpse.

Chapter Three

DCI Steve Burt was back in his office on Monday morning preparing for the bi-weekly meeting of senior officers who met to review their cases. Steve, as head of a unique unit known as Special Resolutions, didn't have much to contribute to the upcoming meeting. His unit had come into being almost by accident, and its task was to take over serious criminal cases other heads of department were finding difficult to solve.

Since its inception, the Special Resolutions unit led by Steve had solved several high profile and difficult cases and he had won the praise of senior officers within New Scotland Yard. Because each case taken on by Steve had tended to be unusual and complicated, he only had a small team of two detectives working permanently with him. What made Special Resolutions so special was their ability to have selected officers seconded to them for the duration of each investigation.

The first of the permanent staff, Detective Inspector Abul Ishmal, had been with Steve since the inception of the unit. The second was a young Detective Constable called Andy Miller. Andy had been assigned to Steve as his admin assistant around eight months ago, mainly due to the fact he appeared at first glance to be somewhat useless, and no one knew what to do with him. Since joining Steve's unit Andy had grown into an intelligent, innovative and dedicated officer. Following his involvement in Steve's last big case and his performance with the task force Andy was now very much in demand by other departments and destined for greater things.

A voice from the outer office called out. "Steve, I'm off to get coffee. Do you want one?" This was Andy.

"Yeah, how much do I owe the kitty?"

There was no answer from Andy who had left, but DI Ishmal chirped up.

"Whatever it is, it's not enough the way you go through the stuff."

The DI was obviously at his desk in the outer office. Abul Ishmal was now a firm friend of the DCI's and had been given the nickname of The Cap by Steve when they first met. The name had stuck.

They carried on a shouted conversation through the open door. "What're you up to Cap?"

"I'm going through statements getting ready for the Hackney murder trial. The CPS want everything buttoned up before we get into it, remember, you're on the witness list."

"I wasn't forgetting but I'm waiting for a date."

"The trial starts in exactly two weeks, hold on." There was silence from The Cap while he looked up the date. "Yes, I was right, it starts on Monday 22nd March."

At that point, Andy arrived with the coffee. "What've you got on Andy?"

"Just cleaning up the files on the American in the Thames case. The new Commander's a stickler for correct paper and procedures. Because that investigation was, let's say, below the radar." Andy looked quizzically at Steve. "He's asking for retrospective reports so he can have a complete file. It's taking time but I've got the data. I only have to sort it." Andy made to leave as he sipped his coffee. "Oh, by the way, Steve, thanks for the wedding invitation." Andy started to blush as he always did where women were involved. "It said, and partner. I'm thinking of asking Samantha Burns. Do you think she'd come?"

Samantha Burns was a profiler the team had used on their last major case. It was obvious from the start that Andy and Sam, as she insisted on being called, were similar personalities, both shy and not too worldly-wise outside of work.

"All you can do is ask Andy, but I'm sure she'll come. After all, you're asking her," Steve smiled.

The Cap who'd been listening called out. "If you don't, I'll make sure Barry from the Murder Squad does."

Andy laughed and gave an embarrassed "Oh! You!"

Steve, a confirmed bachelor, had met his fiancée, Dr Alison Mills while working on the first Special Resolutions case. He'd dated her for ten months before proposing. She'd become involved in his last big case when a heavy called Micky Russ had been hired to disfigure her as a way of getting to Steve. Fortunately, as the result of a tip-off, Steve was able to intercept Micky before he could carry out his orders. Even after all that Alison was still going to marry him in a few months.

"Right, Andy, anything I need to know before I go upstairs?"

"No boss, but it would be nice if you brought us back a case."

The Cap spoke. "Yeah, but one that doesn't require any paperwork." He pulled a sorry face. "Please!"

Steve left the two detectives behind him. He knew he was lucky to have them.

***

Steve entered the office of the new Commander (Crime). Other senior officers were standing around, coffee in hand, waiting for the meeting to start. Steve helped himself to a coffee and nodded to his colleagues as he looked for a friendly face. He spotted Superintendent Alfie Brooks; someone he'd worked for in the past. Alfie was from the north of England and had been a police officer all his life. He was due to retire and had been put on admin duties until he reached his end date. "Hello, Steve, these things don't get any smaller, do they?" Alfie was referring to the number of people expected to attend these meetings. "When Sheila was in charge it was all business and solving crime. Now it's all designed to make our new Commander look important, and for us all to get a lecture on budgets. Bugger catching bad guys."

Alfie was referring to the previous Commander, Sheila Southgate. She'd recently retired and had been replaced by Commander Anthony Bowles.

Steve smiled at Alfie. He liked the old policeman and had enjoyed his company on many stakeouts when they worked together. Alfie had been Steve's immediate boss when Steve was in Serious Crimes. "I know what you mean Alfie. Sheila ran a tight ship. I think the jury's out on this new guy."

The old detective looked menacingly at Steve. "My jury's in. He's a waste of space, bloody graduate entry. He's still wet behind the ears and he knows nothing about real policing. Bar charts and sucking up to those above him, that's all he's good for!"

17

Alfie realised he was sounding off. He drank some coffee and smiled at his old colleague. "Sorry Steve, age is getting to me, but take a tip from an old warrior, watch this fellow. He'll not be there when you need somebody looking after your back." Alfie winked.

"Thanks, Alfie, I'll remember that."

***

Commander Anthony Bowles entered his own office with a flourish. He was accompanied by a civilian clerk. He'd had Sheila Southgate's old office re-configured such that the area for an informal chat had gone. Most of the furniture had been removed leaving the office feeling more like a conference room than an office. A new twelve-seater table had been installed but Sheila's desk was still in use.

"Good morning gentlemen and ladies, please be seated. I'm sorry I'm a little late, but I was called urgently to the Assistant Commissioner's office."

Everyone took a seat as ordered. There had been a few changes in personnel over the past few months. Apart from the old Commander retiring, the second in command of the murder squad, Superintendent Frank Dobson, had resigned due in part to Steve's last major case. Dobson had been replaced by a Superintendent Peter Whitely. Steve had met him a few times at these meetings and he seemed competent enough, but Steve had never worked with him.

The Commander brought the meeting to order. "Let's get started, we've a lot to get through today."

Steve looked at the minutes of the last meeting and the agenda for today. Obviously, the new commander's idea of a lot wasn't the same as Steve's. He saw a fifteen-minute meeting at best. He knew he'd nothing to contribute as his caseload was almost nil. Two hours later they were still at it. Steve and Alfie had exchanged glances throughout the meeting with Alfie mouthing "I told you so".

Eventually, the Commander brought the marathon self-promoting meeting to an end. "Well, I think that's been a very useful meeting. Please remember to update your personal notes and I want your crime stats by the 16th. Thank you all for coming. I'll see everyone in two weeks."

The gathering of detectives gave a collective sigh of relief and started to disperse. The Commander went to his desk and called out "DCI Burt, can you stay, please? I need a word."

Once everyone had gone Steve resumed his seat at the large table. "How are things going in Special Resolutions?" the Commander asked.

Steve was a bit cautious. Alfie's words were still in his mind. "Fine sir."

"Yes, I've heard good reports about the successes you've had with a small team. I've reviewed your remit with Chief Superintendent Charles of Human Resources. It appears you're the first point on any outside request for assistance."

Steve knew this, but also knew it had never been necessary, as all requests from regional forces were usually for specialist officers. The DCI was beginning to feel uncomfortable.

"You've a light caseload at the moment judging from our meeting." This was a statement that didn't require an answer.

"I'm thinking of putting you out to assist a regional force."

Steve sat still but looked directly at the Commander, leaving the senior officer in no doubt the DCI wasn't happy. Commander Bowles didn't seem to notice but carried on.

"Criminal Intelligence has picked up similarities between two murders in Essex. I've spoken to the National Crime Agency to alert them to this." The Commander paused so Steve would be impressed by this decision. He wasn't. He thought everything he'd heard about this excuse for a senior officer was true so said nothing.

"Of course, the NCA was delighted by my intervention and agreed we could offer assistance to Essex with their blessing."

This popinjay was only in his late thirties and, according to the stories, hadn't solved a case in his career. Again, Alfie's words haunted Steve.

"It's nice to think an organisation such as the NCA aren't too proud to listen to us in the Met, isn't it?"

"I suppose so sir." Steve waited to see where this was going.

"You see DCI Burt, part of our job is to keep flying the flag for policing. If we can help our colleagues in the provinces and be seen to solve crimes maybe they couldn't, then we all look good, don't you think?"

"I've no opinion one way or the other sir."

This remark appeared to penetrate the veneer surrounding the Commander. He almost looked shocked. He'd found someone who didn't see the world as he did. His world was all about self-advancement. He didn't understand why this extremely successful policeman sitting with him didn't see things as he did.

The Commander became all business. "Very well, as I said, I've secured the blessing of the NCA to assist Essex whether they like it or not. I need you to solve these murders and make sure the credit is given where it's due." The Commander straightened up.

"You're to see a Superintendent Taylor tomorrow at ten a.m. at Force Headquarters in Chelmsford. You may experience some resistance, but you are acting under my authority and that of the National Crime Agency. Is that clear?" Without waiting for a reply, the senior man continued. "We cannot have our Intelligence Unit collating data simply to have it ignored. These cases are more than six weeks old. If you can crack them then it will be a real feather in our caps."

"Yes, sir, but why are we so interested in a couple of murders in Essex?"

"Ah, yes. The Intelligence Unit thinks they're connected, but apparently, the Essex force doesn't. You've nothing on at the moment and by taking such an initiative it'll show our more senior colleagues that we don't lack initiative."

Both men looked at each other across the table.

"This is one of the roles your department was set up for DCI Burt. You'll be acting with full authority. Carry out your investigation as you would normally and get a quick result. Is that clear?"

"Crystal, sir."

"One final point. We must all be conscious of our expenditure. We're under budgetary pressure all the time. An operation like this should be viewed as an opportunity to divest ourselves of some costs. I'll have accounting set up a separate cost code for you so you can charge all your costs to Essex for the duration of the investigation." The Commander looked smug and very pleased with himself.

Steve rose and left. The Commander remained seated at his table with a broad grin on his face. If this detective could solve the case, then the Commander would have put his stake in the ground for future promotion.

***

Andy and The Cap were still working but the intensity had dropped. Each looked at Steve in anticipation. He returned their look and shrugged his shoulders. "Yes, we've got another case but you're not going to like it. You'd better come in, but first…"

"Yes, I know, Andy, get three coffees." The DC left, smiling.

When Andy had returned, and a few sips of coffee had been taken, Steve briefed his team on his discussion with Commander Bowles. "It seems Essex force has two murders that the National Intelligence Unit think may be linked. Normally the National Crime Agency would be first to take a look, but our glorious leader asked that we get the job. So, first thing tomorrow, Cap, you and I are off to Essex, Chelmsford to be exact. We're to meet a Superintendent Taylor. We're being forced on them, so I can't see too much co-operation coming our way, but let's see.

Andy, until we've scoped out the situation you stay here. I'll get everything sent to you, and if we can work that way, I'd prefer it with you being home-based. But if the locals are hostile you might have to camp out in Chelmsford Headquarters for the duration. Any questions?"

Andy spoke up. "Do we know anything about the cases?"

"No. We're going in blind, but it seems two females were murdered and mutilated and killed two weeks apart. That's it, so be ready to hopefully receive all the usual tomorrow." Steve paused. "If we're lucky."

The Cap, with a grin, asked the most obvious question. "Are we on expenses?"

"Trust you, Abul, yes, but our leader's getting a special code from accounts. He wants everything coded to this new number so it can be re-charged to Essex. Andy, watch out for it today or tomorrow, and for God's sake, make sure everything's charged correctly. Commander Bowles seems a man for his budgets."

All three laughed. "Andy, can you book The Cap and me into a hotel for tomorrow night. I'm hoping we can commute, but better show willing the first day."

The meeting broke up. Arrangements were made for the next morning and the excitement level subsided.

DCI Burt sat at his desk wondering where this case would lead him and why the new Commander was so keen to be seen to be investigating it.

Chapter Four

The journey to Chelmsford proved to be relatively straightforward. The M25 had been kind to them and even the A12 hadn't caused too many problems. Consequently, they arrived before their appointed hour.

After the usual security vetting and handing out of plastic wallets to hang around necks, both detectives were shown to the office of Superintendent Kenneth Taylor, Head of Essex CID's murder unit. The Superintendent was sitting at his desk with his jacket off and his sleeves rolled up. Steve thought he was about sixty years of age. He was a big man almost a typical old-time copper. His hair was thinning, his face was flushed, and he had a large, red-veined nose, typical of a heavy drinker.

He looked up as the two Metropolitan police detectives were ushered in. The WPC who showed them in was just leaving when the Superintendent bawled. "Tell Jenny I need her now!"

Steve placed the accent as North East. Without looking up Superintendent Taylor said "You'd better have a seat at the table. I suppose you'll be expecting a cup of tea." Not waiting for a reply, he lifted his phone and more or less bawled "Tea for four, and hurry, I've got an appointment in half an hour!"

Steve listened to this piece of information with alarm. He and The Cap were here to be briefed by this man, and it would take more than half an hour. The DCI decided to play it down and not be confrontational right from the start.

"Thank you for seeing us, sir. We're here—"

"I know bloody well why you're here. Those computers in London think I'm not up to my job. That's why you're here." They'd got off to a good start. Steve tried again. "Well, sir it's not quite like—"

"Don't tell me what it's like. I've seen it before, high profile double murder. Some computer spits it out as a bit juicy and straight away a couple of suits from the Met arrive to take over and use the local force to do all the work while they take all the glory. I've been around too long not to know why you're here, so please don't soft soap me Detective Chief Inspector Burt."

The door to the Superintendent's office opened and a woman entered without knocking. She stood waiting.

"Ah! Jenny, sit down, my dear. These are the two suits from the Met come to show us how to solve a murder. Gents, this is Detective Sergeant Jenny Fuller. Jenny will be your liaison and contact while you're here. Anything you need Jenny will get for you but anything hooky she'll report to me. Just so we know where we stand. Are we clear?" Before Steve could reply, Kenneth Taylor bawled out to no one in particular. "Where's the bloody tea?"

With an apologetic look on her face, Jenny left the room and returned with a tray containing a teapot, cups and biscuits.

"Right Mr Met, let's hear it, how are you going to show us how to do our jobs?"

The four drank their tea and The Cap finished the biscuits.

"Well sir, I don't want to get off on the wrong foot, but you're wrong about our motives for being here. We know you and your team are more than capable. It's just that our Commander together with the NCA thought we might be able to lend assistance—"

"Yeah right, anything you say." The Superintendent was very flushed and the veins on his face were standing out like rivers. "Look, you're here now and I can't do a thing about it. As far as I'm concerned, both bloody murders are yours to solve. Don't expect too much local help. If Jenny here can't help, then that's it."

He stood and put on his jacket. "I'm off to the hospital, Jen, anything comes in, cover for me. I'll see you tomorrow." He stopped to examine the two London detectives. "Good luck boys, I'm glad it's you and not me." With a chuckle and without shaking hands he left.

The three detectives sat at the table looking at each other. Jenny, as the host, broke the silence. "I'm DS Jenny Fuller." She reached out to shake hands. Steve and The Cap introduced themselves.

Jenny carried on. "Don't mind Ken, his bark's worse than his bite. He's not a well man and knows if he ever sees the Force doctor he'll be out on a medical. Something to do with his heart. I think that's why he's gone to the hospital. I think he needs a bypass, but he keeps things bottled up."

"Thanks for explaining. Now Jenny, what can you tell us about the murders?"

All three sat back while Jenny told the story. "Not much to tell. Victim one. Found six weeks ago by a man walking his dog in Green Forrest Country Park early in the morning. She was in the woods and it was the dog that found her. We've no forensics, no identity and no clues. She hadn't been sexually assaulted but had been mutilated. The killer slit her open and let her innards seep out. All we've got is that she was probably knocked unconscious and transported to the woods. Whoever opened her up did it while she was in the woods and still alive.

The Cap looked shocked. "We must be looking for a real nut job."

"Maybe, our pathologist estimates the first victim was no more than fifteen years old."

Steve had been listening. "Anything from missing persons?"

"No. No one answering her description has been reported missing."

"What about the second one?"

"More or less the same except she was found at the opposite end of the county at Dunmow Common. An engineer going home from his night shift at Stanstead Airport saw what he thought was a rough sleeper. The body was covered in an old bed cover. He was going to give the guy a few quid but when he lifted the cover... well, you can imagine." Jenny stopped to gauge the reaction of the other two detectives. "It's exactly the same as the first. Young girl around seventeen years old, no identity, no sexual involvement and again cut open on-site while still alive. The only saving grace is, that according to our pathologist, both girls would have been unconscious from the blow to their heads so the cutting would have been painless. Before you ask, no, there are no missing person's reports for the second victim."

"And you say this was six weeks ago?"

"No, the first one was, but the second one was four weeks ago."

"Right DS Fuller, it looks like we have some work to do. I take it your Superintendent won't mind if we use you to show us around."

Jenny smiled. "Ken told me to give you every assistance so yes, I'm yours to command, within reason." She smiled a shy lovely smile that lit up her face. Steve thought there was more to DS Jenny Fuller than was obvious. She carried herself with a self-assurance that was rare in a detective sergeant. She was obviously from an African background but listening to her Essex speech pattern she had been born and bred in the UK. Steve thought she was a very impressive policewoman.

They adjourned to the canteen for a quick lunch, and Steve hoped, a decent cup of coffee. Over lunch, they planned their approach to these cases.

Steve was in command. "Jenny, can you get the files over to my office in the Met? I presume they can be sent electronically, and you've got hard copies for us to work with?"

"We're only in Chelmsford sir, not the dark side of the moon."

Steve took the point.

She carried on. "Despite Ken Taylor's not so warm welcome, he's allocated you an office you can use when you're here. I'll have someone put all the files in there."

Steve felt suitably chastised, but it was better to ask. "Yes, of course, thank you. That's the murder files then, plus I want everything the CSIs have got and forensics. I want the full post-mortem reports and the victim's effects in my office at the Met before the close of play today. You'll have to get your exhibits officer to arrange that, so we maintain the chain of evidence. Is that understood?"

"Yes sir." Jenny looked impressed by the decisiveness of this DCI. "If you'll excuse me, I'll get straight on to it."

"Good." Steve produced a business card from his breast pocket. "On the back are the electronic addresses you'll need. Everything goes to DC Andrew Miller at Special Resolutions. Got it?"

Jenny was on her feet. "Got it. I'll be back in about fifteen minutes."

"Thanks, Jenny. Then we'd like to visit both crime scenes."

"No problem. Have you got a hotel for tonight?"

"Not yet but DC Miller's working on it."

Jenny Fuller left the two sitting there. "She's not what I expected Steve. How old do you think she is? Thirty? Forty?"

"Nearer mid-thirties I'd say." Steve wasn't good at guessing women's ages. Especially stunningly good-looking ones.

"Yeah, did you see that ring on her finger? Must have cost a fortune and that jacket and jeans are pure designer. I'd say our Jenny's either got a rich husband or a very wealthy sugar daddy." The Cap loved a mystery.

Steve arched an eyebrow looking at The Cap. "You might find out if you ask her, but I wouldn't."

The Cap was full of fun. "I bet she works out. What height do you think she is? Five-foot nine or thereabouts? And that figure of hers must take some maintaining."

Steve laughed and playfully punched The Cap on the shoulder. "You're a married man and by the look of her she's too much woman for you, and you couldn't afford her anyway, so keep your mind on the job."

Jenny returned and explained where the first crime scene was. Andy had confirmed that he'd booked his colleagues into a hotel in Great Dunmow as it seemed to be nearer to the second crime scene. This was at the other end of the county but not too far from Chelmsford. Steve thought Andy had made a good choice.

Jenny said she'd take her own car if they were to finish in Dunmow. She could leave the detectives there and make her own way home. It seemed like a plan until Steve and The Cap saw the car Jenny was driving. It was a classic Aston Martin DB7 and probably cost more than The Cap's annual salary.

"Don't worry guys, I always stick to the speed limit."

The Cap thought this Jenny was something else. The two-car convoy set off with The Cap driving the Nissan pool car.

DS Jenny Fuller didn't lie. She obeyed all the speed limits, but she didn't say she drove at the maximum speed allowed. The Cap driving the Nissan struggled to keep up, especially on the more minor roads Jenny guided them down.

They parked outside the only gate into Green Forrest Country Park and walked in. The two London detectives noted a large open flat grass area off to the left. They were walking on a wide paved path that separated the grass area from the wooded section on their right. There was nothing special about the place. It was just like any other park.

Jenny explained the geography to help Steve and The Cap get their bearings. As they walked, the path diverted to the left and a rough unofficial path appeared on their right going into the woods. "We go this way."

Jenny guided them onto the rough path and into the woods. They walked about a hundred yards to where the body had been found. There were still a few strands of blue-and-white crime scene tape stuck to some bushes. All three stopped and stared for a few moments almost in respect for the victim.

Steve had the file which he now opened. "Who was first on the scene? It doesn't say in here."

"Apart from the person who called it in a couple of uniforms, I can get their names. They decided it was a case for CID and the duty bloke would have been called."

"It doesn't say any of that in here."

"Sorry sir, it should say. I'll get these files brought up to date." Jenny looked a bit crestfallen. This was a serious lack of protocol. She thought maybe having these two from the Yard wasn't such a bad idea after all.

"If you would please, Jenny. Now this gentleman, Percy Wilson, was walking his dog. The dog ran off and he followed and that's when he found the body. Is that correct?"

"Yes, sir, he said in his statement he found the body around 06.45. He ran home to call us, and his call was timed at 06.57."

"It's a bit muddy here." Steve looked at his shoes which were covered in glutinous brown mud. At that moment Commander Bowles' warning about budgets came to mind and he wondered if the Essex force would stand him a new pair of shoes on expenses.

"Did you get any footprints from around the body?"

"By the time the dog had scratched around, and Mr Wilson had tried to retrieve him, the scene was pretty much compromised. We got a part shoe print that forensics made a cast of. It's with the exhibits but it's not much."

Steve looked around. This was a perfect spot to place a body. If the dog hadn't found it, the corpse could have been there for weeks.

"So, the working theory is our killer struck the victim on the side of the head, brought her here and cut her open. I presume the body wasn't here long so we can assume she was dumped somewhere between say nine p.m. and five a.m. but the pathology will confirm that. After cutting her, the killer leaves her there with no attempt to conceal the body."

"Yes sir, that's what we've got so far."

"And there's only one entry and exit point?"

"Yes."

The DCI turned to The Cap. "What do you think Cap?"

Abul looked into the distance obviously deep in thought. He was searching his memory banks. "I've seen something like this before. It was a drugs case. The gang were using girls as drug mules bringing drugs here, in their stomachs. Usually, a few days after they arrived, they passed the pouches they'd swallowed naturally but every so often it didn't pass. In the case I'm thinking of, the gang killed the girl and cut her open to get the drugs. It's a bit extreme but it might fit."

Steve and DS Fuller looked at Abul. Jenny spoke first. "That's a bit extreme. I know we have a drug problem like everywhere else but to do that for a few packets of smack is a bit desperate."

"You're right, but it happened."

Steve stroked his chin as he'd become prone to do when thinking hard. "So, you think this could be drug-related?"

"It's possible."

"Jenny, has anyone here explored this as a possible motive?"

Jenny could see there had been another failure by her force. Reluctantly, and a bit sheepishly she answered. "No sir, it's not been mentioned."

"We'll deal with that, Jenny. If you don't mind, I'd like to change our schedule. Can we go and see this Percy Wilson now? He clearly lives close by. If we can then we'll look at the second site tomorrow. Does that suit you?"

"Yes sir, no problem." All three detectives looked at their footwear. Only Jenny had changed when they arrived and was wearing rubber boots. No one spoke but Steve and The Cap knew they needed to clean off their shoes before visiting Mr Wilson.

After a stop at a filling station to clean their shoes and have a coffee, the two-car convoy set of for Mr and Mrs Wilson's bungalow, located just outside Southend.

They pulled up outside a neat and typical detached 1930s style bungalow. The architecture could have been drawn by a child. A front door in the middle and two windows on either side. A slanted roof with a dormer window positioned exactly over the front door. There was a neat front lawn and a detached garage off to one side with a paved drive leading to it.

Jenny rang the bell and an elderly man dressed in an oversized cardigan answered. Before anyone could speak, he announced "We don't want any whatever it is." He was about to close the door when The Cap, who was nearest, grabbed the door and said they were police. The elderly gentleman relaxed and allowed The Cap to push the door gently inward. A dog was barking inside the property and the three detectives assumed the old man must be Mr Wilson.

After hurried introductions on the doorstep and flashing of warrant cards, the trio was shown into what Mr Wilson called the front room. Steve was taken back to his parent's house, and his mother insisting the front room was only for best and he wasn't allowed in unless one of his relations or the vicar called. He smiled to himself, nothing changed.

Mrs Wilson appeared drying her hands on a towel. "My goodness, three of you." Looking at her husband she said, "You see, Percy, what you've started, you shouldn't have found that poor girl."

Mrs Wilson seemed to be in charge. The word dragon came to mind but Steve thought that was a bit unkind. After all, he didn't know the woman. She was dressed like any elderly housewife with a floral wrap-around housecoat that didn't button but was tied around her not insignificant waist. The dog still barked outside the room and Steve knew it wouldn't be allowed into this sanctuary of calm.

"Well dear, I couldn't *not* report it."

"But you did and left mud all over my good carpet and the floor. It isn't you who has to clean it up." She looked directly at Steve assuming correctly that he was the senior officer. "I still can't get all the stains out. Can I claim a new carpet from the police? After all, Percy did his duty and because he did, I've got a soiled carpet." Mrs Wilson was a fearsome woman. She appeared to be the same age as her husband but clearly dominated him. Steve felt sorry for the timid-looking man standing in their front room. He understood why Mr Wilson escaped to walk his dog.

Steve saw Mrs Wilson looking at his and The Cap's shoes. Despite their best efforts they didn't look what most people would call clean. A look of disgust passed over Mrs Wilson's face, but she said nothing.

No one was asked to sit. Steve took the initiative and was prepared to suffer Mrs Wilson's wrath. "May we sit down?" Without an answer, Steve sat on a comfortable looking highbacked chair. This opened the way, and everyone sat at once. There were just enough seats.

"Mr Wilson, we're reviewing the murder of the girl you found in Green Forrest Country Park. We've read your statement but wondered if anything else has come to mind?"

Mrs Wilson answered. "No, it hasn't. He's not had a decent night's sleep since he found her, have you, dear?" Without waiting she carried on. "He's been off his food, he's neglected the garden and the dog is down to two walks a day. He's only now getting over it so no, he's not going to remember anything else."

Steve thought this was something from a comedy show. Percy Wilson just sat and let his wife run the conversation.

As diplomatically as he could put it, Steve asked Mrs Wilson not to answer for her husband. "This is a serious murder enquiry and your help is greatly appreciated. Mr Wilson, has anything else come to mind, now you've had time to think about things?"

Out of the corner of his eye, Steve saw Mrs Wilson was about to answer for her husband again. He put his hand up to stop her and gave her one of his best 'don't annoy me' looks.

Percy sat quietly thinking. In a timid voice, he declared "No, I can't get the sight out of my mind, but I told the officers at the time everything I know."

"Did you see anyone during your walk, especially leaving the park?"

"No, it was quiet. It always is at that time of the morning."

"You didn't see anything on the ground beside the body? Your dog didn't pick anything up to play with?"

"No, I'd have noticed, and Tigger usually brings home anything he finds."

"When you're out in the mornings is there anyone around that you see regularly. Someone who might have witnessed something?"

"No, as I said it's always quiet."

All three detectives realised this witness didn't have anything to add to his statement. At the risk of starting Mrs Wilson off again, Steve stood. "Thank you, Mr Wilson. I know it must have been a traumatic experience for you, and we're grateful for your public-spirited assistance." He glanced at Mrs Wilson who had to have the last word.

"Yes well, we've always known where our duty lies, haven't we, Percy."

Percy nodded and the three detectives were escorted to the front door and left.

Out on the pavement standing beside their cars, the three had a quick debrief. They agreed that The Cap's theory about drug mules was worthy of investigation. Steve's team would re-examine all the evidence in the files and he was prepared to bet Andy was now all over it. It was agreed that Jenny would meet Steve and Abul at their hotel tomorrow morning around nine.

As they were entering their cars and as if it were choreographed, all three looked back at the bungalow and shook their heads.

Poor Mr Wilson.

Chapter Five

The pair found their hotel in Great Dunmow thanks to the Nissan's satnav system. Both were tired after their day so opted for a quick dinner in the hotel and an early night. They thought it might give them independently a chance to unscramble their thoughts and hopefully shed some light on the cases in the morning.

Steve phoned his fiancée, Dr Alison Mills. They talked about their wedding plans, where they would honeymoon, and Alison reminded Steve he hadn't yet booked the flights. There seemed so much to organize, and Steve was conscious Alison was doing most of the heavy lifting whilst still running her busy medical practice. They'd decided some time ago that, after they were married, Alison's house would become their family home. Steve still had to list his flat with an estate agent but was reluctant. Selling it would be the end of his independence and although he knew he'd spend the rest of his life with Alison he was still reluctant. After some scolding from his fiancée, he agreed to call an agent before the end of the week.

"Now listen to me, Detective Chief Inspector, like it or not you're coming with me to a function on Friday, black tie, and I've ordered a taxi for seven p.m. from my place."

"Do I have a choice?"

"Absolutely not. It's a dinner I'd not normally go to on my own, but I thought that now I have you, we might step out as a couple. After all, I've been to a few of your get-togethers, but you've never met any of my medical friends. I'm sure you'll enjoy it. You never know there might be the odd pathologist there and you can discuss your gorier cases." Alison knew how to annoy him.

"I wouldn't do that," he said with mock indignation. "OK, but what's so special?"

"A colleague I was at medical school with has just been appointed to the board of the company giving the dinner. It's a big deal for him and he asked me personally to be there. You'll like him, he's a really nice guy."

"Yeah, I'm sure I will." Steve felt something he thought might be jealousy. "What's this big company called?"

"I'm not sure but they pioneered prosthetic limbs and they make artificial knees, hips, that sort of thing. Robbie, that's my friend, he's a surgeon so uses a lot of this company's product. I guess that's why he's been recruited. Say you'll come? It'll be fun and we haven't been out in public yet as a couple."

"How could I say no. I'll make sure to cancel all serious crime in London on Friday night just so I can escort you to the ball." They both laughed and carried on with small talk surrounding their wedding arrangements.

***

Steve and The Cap were finishing breakfast when Jenny arrived. She accepted a cup of coffee and Steve, needless to say, ordered one to keep her company. They reviewed yesterday, but a good night's sleep hadn't taken them any further. Halfway through his coffee Steve's phone rang. It was Andy.

Andy explained he'd received some data from Essex, but he wasn't impressed by how it had been captured nor presented. He was reconfiguring most of the inputs so, as he put it "to get the benefit of future data and make cross-referencing easier."

Steve listened with interest. "Andy, The Cap has a theory that the mutilation of these girls might be drug-related. If they were acting as drug mules, it's possible they were cut open to retrieve the drugs they were carrying. Pull anything you can on this type of action. The Cap says he remembers a case from a few years back. Also, check out known drug gangs operating in this part of Essex. I don't believe newcomers would do anything like this."

"Will do Steve. I've received the effects from both bodies. There's not much but I'll go through it. Any idea on identities yet?"

"No, but we'll work on it. Anything else?"

"No just finishing up the paperwork for the CPS. Remember the Hackney trial starts in less than two weeks. Apart from that, I'm getting on with this new case."

"Good man. We'll be in tomorrow or later this afternoon. See you then." The line went dead.

The same two-car convoy as yesterday set off for Dunmow Common. It was only a few minutes by car. The Cap looked at the ground prepared to put plastic bags over his shoes if the place was muddy, but it wasn't. The Common was just a large field about the size of two football pitches. At its centre was a small man-made duck pond minus any ducks.

Armed with the file the three detectives walked the common until they arrived at the place where the witness Richard Meadows said he saw the body. It was almost at the edge of the grass area and apart from a bush, there was no place the killer could have hidden the body. Steve assumed that was why the corpse had been covered.

"So, we've got the victim laid out here at the edge of the common covered in a bed cover?"

Jenny nodded. "Yes."

"Did you get anything from it?"

"We got a lot of unrelated material but nothing we could tie to any known offenders. We think the killer might have dumped the body, realised it was too exposed and somehow found an old cover to throw over her."

"So, you think it's not related to the killer? Just a convenient find?"

"Looks that way. It was filthy as though it had been outside a long time."

"Our witness found the body at what time?"

"It was called in at 06.34."

"Can we assume the timings of both murders were pretty much the same?"

"I think so."

"Then why? What made our killer hit these girls over the head, move them, only to slit them open, and leave them to be found at more or less the same time? Is it a coincidence or was it planned?"

The Cap and Jenny just stood. They had no answer.

Steve walked around the site but saw nothing that might help.

"Did you do any door to door? The first site was too remote but there are houses around this place."

The Cap had the file and shook his head. Jenny looked embarrassed.

Steve looked at Jenny who in turn looked at the ground. For the second day in a row, her force had been shown wanting in the most basic of police procedure.

"I'm sorry sir, I don't know what to say, except I'll get a team on it now."

Steve saw Jenny was genuinely embarrassed although it wasn't her fault. He let it pass with a "Better late than never."

It was clear they weren't going to learn anything from this crime scene.

Jenny volunteered. "Do you want to talk to the guy who found this victim? He works nights but I called his wife last night and told her we might be round later this morning. She said he'd stay up until noon but then he'd have to go to bed."

She looked at her watch. "It's 10.32 a.m."

Steve looked at this tall very precise detective sergeant with pleasure. She'd brought initiative to this enquiry. Something missing to date. "Thanks, Jenny, yes, let's go. There's nothing for us here."

***

Richard Meadows lived on a small newly built estate just on the edge of Great Dunmow. From the outside, it looked like a pleasant red-brick detached box with a small front garden and an attached single garage. They were welcomed by Mrs Meadows. She seemed a pleasant woman and from the screams coming from inside was obviously a recent mother. She showed the detectives into the living room, asked if they'd like a drink and took an order for three black coffees. She apologised for the baby, explaining it was teething.

"I'll get the coffee and tell Dick you're here. He's having a quick catnap."

With that, she closed the door behind her and was gone. The baby noise stopped within a few seconds of Mrs Meadows leaving.

All three sat on what looked like a new three-piece suite. No one spoke.

Richard Meadows walked in and shook hands with everyone. He introduced himself. "I'm not sure I can help you but please fire away."

Steve remembered yesterday's encounter with Mr and Mrs Wilson and was relieved. This couple was normal.

"Mr Meadows, we're looking into the death of the girl you found a few weeks ago. Is there anything that might have come to mind since you gave your statement?"

"Not really. I keep seeing that poor girl and her guts hanging out. It was horrible. I think I'm still having nightmares. Penny, my wife, says I should have been offered counselling." Steve saw Richard Meadows begin to well up, to the point of crying.

Steve looked over at Jenny. In a quiet voice, he asked if anyone connected to the murders had been counselled.

"I don't know but I don't think so."

This was yet another failure in the investigation. It was standard procedure that anyone involved in violent death was offered counselling.

Mr Meadows was sitting looking on, wiping his eyes, and apologising.

"No need, Mr Meadows, no one should be made to see what you witnessed. DS Fuller here will arrange for you to see someone, if not today, then tomorrow. Are you still working?"

"Yes. I'm on the night shift at the airport."

"Can I suggest you see your doctor and ask him to sign you off from work until our counsellor is happy that you're fit to resume work?"

Mrs Meadows arrived with the coffee but had heard the whole conversation through the serving hatch to the kitchen. "Do as the detective says, Dick, you're not fit to work." She smiled a grateful smile at Steve.

They all sat and drank their coffee. Steve continued but reluctantly. "Did you see anyone on your way through the common?"

"No. It's always quiet but I don't usually go that way."

"Did you see anybody at all, even before the common?"

"No." Mr Meadows was beginning to look sleepy.

"I won't keep you, sir, but did you see anything moving. Car, van, bus. Anything?"

Richard Meadows looked tired, but a sudden flash reached his eyes. He had remembered something. "It might be nothing but there was a van speeding the other way on the Takeley Road. That's the road I take out of the airport. It must have passed me about three miles from the common. It was going well over the speed limit."

"What kind of van?"

"A white transit, and before you ask, I didn't see the driver, nor did I get the registration number." Dick Meadows looked and sounded better. He even smiled.

"Thank you, sir, I bet you watch a lot of TV crime."

Mrs Meadows nodded, relieved to see her husband looking a bit better.

The team left, thanking the couple for their hospitality, and reminding Mr Meadows that Jenny would arrange his counselling sessions.

Outside they decided to return to Chelmsford Headquarters for a debrief and for Steve and The Cap to collect the files.

***

Jenny showed Steve and Abul to their temporary office. True to her word on one of the four desks in the office were several stacks of police files, although none of them looked very thick.

All three sat while Steve summarised. "All we've got as a result of this visit is evidence of shoddy police work and a lack of witness support. Jenny, get onto community support to see if they can fix Mr Wilson up with some counselling. God knows living with Mrs Wilson the poor old bugger probably needs it more than most."

The Cap and Jenny agreed and all three smiled at Steve's comment.

"You've got the issues that need following up and placed in the files, the house to house and so on?" This was directed at Jenny.

"Sir, I know it looks bad, but this isn't like our force. We're pretty much on the ball all the time. I don't know what went wrong but I'll find out and yes, I'll update the files."

"OK, let's say no more. Now, since we got here, we've come up with the drugs angle and a white transit but that's it. Still, it's more than we had yesterday morning. Either of you got anything to add?"

Both detectives shook their heads.

"Right, Jenny, take me to Superintendent Taylor. I just want to say my goodbyes. We'll take this over and any other events that might be connected." Looking at Jenny, Steve carried on. "You're our liaison so anything we get you'll be told about and I expect that to be reciprocated. I don't want any of your gung-ho type CID officers getting involved in this. Make everyone aware this is now a Yard investigation. Can you do that?"

"Yes sir."

"Also, I'll need you at the yard for briefings from time to time and it could be at short notice. Can you give DC Miller at the Yard all your contact numbers in case we have to call you urgently?"

Jenny looked at Steve. With a grin on her face, "I've had men try to get my number before in many different ways but never like this." She was still grinning. "Yes, I'll get them over to him."

"Thanks, let's go see your Super."

***

Superintendent Taylor was at his desk as he had been yesterday. Jenny didn't knock but just walked straight in.

"Ken, the team from London have come to say goodbye."

Steve noted the informality and suspected there was more than a boss-subordinate relationship here.

The Superintendent looked up. "Well, have you solved it?" He had a sarcastic tone to his voice.

Steve stayed calm. "No sir, but I think we've made a little progress."

"Well, bloody good. I only want to see you again when you've got someone charged and behind bars. Only talk with Jenny here. Do not contact any of my officers without my express permission. Is that clear?"

Steve wasn't happy at this outburst and considered pointing out the shortcomings of the investigation so far but decided to leave it. He didn't need this man's permission for anything, and he certainly wasn't working for him.

"Yes sir," he said, adding sarcastically, "Thank you, sir. It's been a pleasure. I'll report when the case is solved."

With that Steve left followed by The Cap. Steve noted Jenny stayed behind.

***

In the car on the way back to London Steve and The Cap discussed things.

"Cap, remember you were drooling over Jenny yesterday and you thought she might have a sugar daddy?"

"Yes."

"Well, I'm not saying Superintendent Taylor is her sugar daddy, but something is going on between them. She calls him Ken in front of us, she walks straight into his office and she's privy to his medical problems. We've got to use her, but let's keep an eye on her until we know she's reliable."

The journey back to New Scotland Yard was slower than they'd hoped. They didn't arrive until after five p.m. Steve said good night to The Cap and headed for his office. He found Andy hard at it, with papers spread over two desks.

"You know Steve if I didn't know better, I'd say there was a conspiracy in these files. They are all over the place and basic procedure's been ignored. It'll take me all night to get things straight and see what's not been done and what's missing."

"Not all night, Andy. Get to a natural break point and call it a night. We'll get an early start tomorrow."

Steve also felt something wasn't right. His new Commander giving him this case. Why? The apparently screwed up investigation deliberate or otherwise and an alluring detective sergeant who seemed unusually close to her Superintendent. There was something niggling him, but the DCI didn't know what.

He tried to put all work matters to the back of his mind as he set off to see Alison for a meal at her place and more wedding planning. He'd also have to call an estate agent tomorrow.

Chapter Six

Steve arrived Thursday morning to find Andy and The Cap already hard at it. Although it was only eight, it was clear the pair had been in for some time. Andy was keying away feverishly on his laptop keyboard while The Cap had the personal effects of the two victims spread across a desk he'd moved to the corner.

Andy looked up as Steve approached. "Sorry Steve, I'm not finished. I need another half an hour or so."

"Andy, I don't expect you to work miracles. I told you last night."

"I know but I don't like not having everything in its proper place. Just give me half an hour."

Steve raised his eyebrows. Andy was his own man and had a unique way of working. Steve was grateful that his DC was as good as he was. He didn't want him to change.

In passing, Steve noted that there was something different about Andy. Gone was the multi-coloured sleeveless sweater. He was wearing a trendy new shirt with what looked like a silk tie. Andy was coming of age.

The Cap stood at the desk and was sifting and recording items as he came to them. "I don't know who these girls are Steve, but they didn't have much. This'll only take a few minutes to go through."

"Right, but don't miss anything."

Steve retreated to his office to think. He had considered a course of action last night and discussed it with Alison. He'd kept his promise to her to keep her involved in his work provided he didn't compromise his cases. She'd agreed with his thoughts but now he was here he was considering the implications.

The DCI made a decision. He left his office. "I'll be back in about half an hour. We'll get started when I get back and let's have three coffees."

Steve went to the seventh floor and the office of Superintendent Alfie Brooks.

He'd known the Superintendent for several years and knew he was an old-style copper. Having renewed their acquaintance at the bi-weekly case review meeting Steve couldn't think of anyone better to approach.

When Steve walked into Alfie's office the old detective was sitting behind his desk drinking coffee and reading the Daily Mail. He saw Steve approach and waved him in at the same time folding his paper and putting it in the top drawer of his desk.

"Well, this is an honour. A visit from a real detective working on real cases." Alfie smiled. He liked Steve and thought he was a first-class officer.

"Sir, can I talk to you in confidence?"

"Not if you stick to sir."

"Sorry, Alfie." Both men looked at each other across Alfie's desk in silence. "Well! Can I?"

Alfie gave a wicked grin. "Of course, you can, I'm all ears."

Steve explained how he'd been given the Essex cases and what he'd found in Essex. He explained The Cap's theory of a drug connection and the relationship between Jenny Fuller and her Superintendent.

"The thing is Alfie, I've a feeling something's not right. This bloke Bowles has set me on a path but I'm not sure why."

Alfie just sat and said nothing.

"I was wondering if you had any contacts in Criminal Intelligence and the National Crime Agency? I'd like to know if Commander Bowles is telling the truth. Did he really get a tip from Intelligence and persuade the NCA to give him the case or is he lying? If he is then why?"

Again, both men sat in silence for several minutes. The DCI took this prolonged period to mean he'd overstepped the mark. After all, telling a senior officer you're worried another even more senior officer is lying is a serious matter. Steve spoke up. "Look Alfie, I know it's asking a lot and you don't owe me, so if it's too much, please just say so, and this conversation never took place."

Alfie smiled a conspiratorial smile. "Steve my boy, I'd be delighted. I know a few old hands that are still actively employed, although the NCA and Intelligence tend to be staffed by bright young things, they still keep a few proper policemen around to keep them right. Leave it with me and I'll get back to you."

With some relief, Steve thanked the Superintendent.

Alfie wasn't finished. "I've been checking up on our new Commander Anthony Bowles. Now what I'm going to tell you is between us, OK?"

"Yes of course." Steve was all ears.

"I've had a peek at his personnel file." Alfie saw Steve was about to question him, but he held up a hand to stop Steve. "I know, all highly improper, but I'm only telling you. Someone I know in HR left it on her desk while I just happened to be in the room. All I did was take a quick look." Alfie drank the rest of his coffee. Steve realised he'd not had a caffeine boost for some time.

"Anyway, our man joined straight from some second-rate university. He spent six months on the beat in uniform as a constable before transferring to planning. A year later he was a sergeant and transferred to admin. He went on an Inspector's course and was promoted as soon as he finished the course, but still in admin. About four years later, he transferred back to planning as a Superintendent. Then on to Chief Super in Crime Liaison before becoming your supreme leader." Alfie sat back looking at Steve.

"So, he's never solved a crime in his career?"

"Correct, but it gets more interesting. His annual reports say he's ambitious, efficient but not a team player. Various people he's worked for describe him as always trying to look good and please senior officers. One even said he only told senior officers what they wanted to hear, and it was fortunate he'd never had command in the field."

"And all this is on his record and he still got the Commander's job?"

"Ah, well, there you have it. You won't know this, but there's a form HRC 667. It allows senior officers, when doing their annual assessments of their subordinates, to record what they really think of them, but their 667 comments don't go on the official record. The 667s are at the back of the file and removed if anybody wants to see the file." Alfie had a smug expression on his face.

"You must have had a long little peek to get all that."

Alfie became serious. "Look, Steve, there's more, but it's all rumour. This guy Bowles is only out for himself, he's political. That means he's likely to get involved in things he shouldn't. He'll attend any function with any kind of people if he thinks it'll help his career or get his picture in the papers. He's the kind of ambitious idiot who's likely to stumble into corrupt situations. Maybe he already has but all I can tell you is beware of him. He's dangerous, not only to himself but to you."

"Well, you have been busy. Thanks for the heads-up, Alfie. You've given me plenty to think about."

"Yes, be careful. I'll see what I can do about how you got these cases and let you know. It might take a few days."

Steve left Superintendent Alfie Brooks office with his mind spinning. He needed his coffee to help sort out his thought processes going forward. He wondered what he was getting himself involved in.

***

Back in his office Andy and The Cap had obviously finished their immediate tasks. Both looked smug, so Steve knew they'd come up with something. He was still thinking about his meeting with Alfie Brooks and needed some discretionary thinking time.

"From the look of you two, you've obviously got something, but give me five minutes and then we'll start. Is the coffee on my desk?"

The Cap who knew the signs when Steve was concerned simply said it was.

Ten minutes later Steve called his colleagues in. "Right Andy, let's not get carried away before we start, so whatever you two have, can we introduce it at the right time? That way we'll not miss anything."

"Yes, fine by me."

"From the top then Andy, the floor's yours."

Andy enjoyed these moments in the spotlight, although he knew he would feel he'd let Steve down if he didn't have something new for them to discuss.

"We know the first Jane Doe was found six weeks ago and the second four weeks ago. To date, we've no ID and both killings were identical, leading us to believe they were murdered by the same person.

I've gone through the files and re-loaded them into our system. The electronic files were as much of a mess as the hard copies." Andy wasn't really annoyed. He loved this work.

"I've had an e-mail from a DS Fuller at Chelmsford. She's given me the names and numbers of the two uniforms first on the scene at Southend, plus the first CID bloke. That at least completed the first page." Andy typed a few keys on his laptop.

"On the second case, there's no house to house. I googled the scene and there are at least thirty properties within a quarter of a mile of the scene. This DS Fuller says she's arranged for it to be done now, but it's a bit late." Andy sat back.

"Now we have the baseline set let's see what we've got." Steve was keen to move things on.

"I input the post-mortem results and the pathologist suggested in both cases death probably occurred within an hour of the bodies being discovered. There's something about the pathology I don't like but we'll come back to that if that's OK?"

Steve nodded.

"The first murder first. The park only has one entrance, and the same exit. I got to thinking it's a bit remote, so the killer had to have transport to drop the body off and he had to go in the only entrance. But this entrance is not for cars, so he'd have to park and carry the corpse." Andy paused to allow his logic to sink in.

"I got onto Traffic's, road surveillance unit. They sent me the location of their CCTV cameras on the roads around the park, especially on the road past the entrance. I called up the images and there on my laptop." Andy pointed to his machine with something resembling pride.

"The witness reported finding the victim at more or less six a.m. and the pathologist thought death had occurred about an hour earlier." Andy was beginning to sound confident. He started hitting keys.

"No cameras are pointing at the entrance, but there's one hundred yards to the north and another fifty yards to the south. They're pointing in different directions. I started with the northerly one and looked between four and six a.m. There wasn't much on the road, so it was quick to get through it. The only vehicle to pass the camera was a white Ford transit van."

Steve looked at The Cap. This was getting interesting.

Andy continued. "The time stamp said 04.22. I reasoned if it passed the northerly camera, it must pass the southerly one. It did. At 04.51. There are only a hundred and fifty yards between these cameras so where was the van for the missing twenty-nine minutes?"

Andy turned his laptop for his colleagues to see and ran the film.

"So, we have a white van in the vicinity at the right time and twenty-nine minutes unaccounted for. I don't suppose you got the reg number or an image of the driver?"

"Sorry boss."

"Never mind Andy. That's good work."

"Should I carry on Steve?"

"Oh! Yeah," Steve was lost in thought but came to when Andy started up again.

"The second victim's a carbon copy of the first. Apart from the missed house to house, the same mistakes were made on the front sheet of the file. I called DS Fuller and she sent over the missing details. The location of the body on the common is better for us. It's more populated and so more cameras but of course, none directly onto the dump site." Andy looked disappointed.

"The witness gave us his route, so I backtracked using the CCTV images and got him. He's telling the truth about his route and times. One of the cameras on the main road, Takeley Road I think it's called, shows our witness being passed by a white transit van similar to the one seen in Southend. I tracked it back and picked it up exiting the road that takes you to the common. The image is timed at 05.27. The image on Takeley Road is timed at 05.34. It's the same van."

Steve was back to stroking his chin. "Did you pick the van up anywhere else?"

"Sorry Steve, the CCTV thins out a bit on the secondary roads. That's the last I saw of it. But I have something else." Andy's fingers once again flew over his keyboard and he rotated his laptop to show Steve and The Cap.

"The definition on modern CCTV cameras is fairly good but not at night. But we got lucky. The Takeley road's pretty well lit. It used to be a main road before they expanded Stanstead Airport. I froze the van's image where it was most brightly lit by the streetlamps and enlarged it." With a flourish, Andy rotated his machine and waited. On the screen was, as expected, an image of a white transit van but this one had a gouge out of its side. It had obviously been in an accident and the dent hadn't been fixed.

"I went back over the images from the first scene, but I couldn't get an image that showed that side of the van."

All three detectives sat back and acknowledged yet again Andy's good work.

"Now all we have to do is find a transit van with a bloody great dent in the side somewhere in Essex, but you know, it's a start." Steve was getting into gear. "Andy put out an all-points. Traffic to stop every white transit in and around Stanstead Airport and to hold any driver if the van has this form of damage. It's a long shot. Our man could have driven north and be in Scotland but if it is drug-related, I'd bet he's still local."

"Will do, Steve, now do you want the really good news?"

"There's more?"

"Oh! Yes, Inspector Ishmal will explain."

Abul smiled and tried not to look triumphant. "I was going through the effects of the victims. Essex said they'd already done it, so I didn't expect much, but when you work for a DCI like ours you learn to double-check everything." The Cap looked mockingly at Steve who smiled back at Abul's statement.

"As you know I'm a happily married man and would never think of fondling ladies' underwear but in this case, it paid off. The second victim comes from Romania or she did her shopping there. In her underwear, there's a small label. I took it to International and they confirm the language is Romanian. I'd say our girl's from there."

"Nothing similar on the first victim?"

"Afraid not, but they may be both from the same place."

"Well done, Cap. Right, Andy, let's get fingerprints, DNA and headshot pictures over to the police in Bucharest. We're looking for missing persons or maybe even wanted persons. Ask if there's a drug connection. If we're lucky we might get a name. We'll assume both our girls are Romanian until we're told differently. If you hit a brick wall channel the request through Interpol."

"Right Steve, I'm also thinking maybe we should get in touch with all body repair shops around Stanstead Airport and maybe Southend and ask them to report body repairs to white transit vans."

"Good thinking Andy, let's do that."

The detectives split up and went to their own desks. Steve sat and pondered what had just happened, and in his mind, reviewed events.

Two identical murders, a white transit van and a possible connection to Romania. It wasn't much but added to his feeling of unease as to why he had these cases. The DCI felt they were making progress, but it was slow.

Steve left early to be at his apartment to meet an estate agent. At least Alison might give him a few good conduct points for getting the sale on the way. He wasn't due to see her tonight as she had a late surgery, so the evening ahead was his.

Chapter Seven

Friday morning was bright and sunny, and Steve had made several notes to remind himself to be at Alison's for seven p.m. He knew the function this evening was important to her and he didn't want to be late.

To his surprise when he arrived at the Yard, DS Jenny Fuller was waiting for him in his office. Steve decided to play it friendly and not be seen as suspicious as to why the DS from Essex was here at all.

"Morning Jenny, don't tell me you were only passing and just dropped in?"

"No, not quite sir, I've come to give you a bit of news."

"Oh, yes, it must be important."

"Superintendent Taylor was admitted to hospital last night. It doesn't look like he's coming out."

"I'm sorry to hear that, Jenny. Is it his heart?"

"Yes, but that's only partly why I'm here."

"Go on."

"Ken was a bit suspicious of you and wanted me to keep an eye on things. He knew the investigation into the two deaths hadn't been thorough enough, but didn't see why you'd forced your way in. He checked with the NCA and they knew nothing about you taking over the cases, but your Commander Bowles had phoned him and told him they had. Ken's a good officer despite his bark." Jenny wiped away a small tear that had formed at the corner of her eye.

Steve sat impassively just listening.

"Ken figured you were only obeying orders, and probably were being a good cop, and not involved in what's going on. He told me to get in touch personally and tell you about the NCA and to watch your back."

"What else did he say?" Steve needed to know more.

"Nothing, he passed out and is in a coma at Chelmsford General. He's not expected to recover."

The DCI was shocked into silence. He heard Andy and The Cap outside talking animatedly. They must have something. Steve was debating whether or not he could trust this Essex detective.

"Let's go to the canteen and have a coffee. I'm sure you could use one."

On the way out, Steve introduced DS Jenny Fuller to DC Andy Miller. The Cap said hello and carried on with what he was doing but before the couple left, he called to Steve. "Boss, we need to look at something when you've got a minute."

He cocked his head towards Jenny with a *what's she doing here* look.

"I'll only be half an hour," was all Steve said to The Cap.

***

Sitting at a remote table with their coffees steaming Steve approached the topic most on his mind. "Jenny, I know this isn't the best of times but Abul and I wondered about your relationship with Superintendent Taylor. What we witnessed wasn't your typical detective sergeant and superintendent's working relationship. We were curious."

Jenny looked at Steve with a sad smile. "I suppose from the outside it must have looked odd but Ken's my father."

Steve put his cup down with an unintentional bang. He was stuck for words, but he knew his next comment might be a bit insensitive. "But your background's not from Europe," was all the DCI could think to say without causing Jenny any offence.

Jenny still maintained her sweet sad smile. "You don't have to tiptoe round me, sir. Ken and his wife adopted me after I'd been abandoned by my own parents. As far as I'm concerned, they are my parents. Ken always wanted me to be the first black senior officer in the Essex Force and encouraged me to sit my promotion exams and generally be a good cop." Jenny had a faraway look in her eyes.

"I'm sorry, Jenny, your father meant a lot to you, but how come you're called Fuller? I'm a detective and I don't see a wedding ring."

"I'm sort of married. I took my partner's surname. You've maybe come across him. He's Ian Fuller, Deputy Head of the Crown Prosecution Service."

Steve was impressed. He'd had dealings with Mr Fuller in the past.

"There's something else Ken said. It was a bit rambling but something about trust and bugs and check the office. He was a bit out of it, but it seemed important to him. I'm sorry sir, that's all I've got."

Steve was coming to like this DS and decided he could after all trust her. "You've done enough Jenny. Who do you report to now in Chelmsford?" Steve was thinking ahead.

"I suppose no one until Ken's replacement's appointed. I was seconded officially to him, so I've no immediate line manager."

Steve sat back, thinking and Jenny was slightly taken aback by the amount of time the silence between them lasted.

Then he began again. "Look, we've found out a few things that you'd better know, nothing earth-shattering but progress. We believe a white transit van is involved. We picked it up on CCTV at both scenes and we're asking Traffic to keep an eye out. It has a gouge on the near side that might need repairing so we're looking at body shops. We also believe at least one of the girls is from Romania but again we're waiting for confirmation."

"That's progress. We didn't get any of that, but there's something else, sir."

"If we're working together please, it's Steve when it's just us and the team."

"Fair enough Steve, I was a bit miffed that you pointed out weaknesses in the initial enquiries. You know, no record of who attended, no house to house, that kind of thing. When I was collecting the info to bring the files up to date, and trying to get the house to house organised, the DI in charge, a fellow called Dean Grantham came to see me. He wasn't very pleasant and more or less told me to keep my nose out of his cases. We had a bit of a stand-to, but he left me in no doubt not to be too clever and keep clear. I don't think he knew about your involvement. He said there was no need for a house to house in Dunmow because the body was found too early in the morning." Jenny had a serious look on her face.

"But here's the thing. I spoke to the two DC's from CID who were the first detectives to attend both crime scenes. I was laying it on a bit about bad procedure and screwing up. One of them told me Dean Grantham had told them these cases weren't important. They were only a pair of foreign scrubbers, so they weren't to waste time. Just do the basics and move on."

"You're sure that's what they said?"

Jenny nodded.

"How come your DI Grantham knew they were foreign when we've only just worked it out?"

"I don't like where this might be going, Jenny. You stay safe, that's the first thing. It's probably best if you carry on in Chelmsford, but with a low profile. Say you need time off because of your father if anyone gets too close. I'll get Abul up to Chelmsford on Monday and he'll work with you. Let's keep all this between us just now. I've a feeling there's a bigger picture we're not seeing."

"OK Steve, and if anything happens to Ken, I'll let you know."

The pair walked towards the lift. DS Jenny Fuller turned in the lift to face the door and waved goodbye to the DCI who appeared to be her new boss.

***

Steve stood outside the bank of lifts. He was thinking about Jenny's last statement. Was it possible his office was bugged or was it just the ramblings of a sick old man? He didn't know but he felt uneasy. He stood for a full five minutes considering what to do. He knew nothing about listening devices and didn't know anybody who did. He reasoned that if his office was bugged it must have been done by someone within Scotland Yard. Not a happy thought. Or was he being paranoid? He decided there was only one way to find out.

Steve entered the huge open plan area reserved for Technical Support. These were the computer and high-tech wizards within the Met. Their senior man, an Inspector Harvey, had been very useful in helping to solve the last big case Steve and his team had worked on. He'd liked the Inspector and thought he could trust him. Inspector Harvey was talking to a geeky looking individual who could have been mistaken for Andy Miller, until a few days ago when Andy had suddenly morphed into a normal-looking human being. Steve walked towards the Inspector who dismissed his colleague and approached Steve.

"DCI Burt, not another computer puzzle?"

"Steve smiled. "No nothing like that. Can we go somewhere private?"

Inspector Harvey raised an eyebrow and guided Steve to a desk in a far corner well away from anyone else in the room.

"What do you know about listening devices?"

"Enough to get by. Why, have you got a bug." This was said without humour, but the DCI was glad this Inspector got straight to the point.

"I don't know, and I've no idea how to find out. That's why I'm here, but I need to keep it quiet."

Inspector Harvey looked happy. He hadn't had a real mystery in months, and as luck would have it, he had a new detector tool that he'd been keen to try out. His response was more than Steve could have hoped for.

"Go down to your office and clear out your staff. I'll be down in five minutes and we'll have a look. I don't have to report experimental or training use of the equipment, so your secret's safe."

Steve was amazed and extremely grateful. He didn't even know this helpful Inspector's Christian name.

***

Steve went back to his office and holding his index finger to his lips indicated neither detective should speak. By sign language, he ushered them out into the hallway and in a low whisper "We may have a bug." Both his colleagues looked at him and The Cap laughed. "Have you been on the weed without telling us?"

"No, but I might be if you don't stop buggering about." Steve grinned at the pair. "Listen, this may be serious. Just don't talk until the office is swept. Go and have a coffee if you want. The Inspector from Technical Services is coming to have a look." Just as Steve finished Inspector Harvey arrived.

In his hand was a small machine not unlike a large mobile phone but with a series of coloured lights on top and a screen that covered the whole of the reverse side.

"You can come in if you like, sir, it won't make any difference."

Andy wanted to stay. Abul would have preferred a coffee but went with the flow. He didn't believe it anyway.

They started in the outer office which at the first pass was clean. It took the Inspector a few minutes to point his machine at each object in the room including the light fittings and the computers. He was just about to declare the area clean when a red light appeared brightly lit on his scanner and an audible noise was given off. Inspector Harvey pointed at the air conditioning duct, located above the door into Steve's office. This pointed into the outer office and gave out cold air in the summer.

"Looks like we've got something."

Steve and his team stood stock-still not believing it. The Cap couldn't say anything now his boss was proven correct.

The Inspector moved a desk and stood on it to reach the air duct. After removing the cover plate, he reached in and produced a small item that looked like a ladies' brooch except this one had lights in it.

The Inspector handed it to Steve and entered the DCI's office. He repeated the same procedure and discovered two more brooches with lights.

All four policemen sat in the outer office whilst the Inspector examined and fiddled with the small devices. Eventually, he laid them down.

"Well, you were right, sir, someone wants to know what you're up to. These are sound activated transmitters only good for say a thousand yards. They must have been put there recently and are only temporary. The battery life isn't great, and it looked like they're almost fully charged. Probably last say a fortnight at best. They're not recordable but transmit only when anyone in the room speaks. They're not real-time so can only go to a recording to be played back later. These days it could be a mobile phone. I've isolated them now so you're safe."

"Who could have put them there?"

"I'm only a technician but I can tell you, they are not police-issue. This was a private job but, given the range, you're being listened to by someone in this building."

Steve was devastated. Why would anybody want to bug his conversations? He almost felt soiled at the thought.

"Thanks. Sorry, Inspector, I'm very rude, I don't even know your first name."

"Don't worry, sir, it's Terry. As I said, no one needs to know that I used this kit today. It's just between us. If you need another sweep just shout. Always glad to help."

With loud thanks ringing in his ear Inspector Terry Harvey returned to his technical den.

***

Steve, with his head full of questions, and even fewer answers, returned to his own office and slumped behind his desk.

When all three were seated The Cap and Andy looked expectantly at Steve. He trusted these two very different detectives and knew he could divulge to them the apparent anomalies in Commander Bowles's statement. But what about the bugs? The Commander's lie had come from Jenny so he wouldn't be breaching the confidence of Superintendent Alfie Brooks who anyway hadn't come back to him. His team of two realised something more than the bugs was bothering the DCI and wisely waited for him to open the meeting.

"Who on earth would want to bug us? It's not like we're discussing state secrets, bloody people." In sheer frustration, the DCI let out a scream. "What's going on!"

No one moved while Steve regained his composure.

"Let's leave the bugs aside just now. We know they've not been there long and luckily we've not made too much progress on these murders to be of any use to anyone."

"I suppose the conversation with the Essex DS in the canteen was secure?" The

Cap was thinking out loud.

"Yeah, I'm sure the canteen isn't bugged. We're working on the theory that whoever put the bugs there has something to do with our current murders."

Steve looked around and everyone nodded agreement.

"Right, there are a few things you should know." Steve felt exhausted.

"As you know I had coffee with Jenny Fuller. This won't mean much just now Andy, but The Cap knows. It turns out Superintendent Kenneth Taylor is her father. She's been seconded to him for a few months. I've brought her up to speed about the transit van and our Romanian idea. From now on she's one of the team."

Both detectives nodded and The Cap looked pleased. Steve continued.

"She said one of her DIs, is a guy called Dean Grantham. He gave her a hard time when she was trying to collect the missing data from the files. You know, Andy, the names of first on scene and so on."

"She got it all to me though and everything is up to date now."

"Right but listen, this is very sensitive, and I know I can trust you, but for God's sake do not repeat it. Certainly not until I tell you."

Both detectives looked at each other and moved forward in their chairs, all ears.

"Jenny's father, that's Superintendent Taylor, spoke to someone in the National Crime Agency to ask why we'd been parachuted into his cases by the Agency. They said they knew nothing about it. The thing is our Commander Bowles told me we were acting with the full authority of the NCA and that Criminal Intelligence was involved."

"Wow, so he lied?" Andy was shocked. He still had a lot to learn.

"Seems so. Then Jenny told me this Dean Grantham, the one who warned her off, had told his investigating CID officers that the cases of foreign scrubbers weren't worth investigating, and they should only do the minimum." Steve waited for the penny to drop. It did with both his team at the same time, but it was The Cap who won the race.

"We've only just guessed one of them was foreign. How the hell did this DI in Essex know?"

"Correct. So, it seems our victims were not UK nationals, we've got our own Commander lining us up falsely for some reason, and our office has been bugged. What else can happen."

"Well Steve, if we add the white transit van, we've got more, but here's the thing." The Cap was centre-stage. "I spoke with a mate in the drugs squad. He confirmed like everywhere else there's a drug problem in Essex, but there are no big gangs that would use mules. He said mules are old hat because the quantities they bring are so small, now it's by the kilogram, not the ounce, so I'm thinking my drug angle might be wrong."

Steve digested this. Andy, who'd been sitting listening and thinking, spoke up. "I've had a quick response from Bucharest. They e-mailed the information on our second victim just before the Inspector came bug hunting." He smiled at his own joke but saw Steve didn't appreciate it. He raced on.

"The Romanian police have identified her as Tatiana Popescu. She's seventeen, comes from a small village outside Bucharest. She was reported missing five weeks ago when she didn't return from the UK. The Romanian police used Interpol to circulate to all forces, but we didn't get a sniff when we asked for a missing persons search, because we assumed the girls were British."

"What do you mean Andy? When she didn't come back from the UK?"

"According to the statements, she left for the UK eight weeks ago and was due back in Romania four weeks later. It seems someone paid for her ticket, but the police said the family claimed not to know why."

"Do they think they are lying?"

"No idea boss, it's only what's in the file."

Steve went into one of his deep thoughts, as did Andy and The Cap.

"Andy, get back onto the Bucharest police. I seem to remember they are Federal. Ask for a full background on the girl and the family. If she had her ticket paid, then someone wanted her in the UK. We need to know why."

"Will do Steve." Andy looked to have something. "It can't be a coincidence that both bodies were found near airports. That's Southend and Stanstead. If our victims are from Europe the chances are they flew into either of these airports.

We know the second victim came from Romania and roughly when. Why don't I get the CCTV from arrivals at both airports, and try and spot our second victim arriving? If we get lucky, we might be able to follow her or see if she meets anyone."

"Not a bad idea Andy, but how long do airports keep their CCTV footage?"

Andy shrugged. He didn't know but The Cap spoke. "It's a CAA and Immigration rule that all arrivals images are kept for six months." He looked smug. "Don't ask, I just know."

"Right Andy, first thing Monday morning." Andy nodded.

Steve turned to The Cap. "Abul, I want you over in Essex on Monday. I've a feeling Jenny Fuller could do with some support. Look up this Dean Grantham bloke. Play a little politics. It sounds as though he knows more than we do. You know the thing, play him along. Make him your new best friend. See if he drops his guard. Also, to keep Jenny out of the way, you and she should hit a few garage repair shops. See if we can get a lead on this transit."

Steve sat back still thinking about the listening bugs.

"Anything else?"

Both detectives said no.

"Right. Let's get a fresh start on Monday. Andy, chase up any outstanding issues including the airport CCTV. I've a feeling next week's going to be busy."

Steve stood up from behind his desk. "In the meantime, I'm going home to spruce myself up, and this evening, attend a gala dinner being given by a wonderful medical company, and to meet a wonderful medical doctor who's just come back into Alison's life. Wish me luck!"

Steve left. He wasn't going to be late no matter what. He'd have the weekend to think things through and hopefully, get a jump on next week.

Chapter Eight

Steve arrived at Alison's house suitably suited and booted. He was even early. The night had developed a bit of a chill and he didn't have a heavy outdoor coat. He shivered slightly as he opened the door and climbed the stair to the doctor's private quarters.

Alison hadn't expected him early and was just finishing off her makeup in the bedroom as Steve arrived. "My, you're early! Is this a first?" she called to him as he entered the bedroom.

"Very funny, I'm fashionably early, as opposed to being fashionably late."

As she sat at her dressing table Steve bent down to kiss her neck. He was about to go for a kiss on her lips when she swung towards him. "Don't you dare, DCI Burt. It's taken me forever to get this face just right and you're not going to spoil it for the sake of a kiss. You'll just have to wait." Alison Mills had a twinkle in her eyes that held out promise for later in the evening.

They went to the living room and Alison poured two glasses of white wine.

"You're so early we've got time for a quick one, the taxi's not due until seven."

Steve looked appreciatively at his bride to be. Neither of them had been married before, both were in their early forties so couldn't be accused of rushing to the alter. Steve felt contented just sitting her looking at the woman he was going to spend the rest of his life with. They were used to each other, and some might say they already acted like an old married couple.

Steve came out of his trance. Alison had been talking but he'd missed most of it.

He looked at her with a look that said my mind was somewhere else.

"Oh, you're impossible sometimes!" The doctor chided. "I was saying I hope you don't get bored tonight."

"What's this all about anyway. All I know is an old boyfriend's been promoted onto the Board of a huge company and you and a friend were invited."

Alison smiled. "He was never my boyfriend. Tonight is only partly about Robbie Symonds. Companies like Eclipse Medical run these evenings all the time and we doctors get invited. They like to get a lot of us together so they can quietly sow a seed for future sales. I don't usually go, and would've given this one a miss, except I have a new fiancé to show off. Plus, I hadn't heard from Robbie for years."

"So, who is this bloke?"

"I met him at medical school. He was brilliant but wanted every other student to know it. I suppose he was a bit arrogant. His parents had money, so he had all the trappings. You know, sports car, designer clothes, enough money always to be buying drinks. On top of that he was very handsome, so had a string of female followers." Steve arched his eyebrow asking a question.

"Yes, I dated him a couple of times, but he was so self-centred. I walked away after the second date. Not my type." Alison sipped her wine.

"So, what did he say when he called you out of the blue?"

"Am I being interrogated by my jealous boyfriend?" She smiled a knowing smile.

"Jealous fiancé please, and no. I'm just trying to understand what I'm getting into tonight."

"All he said was he'd been working for Eclipse Medical for a couple of years in one of their subsidiaries and that he'd been asked to join the main board. It was going to be announced tonight, and he saw my name on what he called a target list. He just thought it would be nice to catch up, but I suspect he just wants to boast."

"Well, I suppose it's a free night out and I'm starving." As Steve drained his wine glass Alison's mobile buzzed. The taxi was outside.

Steve helped Alison on with her coat. He thought it was a shame to cover up her evening gown. She looked stunning. The sky-blue colour of the material and the fashionable cut of the dress showed the doctor was all woman. By contrast, Steve in his hired dinner jacket, couldn't compete.

They set off into what for Steve was the unknown.

***

After Alison had checked her coat in at the ladies section of the cloakroom and Steve had visited the gents to comb his hair and make sure his made up bowtie was straight, they met up in the foyer of the Peacock Grand Hotel just off Pall Mall.

Eclipse Medical appeared to have taken over the entire dining room that was almost the size of an aircraft hangar. People were milling about as Steve and Alison entered. Waiters in white jackets were everywhere, carrying trays of drinks and things on sticks. This appeared to be an elegant gathering with what Alison assured Steve, were expensive designer dresses in evidence, and some jewellery whose insurance premiums must have been more than a month's wages for most people.

Steve was determined not to drink too much tonight. He was here to support Alison and relax. Besides, it had been suggested he might spoil Alison's carefully applied makeup, once this shindig was over.

The couple mingled and Alison spoke to a few people as they passed. An elderly man standing no more than five foot seven inches tall and dressed in the regulation dinner jacket approached the pair. "Ah, Dr Mills, I'm so glad you could come." He took Alison's hand and held it in both of his. He looked at Steve expecting an introduction. Alison did the honours and introduced Steve by his full police title and as her fiancé.

"Ah, another policeman in our midst. You must let me introduce you." The little man guided Alison away from Steve who lamely followed. They approached a group of mainly men who were standing in a circle.

Their self-appointed guide broke into the group without asking permission and instantly started to introduce Alison.

"Tony, may I introduce Dr Alison Mills and her fiancé Chief Inspector Steve Burt, perhaps you know each other."

Steve almost passed out. In front of him stood Commander Anthony Bowles. The Commander was having difficulty focusing but managed to shake Alison's hand and nod a greeting to Steve. It was obvious that Anthony Bowles had had enough to drink already but it was equally obvious that even in a sober state he couldn't remember Steve's Christian name.

Steve remembered being told a long time ago that people who use other people for their own ends are usually only interested in themselves. They dismiss from their memory banks everything that's irrelevant to them, especially names of people they've used. The DCI was reminded of this as he looked at Commander Bowles struggling to recall Steve's Christian name.

They were introduced to the other members of the Commander's circle before the Commander took Steve by the arm and guided him away from the crowd.

In a voice that was slurring its words, the senior Scotland Yard man asked, "What the hell are you doing here? I didn't know you were involved. You'd have saved me a lot of trouble if you'd said." The Commander was dribbling from the corner of his mouth and was swaying slightly.

"What do you mean?"

The Commander offered a conspiratorial grin and punched Steve slightly on the shoulder. "You old dog, the incorruptible detective and here you are. I'm flabbergasted." Steve noted the Commander's attempt at flabbergasted didn't come out right.

It was clear the Commander was being somewhat indiscreet, but before Steve could capitalize on his drunken state, the Commander wandered off looking for another drink, leaving the DCI to wonder and speculate at the same time exactly what his senior officer had meant.

Alison re-joined Steve. "Who was that?"

"That my love was the future of policing in the Met. I'll tell you later. Who was the little guy doing all the introductions? He clearly knew you."

"That's Claude Von Grieser. He's a PR fellow. He must be working for Eclipse. I've met him a few times at a couple of bashes. He's always hanging around trying to network with people. He's pretty harmless but I'm told he has more dirt on the great and the good in London than anyone else."

"Are you one of the great and the good?" Steve teased Alison who replied with a smile that lit up her face and, to Steve, the whole room.

"You'll have to wait and see Detective Chief Inspector."

The couple continued to circulate with Alison nodding to a few faces she recognised, and they took the opportunity to re-charge their glasses. Steve was determined to keep to his self-imposed promise. This would be his last drink of the night.

They stopped to talk to a husband-and-wife doctor combo who Alison had known for several years. After being introduced to them, Steve tuned out the conversation and looked around the room. Most people had split into groups of four or six and all seemed to be smiling and laughing. Steve remembered it was called having a good time.

As he scanned the room, he caught sight of his senior officer having what looked like a heated debate with a man Steve didn't recognise. It was obvious that the inebriated Commander Bowles was angry with his companion who appeared to be doing his best to calm him down. The debate lasted several minutes and ended with the other man taking the Commander's elbow in an attempt to guide him out, and for the Commander to shrug the attempt off and storm out. Steve wondered what that was about and who the Commander had been arguing with and why?

Alison finished her conversation with the two doctors. Steve smiled benignly and they moved on. Steve wondered when the meal was to be served. As they found some space for themselves Steve spotted a tall figure with a full head of fair hair approaching them at speed. Without changing stride, he rushed up to Alison and gathered her up swinging her round before placing her on the spot she'd been standing on before her swing.

The newcomer was gushing. "Alison Mills." He held both her hands and stood back admiring her. "Look at you, as beautiful as ever. It's great you're here. How long has it been? It must be ten years and you look as stunning as ever."

Steve noticed Alison was blushing and he was being ignored despite obviously being Alison's escort. The newcomer talked incessantly for what seemed like ten minutes but was probably only two. When he stopped to draw breath and Alison had retrieved her hands from his grasp, she introduced Steve without his Scotland Yard title.

"Steve, this is Robbie Symonds, I told you about him earlier."

Both men stood and weighed each other up. Robbie was just over six-foot-tall, making him a few inches taller than Steve. He was athletic looking with a handsome face and slim figure. Steve put him in his early forties but acknowledged time had been kind to him. When he spoke, his voice was pure Home Counties.

Steve held out his hand. "Dr Symonds, good to meet you."

Robbie Symonds appeared to stand back in horror, and although about to shake Steve's hand, didn't. "Mr Burt, I'm not a doctor, I'm a surgeon, and as such my title is Mister. If you're coming to my firm's dinner, then at least get to know the difference."

A red mist descended over Steve. This arrogant shop window model was not only rude but disrespectful to Alison who stood with her mouth open not believing what this man she'd not seen for ten years had just said. She hoped Steve was in control. He'd explained to her how he'd previously been suspended for hitting a senior officer. She knew he was capable of flooring her ex-university colleague.

Steve stood forward until he was only inches from Robbie Symonds's face.

"*Mister* Symonds. If you ever talk to me or Alison like that again, I'll have every traffic policeman near where you live mount hourly patrols outside your house, and if you even drive with the wrong pressure in your tyres, you'll be done. Now get off whatever soapbox you're on, *mister*." Steve let this sink in "before I do something here and now that we would both regret. And if I ever hear you talk to Alison in that pompous manner, you're dead meat." Steve stood back and as he took his second step, he adjusted the silk handkerchief in Robbie Symonds' breast pocket.

"Do you understand?"

Robbie Symonds flushed up but stood his ground. "Alison, you do realize I can have your date ejected from here?"

"He's not my date, Robbie, he's my fiancé, and he happens to be a Chief Inspector of Police at New Scotland Yard. I don't think even you are silly enough to try and throw him out."

She stared angrily at this man she'd known previously. "You were always a prig, but what I've seen tonight takes the biscuit. I hope your employers know what a little shit they are employing."

She took Steve's arm and they left the man they thought was the guest of honour, standing by himself looking shocked.

"Well done, you." Steve was smiling and was very proud of his fiancée. "Let's get out of here and get back to your place so I can mess up your makeup." Steve was smiling and Alison was radiant. She'd not been so angry in a long time and the thought of having her make-up disturbed by her fiancé had its appeal.

"Not so fast, Inspector, let's at least have our meal. You said you were hungry and I'm starving." She looked towards the end of the room where the tables had been laid out. "It looks like they are about to start."

The meal was delicious, and both Alison and Steve ate everything that was put in front of them. They sat at a round table set for eight people and enjoyed the company of their dinner guests. Coffee was served and Steve refused a brandy remembering his promise to himself. As the meal was finishing there was activity at one end of the dining space. Microphones were set up together with a small plinth.

The man Steve had seen arguing with the Commander stood with the microphone ready to deliver a speech. Steve thought it was true. There was no such thing as a free meal. He groaned inwardly.

"Ladies and Gentlemen, firstly a big thank you for coming tonight and helping us celebrate another fantastic year for Eclipse Medical. For anyone who doesn't know me, I'm Lars Jenson, CEO and main shareholder in our Company." Lars stopped to play the audience. He was a well-groomed man in his late fifties with a full head of silver hair. He stood about five foot nine inches and was a little thick around his waist. His expensively tailored dinner jacket couldn't disguise that this guy didn't work out. His accent was European, but Steve couldn't place its origin.

"I'm happy to announce that our new transplant venture has been working now for six months under the direction of Robbie Symonds, and in recognition of Robbie's outstanding contribution to group profits in such a short time, he's been appointed to the main board of Eclipse Medical."

Lars stood back and invited Robbie to stand. He did and milked the applause for as long as it continued. When the room settled down Lars began again.

"Our replacement limb business, although not sexy, continues to bring in outstanding profits, but Robbie's division is now geared up to carry out up to thirty human transplants a month, from each of our three new operating theatres in Eclipse Hall in Essex. It's the largest facility of its kind anywhere in Europe and we're very proud." Lars was on an evangelical roll. "We're bringing renewed life to hundreds of souls. This is great and glorious work we're doing and with the Lord's help and your continued support, we'll save many more hundreds of deserving lives." Again, Lars played the crowd and got the applause he was expecting. Steve felt he was at an American-style prayer meeting.

Lars with a great grin on his face held up his arms to stop the clapping. Steve thought what a modest man — not.

"Anyway, enough of us. We're here to honour you, our medical colleagues, tonight. Without your support, no one would use our products, and without your transplant referrals, Eclipse Hall wouldn't be able to do the outstanding work it's been doing. We're very blessed to be able to help you save so many souls. So please, as doctors, think of the benefits transplant surgery can have to your patients with chronic problems. Eclipse Medical is here to help you and your patients. We have the skill and the solutions. Whereas five years ago you'd have struggled to get patients on the donor register, today we can help, and greatly reduce waiting times." Lars gave another great all welcoming smile.

"That's enough of the commercial. Please continue to enjoy yourselves. The drinks will keep flowing until the last man leaves. Thank you very much." Another round of applause before the guests seated at their tables rose and began to scatter. Some to go home, others to the bar.

Alison and Steve were headed for the foyer when Robbie Symonds approached them with Lars Jenson in tow. Robbie seemed a bit flushed but smiled warmly at the couple. He was almost gushing as he held his arms out to Alison but wisely didn't try and embrace her. "Alison I'm sorry about earlier, a pure misunderstanding. Can you ever forgive Robbie?" He put on a pathetic child's pout. Before Alison could tell him what she thought of him he carried on. "And Chief Inspector, we got off on the wrong foot, I'm so sorry. Can I introduce Lars Jenson, CEO and majority shareholder in Eclipse Medical?" Robbie was clearly trying to push things ahead for fear of negative comments about his previous performance.

Up close, Lars was a handsome man with a friendly smile, and as Steve discovered, a firm handshake. "Nice to meet you both. Robbie tells me you're at Scotland Yard. Must be quite exciting?"

"It's more paper than arrests these days."

They talked for several minutes but Steve was conscious it was Lars talking to him as opposed to Alison who as a doctor should have been his target audience. Steve also noticed a small subtle gold cross hanging around Lars' neck. It looked pure gold and in Steve's mind wouldn't be cheap, but also not something he'd expect to see someone wear with a dinner jacket.

After some light-hearted banter, Lars surprised Alison and Steve. "Listen, I'm having a lunch for a few friends on Sunday down at my estate in Buckinghamshire. Nothing fancy, just a BBQ if the weather's nice, and maybe a bit of rough shooting and a gallop if anyone fancies horses. Please say you'll come."

He produced a card and handed it to Steve. "Most people turn up for our early service at nine a.m. It's not compulsory, but we like to acknowledge the Lord's day, when we can. If you're not religious, then around eleven's fine but any time before twelve. Good, that's settled then, see you both Sunday."

Before either Steve or Alison could refuse, Lars Jenson had disappeared into the dwindling crowd. They looked at each other in stunned silence. Steve broke the spell by doing a Laurel and Hardy saying to Alison. "Another fine mess you've gotten me in."

She laughed and thumped his shoulder. "Come on. It's time we went home, and you can mess up my makeup."

***

Saturday was spent in domestic bliss or a version of it. After breakfast and a walk in the nearby park, Alison decided they'd better go and do some wedding shopping. "We agreed that we need to change this place around so it's ours after the wedding and not mine. You agreed and said you'd feel like a lodger. So, come on, let's go." Alison used both arms to pull Steve from his chair. They were both in happy states of mind and set off into the world of joint shopping. A new experience for both of them.

They spent Saturday evening watching TV and discussing wedding plans. Steve was reminded several times it was getting close and he hadn't picked a best man. Saturday evening drifted peacefully by and Steve was again reminded of the thought about looking like an old married couple. He didn't mind. He was happy.

***

Sunday was a glorious day when they set off to Lars Jenson's estate in Buckinghamshire. They took Alison's car with its sat-nav system and a much younger engine than Steve's. Despite their upcoming church wedding, they decided to forego the early morning service offered by Lars in favour of another hour in bed. The drive down was pleasant, and they were tempted to stop off at a few of the inns they passed and give Lars a miss. Alison thought that would be bad manners. Steve agreed and reminded her this was another free meal.

Lars Jenson's estate was exactly that, an estate. The house wasn't grand but was significantly bigger than anything either Steve or Alison had been in apart from visiting National Trust properties. They entered by a gate that opened automatically on their arrival and the house was at the end of a long sweeping road about half a mile long. There were open fields as far as the eye could see and a few small copses scattered around the edge of a few fields. Steve had no idea how much land he was looking at but knew it was a lot.

They parked beside the cars that had arrived ahead of them, although they were slightly early. On hearing the car approach, a uniformed butler appeared and instructed the pair that Lars was at the rear of the house preparing his BBQ.

As Alison and Steve rounded the end of the mansion, they saw at least twenty people milling around and Lars apparently fighting with his BBQ to get it to light. It was under a tent-like awning, and Lars had a bottle of beer in his hand. He saw the pair and shouted a warm greeting. He left his attempts at fire lighting and met Steve and Alison. After getting them a drink each he introduced them to the other guests. There seemed to be a cross-section of society including, Alison noted, two vicars. Steve had a different mindset and noticed apart from the clergy each guest had a position of authority within their own field. Lars was still networking despite the Sunday services. He had however created what felt like a leisurely and friendly atmosphere with everyone seeming to get on.

Robbie Symonds was present and apart from a cursory handshake, he kept clear of the detective.

The afternoon was pleasant, and Steve began to enjoy himself. Alison was mingling and had left Steve to fly solo. He spoke to a few people, admired some of the ladies and learnt a little about futures trading.

He was just about to look for Alison when a voice from behind startled him. "So, you are in then, Chief Inspector?"

Behind him with a bottle of beer in his hand stood Commander Bowles.

"I've no idea what you're talking about now or Friday night, but I'd like to know."

The Commander was silent. From the expression on his face, he seemed conflicted.

"Sorry, but have I misunderstood the situation? You see Lars invites a lot of people and knows a lot of people. Anyone who attends his parties is sure to make influential contacts that can further one's career. That's all I meant. I didn't have you down as an ambitious sort, that's all." He was sweating a little and rubbed his hand over his neck.

Steve formed the opinion that Commander Anthony Bowles was lying and that's not what he meant.

Steve excused himself and wandered into the formal garden to think. The smell of BBQ food was everywhere and a few of the men had gone rough shooting whilst some others were off horse riding. Everyone else was still standing and sitting on the overly large sun terrace that ran along the entire back of the house.

Steve sat on a bench and sipped his beer. There was something lodged in his brain from Friday night, but he couldn't get it out. This was normal for the DCI. He'd cracked a few cases by dislodging a piece of data that stuck in his brain but sometimes it took a while to journey to the conscious side of his brain. He felt whatever it was, it was important, and it had been said at the dinner on Friday evening. He considered the Commander's remarks on Friday. He'd let his guard slip, so there was probably something to his indiscretions. He alluded to Steve being one of them, but Steve had no idea who 'them' were or what they did. He'd said he didn't know Steve was involved, but involved in what, and what did he mean when he said if he'd known Steve was part of it, then it would've saved him a lot of trouble. Was he talking about the listening devices in Steve's office?

Steve tried to clear his head. The Commander was obviously digging his way out of trouble earlier when he realised, he'd spoken out of turn and his attempt to retrieve the situation was good but not good enough.

Something was going on between Eclipse Medical and the Commander. But what? And who else might be involved? He let his imagination take over and ran through a few scenarios in his head, but nothing worked. The two murders, the white transit van, the connection to Romania, a senior officer lying and the bugs in his office. He knew all the pieces must fit together but he needed the key.

He was giving himself a headache and getting frustrated at his inability to see what must be in front of him. And the thing stuck in his brain was still there. It was infuriating because he felt whatever it was, it was vital to the case.

Alison came to find him. She was a bit windswept but looked as though she were glowing. She explained Lars was off shooting and some of the guests were drifting off.

"Come on, loner, it's time to get away from all this fresh air and get you back to London."

Alison went to pull him off the bench but stopped abruptly. She looked at her fiancé. "Oh, no, your mind's working. That means I've lost you for the rest of the day, doesn't it?"

Steve looked up with a sheepish grin on his face. She knew him so well. The thought about them being like an old married couple already came into his mind.

"Oh, well, it was nice while it lasted."

Steve stood and kissed Alison lightly on the cheek. They walked off hand in hand towards her car. Steve's brain was in overdrive.

What was he missing?

Chapter Nine

Detective Inspector Abul Ishmal had collected his pool car on Sunday to get an early start to his journey to Chelmsford the following morning.

Monday had dawned misty and grey with a hint of rain to come. He'd made reasonable time considering Monday morning traffic around London, but the traffic gods caught up with him as he approached the Dartford Crossing. The traffic came to a virtual standstill.

Abul, AKA The Cap, had no choice but to sit and wait. He allowed his mind to consider the two victims whose deaths they were investigating. He considered what they knew and what they didn't. He almost laughed out loud when he told himself what they didn't know was the identity of the killer.

He thought about the two teenage girls not much older than his own daughter. What had brought them to the UK by themselves? He considered the facts, such as they were. The one girl they had identified was expected back in Romania after a few weeks away, but it was unlikely she was on holiday. She couldn't have been here for work. She was too young, and nobody would employ a teenager from Romania for only four weeks if the information given by her parents was correct.

The Cap moved the car forward but only a few yards at a time. He carried on summarizing in his head. There was the white van that must have a part to play, the manner of the killings. Why slit the girl's stomach's open? If it wasn't drugs, then what?

Abul was content to let Steve deal with the bugs and the Commander. Such things were beyond his pay grade.

Then there was the question of DI Dean Grantham and how The Cap was going to approach him. Steve and Jenny were convinced he knew something, and it was up to The Cap to get it out of him. As he continued to move forward towards getting onto the QE Bridge that would take him into Essex, Abul realised he hadn't a clue as to how best to befriend this DI he'd never met.

As The Cap was approaching Essex, Steve was summoned to the office of Commander Anthony Bowles, an experience he wasn't looking forward to. After saying good morning to Andy who was hard at work in front of his computer Steve grabbed a coffee and headed for the twelfth-floor office.

He was kept waiting some fifteen minutes before being ushered into the presence of the great man by a civilian clerk who had not existed during Bowles' predecessor's time. Steve entered and took a seat before being asked. He knew this would not go down well but he wanted this man annoyed. He was more likely to let something slip in the heat of the moment. Steve felt he had the advantage. After all, this excuse sitting behind his great desk had never been a proper policeman whereas Steve was a seasoned thief-taker and knew how the game was played.

Anthony Bowles was clearly nervous but did his best not to show it. He smiled a horrible insincere smile. "Steve! I may call you Steve?" Steve played his game and just sat.

"Steve, perhaps we should have a chat and clear the air. We've come across each other socially twice now in the past few days, and I thought we should get to know each other better, especially if you're joining Lars' stable."

Steve had no idea what Lars' stable was and certainly hadn't joined it. He remained silent. It was best to let guilty men talk without interrupting their flow.

The Commander sat back and picked up a pencil from his desk and started to fiddle with it between his fingers.

"I realize I'd had a few too many on Friday and may have said some things that meant nothing to you, but that you might take out of context, likewise on Sunday. When I saw you there, I assumed things that perhaps I shouldn't have. The fact is Lars Jenson is a great supporter of law and order. He's donated hundreds of thousands to political parties and police charities over the years. He's also a man with contacts that any ambitious officer would exploit." The Commander was back looking and sounding like his old arrogant self.

"When I said the things I did, I was referring to the work Lars and I do together. I'm chairman of the police widows and orphans charity and Lars is a major contributor. We work closely on charity matters but that's all. I can see that as an officer, experienced in solving and possibly looking for crimes, my remarks out of context might lead you to believe that somehow Lars and I are too close for comfort, but let me assure you that is not the case. Are we clear?"

To date Steve hadn't said anything, nor did he believe a word of the explanation Bowles had just given but he wasn't about to blow his cover. Better to have things on a friendly but professional level.

So, Steve told the Commander what he obviously wanted to hear. "There's no need to explain sir. Not for one moment did I think there was anything untoward between you and Mr Jenson. I admit to being curious as to why you were at the dinner on Friday without a medical connection or partner, but of course, it's natural you'd be invited because of your charity work together."

The Commander almost burst with self-satisfaction. He'd convinced this DCI that he shouldn't look any further into what he did for Lars Jenson.

"There we are then Steve, all cleared up." He sat back and replaced the pencil on his desk.

"Now remember, I need your reports on any progress you're making on these horrible murders in Essex. If you need any additional backup," he paused to demonstrate with his arms, "I'm here to help you."

The DCI almost smirked but kept his composure. "Thank you, sir, I'm very grateful."

Steve returned to his office via the canteen where he bought two strong coffees. One for him and one for Andy. They had work to do and one of his first priorities was exposing his new boss. Steve knew he was up to his neck in something, he just didn't know what. Yet!

***

Meantime Abul had arrived at the Essex Forces Headquarters building in Chelmsford. After the usual security checks and being issued a lanyard with his security pass attached, The Cap set off for Superintendent Taylor's office expecting DS Jenny Fuller to be there.

He found her sitting at the small conference table in her father's office working on a laptop. When she saw Abul she stopped, stood and gave a radiant smile that seemed to light up the whole room.

The Cap approached the table and Jenny re-took her seat. Abul pulled out a chair and sat down opposite her.

"Steve was asking how your father was."

"That's kind of him but there's no change. He's hanging on but the doctors aren't too confident he'll pull through."

"Sorry." The Cap didn't know what else to say but decided work was probably what Jenny needed now.

Jenny lifted a sheet of paper from the table. "I've printed off a few damage-repair places that are all within ten miles of here. That just about covers both crime scenes and if our van is central to South Essex, we might find the repair shop on this list, if the driver has had it repaired since you saw it on the CCTV. It's been over four weeks."

The Cap picked up the paper. "What's the significance of the crosses beside some of them?"

"I asked traffic where a dodgy van might go for a quick off the books body repair. The ones with the crosses are the ones they suggested."

"Good, thanks for that. Now, Jenny, I need to tell you something." The Cap wasn't sure how to approach the topic of DI Dean Grantham and his mission.

"We're pretty much where we were late Friday afternoon. A white van, a Romanian connection and not much more." Abul looked straight into Jenny's eyes. He wasn't saying anything about the bugs nor Steve's suspicions about Commander Bowles.

"You told Steve this Dean character told his team to only do a cursory job because foreign scrubbers weren't worth spending time on. Correct?"

"Yes, or something similar."

"Steve wants me to get to know this bloke. The way he put it, I'm to become his new best friend in the hope he'll let something slip. Now I have no idea how to do this so do you have any ideas? What's he like?"

Jenny smiled at the thought of The Cap and Dean. Chalk and cheese, so Abul's task wouldn't be easy. "Well, for a start he's full of himself. He thinks he's God's gift to women. He likes his nights out with the lads, always seems to be flush and doesn't mind standing his round. He's married with a kid, but I don't think he sleeps in his own bed too often. He's an average detective but a bit lazy." Jenny looked at The Cap.

"That's about it."

"Does he have any hobbies? You know golf, vintage cars?"

"No. I'd say his hobbies were women and booze, but I could be wrong." She smiled and The Cap laughed.

"Where will I find him?"

"He'll be in the CID office. He's always there holding court. Like I said he's a bit lazy."

The Cap made a decision. "Jenny, I'd like to get started with him now if that's OK with you? We'll get out later and tour the repair shops. Do you mind?"

"No. I've to call the hospital in ten minutes and bring my statement up to date so you carry on. I'll be fine."

***

The Cap set of to find DI Dean Grantham. As predicted, he was in the CID office with his jacket off and feet on his desk. There were two other officers present, but they seemed to be busy on legitimate police business. Although The Cap had never met Dean, he knew the type from Jenny's summary. He could have spotted Dean Grantham anywhere.

The CID suite was big, housing around ten desks. It was like any other police office in the land, dull, drab and cheaply furnished. Abul went straight over to his quarry and pretended he didn't know who Dean was.

"Morning, I'm looking for DI Grantham?" The Cap sounded cheery.

"You've found him, squire. Who are you?"

"Now don't blow a fuse. I'm with the Met team up here looking into the two murders from a few weeks ago."

"Oh, yes, and you think I'll help you?"

The Cap played the innocent abroad. "Look Inspector, I'm only doing what I'm told. I've been on these kinds of capers before. A complete waste of bloody time. The high-ups at the Yard draft more bodies than you can imagine onto the case." Abul pulled up a friendly chair. "With all that manpower they're bound to find something that you local boys would have got given time." He looked at Dean. "Am I right or am I right?" The Cap sat back.

"Bloody right. We know what these two murders are about. We don't need the Met poking its nose in. Like you said a complete waste of time."

"Exactly, look at me, I'm a DI just like you. They sent me here today to be what they called a presence. Can you imagine, me, a presence! I'd better not tell my wife." Both inspectors laughed out loud. Abul thought he was making progress.

Dean was still giggling away. "Can I get you a coffee?"

"Yeah, if I'm a presence I'll need caffeine." They both laughed again. Dean stood up and went to the coffee machine in the corridor. The Cap noticed he was small for a policeman at about five foot eight inches, he had a bit of a beer belly and rounded slightly flushed face. His hair was brown and receding and he seemed to walk with a slight limp.

When they were back sitting drinking their coffee The Cap asked. "I couldn't help notice your limp. Anything serious?"

"No, I had to jump from a height recently and just jarred my hip. It'll sort itself out."

Remembering Jenny's description of Dean. "I hope you weren't leaping from a bedroom window?"

Dean gave a knowing look. "You're not a detective for nothing, are you? What's your name?"

"Abul Ishmal." The Cap held out his hand.

Dean immediately grabbed it. "Dean Grantham." They shook hands.

"Look Dean, I don't want to be a pain or anything but as a presence, I'm supposed to dig something up. My DCI's a right tyrant. He expects results all the time, even when there's nothing to give him. Can you fill me in on your enquiries? I might be able to drop something in and keep him off my back. I'm sorry to ask but you know how it is or maybe you don't. You've got your own team here so you're a lot more independent than I am in the Met. We've got bosses everywhere."

"Yeah, but the money's better, you get London weighting."

"Yes, but we pay tax on it. To be honest I'd rather be working here with you." Dean's chest swelled. He liked this Met officer and decided to help him.

"Look Abul, I know that these two foreign scrubbers we found are from Romania. Right?"

"Yes."

"I told my boys to visit the scenes, do the minimum and get back sharpish. These two cases ain't worth our time. We'll declare them cold cases, the bodies will be buried in a common grave and that'll be the end of it. No point racing all over the county looking for somebody who doesn't exist."

"Thanks, Dean, that's great." Abul acted like a schoolboy who'd just won a prize. But can I ask a question please?" Again, a schoolboy. "You said running all over the county looking for somebody that doesn't exist. What do you mean?"

Dean looked a bit shocked and realised what he'd said. "Nothing, my son, don't you worry about it. It's just that Essex is a big county and our killer could be anywhere. He may not even be local so what's the point. We'll call them cold cases like I said and get on with real cases that don't involve foreign prostitutes."

The Cap looked at his watch and looked surprised at the time. "Dean, I'd like to stay and maybe we could have some lunch, but I've got to see this DS Fuller. She was appointed our liaison, so I've got to see her. Maybe next time I'm up?"

"Yeah. We could have a night out. I know some cracking pubs up near the barracks. You know, soldiers' wives and grown-up daughters all out looking for it.

"We've had some great nights. Let me know when and I'll round up a few of the lads."

The Cap was leaving when Dean called in a loud whisper. "Watch out for that DS Fuller. She's a cut above and well connected so be careful. Mind your Ps and Qs!"

Both men laughed as Abul went back to Superintendent Taylor's office.

He'd fulfilled his brief from Steve. He had what was needed on DI Dean Grantham, but Dean didn't know it.

Chapter Ten

The DCI and Andy were sitting in Steve's office trying to arrange their thoughts. Andy had marked up the whiteboard but there wasn't much on it. Both were conscious it was exactly one week since the Commander had given the department the case. They were used to making faster progress than this.

"OK, Steve, updates. I've heard back from the Bucharest Federal police. As you requested, they've done a background check on the Popescu family. That's the second victim. They're reporting it's just an ordinary family. Not rich but they make a living from the land, mother, father and another three sisters. They said Tatania was a bit wild and had made several trips to The Capital before announcing she was going to England. Her parents weren't happy, but she was seventeen and wanted a better life. She told her parents she'd be well looked after, and someone had paid for her flight, and she was being housed in England. The police are sure she wasn't being recruited for sex purposes because she said she'd be back in Bucharest within four weeks." Andy looked dejected,

"Sorry Steve, that's not much help."

"Why would a seventeen-year-old virgin, according to the post-mortem, allow someone to bring her to the UK for four weeks? It doesn't make sense."

"We got a hit on the first victim from the fingerprints and DNA. Surprise, she's also from Romania but a different village. She's confirmed as being fifteen and was called Ingrid Baciu. Her parents are dead, and she was living with her aunt. It's more or less the same story. Trips into Bucharest, then a flight to England with a promise of being back within four weeks. There's no background on the family but it's fair to assume someone paid for her ticket."

"Yes Andy, but why?"

Both detectives sat in silence. Steve still had something at the back of his mind but just couldn't draw it forward.

"I've got the images from Stanstead and Southend arrivals. I got everything and have cut it down to the times of flights arriving from Bucharest at both airports. I've assumed if our first victim was found what is now seven weeks ago then she probably arrived at the earliest eleven weeks before if she thought she'd be home within four weeks. So, I've got from eleven weeks ago till the body was found." Andy was looking pleadingly at Steve.

"I've tried scanning them but it's almost impossible. My mate in Tech Services says they've got a new optical face recognition piece of software. He says it's state of the art, almost intelligence grade. I'd like to request them to set up a scan for both images. It's our best bet to maybe catching the girls' arrival in the UK. If we can do that, we might pick them up on other CCTV cameras."

Steve looked in amazement at Andy. "You've done it again. Thinking outside the box. When you told me what you wanted to do last Friday, I knew you'd have a go, but I really didn't think it was possible. Here you are now looking like it might be possible. Andy, what would I do without you, so yes, get it over to Tech Support? Do you need me to speak to Inspector Harvey?"

Andy smiled but was blushing following Steve's glowing remarks. "All done. He's expecting it. I told him I'd ask you and he said just bring the stuff over. They've not tried this software on anything live yet so he can write it off to training."

"Andy, I think you have a kindred spirit in Inspector Terry Harvey. Right, you'd better get off. I've got some thinking to do."

"I'll need more of your time when I get back Steve. I think we've got a problem."

"If it's only one I'll be amazed."

Andy scurried of clutching his CD discs and the post-mortem files so Tech Services could get a headshot of the victims for comparison.

***

Steve closed his door and leant back in his chair. He tried to allow his mind to wander. He was almost unconscious and anyone coming in would swear he was asleep. He was back at the dinner last Friday. He

saw Alison and that horrible Robbie Symonds, the commander and...
something was wrong. He was being awakened but what was the noise.
As he came to, he realised it was his office phone ringing. With an effort,
he shook himself, rubbed his eyes and answered.

"Steve." A hale and hearty man's voice jumped from the phone. "I
hope I'm not disturbing you. It's Lars Jenson, you remember, from
Eclipse Medical. How are you?"

Steve was lost for words. The last person he expected to hear from
was the CEO and major shareholder in Eclipse Medical.

"I'm fine thank you, Lars. I'm sorry we couldn't say goodbye
yesterday, but we were told you'd gone out shooting."

"Yes, only skeets. I can't abide killing animals for sport. I'm sure
you agree?" Steve hadn't thought about it. He was more concerned with
humans killing humans for sport. He didn't answer.

"Listen Steve. The reason I'm calling is I've to be in town tomorrow
and wondered if you might be free for lunch. Just the two of us, a chance
for a chat. What do you say?"

Lars wasn't someone you could easily say no to, but Steve was going
to try.

"I'd love to Lars but..."

"Excellent, let's say the Ritz restaurant at twelve-thirty tomorrow.
I'll see you there, bye." The line went dead.

Now Steve was confused. If Lars and the Commander were up to
something, then why was he being courted? Did they want something
from him? After a few minutes, he realised there was no point in
speculating. He'd find out tomorrow.

***

Andy returned bearing two cups of coffee. Before they'd taken a sip,
Steve's mobile sounded. It was The Cap.

Steve put his phone on speaker so Andy could hear.

After the usual banter, The Cap got straight to the point, almost, he
couldn't resist a bit of humour.

"I'd make a great spy you know. I worked him like a puppet, and
you were right Steve, he's involved. Now listen up. I'm struggling so I'll

go slowly." Abul paused to gather his thoughts. Jenny was sitting with him listening to his explanation.

"Right. Dean tells me, he told his junior CID buddies not to spend time on an investigation. He says he sent them to the scenes to do a whitewash job as two foreign scrubbers weren't worth the time. He didn't visit the scenes, but just sent his juniors."

The Cap stopped talking, waiting for a response.

Steve spoke first. "Go on."

"Think about it. He didn't visit the scene but told his officers they were foreign scrubbers..."

"Oh, you beauty Cap!" Steve was seeing what The Cap saw. "If he didn't visit the scenes but knew who the girls were, he must have either dumped them or knows who did."

Steve sat back. "Jenny, unless it's against police regulations, give Abul a big kiss from me." The Cap had his mobile on speaker so Jenny could hear the conversations.

"Sorry, Steve," she called out. "I think The Cap would prefer you kissed him directly." Everyone laughed. This was a breakthrough, but it needed to be handled carefully.

"Listen you two. Not a word to anyone and I mean anyone. We need to treat this with kid gloves. This DI's probably only a cog. If we're looking at something big enough to bring these girls over from Romania, we're dealing with more than a DI from Essex." Steve was stroking his chin.

"Have you got any visits to repair shops arranged for today?"

"Yes, it's all arranged but Steve, there's more. Dean told me there was no point looking for a murderer who didn't exist. I challenged him on it, but he came up with a story as he realised he'd let something slip."

"What the hell does that mean Cap? A murderer who doesn't exist. Christ, we've got two dead bodies. Somebody did for them." Steve was feeling more than a little annoyed with himself.

"I'm only feeding back the results of my undercover work, sir." The Cap joked, breaking the tension. It worked.

"Yeah! Right James Bond. The pair of you'd better get off and, Jenny, can you come to the Yard tomorrow. I'd prefer if you weren't in

Chelmsford on your own. I've a feeling we're getting somewhere, and it might get nasty."

Steve and Andy sat in silence. Andy stood and marked up the whiteboard with this latest information. Steve noticed in addition to a new white shirt and silk tie his admin assistant was wearing fashionably cut casual trousers and a pair of slip-on black leather shoes. The old Andy was gone.

"What do we make of that then?"

Andy was looking serious. "I'm not sure, boss but he's definitely implicated."

Andy was fidgeting and Steve knew the signs.

"OK, Andy, out with it."

"How do we go about asking for a second post-mortem?"

"You mean any post-mortem or someone in particular?"

Andy gave a slight smile. "I've been inputting the pm results for the two Essex victims. I've got a screen that covers every element, so we don't miss anything. When I was loading the pm data for our Essex girls there seemed to be a bit missing. I'm no pathologist but in every pm report I've dealt with the vital organs have been weighed and commented on, but there's nothing. Also, because our victims were left with open gut wounds it's normal procedure to have an organ count—"

Steve interrupted.

"What's an organ count?"

"I spoke with one of the mortuary technicians. She told me that when a body has been opened and left outside in the wild, it's normal procedure to count all the internal organs in case animals, you know foxes, that sort of animal, have been around and made off with something for their next meal. Apparently, it's to keep a record of missing parts in case a member of the public picks up an odd kidney and a great search starts looking for a body."

"I see, carry on."

"Well, these bodies were left out and had been cut. There was no internal organ count either." Andy looked at Steve with a quizzical look.

"I'm thinking the post-mortem may have been rushed and maybe we're missing something. There are a lot of gaps so maybe a second post-mortem would fill in the gaps."

"You don't ask for much Andy. I'd need approval from our Commander and I'm not about to let him know what we're up to." Steve broke off and considered what his junior officer had just said.

"How important is this?"

"Truthfully, I don't know. I've just finished the reports for the CPS on the Hackney case, and they seemed very hot on the post-mortem evidence. Maybe I'm just worrying too much, but if we get our man, Dean Grantham, into court for these murders, we might have to reveal the pm evidence."

"Mm! Good thinking but I can't use upstairs."

Steve knew he had a problem. Andy was right. If the post-mortem evidence was called into question, then there might be reasonable doubt and the case could fail.

"Leave it with me, Andy, I'll think on it."

"There's something else. I ran Dean Grantham through DVLA to see if he had a white transit. He doesn't."

"OK, Andy, you carry on and I'll think about the post-mortems."

As Andy stood, a figure appeared at Steve's door. It was Superintendent Alfie Brooks. "Come on, young Steve, let's go for a coffee, you're buying!" With that, the senior officer turned and walked away expecting Steve to follow.

Alfie chose a corner table away from everyone in the canteen. The pair made small talk until their coffee arrived and they'd started to get the benefit of a caffeine boost.

"Right Steve, this is what I found out."

Steve already knew from Jenny that the NCA didn't sanction the Essex investigation, but he let Alfie carry on.

"First, the National Crime Intelligence Unit knows nothing about two bodies dumped in Essex. Second, without intelligence, the NCA won't act, so it's impossible that your Commander Bowles was given any authority from either body. He's setting you up."

"Yeah. I'd guessed that could be it. So, what do I do?"

"Nothing. Leave sleeping dogs alone. He's got some agenda, but we don't know what. Until you do just go with the flow. It's odds on that when you get close to an arrest, he'll show his hand. He has to, otherwise why lie to you to justify you taking the case?"

"Good point. Alfie, can I tell you something in confidence?"

"Fire away."

"My office was bugged. Someone's been eavesdropping on our investigation."

"Are you sure? That's pretty serious stuff."

Steve nodded. "Yes, Terry Harvey in Tech Support found them. He reckoned they were short-range so someone in this building's been listening in."

"And you think that might be Bowles?"

"I don't know but given he's sent me off on this case under false pretences, I can't think who else it might be."

"You are in a pickle. What are you going to do about it?"

"Nothing. The office is clean, and I have the bugs, and Terry Harvey, as evidence. I'll sit on this until I can see a way of using it."

The older detective sat in thought. "Leave it with me. I'll have a think and, if anything devious and cunning emerges from my tired old brain, I'll be in touch."

The pair parted and Steve returned to his office.

***

In his office, Steve looked up a phone number he thought he'd never use again.

He picked up the receiver and dialled the number not expecting to achieve much but he thought he would try.

"Good morning. This is the office of Sir Timothy Head. How may I help you?" It was the same man's voice that had stone walled Steve last time he tried to speak with the Head of Her Majesty's Civil Service. It had been on a previous case and Sir Timothy and Steve hadn't parted on good terms with Steve threatening to arrest the Whitehall mandarin.

"It's Detective Chief Inspector Steve Burt from New Scotland Yard. I need to speak with Sir Timothy as a matter of urgency. Please remind him of our last meeting."

"I'll see if Sir Timothy is available, but I think he's in the conference." The line went to funny non-melodic music. Steve had heard it before and if last time was anything to go by Sir Timothy would be too busy.

After about ten minutes of listening to rubbish, the line crackled into life. A very undiplomatic voice appeared on the other end.

"What do you want?" Sir Timothy didn't sound happy. "I thought I made it perfectly clear last time we met I did not expect to hear from you ever again."

"Yes, I remember Sir Timothy, but something's come up and you're the only person who can help." Steve knew he had to remain in control and not let the head of the civil service take the lead as he was used to doing. Steve carried on quickly before the voice on the other end could react.

"Remember the last time we met and the case I was working on? It was, in many ways, off the books, and you pulled the old boys' network to assist you and your friends in intelligence?"

"I did no such thing, as my statement at the time will confirm." Sir Timothy was full of indignation and bluster.

"As you say sir, but I require you to pull the same trick with your old boys' network again. Full denial of course."

"What do you mean the same trick?"

"I'd like you to ask Sir Humphrey Campbell for a similar favour as last time."

"You know perfectly well I did no such thing. It's not within my gift to ask favours from senior Home Office pathologists."

"No sir, but we both know you did, and we both know everything was swept under the carpet. All I need is Sir Humphrey to re-examine two murder victims. I have a situation here at the Yard that means I can't go through normal channels. A bit like the case I was given when we met last time."

"Oh! Is it important? Does it involve national security?"

Steve decided to bend the facts. "It is important Sir Timothy, otherwise I wouldn't have called, knowing how our last meeting ended. As to national security, it's too early to say, but foreign nationals are involved."

There was a long pause before Sir Timothy spoke again. "Listen, Inspector, this is bordering on harassment. If I ask Humphrey to help you then that's it. If I hear from you again, I will file harassment charges. Are we clear?"

"Yes, Sir Timothy and thank you."

A very flustered civil servant huffed and puffed but eventually said. "I'll ask Humphrey to call you but it's up to him. I can't order him to help. You understand?"

"Yes, sir and thank you."

Without another word the line disconnected.

Steve sat back exhausted. He'd not even expected to speak with Sir Timothy Head, never mind get him to agree to his request. As he sat, he recalled Lars Jenson's words about being connected and knowing people who can always help. Maybe this was how it worked.

***

The Cap called to say he and Jenny hadn't had any luck with finding the van and he was on his way back. Unless Steve needed him, he was going straight home and recover from his early start. The pair exchanged their respective views on progress and agreed to meet up first thing in the morning.

Steve called Andy in.

"I may be able to get the second post-mortem but I'm waiting for......" The phone on Steve's desk was ringing.

"Good afternoon Chief Inspector, it's Humphrey Campbell here. I understand you've got a bit of under the counter pathology for me?"

"Sir Humphrey." Steve couldn't believe his luck. He put the phone on speaker so Andy could listen. "Thank you for calling. I presume Sir Timothy called you?"

"Yes, he did. Something about a clandestine post-mortem. As much as I love all the cloak-and-dagger stuff you should know I'm off on my holidays this week. I'm long overdue a visit to my relations in Scotland and a bit of fishing so I may not be able to help you."

This wasn't what Steve wanted to hear. He decided to take a chance and explained in some detail the two cases he was working on, and Andy's view of the pathology in the post-mortem reports. He skipped over any reference to the Commander, only saying events internally required everything to do with the cases be kept secret. He took a lead from Sir Timothy and alluded to national security.

"And you say the original post-mortems aren't complete?" Sir Humphrey carried on in his lilting Scottish accent. "Of course, your man's right about the organ count and the circumstances in which it applies. Every pathologist is aware of it. I'm very surprised any colleague of mine wouldn't abide by the protocol." Sir Humphrey paused. Even down the telephone line, Steve could tell he was thinking.

"I'm not due in Inverness until Thursday. I'm busy tomorrow but Wednesday might be possible. I presume the cadavers are in Chelmsford?"

"I believe so." Steve realised he hadn't a clue where the bodies were, but he decided not to say so.

"As there are two, it's probably better if we go to Chelmsford. I'll round up my assistant and meet you in the mortuary at Chelmsford General at ten on Wednesday morning. I'm assuming that's where everything is. If it's different call me or send a text. I'll need the original post-mortem report sent over today."

Steve looked at Andy who nodded and mouthed, by e-mail.

"We'll get it to you immediately by e-mail and thank you, Sir Humphrey."

"Yes well, it sounds like a Le Carré novel, but I'll do it. Now, what about my report/ Even unofficial post-mortems leave a trail. I suppose you want it for your eyes only."

"Yes sir, if you don't mind."

"I don't mind. It's not my career that'll go tits up if anything goes wrong." The pathologist paused to let this statement sink home. "Ah well, make sure everything's set up. I don't want to be hanging around. Oh! By the by, I don't suppose the original pathologist will be too happy about this. I don't want to walk into an argument especially when this is unofficial. I'm looking to you to sort everything out. Are we clear?"

Steve was now very nervous and wasn't sure he should have started this course of events. "Yes sir, I'll make sure they are ready for you."

The pathologist hung up as Steve replaced the receiver and sat back letting out a huge sigh.

"Well, Andy. You've got the country's leading Home Office pathologist on the case. We're in the collective brown stuff if you're wrong." Steve didn't want to put pressure on Andy. It was his decision, but he was worried about the lack of detail or forward planning.

"Andy, get onto Chelmsford General. Confirm the bodies are still in their mortuary, then speak with Jenny. Tell her to delay her trip here tomorrow. She should sort things out at her end and then come down. If she gets any problems, she can say the Chief Home Office pathologist is attending on higher authority. We can mix the truth with the best of them. I want her at the hospital making sure everything's set up for Sir Humphrey on Wednesday morning, but she should try and keep it quiet for as long as she can."

Andy nodded and was about to leave.

"Andy, remember to e-mail those pm reports to Sir Humphrey." Steve paused. "Listen, Andy, this is getting too close for comfort." Steve made a decision. "I'm going to arrest this Dean Grantham on Wednesday while we're in Chelmsford. It may shake a few things out, but I don't want him running, so you and The Cap will go up first thing Wednesday and lift him. I'll interview him after Sir Humphrey's finished. Is that OK?"

"You really mean it, Steve? I'm out of the office on Wednesday and making a real arrest?" Andy was bubbling over.

"I promised you last time that you'd be more involved in the field on our next case. This is it, Detective Constable Miller."

Both men acknowledged each other and Andy who'd grown another six inches left to sort out Chelmsford mortuary and talk to Jenny. Like Steve, he hoped the bodies were still there.

Steve sat back and played with a ruler. He hadn't been able to bring whatever was nagging away at him forward. It was infuriating. He knew it was important, but he just couldn't grab it.

He decided to call it a night. He wasn't seeing Alison tonight so it would be a take-away, a glass of wine, some meaningless TV and an early night ready for tomorrow and his lunch with Lars Jenson.

Chapter Eleven

Tuesday the 16th of March had dawned as a grey day and had remained grey and overcast. It was depressing weather, and it matched Steve's mood as he got to the Yard. He thought a coffee would help so he went straight to the canteen and bought two strong black beverages, one for him and one for Andy.

Andy was hard at it as Steve walked into his office. He noticed Andy had a coffee but placed another on his desk.

"Thanks, Steve. There's one already on your desk but a second's always welcome."

"Come on in when you're free. Let's update, see where we are."

Andy arrived holding two coffee cups. Before Steve could open the meeting, Andy spoke.

"I sent the PM reports to the Home Office pathologist, and I got a confirmation back. The bodies are still in the morgue at Chelmsford so that's done. Jenny will be at the hospital about now and she'll call before she leaves. They didn't have any joy with the white transit." Andy paused but Steve knew the signs.

"Go on."

"I've been in touch with the Bucharest Federal guys again. I asked them what they knew about how their nationals get to the UK, you know, smuggling gangs, human traffickers and so on. They said they exist, but they didn't think our girls were trafficked. They'd double-checked with the families and both girls separately left their village to spend time in Bucharest before they travelled to the UK, according to the families." Andy paused but still, Steve knew he wasn't finished.

"Remember the Hackney case and how the killer enticed his victims with newspaper adverts?" Andy looked expectantly at his boss. "Well, I thought what if this is similar. Why would young girls living in rural villages in Romania suddenly up sticks and come to the UK, apparently all expenses paid? How does whosoever's behind it find these girls? He can't know them beforehand. The families are convinced it wasn't sex, so what was it? I've asked Dimitri to look over old newspapers four weeks before each girl left and see if there's any advert asking girls to go to the UK on any pretext. It's a long shot but it might throw up a Romanian connection."

Steve sat still. In many ways, Andy had overstepped his authority, but the DCI had to admit he got full marks for initiative. Not wanting to curb Andy's enthusiasm or initiative he let it pass without chastising the young officer. "Good call Andy let's see if anything comes back. By the way, who's Dimitri?"

"He's the station commander in Bucharest and is the only one who speaks English."

"You can find them." Steve sat up. "Right Andy, what've we got?"

"We think we've enough to arrest this Inspector Dean Grantham tomorrow. I'm assuming we'll charge him with murder?"

"Let's see, certainly accessory after the fact. He may not have killed them, but I bet he dumped them. He can tell us a lot, but that's for tomorrow. What else do we know?"

"Not a lot of tangible facts, just a lot of guesswork and supposition."

"You're right. We've got the second post-mortems tomorrow plus Dean Grantham. We'll have to hope something comes from that. The other stuff, like the bugs, is just smoke and mirrors just now. It's not leading to anything or anybody."

They were about to finish their meeting on this low note when Inspector Terry Harvey from Technical Support arrived. He looked pleased with himself, but Steve had noticed the Inspector was always jolly.

"I've got something for you if you're interested?"

Before either Steve or Andy could answer, The Cap arrived holding his coffee and a sticky bun. "What's going on?"

"Terry's about to make our day, I hope."

Terry Harvey grinned. "Well, if you'll accompany me to our new review suite, I'll show you."

Steve thought every time he met Terry, he had something new. Tech Support must have an unlimited budget. Then he remembered, the cunning old fox. Everything he'd done for Steve over the past few days he'd declared either as trials of new equipment or training. All these items came from separate budgets. Inspector Terry Harvey was spending other peoples' money. Steve had to smile at the realisation that someone had found a way of beating the system.

All three detectives plus Terry entered a cinema-like room. It had twelve cinema seats in a row facing a large sixty-inch TV screen. To the left was a desk with a bank of impressive-looking equipment with more flashing lights than a space shuttle. A woman was at the desk typing something onto a keyboard.

Everyone sat while Terry stood front and centre.

"Are you ready Monica?"

Being a detective, Steve deduced Monica was the technician seated at the desk.

"Right, gents, Andy asked us to use our new digital facial recognition software to look out for two girls arriving from Bucharest. One was about eight to nine weeks ago, the other around six to seven weeks ago. He asked us to look at CCTV of passengers arriving on flights from Bucharest, only during these times, and only flights into Stanstead and Southend airports." Terry was talking like a barrister in court, but Steve could see why. He wanted to be sure of his facts.

"Everyone OK so far?"

Andy answered for the team that it was.

"We were given post-mortem head shots of your victims to try and match to passengers arriving at these airports. Now what you must understand is a dead face is no good for our purposes. We need a live subject or at least a picture that shows what someone would have looked like when they were alive." Terry turned to Monica.

"First slide please." On the TV came an obvious pathology head photograph of one of the girls. "What our programme can do is this. Monica?"

On the screen, the image started rotating 180 degrees. It slowly morphed from an obviously dead person to someone alive. The process took about thirty seconds. Terry carried on not inviting questions. "The difficulty is the eyes, but the post-mortem gave them as brown, so we've given her brown ones." The inspector paused.

"Now we have a real-life image we can begin. Our software doesn't need a lot of images to compare. We feed in the image we've just created, and it scans as many subjects as we give it, comparing it to our sample. We use a ten-point matrix and if we get a minimum of six then it throws up a match."

He turned once more to Monica. "If you please, Monica?"

Terry sat beside Steve on the cinema seats holding a remote control while Monica hit a few keys and images of people arriving at an airport appeared.

"This is Southend arrivals dated 12th January."

The images carried on showing people being herded towards Immigration and then baggage reclaim. It was like being at the movies. The Cap thought only ice cream was missing but kept his thoughts to himself.

Suddenly the images froze. There on the screen was their first victim, Ingrid Baciu, arriving at Southend on the 12th of January.

Andy was making notes.

"That's very impressive, Terry."

Terry wasn't finished. He keyed his remote control and the images started to move again. The next camera covered passport control and again the image froze, showing Ingrid in line with other passengers.

"Now watch this." Using his remote, Terry set the TV in motion again. It showed the line of arrivals slowly moving forward and Ingrid was just visible on the left edge of the screen. "Now!" A man was seen approaching Ingrid and escorting her out of the line. The camera didn't pick her or the man again in either the immigration hall or baggage reclaim. "That's the last we see of her or him."

"Can you roll back to where he appears?"

Terry did and froze the image.

All three detectives looked in amazement at the screen. The Cap spoke first.

"Who is that guy? He's airside, so must have something to do with the airport."

"Can you print off these images Terry?"

"Of course, and in high definition."

There was a general easing of tension at Terry's comments.

"Do you want to see the next one?"

This was greeted by a universal yes.

The performance followed the same procedure until the images froze over a girl arriving at Stanstead Airport. Terry gave a similar summary that Andy feverishly wrote down.

"This is Stanstead Airport on 29th January. It shows your second victim arriving from Bucharest."

The inspector moved the images on. There were more cameras installed at Stanstead, so they had more shots of the victim. As before, the image from the camera in the passport control area froze then it picked up Tatania Popescu. The image re-started and showed her in line moving slowly forward.

"Look out, any minute now." The image once again showed a man approach the victim and escort her away from passport control. Terry allowed the images to carry on and the pair were seen landside heading for the car park.

"That's all we've got. We don't see them again."

Steve was pushing his hair back in frustration. "Who is that guy?" He hit the arm of his chair. "Terry, can you get us prints of all images of our victims and that bloke? I presume it's the same guy both times."

Terry smiled. "DCI Burt, do you think we're amateurs?" he mocked. "We've matched the two images and got ten points on the matrix so yes, it's the same man."

Everyone stood to leave but Andy collared the Inspector from Technical Support.

"Sir, can you get everything to me, like now? I've got an idea I need to run by the DCI, but the images would be useful."

Inspector Terry Harvey liked what he'd seen of Andy Miller. "No problem Andy. Monica will have them on your system before you get to your office."

Andy left happy and with a head full of possibilities, except Steve might have to call in one more favour.

***

The team assembled in the outer office, each man sitting at a desk. The excitement level was high, but everyone knew the information they had had only helped move things along. In itself, knowing when the girls arrived wasn't going to crack the case.

Andy was busy with his laptop printing off the information Inspector Harvey had forwarded from the CCTV images. The general consensus among the three detectives was that Terry Harvey was a star. He had the ability to know exactly what people needed and then providing it to them.

Andy distributed the pictures he'd just printed and went into Steve's office to update the whiteboard. He'd just finished putting the last photograph on when he heard a commotion in the outer office.

The Cap was almost jumping up and down. He seemed to be smacking his forehead with the palm of his right hand with some force. In his left hand, he held the picture Terry Harvey had produced confirming the man who met both girls was the same man.

"I'm a bloody idiot. Steve, this is DI Dean Grantham. I didn't spot it on the big screen but now looking at these pictures I'm certain that's him."

Steve was assessing this latest revelation when Jenny arrived. She was a quick learner, as she was holding a cardboard tray with four coffees.

She was welcomed as much for her gift of life-saving caffeine as the news she brought.

"It's all set for tomorrow for the pathologist. You know the bodies are still in the freezers?" Everyone nodded a yes. "I spoke at length with the technician on duty. She'll be there tomorrow." Jenny broke off and digressed with a smile on her face. "She seemed really excited that the Chief Home Office pathologist was going to re-post both bodies. It takes all sorts." After a pause, she continued. "I asked about the original post-mortems. Get this. She said they were done by a retired pathologist who she said must have been in his late seventies or early eighties. She's worked there for six years and had never seen this man before. He told her he'd been called as a favour to do the post-mortems but didn't say who called him. I'm supposing this is why the PMs weren't thorough."

"Interesting. Did you get this doctor's name?"

"Yes, he lives locally in Chelmsford."

"How is it that someone can specify who does post-mortems?" Steve was thinking hard and looking at his colleagues for answers. "Jenny, do you know how these things are allocated at Chelmsford?"

"No, but I could ask around and try to find out."

"Good, do that. Right Andy, let's have a recap again to tell us all what we don't know." Everyone laughed.

Andy taking his role as coordinator seriously, insisted everyone move into Steve's office so he could use the whiteboard for his explanations.

"The bits we know. Victim one, Ingrid Baciu, arrived at Southend Airport on the 12th of January. We know she was met airside by Dean Grantham—"

Steve interrupted.

"Sorry Andy, but a quick question for Jenny. How could Grantham get airside with all the security measures in place?"

Jenny addressed the trio while fishing in her handbag. "Most CID officers in Essex are cleared for airside at these two airports." She held up a lanyard with the usual plastic wallet hanging from it. It clearly said 'airport pass' and had her photograph on it. "It's because both have been given terrorist-divert status so we might get highjacked aircraft landing and we need to react quickly."

"We've got Grantham on CCTV escorting our victims out of the line before they cleared passport control. How could he get them landside?

"Easy, as a CID officer, he'd be checked in going airside. There's a special staff control point going in. If he walked out with one of these girls, he'd just walk back through the same control point to landside. No one would look twice. The issue is people going into the aircraft side, not coming back. There aren't any checks coming back."

"Mm, I see, thanks, Jenny. Sorry to steal your thunder, Andy." Steve held out his arm towards his DC in a gesture that said carry on. Andy did.

"No problem, boss, as I said, the first victim arrived on the 12th January." Andy pointed to the picture on the whiteboard. "Our second victim Tatania Popescu arrived at Stanstead Airport on 29th January and was also met by Dean Grantham." Again, Andy pointed to the victim and Dean Grantham.

"Now, it's our intention tomorrow first thing to arrest Grantham on a conspiracy to murder charge and after the fact. We're not sure he actually murdered these girls, but he must know who did. We know, as a result of The Cap's undercover work, that he knew who the victims were before anyone had even attended the scenes."

As Andy paused, The Cap raised his arms above his head and in a high-pitched voice announced. "I'm auditioning for the new James Bond, a spy extraordinaire." The serious mood that had descended on the room was suddenly lifted by Abul's humour.

Andy carried on. "We've got second post-mortems on our two victims taking place tomorrow and we're still looking for the white transit. I checked with DVLA, but Grantham doesn't have a transit."

Silence descended. Andy started "That's about—"

Jenny put her hand up. "Oh!" She spun around to look at Steve. "Boss, I'm so sorry. With everything going on, and hospital visits, I've not always been thinking straight. Even yesterday, when I was out looking at repair shops with The Cap, it didn't register. Oh! God, I'm so, so sorry." Jenny was distraught.

"OK, Jenny. What are you so sorry about?" Steve was being gentle but at the same time impatient.

"It's his brother. Dean Grantham's brother runs a local delivery business. You know 'Man and a Van' kind of thing." Jenny almost shouted at her colleagues, "He runs a white transit! I've seen him at the station meeting Dean."

All four detectives sat in stunned silence following Jenny's revelation.

Steve wondered if this was a missing piece of the jigsaw. "Let's not get carried away, although I think this could be important. We don't know if it's the van. We need to get eyes on it and see if it has that gouge in the side." Steve stopped to consider. "Do we have a name and address for the brother?" He was looking at Jenny.

"No, he lives in Chelmsford, but I can get it. I'll also get the registration number."

"Jenny, get someone you can trust to do a quiet drive-by once you've got the address. I want to know if this definitely is our van. If it is, it's another link back to Dean Grantham."

No one spoke and Steve reviewed what they'd just learnt. He stood up and went to the whiteboard. "Listen up. I don't want us to get ahead of ourselves. Dean Grantham's looking good for something, but until we interview him and maybe his brother, we don't know what we've got. If this is the van it may give us forensics that we're short of just now." Steve paused before handing out assignments.

"Jenny, get the brother's details, and arrange a drive-by, and check how pathologists are assigned cases. Andy, bring everything up to date, the CCTV and what Jenny's just told us. Cap, get onto Immigration to see if there's a record for our victims coming into the country officially. I'm wondering if Grantham could have spirited them in without going through passport control."

Everyone nodded their agreement.

"Now. As far as we know this DI Dean Grantham doesn't know we're coming for him tomorrow. If the brother's van checks out, then the same for him. We're in no rush, so let's make sure everything's lined up for tomorrow before we go blundering in with our size tens." Steve looked at his watch. It was time he left for his lunch appointment with Lars Jenson.

"We'll meet up here at four p.m. for a final briefing before tomorrow. Andy, double-check with Sir Humphrey that he's still on for tomorrow."

Steve left the team to their tasks and set off for the Ritz and his meal with Lars.

Chapter Twelve

The DCI was exactly on time as he entered the dining room of the Ritz Hotel. It was past its glory days but still commanded a respect from its patrons as being one of the finest hotels in Europe.

The room was large but not as large as Steve would have imagined. The walls were elegantly panelled and gold leaf had been used to highlight some of the intricate carvings blended into most of the panels. One end of the room consisted of floor to ceiling windows to allow light to flood in.

Steve estimated there were around sixty tables, all set for four people. Each table was covered by a crisp white and spotless tablecloth and was set out with fine cutlery and crystal glasses. Steve noticed the uniformed waiters who were dashing around; all wore white gloves.

At the threshold of the room stood a lectern and behind it was an impressive figure dressed in a white dinner jacket. He was studying something on the sloping shelf of the lectern as Steve approached. He explained he was to meet Mr Lars Jenson. The white jacket examined a list and asked Steve to follow him.

Lars Jenson was seated at a table by the windows. He was deep in conversation with another man and on seeing Steve approach he dismissed his partner and stood to welcome Steve.

"Thank you for coming, Steve. It's good to see you again. Have a seat."

The table was set for four people, but a waiter arrived and removed the other two place settings.

"Before we do anything you must have a drink. What's it to be?"

"Oh! Just sparkling water, I'm still on duty."

Steve deliberately dropped this fact into the conversation early in case Lars thought this was just a boys' lunch and the DCI might be less than discreet.

Lars called the waiter and ordered water for Steve and a whisky for himself. "If you're in no hurry we can get the menus just before we're ready to eat. I have a bit of a sensitive stomach and my doctor tells me not to rush things, especially my food." Lars rubbed his flat stomach. "Old age Steve; you're not there yet, but one day you'll know what I'm suffering." Lars gave a tight smile.

Both men passed the time by telling each other a bit about their personal lives. Their hates and their passions and generally feeling each other out. Steve had no idea why he was here but felt sure if he could keep the conversation friendly, he'd find out in due course.

Menus were produced and food ordered. Steve looked at the prices and realised Lars Jenson must be a very wealthy man. Whilst they worked their way through their delicious lunch, they made small talk. Then as they waited for their coffee Lars explained that he had found God several years ago and now his life was totally given to helping his fellow man. He explained he felt he'd been called.

Steve didn't comment but noticed Lars seemed, mentally at least, to have left the room. As a lapsed Christian, Steve was taken aback by the frankness of Lars' statement. He'd heard of such religious conversions but had never met anyone who'd done it.

"So how exactly do you serve God?"

"In any way that I can. I've set the company up to serve the needy and the desperate." Lars sounded like a preacher. "We give hundreds of thousands of pounds to charities and good causes. I set up Eclipse Medical when I learnt our troops were coming back from the Middle East conflicts wounded, shot up and with missing limbs. You know, early on there was little or no help for them. They'd sacrificed so much but this country couldn't help them lead a normal life. Someone had to take responsibility. Someone had to organise for their sakes. Our politicians certainly didn't. Our brave troops had been injured serving their country but were given no help." Lars was on an evangelical roll. Steve was interested and paid respect to this self-declared pioneer by listening quietly, but he was concerned by the intensity of Lars' words.

"I persuaded some of the finest mechanical engineers in the country to come and work for me. I'd inherited money from my parents and used this to establish a research and development unit in Harlow in Essex. Our engineers were brilliant, and we had our first prosthetic limb on the market six months after we started. The new limb was a great leap forward and we've continued to produce better and better prosthetics until today an amputee can do everything with one of our prosthetics that he could do with his own limb. Through me, God's given thousands of young men and women their lives back."

Steve could feel a power coming from Lars that he was uncomfortable with, but he felt duty-bound to comment. "Sounds like a success story, Lars. You must be very proud."

"No Steve, but it's nice of you to say so. It's the Lord's work. I'm only his servant."

Steve had to draw breath. He wasn't sure if Lars was indeed a religious zealot or halfway to being certifiable. On the surface he seemed absolutely normal, but when he spoke about doing the Lord's work his eyes shone and his whole demeanour changed. He spoke with a fierce conviction that was intense and frightening. Even now as the DCI sat at the table, his lunch partner was sweating and looking as though he was coming out of a trance. Steve sat and waited until Lars had collected himself.

When Lars Jenson next spoke, it was as though he had no recollection of regaling Steve with his religious beliefs or his reliance on God.

"Well Steve, that was a very pleasant lunch. Now!" Lars was the businessman again. "You'll be wondering why I invited you today?"

Steve was glad to be back on firm ground. He was uncomfortable in the rarefied atmosphere of religion.

"It did make me curious."

"Yes, just so." Lars paused staring at Steve. Almost weighing him up. Deciding what to say next. "As I said, I'm a religious man and I consider it my duty to help anyone in need. The problem is the government blocks me at every turn with their forms, red tape, British standards and worst of all their select committees. I tried working with them but soon realised if I was to be a force for good, I needed my own organisation. You do see that, Steve?"

Steve thought Lars was wandering again into a part of his brain that might get him certified. The DCI played along. "Yes, I can see why you'd be frustrated."

"Exactly, so I set about recruiting individuals who share my beliefs." Lars waved his arms. "Not religious beliefs but, of course, I always hope to bring sinners into the fold." He looked at Steve with a thin smile. "No, I'm talking about those who believe some other way exists of helping the people of this country. I've retained a few high-profile senior figures in the civil service, the judiciary, the police and the trades unions. We're beginning to make a difference." Lars sat back and examined Steve. After a few seconds of silence, he jumped forward and placed his elbows on the table. He looked directly into Steve's eyes. "I want you to join us."

Lars again sat back and let the silence hang.

Steve was shocked. He hadn't been expecting anything like this and was honest with himself. He wasn't sure what he'd been told. It sounded like Lars wanted to run the country and might be planning a coup, but he hadn't said so. Steve thought he should get out and away from this madman. But how?

"That's very generous of you Lars, but I'm only a DCI. I'm not powerful or senior enough to be of use to you."

"Ah! You see Steve, if you come on board, you won't be a DCI for long. I look after my Disciples and help them with their careers. After all, why keep a load of powerful influential parties if you can't use them. You'd be a Chief Superintendent within a month of coming on board and more besides. Why, Timothy Bowles would still be shuffling paper in admin if I hadn't recruited him and now look at him. He wants an MBE for services to policing. I can get it for him. There's nothing I can't do for my people. We will be running the country soon."

Again, the evangelical side of Lars was showing. He was mad enough to believe he might rule the country, but Steve had to admit, if Commander Bowles was an example, then Lars had some muscle somewhere.

"What would I have to do?"

"Nothing. That's the beauty of our Syndicate. There's no money involved, so no one's open to any potential corruption charges. You just let me take care of your career and when I need something doing that say, bypasses government policy or something that's not strictly legal, but is essential, then you're there in a position of authority to help. You see, we are the leaders. The naturally selected people who can take this country in the direction the people want. Other Disciples are equally important to the Syndicate but they're the foot soldiers. They take care of the less savoury tasks it's often necessary to perform. They get financially rewarded for their efforts but they're still with us. We're an army Steve, not a shooting one but an intellectual one ready to give the country the leadership it deserves. We can do things because of our strength of intellect and by having Disciples in the correct positions of authority." Lars was making a speech Steve suspected he'd made many times before. "Oh! we don't need elections. We already have the people with us who run the country anyway." Lars's eyes were huge almost popping out of their sockets. He appeared calm but somehow distracted. Steve thought Mr Lars Jenson was a nutter but a potentially dangerous nutter.

Lars drifted away but refocused on Steve after a few seconds. "Despite having, shall we say, *benefactors*, like any army, we always need funds. As a Christian, I'm always looking to help my fellow man and occasionally we find we can help and swell our coffers at the same time. That's our latest project. The Syndicate are very proud of the work we're doing in transplant surgery. Robbie Symonds is doing fantastic work helping the sick and earning us badly needed funds. You know Steve..." Lars now looked and sounded like a parish priest talking gently to a member of his flock. "... if you join us, you'll be embarking on the greatest journey of your life. Having another senior policeman as a disciple of the Syndicate will work for everyone. We're finding more and more the present archaic laws sometimes get in the way of our mission. Having Disciples in senior police positions helps us overcome these difficulties." Lars raised an eyebrow as he looked at Steve. He felt he was persuading the DCI to come over. "We all help each other; think of it as a form of the Freemasons except our aims are to run a better country for the people."

Lars suddenly changed tack. "You're getting married soon, aren't you?"

"Yes, in six weeks or so."

Lars was smiling an excited smile. "There you are then. You can get married in my private chapel in Buckinghamshire. I'll lay on a marquee and all the catering. I'll even lay on a band and my helicopter can take you and Dr Mills off on your honeymoon. It'll be a great day. What do you say? Let me organise this for you as a welcome present."

Steve was flabbergasted. He'd never heard anything like it although he could be tempted by the offer of the wedding at Lars's estate in Buckinghamshire. The DCI hadn't mentioned anything about the Commander and decided to ride his luck and lie.

"Lars, that's very kind. I'll have to discuss it with Alison first but if I did join your Syndicate, I'm not sure what you'd expect. You said Tony Bowles was a member." Steve made himself sound as though he were only making conversation. "What sort of things has he done recently?" Steve crossed his fingers hoping he hadn't gone too far, and that Lars might be blinded by the thought of a new recruit.

"He's not had to do much over the years. All he's done recently was get you onto the two murders in Essex. I want them cleared up and someone convicted, otherwise they'll remain open and any snooper could get involved in a few years. Better to get it solved, then it's finished. That's the sort of help our Disciples give."

Steve was about to search deeper, but Lars abruptly stood and said his driver had arrived. He thanked Steve for coming and asked him to consider becoming a disciple of the Syndicate. He said he'd keep in touch, but the movement was on the march. He stopped halfway to the exit. "And Steve, let me know about the wedding, I'd love to host it."

With a wave, he was gone.

Steve sat at the table trying to analyse what he'd just heard. A coup in England. It was a joke, no matter how much money you had, it would never happen. What he had learnt was several senior figures were open to blackmail if their connection to Lars' Syndicate ever became known. He had confirmation of Anthony Bowles' involvement and that was a bonus. Almost worth sitting through lunch with a madman for. He'd have to break this down and debate it with the team.

***

The four p.m. meeting was beginning as Steve arrived back. Everyone was in the outer office again and seated at their individual desks. On his way to the office, Steve had re-run some of Lars Jenson's statements in his mind, and was now very concerned, but hadn't a clue how to proceed. He suspected Lars had admitted to involvement in the murders, but it had been subliminal. There was nothing he could get hold of. He decided to forget about his lunch for now and concentrate on tomorrow.

"I presume you've all had a coffee?" Steve opened with a light-hearted comment.

"And no one thought the poor old DCI might need one?"

Andy chirped up. "There's one on your desk."

Everyone relaxed and sorted their notes.

"Right, Jenny, what've you got?"

"The van. I got a DC I trust to drive by the brother's house. He wasn't in and the van wasn't there. My DC showed a bit of initiative and spoke to the wife saying he had an urgent job but needed to check if Philip's van..." Jenny broke off, "that's the brother, Philip Grantham... was big enough. The wife told him where Philip was working. He was doing a house clearance job."

"The shortened version please, DS Fuller." Steve was impatient to get on.

"Sorry, sir. Bottom line, the transit has a bloody great gouge out of its near side."

The room almost cheered. Jenny carried on. "I spoke with the Chief Medical Officer for Essex. They told me post-mortems are allocated to pathologists on a revolving basis, routine stuff, deaths in hospitals, traffic accidents and that sort of thing. When their name gets to the top of the list it's their turn. There are only four of them. More interesting deaths, you know high profile rock stars and so on, the senior pathologist pulls rank and generally does those. Bringing in the retired old boy was an instruction from the Chief Medical Officer."

"Mm, thanks, Jenny." Steve wondered if the main man in Essex was a Disciple of the Syndicate.

"Cap, how did you get on?"

"You're right, Steve, Immigration have no record of our victims entering the country. This Dean Grantham must have done as Jenny suggested, and taken them through the staff channel."

"Right, so let's plan tomorrow. We need to change things a bit." Steve surveyed the faces in front of him.

"Cap, you'll have overall command and control of both arrests. We need an early start so we get both arrests as simultaneously as we can. Jenny, pick out a place to meet at say, seven-thirty in Chelmsford."

Steve thought about how best to coordinate the arrests, despite the groan from The Cap at the mention of the time to meet. "Jenny, can you take this DC, who did the drive-by Philip Grantham's place, with you? It'll be you and him on the brother's arrest. I want him in custody before his brother. You must lift him from his home before he goes to work. I don't want it to be too early and I don't want his wife alerting her brother-in-law that his brother is in custody. Wait until you see him leaving and do the deed then, OK?"

"Yes, we can do that. Am I arresting him or asking him in for a chat?"

"Good point, try a chat and if he's awkward, arrest him on suspicion of aiding and abetting murder."

"Will do."

"Cap, once Jenny's got the brother, I want the van seized and a forensics team all over it. Use a team from here, but they can work in Chelmsford nick, OK?"

"Right, on it."

"Jenny as you're local, you'll stick with the van and forensics. I want to know the minute they find anything. Clear?"

"Crystal."

Steve noted Andy was smiling like the cat with the cream. "Also, Jenny, when you've got the brother, phone Abul. Cap, that'll be the signal for you and Andy to arrest Dean Grantham. He should be in the office. Jenny says he's a lazy sod, so I don't expect any problems. All clear."

"Yes, if I'm awake. You know seven-thirty in Chelmsford means another crack of dawn start. I'm not made for early mornings." Again, The Cap's humour helped settle nerves.

"Cap, I'll leave you to sort out the finer details. Get both men back here as soon as possible. I don't want them anywhere near Chelmsford cells if we can help it. You'll need additional transport. Cap, can you lay that on? Best get a couple of lads from here to follow you up and meet you before you arrest Dean."

"Yes, I'll talk to traffic. They always like an away day." Another joke but subdued. "Andy and I will take one car."

"Good. I'll go straight to the hospital and meet Sir Humphrey. Andy, if you and The Cap are finished, say before ten-thirty, come to the mortuary. You might learn something, after all you started it. You can come back here with me." Andy wasn't smiling so much now.

"Cap, once you're done, get back here and process our brothers. Leave them sweating until the afternoon. I should be back by early afternoon, and you and I can start on them then." Steve looked at the three faces in front of him.

"All clear?"

"Yes." Nods all around.

"I'm seeing the Deputy Chief Constable tomorrow before the post-mortems, so I'll be in Essex Headquarters between say eight-thirty and nine-thirty. If you get things tied up while I'm still there come and find me. Clear?"

Without waiting for an answer, the DCI retreated. "Good luck, see you all tomorrow."

He went into his own office and left the team to sort out their arrangements.

***

Steve was due at Alison's later. She'd said she didn't have any patients in the afternoon, so Steve had said he'd try and get to her place around seven.

He'd been thinking over all the events and was surprised that it was only four days ago he'd first met Lars Jenson, yet he'd now seen him three times. He thought over what Jenson had told him. It was clear the man was most probably deranged in some way and the shrinks would have a word to describe his megalomaniac character.

Steve debated with himself but didn't think that they were arresting the murderer. He conceded the arrests were of people involved, but his

107

job was to find the killers. He was arranging events inside his head from Alison to Commander Bowles to Lars to the team. He also returned to the thing floating around in his subconscious. The more he tried to recall the events of last Friday and the dinner, the further away whatever it was seemed to go. After about ten minutes he decided to call it a night. Everything was set for tomorrow, so he'd go home, change and comfortably be at Alison's before seven p.m.

A knock on the door frame got his attention. "Steve, got a minute?" It was Andy.

"Yeah, of course, take a seat."

Andy once seated opened his laptop and placed it on Steve's desk but facing himself. Steve thought Andy looked nervous and wondered if it was the prospect of attending two post-mortems that had him spooked.

"Steve, I've been looking at what we got from the CCTV at the airports. We know when the girls arrived, and I've worked back to the flights they had to have come in on. Remember I asked my contact, that's Dimitri in Bucharest, to check newspaper adverts? Well, he did but came up empty. There's clearly a link so I thought what if we could find who bought the aeroplane tickets for the victims? It's not normal these days to pay cash, so we might get a name from a credit card."

"Andy, that's a great thought. You're going to tell me you know who bought the tickets." Steve was animated all of a sudden.

"Ah! I'm afraid not. We can get the airline to open their records and for sure there'll be the booking details — but we'll need a court order. Luckily, the airline is UK based, so a UK court can issue the order. I just wondered if you could somehow get a judge to sign an order?"

"Bloody hell, Andy, you really don't know what you're asking." Steve thought was a very good idea. If they could identify who bought the tickets the victims travelled with, then they would be closer to the killer. But... in the present cloak-and-dagger environment they were working in, getting a court order was impossible. Commander Bowles would have to sign off on it and the cat would be out of the bag as far as the investigation went.

"There's no other way, Andy?"

"No Steve, I phoned the airline and tried smooth-talking them, then I tried, it's only a small request, only take seconds and finally I threatened them with you. Nothing. They're adamant that without a court order we'll see nothing."

"You know we have a problem with upstairs. There's something else I need to let you and the team in on but not yet. Let's just say we should stay away from Bowles for as long as we can."

"I just wondered if you could pull something out of the air the way you did for the second post-mortems?"

"I'm not a magician, DC Miller." Steve smiled at his colleague. "Leave it with me. You're sure you have enough to justify a court order?"

"I think so. Two victims, flying into the UK, avoiding immigration checks. They couldn't have afforded the flight tickets, but we need to know who paid for them hence the request for the court order. Both girls were found murdered. I think that should be enough?"

"Yes, as long as it doesn't look like a fishing trip."

"I've got an idea. Now go home, you've got an early start tomorrow, and a full-on day."

After Andy had left, Steve phoned Jenny's mobile. She answered on the first ring. "Jenny, where are you?"

"I'm just on my way to the garage and then off to meet Ian for a drink and a meal in town. Why? Do you need something?"

Steve considered his next statement and chose his words carefully.

"Yes, I do Jenny, but it's your partner I need to see. Is there any chance we could meet up for a quick drink? I don't want to disturb your plans, but it's important."

There was silence while the DS thought. "It's four forty-five. I'm due to meet Ian in the Swan, off Fleet Street at five. Can you get there?"

"If I leave now, I'll be right behind you. Thanks, Jenny, I'll buy the first round."

Steve set of to meet Jenny and her partner. Andy was still at his desk working away. "If I pull this off DC Miller, you'll owe me a very large drink. See you in the morning."

With that, Steve flew out the door.

***

The Swan pub was a typical central London affair. Very old world, it was tucked up an alleyway off a side street that connected to the main thoroughfare of Fleet Street. It had once been popular with the newsmen and women when Fleet Street was the centre of newspaper production. This had all moved to the outskirts of London at Wapping, and the Swan had reinvented itself as a destination pub catering for office types and lawyers working nearby at Lincolns Inn.

Steve made good time and arrived a few minutes after Jenny. She was at the bar standing next to a tall man dressed in the barrister's uniform of a dark jacket, pinstriped trousers and a white shirt, now open at the neck. The outfit was completed by a waistcoat matching the jacket. The barrister was about forty with a full head of light brown hair and designer glasses that seemed too small for his face.

Jenny introduced Steve to her partner Ian Fuller, and the three agreed to take a table away from the bar. The floor area wasn't big, and people had started spilling out into the courtyard in front of the pub.

"Ian, I'm sorry to interrupt your evening."

"Not at all." The voice was educated and more home counties than Essex. "Jen's told me all about you." He gave his partner a delicate nudge. "I think you have a fan, Detective Chief Inspector."

Steve let the remark pass to spare Jenny's blushes. "Please, it's Steve."

Ian Fuller nodded.

"I have a problem, but I need you to keep this conversation confidential."

Jenny stared at Steve and Ian replied. "Of course, if I can, but you realise as an officer of the court I'm duty-bound to report anything illegal that you tell me?"

"Oh Ian, don't be such a stiff shirt. If Steve needs your help, then unless he admits to murdering someone, you'll help him, won't you?" Jenny was formidable. Her barrister partner seemed to wilt in front of Steve.

"Well, just so we're clear. Of course, I can use my discretion." Ian had become a bit pompous.

"We're working on a double murder in Essex. Jenny may have mentioned it. I've got a situation at the Yard, where a certain senior officer may be under suspicion of being involved. Unfortunately, he's one of the officers I report to. We've been running the investigation under the radar and I've had to bypass him in order to keep our progress to ourselves. I've called in a few favours so that, so far, having to work this way hasn't affected our investigation." Steve paused to make sure Ian understood. After all, he was a lawyer.

"That is until now. I need something and can only get it by involving my superior officer and I don't want to do that."

"And you think I can help."

"Yes. I'm not sure but I couldn't think of anyone else. I know we've just met and it's a real cheek, but Jenny will tell you this hasn't been an easy case because of our issues internally."

"What is it you want?"

Steve gathered his thickest skin around him and ploughed on. "I need a court order to examine some financial records of a UK-based airline."

The barrister almost spat out his beer. *"What!"*

Steve didn't reply knowing Jenny's partner had heard and understood.

Ian Fuller put his glass down and after gathering himself together following the initial shock "I suppose you have grounds for this?"

"Yes. Getting sight of these financial records could be key to solving the case."

"And under normal circumstances, you'd have no difficulty getting such an order?"

"Yes."

"It's highly irregular." The barrister was obviously thinking about how to get out of this predicament. He wasn't a conspiracy theory type. He liked things straight and simple.

He was about to say no when Jenny pulled at his sleeve. "Come on Ian, you know you can do it. It won't cost anything and just think, if we solve the case, and can mention your initiative, the CPS will be very grateful. You might even get a promotion."

Whether or not Jenny's intervention helped no one would ever know. After a few moments and having been preparing to turn Steve down, Ian Fuller looked up at Steve. "Yes OK, if it's within my remit."

Steve could have hugged him. "Thank you, Ian, I really appreciate it. If you give me your contact details, I'll get the case for the order sent over to you tonight. I have a DC who's always working. And can you only put my name on the order and only deliver it to me?"

The Deputy Head of the Crown Prosecution Service gave Steve his card. "Yes, if I have your details."

The three sat and finished their drinks. Steve looked at Jenny and while Ian was looking elsewhere, he mouthed a "thank you" in her direction. She smiled sweetly back knowing she'd helped the DCI.

On his way back to his car Steve phoned Andy who, as predicted, was still at the office. Steve explained what he needed and read out Ian Fullers contact details. "And remember, only my name is to go on the order."

Andy understood. Before Steve hung up Andy confirmed the data had already been sent. "How did you manage that?"

"There's a form I found that you use when requesting court orders. I filled it in as though we were going through official channels and it means all the information's there. I knew you'd come up with something." Andy said this with pride in his voice. "The only things I crossed out were the ranks of the requesting officers and put your name on. You know you need three sponsors, all above Commander rank?"

"Really, no Andy I didn't know that." Steve suddenly felt tired and weary. "Maybe I've been promoted but remember, you owe me a large drink."

"You've got it."

Steve was about to hang up when his mind returned to lunch with Lars and promotion. "Andy, do something else. Pull all you can on a firm called Eclipse Medical. You know accounts, directors, bank accounts, background checks on the directors, the whole nine yards."

"Right. I'll get the request over to Company's House and the Intel unit plus the collator. Always best to cast the net."

"Now, when you've done that, for goodness sake go home." Steve hung up.

He looked at his watch. It was just approaching six p.m. He decided to skip going home and head straight for Alison's instead. An evening talking about wedding plans and guest lists were just the distraction he needed.

A quiet night and an early bed. Or so he thought!

Chapter Thirteen

Steve got to Alison's house just before seven. She was amazed to see him arrive on time. "I've made a salad. I never expected you to be early, your normal seven p.m. usually turns out to be nearer nine." She walked up to him and kissed him. Alison put her arms around Steve for another kiss but then gently pushed him away. "You look tired, darling, why not have a shower and change, the salad will keep."

Steve did as Alison suggested and on his return to the open-plan living and dining kitchen, he felt more refreshed but still tired.

As they ate, they discussed their day, with the by now understood caveat that neither could go into any detail that might be sensitive.

"I spoke with Robbie Symonds today. You remember? From last Friday's dinner party."

"How could I forget the pompous snob, right little prat!"

"Yes. Well, he's still a very good surgeon. Anyway, a patient of mine needs a transplant and I remembered Robbie was working privately for Eclipse Medical." She stopped to laugh. Still laughing she carried on. "Remember that awful speech the man Lars gave. It made my skin crawl."

Steve remembered but he'd heard worse, only today.

"Anyway, she needs a new kidney and has been on dialysis now for over a year. The national database hasn't been any good so out of curiosity and desperation for my patient, I called Robbie. He—"

Steve stood up without warning almost causing his chair to topple backwards.

"That's it! That's what I've been missing."

Alison hadn't seen her fiancé as excited as this about work before. She wondered what was happening.

Steve sat down and looked at Alison. "Sorry darling, but I've had something at the back of my mind since last Friday. Something that was said that could impact on my case." He couldn't sit still, and Alison remained quiet, waiting for her fiancé to calm down and explain himself.

"How many people are on the register for transplant surgery?" Steve was now calm and pleased he had retrieved the information with Alison present.

"It varies, but hundreds at any one time."

"And how many get new organs by transplant in an average year?"

"Not many, low hundreds."

Steve was getting excited again but this time he kept himself under control.

"Remember what the CEO of Eclipse Medical said last Friday? Your pal Robbie was geared to do thirty transplants from three theatres a month. That's ninety a month. Over ten months that's nine hundred organs being harvested for transplants. From the numbers you've given it's not possible, especially if you take the other transplants going on all over the country into account." Steve looked expectantly at Alison.

"Don't you see, they can't be working legally. They must be getting organs from someplace outside the official channels."

Alison became a doctor. "I see what you're saying but harvesting from live donors is illegal. Also, nine hundred a year is an incredible number. Where could they possibly get that number of organs?"

Steve had a sly grin on his face which annoyed Alison. "Romania."

"What! Why Romania, and why do you have that silly grin on your face?"

"It's too early to say with certainty, but the post-mortems tomorrow will confirm it. I bet our two victims are missing some of their internal parts."

Steve went on to explain the cases he was working on and how the girls had been found.

"Certainly, if they'd had surgery to remove organs then slicing their stomachs would be a way of disguising the surgery but it's pretty awful." Alison was visualising the scene Steve had painted.

Alison sat back and studied her empty coffee cup. "I was telling you, before your outburst," she playfully hit him on the arm, "about my conversation with Robbie. What you've just said makes sense. There's no match for my patient on the national register just now but Robbie made an appointment to see my patient. He wants me to go with her. He said he was certain he could help and there were kidneys available if you knew where to look." Alison stared ahead recalling her conversation. "He said a strange thing now I think about it. He said a rejection of the organ was minimised because they could get very close matches. You could read that as him saying he has more than one kidney and he'll use the best match.

"I'd never have thought about that until you told me about your cases."

They moved to the more comfortable sofa, content to enjoy each other's company and continued their conversation.

"You know, darling, when I spoke with Robbie, he had no shame about money. Up front, he said it would cost twenty-five thousand pounds for the operation and another five thousand in follow up care. That's thirty thousand pounds each transplant."

Steve, being a policeman, was ahead of Alison. "That's thirty thousand times say nine hundred. If they do what they claim, that's twenty-seven million pounds a year. I'll add this to things to do tomorrow but I bet Sir Humphrey confirms missing organs. Andy's done it again. The idea to redo the post-mortems is down to him."

Steve told Alison most of the conversation he'd had with Lars at lunchtime but kept back his assessment of the man. He teased her by saying their wedding was now going to be at Lars' Buckinghamshire estate all paid for by him. They'd even be whisked away on their honeymoon by helicopter.

"I hope you said no?"

Steve, playing the miserly groom. "Well, it's all free and it is a stunning location."

"DCI Burt, if you think I'm getting married, in what you've now told me could be a crook's estate, then you'll be the first groom in history to walk down the aisle on your own." Alison pretended to be annoyed but smiled.

"I haven't said one way or the other, but I knew you wouldn't like it, and neither would I. We'll just have to stick to our original plans. Talking of which, you haven't mentioned seating plans or taxis so far tonight."

Alison threw a cushion at Steve and the pair laughed. The laughter finished up with them lying in each other's arms watching something on television that neither was following.

The pair were thinking about a glass of wine and Alison had just gone into the kitchen when the wall-mounted phone buzzed. Someone was at the front door.

"Are you expecting anybody?"

"No, see who it is, darling, and I'll get the wine. If they are selling something I'm not interested."

As Steve went to lift the receiver, he looked at his watch and commented, "If it's a door-to-door salesman at nine at night he deserves to sell something."

He lifted the receiver and a grainy picture appeared on a small screen that was part of the phone. It showed a figure standing outside the front door.

"Yes?" Steve felt this was an obvious greeting.

"Is that DCI Burt?"

A little wary in his answer. "Who wants to know?"

"I'm sorry to intrude, Inspector, it's Patrick Bond. We met a few months ago at New Scotland Yard."

Steve searched his memory banks but couldn't place the name. Maybe if the image on the small screen were clearer, he might recognise the caller.

"I'm sorry, the name's not familiar, and it's nine p.m. If it's urgent, make an appointment with the Yard for tomorrow afternoon."

Steve was about to hang up. Alison had returned carrying two large glasses of red wine.

"Inspector." The voice now sounded more threatening than before. "It's Sir Patrick Bond of MI6. It's important I speak with you tonight."

Steve's jaw fell. He remembered Sir Patrick from their last meeting, but what was this most senior spook doing standing on Alison's doorstep? Steve put his hand over the speaker and gave Alison a quick message about who wanted to come into her house. She shrugged and nodded but with a quizzical look on her face.

Steve pressed the lock release and Sir Patrick entered.

The head of MI6 was an imposing man and quite tall. He was wearing an overcoat that he removed and handed to Alison, who in turn offered him a glass of wine.

Steve was suspicious of this man. Their last meeting had ended badly, and like the other senior government figure he'd spoken to recently, both had declared their intention never to speak with the DCI again, but here he was.

The usual introductions were made, and Alison was impressed that her fiancé moved in such exalted circles. Sir Patrick was fawning in his apologies for interrupting the couple's evening, but he continued to sit. He might be sorry, but he wasn't moving now he was here.

"I'm sorry to intrude but there's something I need to ask and something you need to know before tomorrow," Sir Patrick said to Steve.

"Fine, fire away."

Sir Patrick studied Alison.

"I'm sorry, Dr Mills, but you haven't signed the Official Secrets Act. What I have to discuss with Mr Burt is covered by the act."

Alison looked at both men. Steve's face was blank. "So, you want me to disappear so you two can have a secret talk. Is that it?"

"Very well put, Doctor, it should only take about a quarter of an hour."

"Steve, I've got things to do in the other room. Call me when you're finished." Alison left, but deliberately let both men know she wasn't pleased about being excluded from their discussion.

The architecture of Alison's converted house meant that the door of the bedroom she was now standing in could not be seen from the lounge. She deliberately didn't close the door completely, but left it slightly ajar, knowing she'd be able to eavesdrop on the conversation taking place in her lounge.

Sir Patrick started. "Steve, may I call you Steve? I'll get straight to the point." Sir Patrick pulled a small notebook from his inside jacket pocket. He didn't open it. "You had lunch with Lars Jenson today. What did you discuss?"

Steve was taken aback. Why was the head of MI6 doing the job of an agent? Steve asked Sir Patrick this very question.

"It's a very sensitive operation, Steve. I'll happily explain, but first can you please answer my question?"

Steve wasn't sure how to react. It wasn't every day you realised MI6 must have had you under surveillance. "Why do you want to know?"

"Steve, you're not making this easy." Sir Patrick looked directly into Steve's eyes. Steve saw he was agonising over a decision. Sir Patrick decided to come clean with the DCI.

"I'll tell you everything but must remind you that you signed the Official Secrets Act."

"Understood." Steve settled back on the sofa awaiting a good story.

"Lars Jenson is head of an organisation in this country called the Disciples of the Syndicate. A silly name, but it seems to have been universally accepted. They are linked to several other ultra-right-wing organisations all over the world, Europe, the States, South America. You name a country and there's bound to be a cell of right-wing troublemakers. Lars Jenson sees himself as the leader of all these organisations worldwide." Sir Patrick took a sip of wine.

"I don't know how much of this you already know?"

"Assume nothing."

Sir Patrick nodded. "He runs what looks like a legitimate business called Eclipse Medical, but it's a front for his subversive activities. He believes the democratic system of elected government doesn't work for the man in the street. He believes that there are only a handful of people who run the country and are not elected." Sir Patrick gave a sly smile. "He's talking about people like myself and Sir Tim Head. You remember he's Head of the Civil Service. Well, the theory is that if his organisation can infiltrate the most senior echelons of British public life, then there's no need for parliament nor politicians. You see, he surmises these people call the shots anyway. Parliament and the politicians merely act on their advice." Sir Patrick drained his glass. Steve topped it up.

"You know, in some ways he is right. Take my own case, I report to a Minister who knows nothing about international security. He asks me questions, I answer, and he simply repeats my answers as his own. So, who's running our international security? The Minister or me? I think it's me, and I'm not elected."

"I see that but how can he recruit people like you? You're not silly enough to believe all this world domination nonsense."

"That's what we don't know." Sir Patrick leant forward. "Look, Steve, you asked why am I here and not one of my agents? The simple truth is we don't know who to trust any more. We believe this Syndicate have already corrupted a lot of senior people, even police officers. Normally it would be MI5 that would deal with this or your NCA, but it's international and this guy's reach seems to go all the way to the top. We're at the stage we don't know who to trust. We've got judges dismissing solid cases or handing down light sentences. When this happens, we're looking at them individually to see if there's a link to the Syndicate. Of course, we can't prove anything."

Steve saw why this senior man was here. He had no one he could trust that he could delegate to. "Is this the same all over Whitehall? You don't know if any head of a department, politician or civil servant is or is not a disciple?"

Sir Patrick's eyes lit up. "So, you *do* know something." He allowed a small 'I knew it' expression to pass over his face. "In answer to your question, we don't know if any of the heads have been turned. Most of us have known each other for years and we rely on everyone abiding by our unwritten code, but it's a worrying time. We don't know all senior government or judiciary members personally just as you don't know all your senior officers personally. That's why I need to know what you discussed today at lunch with Lars Jenson. You said last time we met that we were good observers, but the police were better investigators and I need an investigator's take on Lars Jenson." Sir Patrick waited. He'd said enough. He now had to rely on Steve's goodwill and sense of honour.

Steve sat not looking at anything in particular. Sir Patrick told a good story most of which Steve already knew. He knew the bit about the police being the investigators was true.

"OK, Sir Patrick…"

"Please, just Patrick, however, I draw the line at Pat." Sir Patrick had obviously told this one before. He allowed himself a small smile.

"Right." Steve looked over at Sir Patrick. "Patrick, Lars Jenson told me more or less what you've just said. The bit you missed was that he's a religious nutter who wraps everything he does in the word of the Lord.

He told me his Disciples are split into two. The higher ones, like judges and senior civil servants, are rewarded by his ability to pull strings. You know, promotions, honours, plum overseas postings and so on. The second string is what he called the foot soldiers. They are the doers. They get rewarded by cash payments, but he said they were equally loyal to the Syndicate, just not as intellectually attached. He went on about not needing a Parliament, and as you said, he believes a handful of people run the country despite the government or Parliament. He didn't say anything about an overseas element." Steve opened his arms to say he was finished.

"Mm, and that's it. Nothing else?"

"Only to confirm what we suspected that our Commander's part of the Syndicate. He's pulled a few strokes and I'm now conducting a double murder enquiry behind his back because I don't trust him. I also suspect the Chief Medical Officer of Essex might be a Disciple, but I can't prove it." Steve debated whether to tell Patrick about his cases. He decided it was relevant so carried on.

"The other thing that's connected is the cases I'm working on." Steve went on to tell Patrick about the murders, how the bodies were found and about the post-mortem carried out by a retired pathologist.

"We believe our victims were killed for their organs. There may be a supply line running from Eastern Europe supplying spare body parts that this Robbie Symonds transplants into wealthy recipients. Lars went on about helping deserving people and at the same time bringing in funds for the cause. Alison and I calculated tonight that the transplant operation alone brings in around twenty- seven million pounds a year. We've got an operation tomorrow to arrest some people who may or may not be foot soldiers or Disciples, but the Eclipse Medical clinic's definitely involved."

"What did Jenson say your Commander would get as a reward?"

Steve smiled "An MBE for services to the police." Both men exchanged glances that said he's an idiot.

"Lars also said a peculiar thing about the murders. He asked my Commander to get a result so the cases wouldn't be left open and some curious cop could later start to re-investigate them as cold cases. He more or less admitted to knowing about the killings. I got the impression he didn't care who went to court as long as we got a guilty verdict." Steve thought he may have said too much but felt this was now a conversation rather than an interview.

He continued. "Commander Bowles has also been promoted at the behest of Lars Jenson, at least according to Jenson. He said I'd be a Chief Superintendent within months."

Patrick's body language suddenly changed. He was alert. "Hang on, are you saying you've joined him?"

"No. He offered me the chance to become a Disciple. He even offered to host my upcoming wedding at his Buckinghamshire estate."

"Steve let's stop there just now. Can I ask you for another glass of wine? We've got something more to discuss."

With their glasses refreshed, Patrick cleared his throat. He took several minutes to come to a decision. He knew if he opened up to this DCI there was no going back. He decided to take the risk.

"Steve, what I'm about to discuss is so far off the books we wouldn't even have to deny involvement if things went wrong." Patrick had a sincere look.

"I know you've signed the official secrets act so I can be frank." Patrick cleared his throat.

"I was summoned to the Prime Minister's office yesterday. I'd written a report outlining the existence and activities of the Syndicate. The PM was copied in on it and was furious as well as being concerned. Once he understood we could trust no one he ordered me to take personal charge and not involve MI5. As it's domestic it would normally fall to them. He's set up a small team to deal with this and I report directly to him. That's why you have the Head of MI6 acting as a field agent." Sir Patrick looked for signs of Steve's understanding of the gravity of what he'd just said. He carried on.

"The Prime Minister knows the only way to make sure we shut this Syndicate down is to get a list of all of its members. There has to be a record of names somewhere. I've been trying to find a way into this Syndicate since we first came across it. We've had Lars Jenson and this other doctor Robbie Symonds under surveillance for weeks, but they haven't put a foot wrong. Our only way to crack this thing is to get a man on the inside. It's a closed shop but if you've been invited to become a member and, to put it bluntly, we can trust you, then I'm asking you to take up Lars Jenson's offer and become a Disciple."

Steve was amazed that the country's most senior spy would ask him such a thing.

"Patrick, I think you're getting our roles confused; I'm the policeman, you're the spy."

"I realise that, but we have no idea how to get someone invited in. We can't just roll up and say excuse me, we'd like to join, please. No, your invitation is, I'm positive, our best way in, and to crack this. The thing we need to know is how many people have been corrupted into working with this Syndicate. I'm sure some of them do it due to a misplaced sense of patriotism, others for personal gain. But no matter their reasons for becoming Disciples they are betraying their country. The only way to close this down is to round up everyone connected to Lars Jenson. I don't want to pull the patriotism card on you Steve but surely you see you are uniquely placed to help your country."

Steve was still in mild shock. "I've got two murders to solve and other responsibilities. I just can't commit to something like this, besides if I say yes, he'll expect to run my wedding. I can't just say I'm in, but no thanks to the wedding. Also, I'm arresting someone who I believe is a foot soldier in his Syndicate tomorrow. He'll not be best pleased with me after that."

"You said he wanted your cases shut down and he didn't seem to care who you put in the dock. You'll be seen as only doing your job, but if it upsets him and your invitation is revoked then we've lost nothing. Steve, you've got to see it's our only chance."

Steve chewed his lower lip and started to think what Alison would say. After all, if they hadn't gone to last Friday's dinner this nightmare would never have happened.

"So, you want me to say yes to Lars Jenson and become one of his Disciples within his Syndicate. The sole purpose is for me to learn who else is involved, get a list of the Disciples and give it to you? If you say it quickly enough it sounds easy." Steve was being deliberately provocative and sarcastic. He was silent while he considered his options. "I suppose he must have a list. Once you've got the list we're finished. Correct?"

Patrick wasn't totally ready to agree. He dragged out a "Well... If you could also learn something about the overseas elements that would be a bonus."

"You don't want much. Look, I've got an early start tomorrow and I can't give you an answer now."

Just as Steve was about to say he would speak with Patrick tomorrow afternoon Alison appeared. She looked straight at Sir Patrick.

"You've got a bloody nerve, coming here! Snooping and expecting Steve here to betray confidences and then ask him to do your spying dirty work for you all in the name of national security. How can you sleep at night turning people's lives upside down just so you can play at spies?"

"How do you know what we discussed Dr Mills?" Sir Patrick was once again the very proper spymaster. No longer the normal human being having a chat with Steve.

"Simple. As a spy, you shouldn't be surprised, I listened. It's my property after all and you're trying to browbeat my fiancé into helping you. Under the circumstances, I think I have a right to know if my wedding is to be hosted by a crook."

No one spoke but Alison's last remark told Steve he'd have to do as Patrick asked.

Alison was on board with the idea, despite her rant at Sir Patrick.

Sir Patrick also picked up on Alison's remark and visibly relaxed. "Yes, you're quite right, but in my defence, Doctor, I'd no knowledge of Lars Jenson's offer to your fiancé when I arrived. Circumstance and good luck have brought us to this point."

Alison and Steve stood indicating to Sir Patrick that this evening was at an end.

"I'll call Lars tomorrow and tell him I'm in, but I'm not going to push it. I'm not going to be proactive in any way. If I learn things, I'll pass them on but I'm not going to risk my career just for this. I hope that's understood?"

"Yes. And although it can't be official, we're very grateful to you. Let's hope that having a true investigator on the inside brings this to a conclusion soon before any real damage is done to the country."

Sir Patrick Bond left. Steve and Alison stood with their arms around each other. Steve looked at the clock. It was 01.23 a.m. So much for an early night.

Chapter Fourteen

Over twenty minutes a whole gaggle of police officers and forensic experts arrived at a greasy spoon café selected by Jenny as the most convenient spot for the troops to gather just outside of Chelmsford. The spot was off the A12 and the road network leading away from the café meant both arrest sites could be accessed within ten minutes of leaving.

The weather this Wednesday morning wasn't being kind to them. The heavy rain and strong winds would make for a very unpleasant morning. The last to arrive were The Cap and Andy. Andy struggled to close the door behind him, and their arrival was met with "shut that door" shouts from their colleagues. The time was exactly 07.33.

After ordering and paying for coffee and bacon rolls for himself and Andy, but not offering to buy anything for the team, the pair sat and tucked into what they regarded as their breakfast.

"Thanks, Cap, I'll have the same," Jenny sarcastically said.

"DS Fuller you live locally and will have had a hearty breakfast. We've just driven through horrible weather and diabolical traffic to get here, plus I personally was up at four-thirty this morning just to get here by now. I'm having my breakfast and I know you know how to order, so be my guest. I'll even pay, but please let me eat and drink in peace."

Jenny gave a snort of a laugh and the others joined in. "Just checking that you hadn't left your wallet behind. Once we're done this morning it's all back here for a coffee and a bun and you're paying."

The Cap looked around the room at the expectant faces and calculated what kind of a hit his wallet would take. He consoled himself that he'd get whatever it cost on expenses. The pair finished their breakfast in what seemed like record time and ordered another coffee. Once everyone was settled The Cap reviewed the upcoming events. Everyone knew their role. All that remained was to execute the plan.

***

At 08.09 a.m., Jenny and her detective constable left to go to Philip Grantham's house. The forensic team remained behind and would await Jenny's call.

At 08.22 a.m., Abul and Andy left to go to Essex Constabulary's Force HQ building and the office that had previously been provided for their use. The two traffic cars to take the prisoners back to Scotland Yard followed.

Now all they had to do was wait.

***

Steve arrived at Force HQ early and with little sleep. He tried to put the events of last night out of his mind and concentrate on the events of the day. He found the DCC's office, but no one was around. He took a seat in what was obviously a waiting room and as soon as he sat down a rather plain female civilian entered, nodded and took up residence behind what was obviously a reception desk.

She fiddled around opening drawers and removing files. She stood and removed her outside coat before resuming her seat. She continued to rearrange items on her desk before looking up at Steve.

"Yes. May we help you?"

Steve noted the "we". What was this receptionist? He had an idea but kept it to himself. "I've an appointment with the Deputy Chief for this morning at around eight-thirty."

The plain receptionist with royal illusions opened a book that looked like a diary.

"I'm sorry but there's nothing in the diary."

"I spoke to him personally yesterday. It's confidential so presumably, he didn't want it recorded?"

"Well!" Said with more than a hint of disgust "I'm the DCC's secretary. He trusts me implicitly. If you had an appointment, then I would know about it."

Steve wasn't going to argue but noted the emphasis on the "I" in her last put down. "I'll wait until your boss gets in." He sat back down.

At 08.37 the DCC arrived resplendent in his uniform covered in white and silver braid. Steve stood when he saw the senior officer arriving. He noted the plain receptionist was about to stand and her mouth was already open. Before she could comment the DCC invited Steve into his office and ordered the plain receptionist who was called Harriet to bring in two coffees.

The DCC was called Spencer. From his medals, he was obviously an old-school policeman. Steve placed him around sixty, although he looked lean and fit and still had a full head of dark hair. He could be ten years younger, but Steve decided it wasn't important how old this man was.

The plain receptionist called Harriet served the coffee and glared at Steve as she left the room.

DCC Spencer sat back in his overly large executive chair and steepled his fingers. "What's this all about DCI Burt. I get a mysterious call from you yesterday saying there's a Met operation happening this morning on my patch. Here I am, so tell all."

"Well sir, you'll be aware of the two murders of young girls that took place a few weeks ago?"

"Yes. One near to Southend airport and the other out Great Dunmow way beside Stanstead."

Steve felt he had no option but to continue the fiction established by Commander Bowles. "The NCA asked the Yard to investigate and I was appointed SIO. I've been working with their authority. We've been chasing down what few leads there are, but we now believe one of your CID officers, a Detective Inspector Dean Grantham, is involved. Out of courtesy to you and the Essex force I wanted to advise you of this before the arrest is made this morning. We also believe his brother, Philip Grantham, is involved and he is also being arrested this morning."

The DCC sat silently. "What charges do you intend pressing?"

"I'll know exactly once I've interviewed them, but to be getting on with, conspiracy to murder and murder after the fact. The brother we'll start with aiding and abetting. I don't think your DI, or his brother, actually killed the girls but I'm sure they know who did."

Again, the DCC sat quietly.

"You're sure about this? You have enough evidence to proceed?"

"Yes sir. I'm sorry it's one of yours but the evidence is fairly conclusive."

"Mm! If you're sure, then I can only thank you for rooting out a rotten apple." So far, the DCC had spoken in a level tone and seemed relaxed. He leant forward and showed Steve why he was a DCC. In an almost growling tone, he let rip. "But if you've cocked this up and my officer is subsequently found to have no case to answer, I'll hound you all the way to your Commissioner's office and I'll have your pension. Is that clear DCI Burt?"

Steve had expected this reaction and was prepared for it. He had expected it earlier and felt he'd got off lightly if this was all the flak he was going to get.

"Very clear sir and thank you for your understanding." Steve was about to stand and say his goodbyes when his mobile pinged. It was a text message from Jenny. All it said was "Success". He now stood, shook the DCC's hand and made the usual noises about co-operation.

As he left to attend the post-mortems the plain Harriet stood by her desk. "That Dean Grantham's always been a bad one. I could tell you stories. I hope you throw the book at him."

There were no secrets between the DCC and his plain secretary. She obviously listened in on his conversations. So much for security.

As he headed for the car park his phone dinged again. It was The Cap with the same one-word text. "Success". The operation was over and had gone like clockwork.

***

Jenny's message to Steve was timed at 08.56. Abul got the same text. He, Andy and the two traffic officers were in the room allocated within Essex Police Headquarters. One of the traffic officers left to meet Jenny and drive Philip Grantham to New Scotland Yard. Andy and The Cap, accompanied by the second traffic officer, immediately left to find Dean Grantham. As expected, he was in the CID office drinking coffee and not looking too healthy. He saw his new best friend Abul walk in accompanied by a very well-dressed younger man.

"Abul, me old mucker!" Dean hadn't sobered up from his drinking session the previous evening. In fact, if he were to be tested, he would be at least twice over the limit to drive. As he stood up, he swayed and only

129

by holding the edge of his desk did he stop himself from falling over. The Cap spotted the signs but went straight ahead.

He apprised Dean of his rights, read him the charges as they would appear on his arrest sheet and handcuffed him.

"Oh! Come on Abul. We're mates, you and me. This is a joke. Right?" Dean was even drunker than The Cap had realised. His words were slurred, he wasn't steady on his feet and he gave an impression of not knowing what was going on. After a few more attempts to convince Abul this wasn't really happening he shrugged his shoulders in the way of all drunks when they don't understand their situation and left with the traffic officer.

Jenny, after arresting Philip Grantham and before taking him to Essex HQ, phoned the forensic team who met her at HQ, received the van keys and set off to recover the van and drive it back to the garage located under the Police HQ building where they were under orders to rip it apart in the quest for trace evidence that would prove the victims had been in the van.

By 09.14, the operation was complete. Jenny, The Cap and Andy met up at the same greasy spoon to compare notes. As agreed, The Cap paid for the coffee and three large cholesterol heavy sticky buns. They all agreed it had gone according to plan and now all they had to do was get the brothers to talk. They discussed how drunk Dean Grantham had been and couldn't work out how he got away with it. He'd have to sober up before he could be processed and The Cap had called the duty sergeant at the Yard telling him what was coming his way and simply to put Dean in a holding cell based on him being drunk and disorderly. They'd get a doctor to him in the afternoon and then process him. He told the sergeant to process Philip Grantham but to also put him in a holding cell awaiting interrogation.

Jenny had to get back to oversee the forensic team, Andy had to go to the hospital morgue to meet Steve, and The Cap had to get back to the Yard to be on hand should the prisoners want to talk, although he doubted Dean was in any fit state.

All three left and Jenny gave Andy a lift to the hospital.

***

After leaving the Deputy Chief Constable, Steve headed straight for the hospital and the mortuary. It was like most houses of death he'd been in before, very cold, sterile and smelling of death. He complied with the written instructions in the waiting area and got himself gowned up so as not to contaminate any evidence found on the bodies. There was no one around so he pushed on one half of very heavy double rubber doors that lead to the inner area where the pathologists performed their gruesome tasks. He called out in what sounded like an echo chamber.

A voice replied before a girl in her late twenties appeared dressed in green hospital scrubs, regulation white rubber boots. Her appearance was completed by a green plastic apron, a green plastic cap and rubber gloves. She introduced herself as Connie the theatre technician.

Steve introduced himself and explained he was awaiting Sir Humphrey Campbell.

"That'll be for the autopsy of the two murder victims. A detective sergeant came by yesterday. I've got them out and set everything up. It's really quite exciting having the Home Office's senior pathologist here. Shame I was asked to keep it quiet. I know our regular guys would love to meet him and watch him work." Steve thought Connie was a bit nervous and this showed by the speed of her word delivery.

"I'm a bit early but thought I'd just come over." Steve paused wondering how best to phrase his next question. "You were here during the first post-mortems."

"Yeah. That was weird."

"How so?" She was clearly willing to talk and Steve stood and let her.

"Well, the first one was down as a regular job. Nothing special except it was a murder victim. I was getting things ready when I got a phone call from County Medical. They said the post-mortem was being delayed by twenty-four hours and that an outside pathologist would be doing it."

"Was that unusual?"

"No. It's happened before but it was very short notice. The next day this old bloke turns up. No joking, he was almost doubled up. He could hardly walk never mind stand at the table for an hour. Well, he didn't, did he? He sat on a stool and only made the most cursory of examinations.

It's not my place to say but even I know you can't do a proper examination in ten minutes. That's about as much time as this old boy gave it. He asked me for the forms and signed them as cause indeterminate but probably due to blood loss."

"Did he do anything?"

"Not much. The stomach was already open, so he pulled out a few organs but didn't weigh anything nor examine the stomach contents. That's all, standard procedure."

So, you think he hurried it?"

"Oh, yes! No doubt."

Steve knew from Andy that the examination probably hadn't been thorough and that was why they were here today.

Connie, who seemed to work alone except when an autopsy was being performed, seemed to need to chat. Steve stood back and let her continue.

"When we got the second cadaver and were told the same old pathologist would do the pm, our senior guy went ballistic. He complained to County medical and the Chief Officer but was told the decision on the pathologist had been made."

Connie laughed. "You should've seen his face. He was livid but the old boy still did the post."

"What happened the second time?"

"Nothing. It was a re-run of the first only this time I don't think he even examined any internal organs. He signed off as before and left. It was all very strange and then we were told to keep the cadavers because they were foreign, and nobody knew about burying them. That's why there still here. A lucky coincidence, don't you think?"

Steve agreed and thanked Connie for her frankness. The rubber door opened, and Andy appeared dressed exactly like his boss. He explained about the operation, that Jenny was with the forensic team and that Dean Grantham was still drunk from the night before.

Steve was about to ask Andy for more details when from the other side of the room, Sir Humphrey Campbell appeared with his assistant in tow. Sir Humphrey was dressed for work. He was a big man with a big personality. He seemed to fill the room yet there was a softer side to him that Steve had witnessed last time they met.

"Good morning everyone. What a bloody awful day for a drive into darkest Essex. Inspector, you shall owe me several large single malts next time we meet." The voice was overly loud and echoed around the mortuary, but the face was gentle and smiling.

Two metal tables stood side by side with the victims laid out on them. Connie had been diligent and had identified each one by placing a label on the big toe of each.

"Right. Which one first?"

Connie stepped forward and introduced herself stuttering how it was an honour to be assisting Sir Humphrey. Humphrey Campbell, like all great men, acknowledged the sentiment in a way that pleased Connie. She suggested the first victim might be looked at first.

Sir Humphrey pulled back the sheet covering the body of Ingrid Baciu. He'd just placed his face visor onto his head when he immediately pulled it off. He turned to look at Steve. "Inspector, can we have a word please?" The pathologist stormed rather than walked back through the door he's entered from.

"What the hell's going on here. If you're trying to get me involved in your petty political police games, I'll have you suspended."

Steve was taken aback. "I'm sorry Sir Humphrey. I've no idea what you're talking about."

"That body has never been posted. You led me to believe I was only to examine the bodies for anything the previous pathologist may have missed. That young girl hasn't felt a scalpel in death. So again DCI Burt. What's going on?"

Steve explained about the older pathologist and Connie's remarks about how the post-mortems were performed.

"Who in their right mind would employ a geriatric for such a task?"

Steve debated with himself how much to tell this very likeable pathologist but one who was senior enough to be a Disciple of the Syndicate. He reasoned, based on his reaction, that Sir Humphrey probably wasn't and could be trusted.

"Sir Humphrey, I'll tell you what I can but please treat this information as top secret."

"I'm not a fool man. Spit it out." The voice was loud.

"I'm afraid something is going on with high-ranking officials who may be interested in subverting the Government. We believe they're in all walks of life and they exist to help each other as best they can, even breaking the law if they have to. The reason you're here today is that some of these people work in Scotland Yard and I'm trying to conduct my enquiry without their knowledge. I'm not sure but I believe using the geriatric pathologist was part of this group's strategy. They're somehow responsible for these murders and didn't want them looked into too closely." Steve paused to make sure the pathologist understood.

"If it hadn't been for my DC, they'd have gotten away with it. He spotted inconsistencies in the pm report. That's why I asked you, shall we say, for a favour. We suspected the post-mortems were a work of fiction, but I couldn't ask for a second opinion through official channels."

Sir Humphrey looked pensive. He paced in a circle mumbling to himself. This lasted for a few minutes and in complete silence. Eventually, the pathologist spoke.

"And you say these senior people are plotting against the government?"

"No, not exactly. At least not actively planning to topple the government. At the moment they just seem to want to act in what they think is best for the country regardless of government policy. They believe they rule the country anyway, so they bypass government instructions if they think they are against the national interest."

"And you've no idea who these people are?"

"No."

"But they're definitely in positions of authority?"

"Yes."

"Positions like the Head of the Civil Service?"

Steve's jaw dropped. He'd meet the head of the civil service and knew Sir Humphrey and Sir Timothy Head were close friends.

"Well, that's the level of authority these people target. It could be you are on their target list and for all I know, Sir Humphrey, you may already be a Disciple of the Syndicate. No one knows who they are."

"I can assure you Chief Inspector that I'm not a member and am unlikely to be." Humphrey paused to examine Steve. A bond was forming between the two and Sir Humphrey decided to confide in Steve.

"I had a call from Tim Head last night. He knew I was doing the posts here today. I thought nothing of it at the time but what you've told me about this Syndicate I'm beginning to wonder. He asked for a copy of my results to be sent to him and he would forward them to you. From what you've told me, that's a bit strange and conspiracy theory might suggest he was a member. I've known Tim Head for years and am sure he's not involved but why ask for the reports. It's all very strange."

"Now you see, sir, what we're up against. With a little inside knowledge, you start to suspect the actions of any senior figure but, getting back to your original question." Steve paused and looked the pathologist straight in the eyes. "I am not setting you up for anything. I believe by asking you to examine these bodies we can confirm what I now suspect, but I need your expertise."

"Yes. Sorry for being a bit abrupt. I suppose you want my reports sent directly to you?"

"Yes, and can I ask for only one copy? I don't want anyone else seeing your findings until I'm ready to publish them."

Sir Humphrey nodded in acceptance. He put a powerful arm around Steve's shoulder and guided him back towards the mortuary. "What's this world coming to when you suspect everyone you've known for years of being up to no good?"

"Now then, let's get started. Who's this poor wee soul?" Sir Humphrey pointed to victim one.

Connie stepped forward. "This is Ingrid Baciu. She was the first victim." Connie stood back and allowed the Home Office pathologist's own assistant to take over.

Sir Humphrey was quick with a scalpel. He completed the Y shaped incision and within twenty minutes almost every organ had been removed, weighed or cut open and were now neatly laid out on a stainless-steel topped bench.

"No need to do a cranial investigation given the injuries are not connected." The pathologist carried on checking minor organs and talking into the overhead microphone.

Andy, who was a little reticent at attending his first post-mortem, seemed to be mesmerised by the whole experience. As Sir Humphrey was cutting, Andy had moved closer for a better look. Steve always felt uneasy at post-mortems, but Andy appeared in his element. This was another side Steve hadn't seen in his junior.

Sir Humphrey was finishing up and was giving instructions to his assistant about stomach content analysis and sufficient material for toxicity screening. He moved to the second table while removing and changing his green plastic apron and blue rubber gloves. Steve noted Andy followed and took up a position in front of the body so he wouldn't miss anything.

The second post-mortem followed the detail of the first. The body of Tatania Popescu was dealt with as swiftly as her fellow Romanian's. Sir Humphrey had all the major organs listed and placed on another stainless-steel topped table and he gave the same instructions to his assistant.

"Right, that's that. Let me get a shower and out of this uniform and back into my street clothes. I'll let you have my preliminary findings over a cup of something hot." He turned to Connie. "Thank you for your help and superb preparation, my dear, very good. Now is there some form of café in this hospital?"

"Yes, sir. It's on the fifth floor."

"Splendid. Perhaps we can gather up there in say fifteen minutes. I'll have a strong black tea if anyone's buying." Sir Humphrey marched off leaving everyone else standing looking at his back.

Steve and Andy found the canteen or café as the hospital described it on a large sign by the entrance. Andy stood in line and bought two coffees. While Andy was performing his most important task, Steve called Jenny. She answered on the first ring.

In answer to his enquiry she said, "Yes Steve, they are getting on with it. They've found hair and bits of thread that might hook back to our victims although they're saying the van's quite clean. They'll keep at it and get the samples back to their lab this evening. I'll leave the van in the pound in case they need to look at it again."

"Good. How's your father? I'm sorry I should have asked earlier."

"He's holding on. The doctors say he's even showing signs of improvement. I was going to ask if I could take some time later and go see him."

"Of course. Tidy up with forensics and take the rest of the day off. When you get into your own office tomorrow, we'll speak then. I'm thinking there may be things to do up here after we've interviewed the brothers so best if you're on site."

Jenny agreed and thanked the DCI. She broke the connection.

Andy appeared with the coffees. They discussed the events of the last ninety minutes and Steve explained what the morgue technician Connie had told him about the geriatric pathologist. He made no mention of any links to the Syndicate. Sir Humphrey arrived and Andy was dispatched to get a strong tea and two more coffees.

Drinking his tea with a reverence normally associated with fine wine, Humphrey Campbell told the detectives, "Until we get the lab results back, I don't know, right at this moment, how these girls died, but I can tell you both had a kidney removed recently and it was done professionally. Now it could be the kidney that was removed was diseased, but in both cases, the remaining kidney was healthy. I'd say you're looking at organ harvesting but the surgery appeared to be fine. The removal of the kidneys didn't kill them. I'd say it's more likely post-operative complications took over. I'll wager the tox screen will show high levels of morphine and antibiotics, and sepsis was your killer."

"So, on the cause of death, you'd put...?"

"Misadventure. Certainly not murder unless you can prove the removal of the kidneys wasn't for medical reasons but was organ harvesting. I believe both victims were dead before their stomachs were slit. I'm equally sure the slitting was to disguise the surgical scar from the operation to remove the kidneys. Show perfectly healthy kidneys were removed and I'd say murder. The poor wee things wouldn't be dead if they hadn't gone under the knife."

Steve looked at Andy and while Andy hadn't been read into the latest developments Steve trusted him. He decided to plough on while he had this renowned medical expert here.

"Sir Humphrey I believe there's a clinic close by that's bringing young girls and probably boys as well into this country for the sole purpose of harvesting organs for transplant. I believe it's being done on an industrial scale and we could be looking at up to say nine hundred transplants a year. Is that feasible?"

"That's a lot but perfectly possible. The problem in this country is the lack of donors. The last time I looked there were several thousand on the waiting lists for transplanted organs. If this clinic you're referring to is indeed bringing in live donors and this is giving them a steady supply, then subject to correct tissue matching the numbers are possible."

"What about tissue matching? Just because they have, say a kidney, doesn't mean it's suitable for every patient. Or does it?"

Andy was listening intently. Steve could almost see him analysing this information and hatching a plan to help with the investigation.

Sir Humphrey finished his tea. "These days with better drugs it's more possible to transplant an organ that doesn't quite match but it's risky and means the recipient would be on medication their entire life."

"Can organs be stored to await the correct match?"

"Mm! Good question. A lot of work has been done on storage and progress has been made but even so, I'd say forty-eight hours in cold conditions is about all you'd get away with now."

As Steve thought about that the table went quiet. How could the Syndicate perform nine hundred transplants a year if the organs couldn't be kept? Surely Lars Jenson was wrong when he gave the numbers of possible transplants at the dinner last Friday. Had he and Alison overcooked the numbers and how did the Syndicate get nine hundred donors in and out of the country without arousing suspicion. It came to him in a flash. Jenson had said it was a new facility and could do that number. Maybe they were only gearing up and the operation wasn't in full swing yet.

The DCI made a note to check out the new transplant clinic.

"Well gents, it's been interesting. I'll get my report to your office only once the lab work is back. I'm off to Scotland but I'll make sure my assistant forwards the data. It'll only take minutes to finish the report, but I shouldn't think it'll say anything other than I've told you."

"That's very kind Sir Humphrey. I appreciate your help and I'm sorry if we're interrupting your holiday."

The pathologist looked amused as he stood. "Remember you owe me several single malts next time we meet. I'll just add the interruption to my holiday to the bill."

All three men shook hands and Sir Humphrey left.

"Steve, what was that all about, what clinic?" As predicted Andy was curious.

"It's something I'll have to tell the team about soon Andy but for now it's a bit sensitive. Come on. Let's get back and see what we can charge our brothers with."

The DCI knew he was looking for more than a confession of involvement with the girl's deaths. He wanted information on the Disciples of the Syndicate and was certain Dean Grantham had some of the information he wanted.

Chapter Fifteen

Steve and Andy arrived back at New Scotland Yard at exactly three p.m. The traffic had been kind to them although the final part of their journey through London had been slow.

Carrying three coffees in cardboard cups they found The Cap in the office. He was going over remarks made by Philip Grantham and recording them for his own use. Nothing of what the prisoner had said so far could be used in court. This was because although he'd been processed, he hadn't been made aware of his rights nor offered a solicitor. Jenny hadn't arrested him as he'd agreed to help with enquiries.

The Cap also had a pile of papers on his desk relating to the upcoming trial of the killers in the Hackney case. This had been their last major case and the CPS had returned various statements with queries that only Abul could answer. The expression on The Cap's face told how much he liked paperwork.

The Cap was glad of the break when Steve invited his colleagues to drink their coffee in his office.

"We need to get going on this but I'm not sure we're looking at the original case."

Steve was all business.

"According to Humphrey Campbell there's no murder here, only misadventure unless we can prove these girls had a healthy kidney removed for profit, and it was this act that led to their deaths. Frankly, I think the best we'd get would be a manslaughter charge, so a change of direction. We've still got serious crimes here that need solving."

No one spoke. Steve debated yet again on how much information to pass on. He trusted these two with his life and knew they could be trusted. He made a decision.

"I want to plough on as we were, so I'll explain later. Andy, did you get all the financials on Eclipse Medical?"

"Looks like it. I haven't checked but I got an e-mail on my phone from Companies House."

"Good. What about the court order?"

"Yes, checked that just before we came in here."

Steve had to work out a plan. He approached the whiteboard and started to write.

"Andy, follow up on the court order. It's your idea, but if we can trace the credit card that paid for the victims' flights, we might get a handle on those involved in this organ business."

Steve hadn't finished, but Andy interrupted anyway. "If what you said about the numbers of transplants is true, then there must be a load of young people arriving and leaving from Stanstead and Southend airports. I could go back a few months and get the manifests of flights from Eastern Europe and see how many passengers fit the profile of young and travelling alone." Andy was on one of his rolls.

"Remember this Dean bloke was seen on CCTV collecting the victims. If I can identify young people travelling alone, arriving on specific flights, then I could call up the CCTV and see if Dean Grantham had pulled out any other people before Immigration. It would probably mean the ones he pulled out are probably here to sell an organ." Andy looked pleased with himself despite having volunteered for a lot of extra work.

Steve yet again admired his young DC.

"Good thinking. If you've got time, then do that, but serve the court order first. Let's see what it throws up. Hold onto the financial stuff until I've spoken with Financial Crimes. I want them to look at this company."

The Cap laughed. "I can see a certain roadblock arriving anytime soon."

"You've read my mind. I'm going to call her and check she's free." Steve felt relaxed now they had a plan. He decided to carry on.

"Now, listen up you two. What I'm about to tell you is for your ears only. It's not for broadcasting in the pub or even discussed with your wife, Cap, or your serious other half Andy." As predicted Andy blushed.

"Is that understood?"

Both detectives nodded.

"I can't go into too much detail and some of what I'm going to say you already know. We were handed the double murder case by Commander Bowles under false pretences. He said the NCA, on guidance from the National Intelligence Unit, had asked the Yard to step in and control the investigation. This wasn't true. I found out he set us up and the NCA knew nothing about it."

Both detectives listened and their faces were solemn.

"I've discovered there's an organisation called the Syndicate." Steve stopped to let this sink in. He smiled "I know it sounds farfetched but this organisation has recruited senior officials to undermine the government. Bowles is a member and I suspect it's this Syndicate that's responsible for the girl's deaths." Steve wasn't about to divulge how much he knew about the Syndicate, at least not yet.

"These guys do each other favours, and we got the case so Bowles could get a result, and get the case closed without any heat being directed at the Syndicate. The Syndicate seems to be run by a Lars Jenson. He's CEO of Eclipse Medical." Steve paused and looked directly at Andy. "That's why I want to get into their financials."

Andy nodded his understanding.

"The problem is we don't know who's involved with the Syndicate. All we know is they are important decision-makers in the police, judiciary, government, industry even universities. They refer to themselves as 'Disciples of the Syndicate'."

Another pause to allow his audience to absorb what he was saying.

"A good example of how they work is the post-mortems this morning. A retired pathologist was brought in, instead of the regular one, on the instructions of the senior man at Essex Health Board. It's suspicious, especially given the cursory examinations of the bodies, but knowing about the Syndicate makes you wonder if the head man in Essex who put in the replacement pathologist is acting as a Disciple of the Syndicate. We don't know but it raises a question. Do you follow so far?"

Abul answered. "Sure, Steve but what are we doing? Is this now the focus of our investigation or what?" Steve didn't want to answer this directly.

"What we're doing is making a case against the two downstairs for involvement in the two deaths. That's our priority. I suspect Dean

Grantham at least is a member of the Syndicate. Think about it. If the Syndicate are behind the transplants and we have Dean meeting our two victims, it ties him directly to this organisation. I know they operate with what they call foot soldiers and I believe that's where he fits in. But first, we have to get him to admit to being involved in the deaths and get him charged. That's our primary focus. Whether we can prove murder remains to be seen, then we'll see what he can tell us about the Syndicate. Agreed?"

Nods all round.

"We'll pursue the court order Andy and see where that leads us, but we're now looking for links to Eclipse Medical unless the credit card information tells us something different. That means two investigations, but the second is secret. Any questions?"

Andy was on his feet ready to get started. "No, I'll get going. What do you want me to do with the financial stuff on Eclipse?"

"Hold onto it until I tell you where to send it. Cap, we'll make a start downstairs but give me a quarter of an hour. I've got a few things to do."

***

On his own, Steve called Lars Jenson. "Hello Lars, it's Steve Burt."
"Ah, I wondered when you'd call. Good news I hope?"

"If you call me wanting to join you and take up your offer of hosting our wedding good news, then yes, I suppose it is good news."

"Excellent. You know Steve, God directs my every move. He told me you would make a first-class disciple and now here you are, on the brink. I'm really pleased."

Steve wasn't sure God had much to do with it and he wondered, given his real reason for joining the Syndicate, whether God might grass him up to Lars!

Lars was in full flow. "We'll arrange your signing ceremony for this weekend. It's just a ritual all Disciples go through when they join. Nothing satanic, no getting dressed up in funny clothes, just a simple ceremony to welcome you." Lars sounded happy.

"Steve, I'll arrange our Sunday service for eleven a.m., bring Dr Mills again, she seemed very pleasant last week, and a lot of my guests

143

were asking after her. If you arrive just before 11.00, you'll join us for our service and then we'll go into the library for your signing ceremony. That all seems most satisfactory.

"We'll do an under-cover barbeque as the weather forecast isn't too good. I suppose that means I won't be eaten out of house and home as usually happens when the weather's kind to us." Lars was chuckling down the line.

"What convinced you to join us, Steve?" Lars had suddenly switched from being his jovial new best friend to speaking in a very serious voice. Steve knew he had to be careful of this unstable man.

"It was as you said. There are only certain people who rule this country and not one of them has been elected. They've been successfully running things for years, so why do we need puppets to simply repeat and endorse what our real rulers are deciding."

"Bravo Steve, the Lord guided me wisely. You'll be a great asset to the Syndicate, and we may have something for you to do for us, but let's not get ahead of ourselves. I'll see you and your fiancée on Sunday. We might even have time to talk about your wedding arrangements." Lars drew a breath. "Goodbye Steve and welcome." The line went dead.

The DCI sat, gazing at nothing, hardly believing what he'd just done. He had a feeling Alison wouldn't be too keen on another Sunday trip to Buckinghamshire. He smiled to himself. "She'll probably kill me!"

***

Steve next went to the area occupied by Financial Crimes. This was the place where the Financial Times was preferred reading over the Police Gazette. They employed mostly civilian analysts but had a few very bright specially trained police officers. The analyst he'd come to see was unique. She was Honorary Inspector Florance Rough. He spotted her in a cubicle made from free-standing partitions about five-foot-high, perched on the edge of a chair typing away into a computer. Until just over a year ago she was Detective Constable Florance Rough. She'd been one of Steve's first colleagues when his Special Resolutions Unit was set up. At that time, she didn't fit the profile of a woman police officer in the Metropolitan Police service. It wasn't her intellect but her size. Steve had affectionally christened her "Twiggy". When she worked for him, he estimated her weight to be around two hundred pounds, but looking at her now he felt she'd gained a few pounds and despite wearing long tent-like dresses she could never be called thin. The powers in charge at that time had decided to make her redundant, along with Steve and his other inaugural colleague Abul Ishmal, AKA The Cap. Things hadn't gone to plan for the scheming commanding officer and now they were all still working for the Met in senior positions.

Twiggy had shown an aptitude for solving complicated financial puzzles and had been recruited into the Treasury as a civil servant and loaned back to Financial Crimes with the rank of Honorary Inspector. This meant she didn't have to worry about being a front-line officer but was still involved with the job and organisation she loved.

Steve approached her office space and standing behind her he coughed. Looking up and around Twiggy almost fell off her chair. Steve was pleased when she regained her balance. He'd seen Twiggy close up when she had driven him in her old Fiat 500, and he had no wish to even contemplate assisting her to her feet if she'd stumbled and landed on the floor.

"Bloody hell, sir, you startled me. To what do I owe the pleasure?" Twiggy was genuinely pleased to see her old boss.

"Have you got a minute? Somewhere more private."

"Oh! All very cloak-and-dagger." She heaved her great bulk out of her seat. "We can use the boss' office. He's over at Treasury for a meeting."

The pair walked around cubicle's exactly like Twiggy's, until they reached a free-standing box tucked into a corner of the office space.

In deference to her visitor, Twiggy took a chair on the visitor's side of her boss's desk intending that Steve should be seated in her boss's chair. Steve pulled another chair sitting against the office wall and sat beside Twiggy. The pair spent several minutes catching up and reminiscing about their previous working relationship. It was clear they had a deep bond with each other. Eventually, the DCI brought the conversation back to why he'd sought his old junior out.

"I've got a case that's taken us into uncharted waters, and I need your help."

"That's nothing new. I don't know if you're aware but that's exactly your reputation and the reputation of Special Resolutions. You get a case, but you always finish up looking into another case." Twiggy giggled her schoolgirl giggle.

Steve found he'd missed the sound he'd first heard over a year ago.

"But go on, you know I'll help."

"This is a bit more serious than anything we've looked into before."

Steve proceeded to tell her about the bodies and how he was suspicious the Commander had set him up. He explained about the post-mortems and how Sir Humphrey had said the victims had not been examined by post-mortem but there was a full post-mortem report stating the victims had died from loss of blood caused by having their stomachs ripped open. Steve wasn't sure how much to tell Twiggy, but he did tell her about the Syndicate, Lars Jenson and Eclipse Medical. He reminded her she could trust no one, not even her boss.

"From what I can see Eclipse Medical hold the purse strings for the Syndicate and I'm convinced something is going on with money, but I can't get to it. If we can show that Jenson is benefitting from the illegal trade in human parts, then we've got something to run with. At the moment we've nothing on him, other than we believe he's corrupted various senior officials with his beliefs and promises of a better world."

"Wow! That's a lot to take in Steve, but I see your problem. What do you want me to do?"

"Look Twiggy, this could get dangerous. I've no idea who's involved or how far Lars Jenson will go to protect his Syndicate."

"As you can see boss, I'm a big girl." She smiled more to herself than at Steve. "I can take care of myself and deep down you're still the boss so please just spit it out."

"Thanks. Right, I've had DC Andy Miller pull all the financial records for Lars Jenson's company, plus bank records, company and private and director backgrounds. I need you to delve into them. Look for anomalies, anything that looks dodgy, maybe even track money coming from third parties. Anything that will aid a conviction when we land something on this Syndicate."

"Does this DC Miller have the files?"

"Yes, they're electronic. I can have him send them to you now if you want?"

Twiggy reached over her boss's desk and retrieved a pen and a piece of paper. She wrote something and handed it to Steve.

"If this thing goes as deep as you say then best not to use official channels. Get your man to send everything to that web address." She pointed to the paper she'd just handed to Steve. "It's my personal set-up and is one hundred percent secure. Do you want me to report straight to you?"

"Yes, but you can include Andy Miller. He's a bright lad and is up to speed on what's going on. If you need any information just speak with him. I think you met him anyway, a few months back on the Formula case."

"Probably, but since I've been here, I've met so many people it's hard to keep track."

"Thanks, Florance, I'll get Andy on to it but remember, be careful."

The pair parted. Steve felt good having met Twiggy again, and he knew he could trust her. On his way back to his office he was overcome with a feeling of being fatigued and didn't really relish interviewing Dean and Philip Grantham.

Little did he know!

Chapter Sixteen

After telling Andy to forward all the financial data he'd gathered on Eclipse Medical to Twiggy's secret address Steve and Abul visited the interview rooms and sought out the custody sergeant.

"The Doc visited the drunk this morning sir, about an hour after he were brought in." Steve hadn't met this sergeant before, so he introduced himself and The Cap.

"The bad news is he's signed the prisoner as not being fit to be interviewed until tomorrow after eight. He says the blood alcohol level's too high and anything you got out of him today would not be admissible in court." The sergeant looked seriously disappointed at having to pass on this news. "I'm afraid you've only got the second one for now."

"Thank you, Sergeant, these things happen. Can you bring Philip Grantham from the cells.?"

"Yes sir. You can use interview room one."

***

Steve and The Cap sat on one side of the metal table that was screwed to the floor. From previous experiences, they knew all six interview rooms were identical and each had an observation room attached to allow interested parties to view interrogations through a one-way mirror. Apart from a dual recording machine and a panic alarm that ran round the room, there was nothing else in the room.

The custody sergeant pushed a man they presumed to be Philip Grantham into the interview room, then stood aside to allow a uniformed constable to enter and take up his position beside the door. Steve invited their suspect to take the seat opposite the two detectives.

"Now Philip, do you know why you're here?"

"No, I bloody well don't. Your woman turns up as I'm leaving for work, says she wants a word and my van keys and the next thing I know I'm here and I don't know why." Philip seemed genuinely upset.

"Oh! Come on Philip. You know exactly why you're here. Tell us about the girls."

Philip's face fell. Steve got the impression he'd not thought the police would know of his involvement.

"What girls? I don't know anything about any girls." The suspect had recovered some of his composure but now looked shiftier and less sure of himself.

Steve ploughed on. "Yes, you do, the bodies of the two scrubbers you and Dean got rid of and probably murdered."

Philip Grantham was a tall slim man with no real distinguishing features. His teeth were yellow from smoking, he hadn't shaved in a while and his thick black hair needed cutting. Steve's reference to murder hit the spot.

"Hold on." Philip had raised his voice. "What are you trying to do here. If you think you can stitch Dean and me up for murder, then you're wrong. We never had nothing to do with killing them girls."

"So, you admit you did know them?"

"I never said that. All I said was we didn't murder them."

"So, they were dead when you picked them up?"

"I never said that," Philip Grantham was proving easy to break down. Steve felt he could crack this suspect now and get him charged.

Steve went into friendly mode. "Look, Philip." He sat back making the interview less formal. "You said they were dead when you got them, so that tells me you're involved. I'm prepared to believe that you didn't kill them, but I'm confused by what you're saying." Steve paused to let Philip absorb this now friendly policeman. "Just tell us. Did you move the two bodies in your van?"

"No. I'm not saying anything. I've seen them TV programmes where the cops get some poor innocent fool to confess. Well, I ain't saying anything and I want a lawyer."

"That's your choice but Philip…" Steve was still trying to portray himself as a friend. "You've not been arrested. Detective Sergeant Fuller told you that you'd be helping us with our enquiries. Now, we appreciate your help Philip, and I don't want to keep you here, any longer than I have to. But look at it from our point of view." Steve put on what he hoped was a concerned look. "You've told us you know about the bodies, so as you're here to help, I thought you'd be pleased to tell us what you know."

"Yeah, so you can stitch me and Dean up." Philip crossed his arms in front of him in what looked like an aggressive manner.

Steve persisted as a friend. "Look Philip, we know you're a good guy. I've checked and you don't have a criminal record. I'm sure Dean maybe just asked for a favour or maybe he borrowed your van and you really don't know a lot." Steve drew breath. "But you've told us something, so we have to follow it up, even if we're here all night and we have to arrest you. Come on, we all want to get down the pub. Just tell us and this'll all be over."

Steve saw he was getting through. Philip was biting his bottom lip, considering what the DCI had said.

He slowly looked up and, equally slowly, started to talk. "You're right. I've never been in trouble. With a big brother in the police, I wouldn't dare. Can I have a cup of tea?"

Steve signalled to the officer by the door, one tea and two coffees.

"Your tea will be here shortly Philip. Carry on. You were saying with Dean as a copper you'd not dare get into trouble."

"That's right. I deliberately kept my nose clean even when some of me mates were pulling off a job and wanted me along. I've always looked up to Dean so when he asked me to drive the van for him, I agreed." Philip pleaded. "But you must believe me. All I did was drive Dean. I'd no idea we were moving a dead body."

"So, you're saying Dean asked you to drive and it was him who put the body in the van. You didn't help or touch the body?"

"No! No! I just drove."

Steve wanted to push on but didn't want to lose this statement. "What happened. Tell us about the first time?"

Philip was almost crying. It was obvious that, despite Steve's friendly approach, Philip Grantham knew he was in trouble.

"Dean came round one night. It was January, but I can't remember the date. My wife was at the bingo and the kids were at her mother's.

Dean said he needed a favour. He had something to do and it was secret, but he'd need the van. He's my brother see, so I agreed."

The tea and coffee arrived, and everyone sat in silence sipping the hot liquids until Steve asked, "What then?"

"Dean told me to drive to this big house just outside Harlow. It had gates and a long driveway. I drove in and Dean said to go round the back. It must have been about ten. I opened the back doors of the van while Dean went inside. Him and another bloke came out pushing one of those hospital trolley things. There was a girl on it. She looked dead. I almost threw up. I've never seen a dead body before. The bloke had a big sheet of plastic. Him and Dean laid it on the floor of the van and then lifted this body into the back. I heard the other bloke and Dean talking. I'm sure the other guy was telling Dean what to do."

"Do you know where this big house was?"

"Yeah, outside Harlow. I could take you there, but I don't know the address or anything."

Steve stroked his chin. A thought had just sprung into his mind.

"Then what?"

"Dean says to drive to Southend Airport. We had words on the journey. You know, I'm asking what's going on, but Dean just says not to worry. We won't get into trouble because somebody's looking out for us if we just obey orders. I'm telling you I was scared and I'd no idea what my brother was going on about."

Philip took another drink of tea. "We got to the airport and Dean directs me to a park gate. I can't get the van through the gate, so I park up just opposite the gate. Dean says to give him a hand and we carry the body into the park and then into the woods. Honest, I was shaking. Dean got out a knife and cut the girl's stomach. He said he'd been told to do it, but I was feeling sick, so I didn't question him. We left the girl in the woods and I drove Dean back to his house."

Philip Grantham seemed remote from his tale. "After I dropped Dean home, I went home, but next day I cleaned out the back of the van and put the plastic sheet in the bin." Philip sat back looking exhausted.

"Thank you, Philip. That's been very helpful, and shows you really are a good man." Steve may have been overdoing the praise, but Philip seemed to react more positively to these remarks.

Steve carried on using a gentle tone. He genuinely felt sorry for this man who it appeared was only helping his brother. "What about the second victim, Philip?"

Philip Grantham was all in. The effort of reliving the horror of dumping the first body was too much for him. His eyes welled up and he sobbed uncontrollably for several minutes. The detectives waited. Eventually, he regained some composure and answered Steve.

"It was much later when Dean called, I think after midnight. I was in bed and I remember my wife wasn't too pleased. I had to collect him, but he was dressed and ready when I got there."

Philip told his story which mirrored the handling of the first victim. They collected the body from the same country house outside Harlow in Essex. Another plastic sheet was used to cover the floor of the van and they set off for Southend. Philip explained that Dean had told him it wasn't to collect another body, but the clinic needed to dump some waste. Philip was surprised when another body appeared but couldn't do anything about it. He was there and committed.

"You're saying Dean told you it wasn't to collect another body?"

"Yeah, like I said."

Steve tucked this piece of information away. It might help Philip at trial. The Cap was taking notes as Philip resumed his narrative.

"It was getting late, so Dean said we'd not bother going all the way to Southend. He told me to head for Great Dunmow. After all, it was getting on for five in the morning. We found the Dunmow Common and Dean told me to stop. We got the body out, but it was too obvious. Dean took one of the old covers I use to protect furniture when I'm moving it and covered the girl with it, but he cut her stomach first, just like the first one."

Philip went on to explain that after dumping and covering the body he dropped Dean at his house, and he went home.

Philip had answered a few questions, such as, where did the cover used to hide the second victim come from. Again, Steve made a mental note to have forensics re-examine it. It must have traces of Philip on it and that would tie him to the body when the case went to court.

"Thank you, Philip, that couldn't have been easy, but why didn't you go to the police the first time, when you realised Dean was collecting a body?"

Philip appeared to gather strength. "I'm no grass. I'm not going to shop my own brother, am I?"

Steve was aware that Philip Grantham had done just that.

"Now Philip, here's what we're going to do. This officer..." Steve pointed to the policeman standing beside the door, "... will bring you a pad and pen and I want you to write down exactly what you've told us." Steve, still acting as a kindly detective, spoke quietly as though Philip were a ten-year-old child.

"Can you do that for me, Philip?"

Philip nodded. "What happens now?"

"Once you've finished writing we'll see. I know you're not guilty of anything other than helping your brother so I'll see what I can do for you. Is that OK?"

"Yes. Will I get home tonight?"

"Finish writing up your statement and as I said, we'll see where we go."

The PC had left and returned with an A4 pad and a biro pen. He was joined by another officer as Steve and The Cap left the interview room.

Outside The Cap smiled at his boss. "You know Steve, you're a devious bugger. You played that poor soul like a cheap fiddle. I've no idea how you do it but it sure is effective."

"A misspent youth telling tales and trying to get into trouble with the opposite sex helped hone my skills." Steve laughed at his own joke.

***

The pair returned to the office via the canteen for a much-needed coffee. They arrived with a cup for Andy to find he was missing. It seemed strange not to see Andy at his post. They went into Steve's office and sat at his desk. Steve saw a handwritten note had been left and from the writing, he knew it was from Andy.

"Andy's serving the Court Order. Says he left at three forty-five and should be back by five." Steve looked at his watch. The days were getting longer. It was five minutes past five and they still had to charge Philip Grantham.

"What do we charge him with Steve? The poor sod's not guilty of anything other than helping his brother."

"True but he didn't call us when he knew they were dumping a body and he handled the corpse. That takes it out of the misdemeanour, and straight into an aiding and abetting charge as a minimum. We could go for after the fact or conspiracy but let's put it together and give the CPS the option of additional charges. I think we go for aiding and abetting in the unlawful disposal of a body. You'd better look up the statute."

The Cap stretched his arms above his head. "It's been a bloody long day. I want to go home." The Cap yawned and shook himself.

"You're right Abul. Let's go and charge chummy downstairs and hope he's written what he told us. I'll leave a note for Andy. We can all do with twelve hours of sleep.

***

Philip Grantham had indeed written exactly what he'd confessed to. Because he hadn't been arrested the confession without a solicitor present would stand. He was read his rights, formally arrested then charged and returned to the same holding cell to await transfer to a local police station awaiting an initial court date. Steve had left a note for Andy telling him to go home and that they would meet up in the morning as usual.

Steve wasn't seeing Alison, so he went straight home via a Chinese takeaway and was sound asleep by eight p.m.

Chapter Seventeen

Despite being exhausted, the DCI had a restless night's sleep. His mind went round and round trying to make sense of what he was doing. What started as a double murder had turned into a John Le Carré novel. A Syndicate trying to control the government, an industrial-size business in human parts, senior people as Disciples of this Syndicate working against the government, his upcoming role as an insider and the murders weren't even murders.

He woke early feeling slightly better than he had the previous evening. This Thursday morning looked like it held a promise of sunshine and blue skies.

He decided to walk to the Yard. It would only take an hour and the exercise and fresh air would do him good. He arrived at 07.32 feeling more invigorated than he should after his fourteen-hour day yesterday and his broken sleep pattern.

As usual, Andy had beaten him in. Andy, dressed in his new wardrobe and with stylishly longer hair, looked equally refreshed. He told Steve he had a few things to discuss but volunteered to get coffee before they started. Steve wasn't surprised The Cap hadn't arrived. He'd probably get in sometime after eight. Long days and early starts weren't his style.

***

Seated in Steve's office Andy was keen to get on. "Right, boss, I served the court order on the airline yesterday. Luckily, their head office isn't too far away."

Steve could see Andy was enjoying his newfound status as what he saw as being a real detective.

"It's amazing how people react to a piece of paper. Anyway, they gave me what I asked for, that was access to their records of payment for specific passengers. It took a while, but I found our two girls. The tickets were bought directly but the booking was made in Bucharest but using a UK-registered card."

Steve sat up. This was interesting. He hoped Andy had more.

"I got the name of the guy who ordered the tickets from Bucharest. Turns out he's a travel agent so he's not the bloke. He only sold the seats but someone else using the UK credit card must have paid."

"So, who's the UK card registered to?"

"That's the thing, Steve, it's not registered to anyone. It's listed as a card registered to the Anglo European Bank. You know them as AEB. It seems any charges on the card are paid by the bank."

"Is that normal?"

"Not at all. So, we know the tickets were purchased in Romania through a Romanian travel agent and paid for by a UK bank bypassing the agent."

"Sorry to be a bit dense. What do you mean, bypassing the agent?"

"A guy goes into a travel agent, buys a ticket for one of our victims, and obviously her name is on the ticket. The agent uses the buyer's UK credit card to pay the airline for the ticket instead of it being charged by the airline to the travel agent. That's the more normal procedure. But the Romanian travel agent still gets his commission from the airline and probably a back hander from the buyer for bending the rules." Andy paused.

"Bottom line. We don't know who bought the tickets in Bucharest and we don't know whose credit card was used to purchase them. Sorry, Steve."

"No, no Andy, it's not your fault." Steve sat back and sipped his coffee. "We need to find out from AEB who's paying the credit card bill. Is that about it?"

"Yeah, but we'd need another court order and I'm not sure you can work your magic again."

"True. Unfortunate but true." After a long pull on his coffee, the DCI sat more upright in his chair. "Leave it with me, Andy, there must be a way. If we can discover whose account the credit card is registered to, then we're well on our way to understanding what the hell's going on."

Steve noticed Andy was fidgeting. This was a sign he had more but was reluctant to speak up. "Go on Andy, let's have it."

Andy smiled a relieved smile. Somehow his boss always knew when he wanted to say something. "I was thinking that if I contacted Dimitri, the Inspector in Bucharest, and gave him the name of the travel agent and briefed him on at least part of our case he might find the guy who bought the tickets."

"Yes. Good thinking Andy. Do that but be very circumspect about what you tell him. Keep it simple and keep it to the two victims, nothing else. Got it?"

"Yes. Now I've got something else." Andy looked at Steve with an expression that said 'you'll like this'.

"When I was at the airline, I asked for all transactions using this credit card." Andy held up his hand before Steve could speak. "I know, it was outside the scope of the court order but as I was there, I figured it would save me a lot of time trawling through flight manifests and hours of CCTV."

"DC Miller, one day you'll get caught, but not today." Steve admired the young DC's initiative. He was almost coming to expect the extraordinary from Andy.

Andy smiled and shrugged. "I got them to go back six months. I've got a printout, but it looks like the first flights were booked about four months ago in early December. Just four tickets all for young girls. I've got the names and dates, so I'll check with immigration. In January there were eight, February fourteen, and so far, this month sixteen. All mostly girls but a few boys, but no one older than seventeen."

"Good work. You said you got all the information, names, dates and so on, and all these young people travelled alone?"

"From what I could see, yes."

"Get Tech Support to help but go through the CCTV for the arrival dates of these kids. Look and see if Dean Grantham appears and takes them out of the passport control queues. Good work, Andy."

Steve started to stroke his chin, a sure sign he was thinking. "Tell you what, Andy, give your pal Dimitri in the Romanian Federal Police department the names of all the kids you've found. See if he can track them down from the flight data. If he can get them to talk, we might learn more of what's going on at this end and possibly he might crack something at his end. I'm sure even in Romania it's not legal to solicit young people to sell their organs."

Andy nodded, seeing the sense in Steve's thought. He left holding his empty coffee cup.

Steve's internal phone rang. It was Commander Bowles. "Steve, can you come up and see me now please?"

"Well, I'm just getting ready to conduct an interview. Can it wait?"

"Afraid not. I'll see you in five minutes." The line went dead.

The Cap arrived and as predicted looked as though he'd only just gotten out of bed. Not one of nature's early risers.

"Ready to take a run at Dean Grantham, Steve?" There didn't seem to be much enthusiasm coming from The Cap. He looked half asleep.

Steve decided to make some capital out of his surprise summons to the twelfth floor. "You look like death warmed up. Tell you what, go and have a lie-down and I'll wake you when we're ready to start."

"Ho, ho, very funny. I'm ready. It's just my brain's stuck in yesterday."

"Just catch your breath and relax for a few minutes. Write up your notes from yesterday's interview of Philip Grantham and give them to Andy." Turning to Andy who appeared lost in his speed typing. "Update the file Andy, once The Cap gives you his notes. I've been summoned to visit the twelfth floor. Shouldn't be long. We'll interview Grantham when I get back."

***

Steve entered the office of Commander Anthony Bowles. He knew the commander was a member of the Syndicate but so far couldn't prove it. He didn't like his superior officer and felt it was reciprocated. Without being asked and as a small gesture of defiance Steve sat opposite the Commander who was seated at his desk.

"How's the double murder enquiry going?" No small talk, just straight to the chase.

Steve knew his superior was unaware of the second post-mortem and that the girls hadn't been murdered by any legal definition. He knew he had to box clever with this man.

"Fine. We're making progress."

"Good. I hear you've got a couple locked up?"

"Yes. I'm due to interview the second suspect when I leave here." Steve didn't hide his frustration at not being allowed to get on with it.

"That's what I wanted to talk to you about."

Steve had no idea what was coming but he noticed the Commander was nervous. He kept playing with a ruler on his desk. "You're going to be signed in as a Disciple of the Syndicate on Sunday. It's a great honour." He fiddled with the ruler. "You know the rules and how the Syndicate works. We all look out for each other and when the Master asks us to do something we obey unquestioningly. This is the world you will enter on Sunday."

Steve didn't like the way this was going.

"Although you're not officially a Disciple, the Master is asking you to do something for him. I suppose it's a bit of a test."

"What do you mean the Master?"

"Oh! You'll find out on Sunday, but Lars prefers to be referred to as the Master when we're discussing Syndicate business."

Steve thought they must all be mad or simple in the head to be part of an organisation run by some megalomaniac. This whole situation was getting weirder and weirder, but he'd promised the head of MI6 to infiltrate it if he could, so he'd play along but reluctantly.

"What is this test?"

"You were given the two dead girls cases in order to get a result. The Master was made aware of them and I advised him that the cases should be closed as quickly as possible. We've seen unsolved cold cases resurrected years later to the discomfort of the perpetrators. You now appear to have two suspects in custody but unfortunately one is a Disciple. He's just a foot soldier but a valuable one. You are instructed to throw the book at Philip Grantham for the murders but to find no case to answer against DI Dean Grantham."

"What!" Steve jumped out of his chair. "Are you telling me officially to stitch up a suspect and let the real culprit walk?"

"In essence, yes. You know the way the Syndicate works is we look after each other. The Master tells me he wants Dean Grantham freed. I tell you and as the officer with the authority and as a member of the Syndicate you oblige the Master and find a way of not bringing charges against a fellow Disciple."

"But you're a police officer. How can you condone this?"

"I'm also a Disciple, Steve. This is only a small example of how we operate and how one day we'll be the ones in charge. Not some lame elected government. And there's no foul here. You put away a nobody. The world won't miss him, but you give one of your fellow Disciples another chance to serve. It's a great and glorious thing we're doing." Anthony Bowles was beginning to sound like Lars Jenson. In Steve's opinion that meant he was *also* completely bonkers.

The Commander carried on. "Of course, Disciple Grantham will face some form of punishment. He was supposed to make the victims disappear. After all, who would miss a couple of bits of human trash who weren't even in the country legally? If he'd buried them or dumped them into a lake, we wouldn't be having all these problems, but the fool left them for all to see, but luckily, the Syndicate can resolve all problems."

The Commander sat back and stared at Steve. "There you have it, DCI Burt. Your first chance to please the Master and me. The Master is very generous towards those who obey him and get results." He stood up indicating the meeting was over. "Go forth and please our Master and your signing ceremony on Sunday will be a great triumph." The Commander smiled but Steve saw a leer.

Steve was speechless. He knew better than to comment but was already trying to work a way out of his predicament, but his mind was blank. As he walked down the stairs to the eighth floor and his office, he ran the conversation over in his mind. He had no answer.

Chapter Eighteen

As soon as Steve entered his office suite, both Abul and Andy knew something was wrong. Steve didn't acknowledge either of them or crack some form of a joke. He went straight to his own office and closed the door. Neither detective had seen him do that before. Whatever was up must be serious.

"Best stay here, Andy, we'll give him half an hour and if he doesn't surface, I'll give him a knock."

"Right Cap, I wonder what's up?"

The Cap shrugged his shoulders. "I'm off to the interview suites to check up on Dean Grantham. At least we'll be ready when Steve wants to start."

The Cap left the outer office. Just as he left Steve's office door opened and he stepped out. "Where's The Cap?"

"He's just left. He's gone to check up on Grantham."

"Andy, come in please."

Andy was concerned. He'd never seen his boss so gloomy nor so formal. He noticed he wasn't invited to sit so he remained standing. This was going to be quick. "You know that credit card info you got'"

"Yes."

"I want you to send it to Twiggy, sorry, Miss Rough." The DCI allowed a slight smile to crease his face. "Send it to her secret address, the one I gave you." A deliberate pause. Andy knew his boss was worried about something. "I know you'll have the file up to date on the Essex cases. I don't have to ask. Get me a hard copy of everything on file and can you get it now, please, Andy?"

"No problem." Andy was concerned so threw caution to the wind. "Is everything all right Steve? You seem a bit off colour."

"I'm fine Andy. Please just do as I ask and close the door behind you. When The Cap gets back tell him to hang around. I'll need about an hour."

The DCI took an A4 pad and started to write detailing every interaction he'd had with the Syndicate, MI6 and Commander Bowles. He laid out in clear statements his thoughts on the case, his recruitment by Sir Patrick Bond to infiltrate the Syndicate with the task of getting the details of its members. He recorded his last conversation with Commander Bowles and the actions he proposed taking.

Steve felt he was writing his obituary. He'd never before felt the need to prepare such a document and it didn't sit well with him. Finally, he explained why he was proceeding with his actions and finished with a justification for them.

He signed and dated what was now a six-page document. Next, he pulled his mobile from his jacket pocket and speed dialled Sir Patrick who answered on the second ring.

"It's Steve Burt, Sir Patrick; please listen and say nothing. I've been put in a position as a result of your asking me to get close to the Syndicate, where my career could be in jeopardy. I said at the beginning that, if this happened, I was pulling out."

He stopped momentarily to allow the head of MI6 time to digest what he was saying. "However, I'm now of the opinion that this Syndicate are a serious threat. They've asked me to, at the very least, pervert the course of justice and the scary thing is they expect it to be done, and it came from a senior police officer. I'm no boy scout but this episode has shown me how they can manipulate the system for their own ends."

Again, Steve paused to make sure Patrick Bond was following. "I've prepared a dossier to be opened in the event things go wrong and I finish up on the wrong side. It details everything to do with the case and your involvement, plus your suspicions surrounding Sir Timothy Head. It's a full expose. I'm leaving it with someone I can trust, but be aware if anything happens to me, or mine, or my staff, then the dossier will be made public." Again, a pause.

"I'm embarking on a course of action to try and get you the list of members of the Syndicate. After my experience, this morning I now believe them to be dangerous and corrupt. I just hope to God you're being straight with me because if you're not I'm cooked." Steve paused for the final time. "Now you can answer. Did you get all that?"

"Yes, I did but—"

"That's enough, I'll be in touch." Steve hung up.

After a few minutes of agonising with himself over his actions, Steve opened his office door. Andy and The Cap looked expectantly at him. There was silence. Steve broke it by asking Andy for the hard copy of the file and suggesting they all needed a coffee.

Back in his office Steve placed the file and his hand-written dossier into a large white envelope and wrote a name on the front. He sealed the envelope and signed across the sealed flap for extra security.

Having reached his decision, the DCI felt better. He had a plan, and that gave him purpose. If things worked out, he'd be fine but, if things went wrong then his days as a police officer could be numbered. It was a risk.

Sipping coffee, all three detectives were now sitting in Steve's office. He was more like his old self.

"Andy, the names of the unaccompanied children you got from the airline. I want you to send them to Jenny." As Steve said this, he speed-dialled DS Jenny Fuller using his mobile.

"This is DS Fuller."

"Hi, Jenny, it's Steve and I've got the gang here." Everyone said hello, and the mood was lighter. "Jenny I've asked Andy to send you a list of names of unaccompanied youngsters arriving from Romania today. Luckily, there's only one main airline that flies the routes to Stanstead and Southend. I want you to go airside and meet the flight. Obviously, we don't know what they look like but shadow the passengers and see if any of them are pulled from the queue at passport control. We think the names you'll get might be here to sell their organs. The same credit card that bought our two victims' tickets was used to buy the tickets for the ones arriving today."

"Understood. I suppose because you've got Dean locked up, we'll be looking for his replacement, if there is one."

"Exactly. If they're picked up before passport control step in and lift whoever the new Dean is. Take the kids through passport control and take them to Chelmsford. If no one meets them, get the Border Force guys to look out for them and give you the nod when they get a matching name."

"And you want me to follow them landside?"

"Yes. It could be the new Dean can't get airside. If no one shows, I'm guessing the kids will be a bit lost. Step in and take them to Chelmsford."

"Will do." Jenny raised her voice to get Andy's attention. "Andy, you'll give me flight numbers and arrival times?"

"Yes. The good news is the airline is going to e-mail me each days' passenger manifest and highlight the names whose tickets have been paid for using the credit card." Andy chuckled. "You could be on airport duty for weeks. The good news is the credit card isn't used every day, so you'll get time off."

"Not funny but I get your point. Leave it with me and I'll be in touch." The line went dead.

"That'll keep Jenny out of mischief for a while, but if we can get these people to talk, we might move this thing alone." Steve sat back and considered his next statement.

"I want you to listen closely to what I'm going to say. I don't want questions unless you're desperate. Is that clear?"

Both The Cap and Andy said yes simultaneously.

"Over the next few days, maybe longer, you might think I've gone a bit mad. I can't tell you why, but I'm into something that requires some odd decisions to be made. Decisions that you both know are wrong and maybe even illegal. But I need you on board. Don't question anything I decide; not in private nor in public. We'll keep working the case and keep what we've learnt secret as before. All I can say is this is important, and you should both be careful. If either of you or your family are approached by any unusual or shady characters you must let me know. Clear?"

Both detectives nodded.

"What I'm into might become dangerous, depending on how things pan out, so keep your heads down. Trust no one and I include Commander Bowles in that."

The DCI sat back. "We'll go see Dean, when I get back. Andy, find out where Philip Grantham is. I want him back here. Cap, sort out Dean and get him into an interview room."

Steve took his envelope with the dossier and headed for Financial Crimes. It wasn't that he didn't trust The Cap but Twiggy was removed from the investigation and was less likely to come in for serious scrutiny if things went wrong.

He saw her in her usual spot working away on her computer keyboard. He approached her cubicle in a way that she could see him coming. He still didn't fancy having to help her to her feet if she were surprised again but couldn't regain her balance. She waved and signalled Steve to go in the direction of her boss's office. Like last time he was out.

"I'm glad you came, I've got a few interesting things for you." Twiggy perched on the chair she'd used at their last meeting in this office. She looked at the envelope Steve was carrying. "What's in the envelope?"

"Something I need you to do for me, but it can wait. What've you got?"

Twiggy smiled. Steve remembered the first time they met and being amazed that someone so large could have such a pretty face and a genuinely warm smile.

"I've made a start on the accounts. Let's just say I think they are a work of fiction."

"Nothing new there then." Steve faked a grin he didn't feel. In truth, he could do without Twiggy's natural enthusiasm, but he let her carry on.

"I've not had long, but it looks like large sums are arriving in these accounts without any obvious goods or services being supplied in return. There's a connection to various banks in dodgy jurisdictions and again no obvious reason for sums in or sums out. I'll get to work behind the scenes and see what crops up but for sure Eclipse Medical is up to no good." Twiggy tried to sit back but her bulk on a standard chair meant she just shifted her weight.

"What do you think they are up to?"

"Steve, your guess is as good as mine. I don't think it is money laundering, but there's always a chance. They are spending big on something. There's a monthly payment to the Royal Bank of Jersey. No idea what for, but the good news is we have the powers to examine their accounts. That's next on my list."

"Good job, Twiggy. You obviously made the right move?"

"Yes, and it was thanks to you, Steve."

Steve felt embarrassed by the compliment even though there was an element of truth in it, but he didn't want to dwell on this topic.

"Twiggy, I need a favour but it's hush-hush. You can't tell a soul. I should say things might get a bit hairy round here, so if you say no, I'll understand."

"Steve." Twiggy was laughing a deep belly laugh. "You are in the presence of a Fiat 500 driver. Things getting hairy doesn't apply. Scary might be nearer the truth. Whatever you need just ask and it's yours."

Steve explained what he could and gave her the same information he'd passed onto The Cap and Andy. He told her about the Syndicate but held back on his involvement. He explained about the sale of body parts, but not about having to let Dean walk. He explained he'd been put in an awkward position, but he was working his way out of it. Finally, he told her she might hear he was making some odd decisions but asked that she ignore any gossip.

"I've prepared a dossier on everything that's happened. I've explained my reasoning and named the people involved. It's the sort of document people could get hurt over if the wrong people knew it existed. It's my insurance in case things go horribly wrong." He handed the envelope to Twiggy. "It's all in there. I need you to keep it safe and away from the Yard. If I seem to be in trouble, I'd like you to go to The Cap and Andy and decide how best to use this. Hopefully, it will bail me out." Steve looked at a serious-looking Twiggy. "I know it's a lot to ask, but I wouldn't trust anyone else, especially as you're two steps removed from Special Resolutions and less likely to come up on certain people's radar."

"I think I see, but regardless Steve, you can count on me. It sounds a bit cloak-and-dagger but I'm sure you know what you're doing. I'll take it home and hide it in a place no one will ever find it and before you ask, it's not my knicker drawer."

They both laughed. Twiggy took the envelope. "I'll have more on these accounts later today. Should I come across to you or do you want to be briefed off-site?"

"Mm! Let's see how we go and how the time works out. If I'm not around talk to Andy Miller, but hopefully I'll be here."

They parted and headed their separate ways. Steve thought about the irregularities in the accounts. He recalled they'd solved a case in the past based on accounting evidence but deep down he couldn't see how a set of dodgy numbers would help with his present predicament.

Chapter Nineteen

When Steve arrived back at his office he was met by an excited Andy.

"Steve, can you call Jenny urgently?"

The Cap who was waiting for Steve to start the interview of Dean Grantham looked worried. "I got the idea that she's got the girls Steve."

From his office, Steve phoned Jenny and put her on the speaker to let The Cap and Andy listen in.

Jenny was talking in a whispered voice. "I've got the people we were looking for in sight. It's two girls again. There was no new Dean airside, so they've gone through passport control. The immigration guys were good, and I got the heads-up. They didn't have any luggage, so they went straight to the exit." Steve could hear the tension in Jenny's voice. "I'm following them and we're just getting landside. They look lost. They are standing in the middle of the concourse talking to each other. It looks like they are arguing. Hold on." The line went quiet only punctuated by background airport noise. The line was silent for several minutes before Jenny started talking again. "There's a guy turned up holding a cardboard sign with the girls' names on it. They are talking with him... Hold on, now they are moving towards the exit. What do I do, Steve?"

"Keep them in sight, but remember, don't let these girls go anywhere except Chelmsford Headquarters."

The line to Jenny was still open. Everyone in Steve's office could hear Jenny breathing. Silence. Then suddenly "Steve, it's a taxi. The guy who met them is a taxi driver, they are getting ready to go with him."

Steve immediately burst into action. "Right Jenny, get the girls NOW! Then pull the taxi driver. I want to know everything about who hired him. Got it?"

Jenny was obviously running. She was a bit breathless and her heavy breathing filled Steve's office. The Cap and Andy sat and listened to the drama being played out. They heard the muffled tones of Jenny talking and then shouting.

There was silence for a few seconds until Jenny came back on the line. "Got them! The taxi driver's not too keen to help, but the uniforms I brought with me have shown him the error of his ways in not helping the police. Hold on Steve."

More silence and a muffled conversation. Jenny sounding in control and breathing normally returned. "Right, the girls are on their way to Chelmsford in a patrol car. The DC whom I've used before has blagged a room at the airport that we can use to interview the taxi driver. He's taken him there now. I'll follow on and let you know what we get out of him."

"Good work Jenny. What I'd really like to know is who hired him and confirmation of where he was taking the girls."

"Understood. I've put Social Services on standby to take care of the girls. I couldn't get an interpreter though."

"Not to worry. Get them sorted and bring them to the Yard tomorrow at say eleven a.m. We'll sort out an interpreter."

"Got it."

"And Jenny? Let me know what the taxi driver says. It doesn't sound like he's involved but if you've any suspicions, pull him."

"Will do. I'll be in touch."

All three sat in silence. The Cap thought he'd just been listening to a detective programme on the radio. He had quite enjoyed it and it sounded as though progress was being made.

"She's doing good work," was all Steve said.

"Andy, has Philip Grantham been brought here yet?"

"Yeah, he's downstairs."

"I've checked with the medics and Dean is now fit to be questioned." The Cap was ready to get started.

Steve was still conflicted and regretted not telling his colleagues everything he knew. But he realised it was for their own safety and it didn't matter if he were ploughing a lone furrow.

"Cap, you and Andy go make a start with Dean. I've got something to do first, but I'll be down as soon as I can."

Andy looked shocked. He'd never been involved in such a high-power interrogation before. He reverted to the Andy of a few weeks ago. He was excited and it showed. Steve smiled inwards.

The Cap looked at the DCI. "I suppose this is the 'now don't ask' phase."

"There's no fooling you Abul." Steve shrugged. "Just get on with Dean and I'll be along when I can."

The Cap looked at Steve with something approaching pity. Then turned to Andy as they both stood.

"Andy my boy, you're about to see a master at work. Your job is to sit there, take notes and admire how I can get suspects to talk. Watch and learn." The Cap put an arm around Andy's shoulder and steered him out of the office. Both were laughing but Steve doubted Andy would learn anything from Abul's interrogation technique.

Alone, and with the door closed, Steve dialled the number for Jenny's significant other. Ian Fuller was Deputy Head of the Crown Prosecution Service. With a bit of persuasion from Jenny, he'd pulled a few strings to get the court order that allowed Andy to have access to the airline's credit card records.

Steve tried the mobile number he had but it was switched off. He then tried the landline number and after the usual explanations, the mindless music, more explanations, a voice came on the line.

With an abrupt tone full of self-importance, the voice announced. "Fuller!" Steve was looking for advice so didn't want to start on the wrong foot. He had only met Ian Fuller once, and his recollection was that unless Jenny prompted him, he was a by-the-book man. Not good for Steve's purposes at this moment.

"Ian, it's Steve Burt. You remember I met you and Jenny the other evening?"

"Yes, I remember; you needed a court order."

"Yes, and thank you for that, it allowed us to make major progress with the two cases." Steve lied. It had helped but there certainly was no breakthrough. "I know you're busy, but I could do with some advice."

"Mr Burt, I work for the CPS. I'm not a commercial lawyer and therefore do not give ad hoc advice."

"I understand." Ian Fuller was confirming what Steve thought about him. "But when we're presenting cases, you advise on all aspects of our evidence." Steve didn't want to be seen as being a smart arse.

"Perfectly true; does the advice you're looking for come within that category?"

Steve had to box clever. "Well, almost." He knew he had the man from the CPS' attention. "Can I just explain and then you decide? I believe the advice I'm looking for is covered by your remit."

"Oh! Very well but be quick. I have a conference call in ten minutes."

Steve took a deep breath and began. "You'll recall the reason I asked you to get the court order rather than go through normal and official channels?"

"Yes. You've got some cloak-and-dagger project going on."

"Yes. Well, it's still going on and I'm in a bit of a pickle. What would happen from the CPS' perspective if I had a prisoner that I have enough evidence to charge with a serious crime, who is currently in custody, but I release him and re-arrest him in say a week's time on the same charges, and on the same evidence?"

Ian Fuller was clearly thinking. There was no sound from the other end of the line. Eventually and with a great sigh, Ian was back. "Well, you'd be open to criticism about why you let your suspect go and then arrest him later. It's not common practice but from a legal point of view, it's not criminal, although as I say, you could leave yourself open to questions about your competency. On the other hand, the suspect could file a case for delayed justice and probably exaggerated stress due to having been released thinking he was free and then being re-arrested on the same evidence."

"Hm! I see that. Is there anything that can be done to get around such a situation?"

"I presume this isn't a hypothetical problem?"

"No."

"I thought not. Then, I suggest you release your prisoner on police bail. Notate your file that you intend to make further enquiries as the reason for granting him bail. In any normal situation that should keep you clean. Now I really must be going."

Steve wasn't finished. "Sorry, Ian but just one more, please."

"Oh! Very well." The voice was now very full of self-importance.

"It's almost the same thing but in reverse. If I have a suspect who's involved in a crime, but only on the margins... Under normal circumstances, he would be looking at a minor charge, but I want to send him down on more serious charges for say a week and then revert to the minor ones. How do I do that and what are the consequences?"

"My, my, you *do* lead a complicated life, Chief Inspector. I presume you intend holding your second prisoner on remand?"

Steve was beginning to see why Ian Fuller was with the CPS. "Yes, it's necessary."

"Well, I'd advise against it. You're telling me you are going to charge a man with a serious crime without evidence. I'm presuming this is the case?"

"Yes."

"I'm not sure how you could justify it if there was an enquiry. In the first scenario, you have the seeking-more-evidence ruse. In this second one, you are totally exposed. The only way you might survive is if you played the circumstantial evidence ploy. In my experience, cases that rely on circumstantial evidence get very messy. Everything's up for interpretation. I suppose you could frame charges based on circumstance and after a week fail to make the pieces fit. It would give you a more plausible story but please do not fabricate hard evidence. If you do, you'll be hung out to dry, even if after a week you admit you were wrong and your prisoner's freed. Wrongful arrest suits are messy even when they are genuine. Faked charges are certain jail time for the officer."

Steve listened but couldn't see a clear way forward. "So, your thoughts, Ian, are to release the first suspect on police bail and to look for enough legitimate circumstantial evidence to hold the second suspect? Then after, say, a week, I throw the book at the first one and release the second. Is that about it?"

"It's not ideal but yes. At least you might save your career if either of them creates a stink... but bottom line, play it straight." Ian Fuller sounded genuinely concerned. He carried on to Steve's surprise. "Jenny's told me a few things and she rates you as one of the good guys. Please don't make me have to prosecute you for conspiracy to pervert. I'm also good at my job and I've no internal politics to hold me back." The man from the CPS sighed. "I must go now. This conversation never happened. Good luck but be careful. Goodbye."

The line went dead. Steve needed to think. He pulled his A4 pad out and started to write, listing what he knew and what he could do. The next fifteen minutes could decide his whole career.

He listed the advice Ian Fuller had just given him, the need to satisfy Lars Jenson, the involvement of Commander Bowles, the murders of the two dead girls, and Dean Grantham's involvement. Then he added the link to Romania and the credit card with the word 'anonymous' beside it, and the clinic beside Harlow and the organ transplant operation. Some of the connections were obvious but he couldn't see a way through. How did Lars Jenson manage to recruit his Disciples and how did men who appeared at the top of their profession succumb to the utter nonsense of the so-called Master?

The DCI's head was spinning. He had to make sense of what he was getting into. The one thing he jotted down that was relevant was that Commander Bowles had told him to make sure he didn't charge Dean Grantham, but he was expected to charge someone with the girls' deaths in order to ensure the cases were closed. Steve didn't like this abuse of power and it was this that would make him carry on even at the expense of his career.

He was about to visit the interview suite when Jenny called.

"I've got everything I can from the taxi driver. He seems quite innocent, just doing a job. He was told to collect two girls from Stanstead Airport and take them to Eclipse Hall outside Harlow. He was paid in advance by credit card, told to write the names on a piece of cardboard and to meet the afternoon flight from Bucharest. That's it, nothing more."

"Thanks, Jenny. Can you chase up forensics? I haven't heard anything about what they may have found in Philip Grantham's van."

"Will do. The girls are staying in a B&B tonight. Immigration at the airport, are keen to send them back so we might get into a turf war later. I'll be there tomorrow with them if you've managed to find an interpreter."

"Thanks for the reminder. See you tomorrow around eleven." Steve hung up and immediately called Human Resources. He requested a Romanian speaker to be available at eleven the following morning. After a bit of "they don't grow on trees you know", and after a lot of frustration and unnecessary threats, it was eventually agreed an interpreter would be in his office as requested. You had to love pen pushers.

**

At long last Steve arrived at interview room four. He knocked and entered. The Cap looked exhausted as did Andy. Dean Grantham was lounging in his chair with a smug grin on his face. The ever-present constable was standing just inside the door.

When The Cap saw Steve, he informed the tape being used to record the interview of his arrival. Steve said nothing but signalled both The Cap and Andy to meet him outside the room. The Cap told Dean the interview was being suspended.

All three officers gathered round in a circle.

"How's it going?"

"Not well, Steve, the slimy bugger knows all the tricks. All we're getting is 'no comment' and 'you can't prove a thing'."

"Is he admitting to anything?"

"No, he's hardly admitting to his name."

"You told him we have him on CCTV at the airport?"

"Yes, and the cheeky sod said it wasn't him. Just somebody who looks like him."

"How long have you been at it?"

The Cap looked at his watch. "Just over an hour."

Steve was uncomfortable with his decision but pressed on. "Get him back to a cell. We'll have another go later."

"But Steve, he's warmed up. You know the longer we go at a suspect the more likely they are to slip up." The Cap wasn't ready to throw in the towel.

Steve looked at Abul. "Please just do as I say. Andy, with me." The DCI waved a 'follow me' arm towards Andy and left Abul standing outside the door to interview room four.

Chapter Twenty

Andy was now back at his desk dealing with his e-mails and other data that had landed on his desk. The Cap arrived back and slumped down in his chair after he had distributed the three coffees, he'd bought on his way back.

Steve was contemplating his next move with Dean Grantham when he heard an excited shout from the outer office followed by Andy almost running into his office. The Cap obviously curious followed but at a more leisurely pace.

"I've had an e-mail from Romania." Andy was holding his laptop in the air like a trophy. "My contact Dimitri has just said they've identified the guy who's been buying the flight tickets and using the credit card. They've arrested him but so far he's not talking, except for one thing." Andy was jubilant. He lowered his laptop and placed it on Steve's desk but not for Steve to look at. Still standing in the centre of Steve's office he announced, "He works for the British Embassy in Bucharest. He's Romanian and works as a driver."

"Bloody hell, where are we going with this, boss?" The Cap was remembering Steve's warning, but this seemed to be getting out of control. A routine enquiry now had international elements no one had forecast.

"Mm! Interesting," was all Steve said, as he considered this latest information.

"So, we now have a link to our Embassy in Bucharest, but where does this take us?"

The room was quiet. Steve sat whilst his colleagues stood.

The phone on Steve's desk rang indicating it was from someone in the building. "Yes, Steve Burt."

"Steve, it's Twiggy." Her voice was low, low enough to be a whisper. "Can we meet away from the Yard?"

"Yes of course. What's up?"

"I said I'd have something for you on the Eclipse accounts this afternoon, but I don't. I've been pulled away on something else relating to your case and it's something you should know, but I can't tell you officially, if you get my drift?"

Steve sat and contemplated for a few seconds. "Sounds a bit intriguing, can't you just come over here?"

"Trust me, Steve, you need this information, but you don't want it on site."

"Sounds serious. What are you thinking?"

"I'm going to be here until at least seven. Could we meet up for a drink or something?"

"I'm having dinner at Alison's place tonight. Why don't you come over? I'm sure there'll be enough food and you haven't met her yet."

Twiggy considered the second-hand dinner invitation. "If you're sure then it's a date. Give me the address."

Steve did and they agreed Twiggy would arrive around seven-thirty. As he was about to hang up Twiggy carried on talking.

"Steve, you'll get a call anytime now to attend a meeting tomorrow. It's all to do with the original murder enquiry. I can't say any more over the phone, but I'll see you tonight." The line went dead.

The Cap and Andy were still standing and had been listening to one side of the conversation. Steve ignored the curious looks on their faces.

"Cap, let's go see Dean and then I want to re-interview Philip Grantham."

Steve stood but Andy raised his hand and turned to his laptop. " Steve, we've got the forensics back from the transit van." Andy keyed in for a minute or so and turned his machine so everyone could see the screen.

"Looks like they found hair samples that match the two victims, so they were definitely in the van. There's not much else. They say the plastic sheet did its job and the van's more or less clean."

Steve looked into the far distance. This would help with his plan. "Right Andy, add it to the file. Again, it's helpful but we're no longer dealing with murder. At best manslaughter, and I'm convinced this Eclipse Clinic in Harlow is at the centre of everything. Jenny told me the taxi driver she questioned was told to take the latest two girls straight there." The DCI stopped remembering something. "Andy, get onto Jenny and get her to contact the taxi driver again. He said he was paid by credit card. Get the number and trace it."

"Right."

All three left his office. Andy to his desk and Steve and The Cap back to interview room four. When they arrived the custody sergeant had already had Dean brought from the cells. He was seated as before but had a paper cup full of tea in front of him.

"Well, well, I am honoured. An even more senior officer to come and waste his time talking to me."

Steve and The Cap ignored Dean's attempt to wind them up. They complied with protocol regarding taped interviews and interviews under caution.

Steve had previously agreed The Cap would continue to take the lead.

"Now, Dean, anything to say yet?"

"Apart from 'no comment', you mean?"

"You are an experienced officer, Dean. You know how the system works. We've got enough on you now to charge you but as one officer to another we're giving you a chance to tell your side of the story."

"You've got nothing!" Dean was sneering at Abul. "You pulled this I'm your friend stunt in Chelmsford, so I know your style. Just accept you've got nothing and get me a lift back to Chelmsford."

"Sorry Dean, that's not going to happen."

Dean continued to sneer and sat back.

"You know Dean, an ex-police officer in prison doesn't usually have an easy time. Cooperate with us now and we might be able to make it possible for you to do your stretch in a soft prison."

"Rubbish, I'm not falling for that old one. I've used it too often myself."

"Well Dean, if you won't help yourself, I'm afraid we'll have to let the CPS cherry-pick the charges we can land on you. Everything from murder, to conspiracy, all the way to perverting the course of justice, sounds like at least twenty years. Of course, if you give us something to work with, I'm sure we could forget a few charges and you'll get maybe ten to fifteen."

"I have to hand it to you. You're a persistent bugger. But like I said, 'No comment'. See, I have connections and I'll be away from here before morning."

The Cap was about to launch more statements at Dean to try and wear him down. Steve decided the time was right but was fearful of Abul's reaction to what was to come.

Steve sat forward. "DI Ishmal, has this suspect been formally charged?"

"Yes, sir, charges as discussed."

Steve looked Dean squarely in the eyes. "Detective Inspector Dean Grantham you will be released on police bail in order for us to carry out further enquiries and gather evidence as to your guilt. You remain charged with conspiracy and leaving two dead bodies in unauthorised places. As a result of on-going enquiries, further charges may follow. You are required as a condition of your bail not to leave the country and you are to report to Detective Inspector Abul Ishmal at New Scotland Yard next Thursday exactly seven days from now at three p.m. Failure to comply will result in an immediate arrest warrant being issued. Is that clear?"

Dean suddenly smiled. He gave Steve an odd look before pointing his index figure at the DCI and pretending it was a gun, he clicked his tongue. "Click, got you Mr Disciple; now can you get me a lift?"

The Cap and Steve left Dean behind and entered the adjoining interview room, number five. As it was empty, and they waited for Philip Grantham to be brought to them, The Cap let fly. "Steve, what's going on? We can't let a murder suspect go on police bail. We'll be lynched if anything goes wrong. Are you mad or what?"

"I don't think I'm mad and remember our discussion about odd behaviour and the need for your support."

"Yes, but—"

Steve cut him off. "Well, you've just seen a practical demonstration of what I meant."

Abul realised Steve must be in a difficult position, so decided to keep his own counsel. He simply said, "I hope to God you know what you're doing."

Steve smiled. "So do I, Cap, so do I."

The Cap had noticed the use of the word 'Disciple'. He stored it away to seek clarification at a later date.

**

Philip Grantham arrived with an escort who took him to his chair and then took up position by the door. Steve and The Cap sat opposite. The detectives hadn't discussed how they were to orchestrate this interview, and The Cap had no idea why Philip had been brought back for questioning. He organised the tape recorder and sat back to let Steve take the lead.

"Hello, Philip." The DCI was using his gentle 'I'm your best friend' voice. "Are you being treated OK?"

Philip Grantham looked a little unsure. He was nervous and wasn't making eye contact. Steve hated what he had to do next.

"Yeah, I suppose, the food was better than I thought." He gave out a weak giggle.

"Philip, you remember last time you told us what happened with the two girls, and how Dean was really the leader?"

"Yeah."

"Well, we've just had to let Dean go. You see, he didn't tell us the same story." Steve knew this was a stretch but at one level it was the truth. He didn't look at The Cap but could feel his alarm. Fortunately, Abul remained silent.

Philip's expression didn't change. He just shrugged.

"Philip, do you know what a forensic scientist is?"

"Not really. I've seen TV programmes where the main cop always asks for forensics but I've no idea what it means." Philip was chewing his bottom lip.

"Well, they are very clever people who can find the smallest clue. They've been working on your van and they found hairs that match the two dead girls in your van. How can you explain that?"

"I told you Dean and I took them from the big house in Harlow so there must be hairs."

"No Philip, you said Dean and another guy put a plastic sheet down. Now if that's true then no hairs should have been found. Isn't it true you murdered them in your van and that's why we found their hair?" Steve knew he was pushing it, but he had to finish.

Philip almost jumped from his chair. "No, I didn't touch those girls. It was all Dean."

"But you told us yesterday you *did* touch them. In fact, you said you carried them from the van. Isn't that correct?" The DCI hated deliberately twisting an innocent statement into something that sounded sinister.

"Well yes... I mean no... I told you I only helped."

"But the evidence is mounting, Philip. You admit you handled the bodies; we've found hair from the victims that you say couldn't be there because there was a plastic sheet on the floor of the van and we've only your word that Dean was involved. You see how it looks?"

Philip started to cry. "No, you've got it wrong."

Steve pressed on. His voice was no longer the friendly version it had once been. "No Philip, I think we've got it right. It was you who murdered these girls and you're trying to pin it on your brother. Just tell us, Philip. Did you kill these two girls?"

The tears were in full flood. It was clear Philip Grantham was in no fit state to carry on.

Steve steeled himself for what had to come. "Philip Grantham, I'm arresting you for the murders of Ingrid Baciu on or about the 24th of January this year, and the murder of Titania Popescu on or about the 14th of January this year."

He went on to advise him of his rights and finished up asking The Cap to arrange transport to return him to the local police station where he was being held.

Although The Cap complied, it was clear he wasn't happy at the turn of events. He'd never seen any senior officer railroad a prisoner as Steve had just done. This was the same DCI Burt that he looked up to and admired, but he didn't recognise this current version of his boss.

***

Andy was waiting for Steve as he entered the office. Steve was exhausted and not at one with himself. He hated what he had become or at least what he had become to his friends and colleagues. They took up their usual positions when it was just the two of them.

"Jenny got back to me with the credit card that was used to pay the taxi driver at Stanstead. It's registered to a Mr Robert Symonds. He lives in Essex near Harlow. I did a background check. He's listed as a surgeon and a Director of Eclipse Medical and the Medical Director of Eclipse Transplant Surgery Ltd. It's shortened to ETS. Jenny said the cabbie only got the call minutes before he had to set off. She thinks the taxi wasn't planned and was a last-minute fix. The girls had mobiles and an emergency number to call. With no Dean Grantham to intercept them, she thinks the clinic panicked, made a mistake and used a credit card not normally used by the business and sent the taxi to collect them." Andy waited for Steve to comment.

"So, we have a direct link to the director of the transplant clinic. Get it onto the file Andy. It's all building a picture. Jenny's bringing the latest two girls here tomorrow at eleven and I've laid on an interpreter. What's happening with incoming flights from Bucharest tomorrow?

"Nothing. The credit card wasn't used to book any of the passengers on either of tomorrow's flights so Jenny wouldn't be on airport duty anyway."

"Good. Now call it a day. I've a feeling tomorrow's going to get exciting. We'll…"

Abul stormed in.

"DCI Burt. I don't know what the hell that was all about, but you'd better have a bloody good explanation, otherwise, I'm off to Professional Standards and lodging a formal complaint."

Andy was physically shocked. He'd no idea what had happened, but he knew he didn't like it.

"Close the door Cap, and both of you sit down." Steve sat down in his chair behind his desk again. This was going to be official.

"I can't stop you going to Professional Standards. It's your right and in your shoes, if I'd just witnessed my governor pulling a stunt, like the one I've just pulled, I'd do the same thing. It shows we're decent straight cops. Think back to earlier. I said I was working on something and, for your own safety, I asked you not to question my decisions which might seem odd at the time, and to trust me. I'm asking for that trust now. All I can tell you is that greater powers than we can even begin to understand are at work and without your trust, we'll never get to the bottom of what's going on. I promise that as soon as the time is right, I'll tell you all about it." Steve hadn't prepared a speech but inwardly he was pleased with himself.

The Cap was a little ashamed and said so. "But you've just railroaded that poor bugger on a murder charge."

"As I said, Cap, I'll explain everything when I can but, trust me when I tell you Philip Grantham will be OK, and his brother will do some serious time. He's not off the hook."

Andy looked worried. "Steve, I remember what you said, and I don't know what's happened, but do you still want us to pursue legitimate enquiries?"

"Absolutely Andy." Steve looked at his two colleagues. "Just give me some space and time over the next few days. That's all I'm asking."

The Cap stood up followed by Andy. "You know we will, and we trust you. It's just that I for one have never known you break the rules, that's all."

The pair left. Steve sat behind his desk and closed his eyes. He needed to escape work even for a few hours to try and make himself feel better about his actions and what was to come.

***

Thursday had become a bit of a tradition between him and Alison. She'd order in pre-cooked meals, place them in the oven and produce the feast as though she had cooked it all from scratch. Steve pointed out to her early on that he was a detective and leaving the delivery boxes in full sight wasn't smart. This form of banter had survived and was now firmly part of their relationship.

Steve was just getting up when his internal phone rang. It hadn't rung for weeks and here it was twice in one day.

"DCI Burt."

"Chief Inspector Burt, this is Cecil Younger. You do know who I am?"

Steve knew this was the Assistant Commissioner of the Metropolitan Police. He held the receiver to his ear and sat down again.

"Yes, Sir Cecil, I know who you are."

"Good. You're to attend a meeting in my office tomorrow morning at eight-thirty sharp. No ifs, no buts; be there, and tell no one. Clear?"

"Yes Sir."

The line went dead. Steve replaced the receiver and remembered Twiggy's words, "You'll get a phone call later". That was the phone call. You didn't get a summons from the Assistant Commissioner every day of the week. Steve was concerned. Had his involvement with Lars Jenson been discovered? Had Sir Patrick Bond of MI6 shopped him? He had no idea, but he knew he had a very interrupted night's sleep ahead of him.

Chapter Twenty-One

He'd called Alison to say Twiggy was joining them for dinner. He explained it was work-related, but it was time she met Florance anyway. Alison took most things in her stride and simply said she'd lay another place, but Steve had better buy an extra bottle of wine.

The DCI remembered he hadn't explained about Twiggy's size and that she was probably still on a permanent diet. Judging by her present dimensions he didn't think the diet was working, and he didn't tell Alison that part of her diet was no alcohol. He was happy to top up the wine stock so said he'd pick up a couple of bottles on his way.

Steve arrived bearing the wine and was met by a delicious smell of cooking. Before his fiancée could give him a welcome kiss he asked "What's cooking? It smells delicious. Supermarket pre-cooking must be getting better."

He was met by a towel thrown by Alison. "If you say any more, I'll switch the oven off."

They both laughed, happy and content in each other's company.

***

Twiggy arrived on time, and after the introductions, the three settled down to a delicious dinner. Alison and Florance seemed to hit it off and Steve felt like a spectator. Twiggy embarrassed her ex-boss with several tales from when they first worked together. They got on so well Alison enquired about Florance's weight issues. She offered to treat her if she ever felt the need for radical solutions. The evening went well, but it was difficult for Steve to enjoy it fully, knowing Twiggy wasn't here just to be fed, but to pass on information he needed.

"If everyone's had enough, I'll clear the table. I know you two have business to discuss. Why not go over and use the lounge?" Alison was being practical as always. "I'll make myself scarce and promise not to eavesdrop."

"Are you sure I can't help?" Twiggy's domestic side was showing.

Alison shooed her away while Twiggy and Steve sat on one of the sofas. Or at least Steve got the twenty-five percent that was left.

Suddenly Twiggy was very serious. "Steve, we've got a problem."

This wasn't the opening remark he'd hoped for. Twiggy carried on. "Your man Andy passed over a credit card and asked if I could trace it. Well, I did, and it's caused an uproar within Financial Crimes, the Government and the twelfth floor." Twiggy drew breath. "Did you get a call to attend a meeting tomorrow?"

"Yes, with the Assistant Commissioner no less."

"It won't be a happy meeting. This credit card has brought a lot of trouble." Twiggy could see her ex-boss wasn't following.

"Let me explain. Andy told me this credit card has been used to purchase flight tickets from Bucharest to the UK. The people using these tickets to get here are young Romanians. We don't know why they're here, just that the credit card paid for their flights."

Steve didn't interrupt but it was obvious Twiggy and whoever she was working with didn't know about the clinic, the organ transplants or Lars Jenson.

Twiggy carried on. "We traced the card to the Anglo European Bank in Jersey. You'll know it as AEB. I spoke to one of their directors. Jersey was on the money laundering list for years but as of four years ago, they're duty-bound to assist us. Officially we need court orders but usually, they cooperate without one." Twiggy sipped what was left of the herbal tea she'd brought from the table. "It seems that someone in Bucharest is using the card. He purchases the flight tickets from a travel agent using the card, but then strange things happen. The name on the credit card is AEB. In other words, they're paying off the balance each month themselves on a credit card they issued."

"OK. So that's a bit unusual, but why is that causing all the uproar?"

"Well." Twiggy raised her eyebrows. "The bank processes the payments. They clear off the balance each month using bank funds. But the question is, as the bank's not a charity who is ultimately paying?"

184

"OK Florance, you've told a good story so far, but I don't see where you're going."

Twiggy gave a long, exaggerated sigh. "The monthly statements are sent to Whitehall. It's a *government card*, Steve. The UK's done a deal with AEB and appears to be paying to bring girls into this country. That's what's got everyone excited." Twiggy tried to sit back but could only perch on the front of the sofa.

Steve sat back on his small section of the sofa. "You're saying someone in Bucharest is using a British government credit card to bring girls into the UK and you don't know why?"

"That's it, and tomorrow you're going to be asked to explain any progress you've made, knowing I've been helping you look at this credit card. It seems the powers that be don't understand where you fit in."

Steve considered telling Twiggy everything, but he hesitated. If she saw the whole picture, she might be in danger, but Steve couldn't understand why he thought that. "Is that it? A credit card being paid by HM Government, and that's going to cause me grief tomorrow?"

Twiggy shrugged her shoulders in a 'that's it' unspoken statement.

Alison reappeared. Despite what she said Steve knew she'd been listening. "Right, everyone, I'm sorry Florance, but I'm throwing you out." This was said with a smile. "I've got an early start tomorrow and a heap of work to do before I go to bed, but it's been lovely meeting you."

Twiggy took the hint and struggled to her feet. The sofa sighed.

"No problem Alison, and if I can take advantage of your weight-loss advice, I'd be really grateful."

"I'll get your contact number from Steve and give you a call."

Twiggy left smiling. Clearly, she was still looking forward to the day when her weight wouldn't be a problem. However, she feared for Steve in the morning.

Steve and Alison sat wrapped up in each other. Alison volunteered she'd listened and wanted to help. She already knew Steve was working on behalf of MI6 trying to infiltrate the Syndicate and learn who the members were. But she didn't understand too much of what Florance had been alluding to. She prompted Steve to open up to her.

"I need a sounding board darling, and you're about the best I can think of."

"Good, now tell me everything."

Steve cleared his brain of everything not related to the case. After a deep breath, he began. "I was set up by Commander Bowles to investigate what looked like two separate but similar murders over in Essex. The local investigation was cursory at best, and by having a second post-mortem we learnt the girls weren't murdered in the conventional sense. We know who and how they dumped their bodies." Steve was staring off into the distance and Alison was holding his hand.

"You remember I met Lars Jenson with you at that dinner last Friday and again on Sunday down at his Buckinghamshire estate? Well, you know he invited me to lunch and asked if I would join his Syndicate. The Syndicate want to rule the country and believe they already do. They say members include very senior people from all walks of life. They help each other out, including bending the law. While we were looking into the two deaths, we were able to prove a DI in Chelmsford was involved with the Syndicate and was meeting girls off flights from Bucharest. We also discovered that these girls were probably selling their organs for transplant to the Eclipse Transplant clinic in Harlow, that's your friend, Robbie Symonds.

"As you know, Sir Patrick Bond of MI6 knew I'd met Lars Jenson and convinced me to do a little undercover work, so I've agreed to join the Syndicate to try to get a list of members. Sir Patrick's looking after the investigation personally because he doesn't know who to trust. Any senior figure could be what they call a Disciple of the Syndicate. This thing goes deep." Steve looked at Alison who squeezed his hand and nodded for him to continue.

"Then Lars asked me to do something almost by way of a test. He wanted the DI from Chelmsford released and someone else stitched up for murdering the two girls. You see the DI is a Disciple. This message came from Commander Bowles who's quite relaxed about breaking the rules." Steve shook his head in disbelief even now.

"Then Andy made contact with the Romanian police and fed them what we had. It seems they've arrested the guy who booked the flight tickets for the girls coming here to sell their organs. He's Romanian but works as a driver in the British Embassy in Bucharest. Now we've got Twiggy telling us the UK government is actually funding the airfares to bring these young people from Bucharest. We interviewed a taxi driver who confirmed he was to take the most recent arrivals to Harlow and the Eclipse Clinic." Steve looked exhausted.

"That's it as far as it goes. I released the DI from Chelmsford and have stitched up a patsy on murder charges just to keep in with Lars and his Syndicate. I'm no boy scout but I feel really terrible about it. Even worse, I've not told Abul or Andy what I'm up to. Technically and practically, I've broken more than a few rules and laws, all to try and get in with the Syndicate. I spoke with Ian Fuller of the CPS and sort of told him what I had to do. He's given me advice and I've written a dossier explaining all this should things get nasty. Twiggy has it." Steve knew he had to be strong to finish this thing wherever it led.

"My poor darling, no wonder you look as though you're carrying the weight of the world on your shoulders. You probably are. Is there anything I can do to help?"

Steve had been thinking Alison could help but was reluctant to involve her especially as a few months ago she had narrowly missed being beaten up by a low-life thug who was involved in one of Steve's cases.

"I've not pressed the buttons on the clinic in Harlow yet." Steve looked defeated but was still reacting to events.

"I don't want to let Lars see we know about his operation just now. I need to be seen to be a Syndicate player and a good Disciple if I'm to get to his list of members. But I can't leave it much longer. I need to get inside the place and suss it out. You said you have a patient who needs a transplant and your buddy Robbie wants you to go with her. What if I went with you just to act as your driver? It would give me a way in without alerting suspicions."

"Oh! Steve, what a good idea. This all sounds a bit 007. It may not feel like it to you, but I think it's quite exciting and I want to help. In fact, I've got an appointment for next Tuesday the 19th."

"I don't want you doing anything out of the ordinary and putting yourself in danger. We've done that once and I promised you it would never happen again."

"Yes, you did my darling and it was very gallant of you. But on this occasion, unless you go charging in with your big boots, I'm your best chance to see what goes on in Harlow."

Steve looked at his fiancée in another light. This lovely lady wasn't only smart but brave. He told himself he was a lucky man.

"Right Mr Detective, I'll put the kettle on, and we'll have a nice cup of tea, then bed."

Alison gave Steve a peculiar look he couldn't interpret. She went into the kitchen area to boil the kettle.

***

Steve sat still trying to make sense of everything when his phone rang. The caller ID told him it was Sir Patrick Bond, Head of MI6, and the person who'd put him in the position he was now in. Reluctantly he answered.

"Steve, I'll be brief. You know about this meeting tomorrow?"

"Yes. I had a call from the Assistant Commissioner. Eight-thirty tomorrow morning."

"Right. Do you know what it's about?"

Steve thought this was an odd question. Twiggy had broken the rules by telling him, so officially he shouldn't know. He played dumb.

"No, not a clue." The DCI was now looking on this conversation as a test of just where the head of MI6 fitted into this puzzle. If he came clean about the government credit card, then Steve could trust him. If he didn't then he was under suspicion.

"Look, I'm not sure if it's to be spoken about before the meeting, but the credit card you asked your Financial Crimes people to trace has stirred up a hornet's nest. You should be ready to explain it tomorrow. Understand?"

Steve was relieved. Sir Patrick seemed to be one of the good guys.

"Thanks for the heads-up."

"Yes. Well, it's the least I can do but listen, I don't think anyone, apart from us, is on to the Syndicate thing. I'd like to keep it that way, so tomorrow don't mention anything unless I bring it up. We should keep what you're doing on a need to know only. Are we agreed?"

"Good idea. I presume you'll be at the meeting tomorrow?"

"Oh yes, I'll see you there. Good night Steve."

Over a cup of hot tea, Steve updated Alison who agreed it put Sir Patrick squarely on-side, then they moved to the bedroom and a good night's sleep as ordered by the doctor.

Chapter Twenty-Two

Because the world was split into different time zones it was possible to be at work in one part of the world while people slept in another. This wasn't quite the case between the time in London and the time in Bucharest, but it meant Romanian businessmen were in their offices as the DCI stood in the shower in Dr Alison Mills' house.

On the top floor of one of the tallest buildings in Bucharest were the offices of The World Trading Company or WTC as stated on its letterhead. WTC was one of Romania's oldest and most well-established businesses. It had been run by the same family since inception and the current head was the grandson of the founder.

Luca Radu inherited the business from his father, who in turn inherited it from Luca's grandfather. Old man Radu set the company up after WW1 as a means of making ends meet. He would trade anything and hope to make a profit on each transaction. Times had been hard and there were occasions when it was difficult to feed his wife and young child, but they survived. Eventually, things improved and although the Radu family were never rich they at least got by.

When Luca's father took over the business Luca was newly born. His father had the advantage of being better educated than old man Radu and quickly saw how to survive under a dictator and a communist regime. He set about making himself useful to the government and was rewarded by being awarded state contracts and eventually being handed state assets. The first of these were two coal mines that came with state supply contracts to supply coal at inflated prices per ton.

WTC flourished under this arrangement and the family prospered. Other assets were gifted to the company due to the patronage of the leaders of the dictatorship.

Luca's father didn't enjoy the best of health and retired, passing on the business to his only son. Luca was diligent but during his watch, the Romanian state apparatus started to crumble, and Luca was smart enough to distance the business from the regime. As things became more liberal, the company looked for opportunities within the new Europe. The Europe of the Common Market.

Luca was smart and still rich. He was young enough at just thirty-six to take the business forward and enjoy the fruits of its success. He had been married for two years but the marriage wasn't working. He had taken his father's advice and married a plain girl not suited to the more glamorous life Luca led. He compensated himself by keeping a string of more attractive mistresses. He was also very ambitious and had set about extending his reach well outside Romania.

However, Luca had a secret. He wasn't the most honourable of men. He knew the value of a bullet in settling disputes. This philosophy took him to similarly minded businessmen throughout Europe, and WTC was now part of a Europe wide organisation that thought only of their profits. They weren't as strict as, say, the Mafia, but they could be just as violent and usually found the same solutions to problems as their Mafia counterparts.

***

It was eight-thirty Romanian time on Friday morning. Luca Radu was sitting at the head of a long and highly polished table opening the company's weekly meeting. It wasn't a board meeting because there was only one director. It wasn't a shareholders' meeting because there was only one shareholder. It was a meeting designed to keep the executives of WTC afraid enough so that they performed at maximum efficiency.

There were four executives at this particular meeting. They were responsible for various aspects of Luca's empire. They looked after his interests in drugs, prostitution, extortion, international expansion and people trafficking.

As Luca opened the meeting, he was interrupted by the executive responsible for international expansion. He was called Andrei Popa. Andrei wasn't sitting around this executive table for his intellect, but rather for his undying loyalty to Luca and his father before him. Andrei was an assassin. He'd taken care of several disputes WTC had found itself embroiled in over the years and in each case, WTC had expanded due largely to Andrei's skill with weapons.

"Boss, I think we have a problem." Andrei was solidly built with broad shoulders and, at just under six feet, was an intimidating figure.

"What kind of a problem?"

"The last two sample girls didn't reach the UK, or at least didn't reach the clinic."

"So, what happened to them, they can't just disappear?"

"You're right, but according to that doctor guy he's not seen them, and we've lost money. He says he needed them for the transplants, but his patients are now too sick."

Luca didn't have time for details or problems. He expected what he said, and what he wanted to happen, would happen. "You get back to them and tell them it's their problem. We saw the two onto the airplane. We did all the testing for matches and the clinic here needs to be paid, so we want paying. We're not..." The door opened and an attractive woman in her late twenties entered and went straight to Andrei. She whispered in his ear, smiled at everyone present and left.

"Boss, they've arrested the driver from the UK embassy. He's being held at central and they've taken the credit card."

This was not news Luca needed to hear. His usual response to bad news was to throw things at people or to smash something against a wall. With difficulty he held himself in and for once tried to rationalise things.

"What the hell's happening here. That clown Constantine has gone and got himself arrested, and we've lost two lots of transplant profits, and you're telling me the idiot in the UK says we'll never be paid because his patients are now too sick."

Luca didn't do thinking. He saw himself as a man of action and decisive decision making even though in times of trouble his decisions usually meant someone dying.

"Andrei, get yourself over to England. Go today. I want to find out what's going on. Get in touch with this Lars Jenson. You know the guy. He's the Syndicate Head. You tell him, I expect to be paid, and he must sort out things at his end. This is too good a racket to let anything get in the way. We're only getting started.

"Remember this is worth millions. If you get any resistance or, if you find some bright spark is interfering, you know what to do. Got it?"

"Yes, boss." Andrei was looking at his mobile phone and stumbled over his next statement. He wasn't confident in this office environment. "I'll have to leave now boss. The flight I leaves in two hours and I've..."

"Yeah, yeah, Andrei, just go and sort this out. I'll talk to the Chief of Police and get the fool Constantine out, but he'll pay for handing over that credit card."

Luca waved goodbye to his fixer and carried on with his meeting.

Andrei Popa left, but as soon as he was outside the office, he dialled a London number. His contact would get him a suitable weapon. Just in case.

***

Steve arrived at the Yard at exactly eight a.m. just as Andrei Popa was being driven to Bucharest Airport. Seated in his office, and drinking his third coffee of the day, the DCI was contemplating the next few hours. He'd decided to play dumb if things got too difficult. He'd rely on Sir Patrick for backup. He was daydreaming a little and thought he heard Andy or The Cap arriving in the outer office.

A tap on the door frame and there stood Superintendent Alfie Brooks. "Good morning," was all he said. His features were neutral. This was unusual because the Superintendent was known for his cheerful outlook on life.

"Morning sir, I'm sorry but it's not a good time. I'm just—"

Alfie interrupted. "Yes. You're off to the twelfth floor for your eight-thirty meeting. I know."

Steve remembered Alfie was the font of all knowledge and a good keeper of secrets.

"I just needed to bring you up to speed about our friend Commander Bowles. He's been to see Professional Standards and dropped you right in it. He's claiming he told you not to release this DI from Chelmsford, and that you've charged an innocent man with murder."

Steve was struck dumb. What was happening here? How could Bowles as a Disciple do such a thing? Steve's stomach was churning.

"But why?"

"He's likely to face a disciplinary. It seems the Deputy Chief Constable of Essex has reported your involvement in two of their cases and that you told him you were acting on the direct orders of Bowles and the NCA. Bowles lied about the involvement of the NCA and one of their blokes got to hear of it and wants blood. Bowles thinks by selling you out he'll survive."

Even in this time of adversity, Steve managed a small smile. "I wonder who tipped off the NCA?"

Alfie Brooks just shrugged. "But Steve, be careful up there. I don't think they know about Professional Standards yet so you're still one step ahead."

"Thanks, Alfie, I owe you one."

"Yes, you do, but make sure you're still around for me to collect." He made to leave and with a swish of his arm added, "Good luck. Keep me posted."

Steve arrived in the anteroom of the offices of Sir Cecil Younger, one of the most senior policemen in the Metropolitan Police Force. There was no one around, so he knocked on the door that led to the Assistant Commissioner's main office and turned the handle. He pushed the door open a fraction and heard voices. He pushed further and with the door open halfway, he heard a voice call him in.

He recognised the AC resplendent in his uniform and recognised Sir Patrick and Twiggy. The pair appeared to be deep in conversation. The AC was talking to a man Steve didn't know. He was of average height and dressed in a cheap suit. His brown hair was too long, and he had the look of a second-hand car salesman about him.

Without any preamble, Sir Cecil called for order and everyone to be seated around his large dining room style table. He introduced everyone and Steve discovered that the used car salesman was called Peter Dunlop, and that he was a politician and a junior minister in the Treasury.

"There are to be no notes taken today and no gossiping about what we're going to discuss. Clear?" Sir Cecil looked at each person in turn for confirmation.

"It's a little unusual to have the head of our counter-intelligence force with us. We can only assume Sir Patrick has good reason to take a personal interest in this credit card." The AC looked directly at the Head of MI6 who in turn looked across at Steve.

"We have worked closely with your colleagues in MI5 in the past, as you might imagine, as they are responsible for domestic issues. Our collaborations have for the most part been cordial. I hope our relationship with your more international force will be equally cordial and mutually beneficial."

Steve wondered if the AC were laying down some form of invisible marker or if he knew more than he was admitting to.

Sir Patrick smiled. "Thank you, Sir Cecil, I'm sure we will all work well together and have this affair resolved in no time."

The AC bowed his head towards Sir Patrick. "Good. Now Miss Rough, can you inform everyone what you've unearthed concerning a credit card, but *only* the credit card. Do not wander into areas of speculation, only the facts."

Twiggy proceeded to tell her story of how DC Andy Miller, acting on instructions from DCI Steve Burt, had asked her to trace the owner of a credit card. She explained the process by which she'd achieved this and told the meeting the card had been registered to the Anglo European Bank in Jersey but that the payments were being made by the Treasury in London.

This last statement caused a bit of a stir but a lot of it was cosmetic. Steve knew everyone already knew who was paying the bills, except perhaps the politician in the bad suit.

Sir Cecil took up the narrative. "DCI Burt, why did you ask Miss Rough to investigate the pedigree of this card and how did you know of it?"

Steve was now firmly on the spot. It was career suicide to lie or tell half-truths in this setting but given his involvement with Patrick Bond, he had no choice.

"My team and I were investigating a double murder in Essex. We came to believe the victims were from Romania. One of my officers, on his own initiative, learnt that the victims had travelled on air tickets paid for in Romania and he managed to track down the credit card number that was used. We then asked Miss Rough through Financial Crimes to trace the owner of the card as a link in our investigation." Steve sat back indicating he'd finished.

The AC took things up again. "Mr Dunlop, we appear to have a government-funded credit card being used in Romania to assist in the crimes being committed here. How is that possible?"

If Steve had felt he was in trouble, now he felt sorry for this politician. The AC was a cop, not a political appointee and he knew how to ask searching questions.

"I simply don't know. All expenditure is tightly controlled in these stringent times. We're spending several million upgrading our computer system."

"Spare us the party political please. Just answer the question." Sir Cecil seemed to be enjoying himself.

An embarrassed treasury minister had no answer. "I'm sorry but I don't know. To the best of my knowledge, it's impossible."

"I see. How do payments work at the treasury?"

Again, the junior minister didn't know.

Sir Cecil ploughed on. "It appears you don't know a lot, Mr Dunlop. Perhaps we shouldn't be surprised that our government appears to be funding international crime."

Mr Dunlop looked sheepish but made no attempt to defend himself.

Twiggy spoke up without being invited. Steve wondered if this was a wise move.

"Sir Cecil, the procedure is that any invoice or bill below one thousand pounds is just paid through a petty cash bookkeeping system. Anyone can sign off on such payments. Between one thousand and five thousand. It's pretty much the same system except each payment must be approved before being entered into the system. The work is done by junior clerks, and unless something doesn't look right, everything is signed off. In answer to your question, I suspect a credit card statement from AEB would be below the five thousand limit and would be processed automatically."

The AC looked at Twiggy and smiled. "Thank you, Miss Rough, now perhaps you can tell us who set this up and why?"

"I'm sorry, Sir Cecil."

"Mm, and I don't suppose, Mr Dunlop, you would know?"

Dunlop just sat in silence.

"Now we come to the reason this credit card thing is so important. Sir Patrick perhaps you'd like to explain?"

Patrick Bond sat forward. Steve was interested in what he'd say. "This is extremely confidential but national security is involved."

Steve thought *good man*. The use of national security as a shield was always good. It limited questions and gave a natural defence if questions became awkward.

"We had been shadowing a group of individuals for some time who appeared to be involved in bringing down our government, but not through the ballot box. We became aware that DCI Burt's investigation into the killing of two girls in Essex appeared to be running on parallel lines. My agents are good observers but would never claim to be good investigators." Where had Steve heard that before?

"I approached DCI Burt and he shared information with us that has been very helpful in our understanding of how this group operate. We agreed that DCI Burt's investigation should follow normal lines of enquiry while we continued to monitor. I am aware of a connection with Romania that involves young people from that country being sent here to have at least one organ removed for transplanting into another human being. This trade is of course illegal but has nothing to do with MI6. Our remit is international security, but in this case, both DCI Burt investigation and our own are linked, because we believe the group we are interested in is involved in this organ transplant business."

Sir Patrick Bond sat back but glanced quickly at Steve and gave the slightest of nods.

Sir Cecil Younger also sat back and steepled his fingers in front of his face.

"Let's see what we have. MI6 are looking out for an international group hell-bent on subversion." Patrick Bond nodded. "And DCI Burt's murder enquiry cuts across MI6's surveillance?"

"That's correct," Patrick Bond answered.

"As a result, you shared information and this sharing resulted in DCI Burt unearthing a credit card that's used to purchase flights from Bucharest to bring people here to give up their healthy organs for transplant?"

Again, Patrick Bond answered yes.

"DCI Burt asked Miss Rough to trace the credit card which she did back to this AEB bank and our own Foreign office…"

Twiggy stepped in. "Not quite sir. All we know at the moment payment to AEB bank comes from HM Government. We've no proof it's from the Treasury. They pay money out on behalf of all government departments."

"Yes, I see. So, DCI Burt if you have proof supplied by MI6 of this gang's activities, why haven't you arrested them?"

Before Steve could answer, Sir Patrick spoke. "I asked the DCI, in the interests of national security, to hold off. We have the main players under surveillance and only need a few more days to complete our investigation. DCI Burt is aware of our request."

"That's all very well, Sir Patrick, but DCI Burt doesn't run a private investigation company. He's a member of the Metropolitan Police Force and as such works within a chain of command. He can't do side deals with every Tom, Dick or Harry." The AC was visibly annoyed by this revelation.

Steve thought that to tell the AC that he couldn't trust his senior officers may not go down well. Trying to conceal the real objective of the Syndicate and the identity of known Disciples was beginning to prove difficult to justify and their cover story was non-existent.

"DCI Burt, are you ready to proceed against this subversive group?"

"No sir, we have too many loose ends." Steve decided to push his luck and lie. "I spoke with the Deputy Head of the Crown Prosecution Service only the other day and his advice was not to do anything." If the AC were to check this with Ian Fuller, then Steve was cooked.

"Well, if you've checked it out, I suppose I'll have to sanction your ongoing involvement with MI6, but take care, Detective Chief Inspector, no more private arrangements, otherwise you could find yourself hung out to dry. Am I clear!"

A very relieved Steve Burt simply said, "Yes sir."

The Assistant Commissioner returned to the reason for the meeting. He addressed the group at large. "There are a few answers we need now. For example, how do we track down the person who set up this credit card arrangement? Where is this card, and why was this allowed to happen?"

Twiggy raised her hand. "I believe I can trace the flow of funds back to the beginning, but I've no idea how long this arrangement's been going on. It'll take a while, but it should give us the name of the person who sanctioned it in the beginning. If we can identify who, then I'm sure DCI Burt will get to the why."

Twiggy actually winked at Steve. Luckily only Sir Patrick noticed.

"Very well. That sounds a sensible move. DCI Burt, I'm putting you in charge of resolving this credit card fiasco. If the press got hold of this, we'd be crucified."

Sir Cecil turned to the hapless Mr Dunlop. "Dunlop, please return to your masters and inform them of this meeting and warn them that if I hear a sniff from anyone that this meeting even took place, I'll personally file charges. Is that clear?" Without waiting for an answer, the AC carried on. "I sometimes wonder why we have elected politicians. If you're the best the government can appoint as a treasury minister, we'd be better not electing politicians but appoint people we know can do the job."

Sir Patrick and Steve exchanged glances. It sounded as though it wouldn't take much to turn the Assistant Commissioner into a Disciple.

The AC wound up the meeting. "Action plan. Miss Rough, you'll work back and try to discover who set up the arrangement whereby HM Government funded this credit card. DCI Burt, you'll be her liaison and the officer in charge. Sir Patrick you'll continue to work with DCI as you have been but now it's official. MI6 clearly need the Met's help. I'm relying on you both to get this over and done with. Talk of subversion and links to government doesn't sit well with me. Put this to bed quickly before we really have a major incident on our hands. I'll have to brief the Commissioner before she meets the Prime Minister for their weekly briefing, but I'll keep it clean. That's all." Sir Cecil remained seated. "Good day lady and gentlemen."

Just to show he was human he touched Steve's sleeve as he was walking past and in a gentle whisper told the DCI. "Keep me posted Steve, and watch yourself; I know you held back and I'm sure you have your reasons. Just don't do anything silly."

***

Sir Patrick, Steve and Twiggy adjourned to the canteen for coffee and a council of war. Steve pulled the head of MI6 to one side and told him Twiggy knew nothing other than the credit card issue and that she had been asked to look at the accounts for Eclipse Medical.

It was agreed that for now, MI6 would shadow those senior members of the Syndicate and Steve with Twiggy would carry on with the investigation.

The beginning of the end was about to be planned or so Steve hoped. With Bowles informing on him to Professional Standards he'd have to move quickly to get a result before he was closed down and probably suspended from duty.

How wrong he was. If he'd known what was coming, he'd have resigned there and then. The future wasn't bright.

Chapter Twenty-Three

Steve returned to his office to be greeted by Jenny. She'd arrived early with the two girls from Romania. Neither spoke any English and Jenny had confirmed the interpreter was on her way. The girls were in the canteen having a drink in the company of a WPC.

Jenny looked upset as Steve went into his office. She followed him in and closed the door. "I hear you let Dean Grantham go. Can I ask why?"

"Look Jenny, there are things going on I can't explain just now, but hopefully once this is over, you'll see why I did what I did."

Jenny looked suspiciously at the DCI. She thought she knew him and had trusted him as a good cop but now she wasn't so sure. They had had Dean Grantham bang to rights on a variety of charges, but Steve had released him on police bail. It didn't make sense to Jenny and she told Steve what she was thinking.

"I know how it looks Jenny but please bear with me. I've asked The Cap and Andy to trust me and now I'm asking you. I haven't suddenly gone over to the dark side. It's just I've gotten myself involved in something and I have to see it out."

Jenny wasn't convinced. "You know my father said he thought you were one of the good guys. I'm glad he's not around to see what's going on."

Steve remembered Superintendent Kenneth Taylor. He'd only met him once. He was an old cranky copper who didn't exactly welcome Steve and The Cap to Chelmsford. He was also Jenny's adopted father and according to her was a decent copper whose bark was worse than his bite. He'd suffered a stroke and was now in hospital.

"How's your dad doing?"

"He's coming along. The doctors think he'll be conscious again soon and then it will be a slow recovery. Thanks for asking." There was no warmth in Jenny's words. It was clear she didn't like what was happening but was going through the motions of supporting her senior officer.

The interpreter arrived on time at eleven. Steve had booked a conference room on the 7th floor. It was more friendly and less intimidating than the interview suite in the basement. Steve, The Cap and the female interpreter arrived first followed a few minutes later by Jenny and the two girls.

The interpreter sounded Romanian. She introduced herself as Svetlana. She looked in her late twenties and was strikingly beautiful. At a few inches under six foot, she could have passed for a model. The Cap appreciated her beauty and nodded to Steve. Despite his troubles, Steve smiled inwardly. The Cap enjoyed looking at beautiful women but knew if he ever strayed his wife would kill him.

After the introductions, Steve gently opened the questioning. Svetlana would translate the questions and the answers. Steve wondered if he should have interviewed them separately. It was standard procedure within the Met not to allow witnesses to listen to each other's version of events. After the morning he'd had he thought he might be getting a little paranoid. After all these girls were unlikely to give evidence in a UK court. It was too late anyway, and he really didn't think there would be a problem. He decided to deal with them one at a time.

The first girl called Pushta told her story. She was the taller of the two but looked too thin for her height. She would never be called pretty with her acne-blemished face and her pale skin. Her hair looked to have been cut by herself and her clothes looked fit only to put on a scarecrow.

She answered Steve in a firm voice that belied her appearance. Pushta was a student at a college for design in Bucharest. She was sixteen years old and her family were poor. She knew they couldn't afford the college fees, but they wanted the best for their daughter. One day a travelling medical unit had arrived in the college to offer free health checks to the students. After Pushta had been examined, the doctor told her she could be suitable to go to England and be paid the equivalent of £1000.

The doctor got her to sign a form and took a large blood sample from her. He noted down her mobile number and said he'd be in touch and gave her some money, she thought around twenty pounds. She was told not to say anything to anyone, particularly her parents.

This doctor called about two weeks later. He gave her a hotel address in Bucharest and told her to bring some clothes for a short journey to England. She was to say she'd won a prize and would be on holiday in England for two weeks. She said her parents weren't convinced, and begged her not to go, but she did. At the hotel, they told her to stay in her room and wait. They took more blood and after three days she was taken to the airport and flown to Stanstead Airport. The doctor told her she'd be met in England and taken to a large country house. If she did what they asked she'd have her money when she returned to Bucharest.

Steve was surprised by the apparent gullibility of this young woman.

He turned to the interpreter. "Ask her what they told her would happen when she got to England."

Svetlana explained the girl was told she was taking part in a medical experiment and they needed young girls with her specific blood group. They took samples of her blood, and said nothing would happen to her and she'd get paid.

Svetlana, the beautiful interpreter, spoke. "Mr Burt, you have to understand, these are simple country girls looking to better themselves and help their families. They've led sheltered lives and something like this is a big adventure. They wouldn't know which questions to ask."

"Yes, I see." Steve was scratching his head. "Apart from the first piece of paper they asked her to sign when they came to her college was there any other paperwork?"

Svetlana asked. The girl called Pushta said she had signed a contract at the hotel but the people in Bucharest kept it.

Steve asked if she knew any of the people she'd met in Bucharest.

Pushta said no.

The DCI felt he was banging his head against a brick wall and in the absence of anything else to ask he said. "Which hotel was she staying in?"

After Svetlana asked the question Pushta replied it was the Fountain Hotel, but that the people involved took her from the hotel to an office in Petter Street. That's where the doctor examined her and took her blood.

"The place in Petter Street. Was it an office or did it look like a doctor's surgery?"

Again, Svetlana asked and Pushta answered. "She said it was a doctor's office."

Steve signalled to The Cap that they should leave the room and turned to ask the four remaining ladies if they needed anything. The reply was nothing.

Outside the conference room, Steve turned to Abul. "I wonder if we've got something here. The surgery in this Petter Street must be of interest to Andy's buddy Dimitri. From the other end of this thing, the Romanian police must know who runs that practice. If nothing else we've saved these two girls and can give a lead to the Romanians. Is there anything else you can think of?"

"To be honest I'm surprised you got that much. They don't know very much but you're right. This could confirm the identities of the people involved in the supply line from Bucharest."

The two detectives returned. Steve asked the second girl called Uza to tell her story.

She looked shyly around the faces at the table. Her hair was dark as were her eyes and she was clearly very nervous. She began her tale in a low voice that meant Steve had to strain to hear her. She was fifteen years old and studying at high school. She was a member of a gymnastics club and a mobile laboratory had arrived late one afternoon offering free health checks. Like Pushta's, her family was poor. Her father had had an accident several years earlier and couldn't work. They lived in a village ten miles south of Bucharest and she had five brothers. She was the only girl in the family.

Her story followed exactly that told by Pushta right down to the doctor's surgery and the money she had been offered.

Steve was on the point of winding up the meeting when The Cap asked a question. The DCI wasn't sure if this was to impress Svetlana or if he really had thought of something.

"Did they know the man who took them from the hotel to the airport and did they go by taxi or private car?"

Abul smiled sweetly at the interpreter who returned the gesture.

Both girls started to talk at once. Svetlana said something and Uza took up the narrative. They were taken by car and the man who took them was called Constantine. The car was large and black and at the airport, they went straight to the aircraft. Both girls giggled when Pushta interrupted to say they both felt like film stars.

Steve looked at The Cap and nodded. Another piece of the jigsaw had just fallen into place.

There was no more to learn. Steve brought the meeting to a close and thanked the girls through Svetlana. He thanked Svetlana and told Jenny to see the girls got safely back to Chelmsford and to let him know when they were going back to Bucharest.

Steve sensed Jenny still wasn't happy with him and he regretted it, but he told himself there was nothing he could do. He just hoped when this was all over his explanation would be enough.

As The Cap and the DCI entered the office Andy was standing waiting. With his new more-trendy look he still managed to convey some of his inherent boyishness when he was excited. No amount of good tailoring could suppress his basic charm and enthusiasm.

"I'm glad you're back, I've got something."

Steve was in no mood for games but asked Andy into his office. The Cap followed.

"Right Andy." Steve forced a sigh. "What've you got?"

Andy didn't read Steve's mood nor see his exhaustion. "I got the manifest for today's flight from Bucharest to Stanstead. The one to Southend doesn't fly on Fridays. I checked for the credit card bookings and single young people but there aren't any. By the way, I've told Jenny. But looking at the list, there was one booking that caught my eye. A Mr Andrei Popa is on the flight with a ticket paid for using the same credit card. I did a quick check back and this guy has made more than a few trips over the past few months and has always been booked using this credit card." Andy glowed. As proof of his increasing maturity, he volunteered. "I think this Popa's connected to the girls at the Bucharest end."

Steve's fatigue suddenly vanished. "What time does that flight get in?"

"The ETA is Stanstead at 13.22."

Steve pulled out his mobile phone, pressed a pre-set number and stalked out of his office with his phone to his ear. By the time he reached the relative privacy of the corridor Sir Patrick answered. Steve told him what Andy had unearthed and asked if one of MI6's agents could meet the flight and tail this Romanian.

"We've got assets there, so yes. You only want him tailed?"

"Yes, just now. Let's see what he's doing here. His connection to the credit card is more than a coincidence. We've removed their last consignment of human parts. Don't you think they might send someone to find out what happened?"

"Steve, you're right. Leave it with me and I'll keep you posted." The conversation was over. Steve looked at his watch. It was one p.m. exactly.

"Sorry about that, Andy, but your info needed to be passed on. Now, The Cap will write up the notes on our interview with the girls and you can get it onto the file." Steve was conscious life had to go on.

"Has your buddy Dimitri come back with anything?"

"No. Just that the card was being used by this driver who works for the British embassy." Andy gave out a small cry. "If the credit card has been with the Romanian police since yesterday how did this Popa character get to use it today? He was only added to the manifest hours before the flight?"

"I suspect the travel agent keeps the details and anyone authorised to use it just tells them to charge it. Remember we've deliberately not put a stop on the card."

"Yeah, I suppose so."

Steve was back in full flow. "Andy, get onto Dimitri. Tell him to look at a doctor's surgery in Petter Street. That's where the girls are taken, presumably for type matching. Whoever runs that place is involved."

"Wow, good work boss!"

"Yeah, it is." The Cap spoke up. "I got it out of the girls." He laughed and again the Cap's wit was invaluable in keeping this small team together.

"What was the name of the driver, Andy?"

Andy looked it up on his laptop. "It's Constantine."

Steve and The Cap gave each other a high five. "That's the guy who takes the girls to the airport. He must have diplomatic immunity as a driver because he picks up VIP's and diplomats all the time from the airside of the airport. The girls said he drove them straight up to the plane. You'd better pass that nugget onto Dimitri as well."

"I'm on it." Andy disappeared.

The Cap sat down. It was clear he wanted a heart to heart with his boss who was also his friend. "Steve, I'm worried. You're not telling us everything that's going on. Our original brief was to solve the two murders in Essex. We now know they're technically not murders so why are we still shuffling around. Granted, there seems to be a connection to some clinic that's bringing girls in to harvest their organs and granted, our two Essex victims were part of that, but our job's done. We've got Dean Grantham. Why not get him back in, charge him and close the cases?"

Steve saw Abul was as tired as he was but realised The Cap didn't have the responsibilities he'd just agreed to take on, nor the content of the meeting with the Assistant Commissioner this morning.

"Abul, I know you're concerned, and you want to help. Just by being here, you're helping. There are things are going on that I really can't tell you about. We are making progress with the cases. We've just passed information to Bucharest to help them clear up at their end. That's good police work Abul. We can do that and despite what you think we're still working the original case."

Steve felt he needed to sleep. He was just about to announce he was going home when his phone buzzed. He saw the number. "Cap, I have to take this and it's a bit sensitive." He pointed towards the door. "Do you mind and can you close the door, please?"

"Steve, it's Patrick Bond. My man picked out this joker from Romania. He tailed him to a car hire desk and guess what? Your DI Dean Grantham met him there. Luckily, we have cars in the area, so we tailed them to a Holiday Inn just off the airport. The pair went to this Andrei Popa's room. They're still there. Any ideas?"

Steve thought it was ironic. The Head of MI6 whose pay grade was well above Steve's was asking for advice.

"Can you keep someone on him twenty-four hours?"

"If we have to. What are you thinking?"

"He's obviously here to find out what's going wrong. I'm assuming the Romanian end are sharing in the profits this thing is making. We've estimated the loss of the two girls we picked up equates to around sixty thousand pounds. Overall, we think the whole operation could be worth tens of millions when it's fully up and running, so if there's a glitch now, I'm guessing they'll want it sorted. What I don't understand though is why Dean Grantham. He's a foot soldier, not a leader."

"Mmm. It could be Popa's a foot soldier and doesn't know the leaders?"

"Possible but if he's here to fix things you'd imagine he knows who's who."

Sir Patrick was silent for a few seconds. "All right. I'll cover Popa with twenty-four-hour shifts until twelve noon Monday. If there's nothing by then I'll call it off. Fair enough?"

"Yes. Fair enough." The connection was broken.

Steve kept his promise to himself and left his office early. He'd phoned Alison to say he wouldn't be over but was heading home and an early night. They arranged he would go round to her place in the morning. Being Saturday, they would continue their wedding plans and shopping. This reminded Steve he hadn't heard from his estate agent about the sale of his flat.

Something else to do in the morning.

On his way out he had a sudden flash. This wasn't his normal slow-burning inspiration that usually he worried out of his brain over days. This was an instant solution to a question he's been aware of but hadn't formulated. Despite his exhaustion, he headed upstairs to the offices of Human Resources.

Steve had had, on past occasions, to be thankful to the head of Human Resources, and although he didn't regard Chief Superintendent Charles as a friend, he couldn't believe the upright and pompous officer would ever be connected with the Syndicate. But you never knew, so Steve was heading to see a Miss Hawkins. She was the Personal Assistant to the head of Human Resources. A title she often used to inflate her own self-importance.

Miss Hawkins had, over the months since her first meeting with the DCI, mellowed towards him and at their last meeting had been very helpful. Steve hoped she was in the same frame of mind.

On entering the quiet oasis of calm that was Human Resources Steve immediately saw Miss Hawkins. She insisted on dressing in tweeds that her shape just didn't suit. She was a thin woman and a confirmed spinster whose whole existence was to please her boss. Steve wickedly allowed a picture of Miss Hawkins dressed in tweed and Chief Superintendent Charles in his best, tailored uniform somehow having fun. The picture wouldn't come.

"Miss Hawkins, remember me?" Steve stood in front of her desk which was remote from others.

"Of course, Detective Chief Inspector, what can I do for you?"

Steve was confident Miss Hawkins wasn't part of the Syndicate. The DCI lowered his voice and in a conspiratorial whisper "Can I run something hypothetical past you?"

Miss Hawkins looked surprised but allowed a small smile to pass over her usually austere face. "I see no reason why not."

Steve thought a simple yes would have done. "Suppose a DCI was being recommended for rapid promotion to say, Chief Super. How would that be done?"

"Oh, it's not very likely. Such accelerated promotion within these senior ranks is practically unheard of."

"Granted, but just suppose, who would sanction such a thing?"

"Well — first a recommendation would have to come from Commander rank or above, and the individual would have to have performed some outstanding act. Then Chief Superintendent Charles would do a full background check, in case the individual had any skeletons, and finally, the Assistant Commissioner would interview the officer before confirming his promotion."

"So, there's no one person who could just announce such a promotion?"

"Oh, no." Miss Hawkins was curious. "Is there something Chief Superintendent Charles should know?"

Steve was thinking. His tired brain spinning. If Lars Jenson had promised him, he'd be promoted Chief Superintendent within months, how would he do it? Commander Bowles could start it off but how could he be so certain the Assistant Commissioner would sign it off... "Unless?

"No, Miss Hawkins, it's just a theoretical puzzle, nothing important, many thanks." With a wave, Steve left Human Resources and went home.

***

At the same time Steve was talking to Miss Hawkins Andrei Popa and Dean Grantham were having their first drink from Popa's duty-free whisky. They were in room 106 of the Bishop Stortford Holiday Inn. Popa was listening to Dean's story of arrest and release and the actions of the Syndicate.

Popa poured another round of drinks and sat back on the bed listening to Dean's tale.

"Who is it who's causing the problems?" Popa's English was very good and only slightly accented. Considering he was more or less self-taught this was an achievement.

"We were going along nicely until this DCI Burt came along. He was the investigating officer on the deaths of the two girls, but instead of just closing the case he kept digging. He's dangerous and he's getting closer."

Andrei Popa sneered at Dean and poured his third whisky in fifteen minutes. "Such men are a nuisance, but such men are fools. They are boy scouts making the world a better place, my friend. This policeman will not be a problem. I will take care of him and we can all go back to how things were. Luca has decreed he wishes to maintain our little enterprise." Popa's eyes were glazing over. "I like to please Luca because a happy Luca means a happy me."

Popa stood up, poured his fourth whisky and threw his arms around Dean. He was laughing loudly. "My friend." He staggered holding onto Dean. "I am your saviour. I will solve all your problems." He was dribbling saliva from the corner of his mouth. "Your policeman will be a dead policeman."

Chapter Twenty-Four

The DCI was asleep in his favourite chair within five minutes of returning to his flat. He checked the time before drifting off. It was only three-thirty p.m. but he was exhausted.

He fell into a deep dreamless sleep for over two hours and started to regain consciousness around 5.50 p.m., then drifted into that happy state between sleep and consciousness for a couple of hours. In this state, his thoughts began to surface, and he replayed events in his mind. He saw Lars Jenson as the head of a corporation that did genuinely do good work. There must be hundreds of ex-servicemen grateful for his work on prosthetic limbs plus others who were pain-free thanks to his hip and knee replacements. The DCI thought Eclipse Medical must be a good business so why would a man like Lars jeopardise all he had worked for?

Then his thoughts turned to Robbie Symonds. He hadn't given the surgeon much thought, but in his mind, he saw a successful surgeon who was involved in illegal trade in body parts. As he continued to drift, he asked why?

He pictured his wedding day and Alison standing beside him in church, he saw them on honeymoon, happy and smiling. His mind called up various people and events all at once. He imagined Patrick Bond meeting the Prime Minister, and Twiggy with mounds of paper, looking through the accounts for Eclipse Medical. He saw Andy's contact in Romania raiding the doctor's surgery on Petter Street, and the driver at the British Embassy in Bucharest delivering girls to the airport, and even Commander Bowles in handcuffs. Then a credit card suddenly appeared. It seemed to fly past him and crash into a wall, making a terrible noise. The imagined sound woke him up with a start.

He panicked as he realised for a split second he didn't know where he was. There was a banging sound in the distance and, he realised someone was knocking at his door.

He looked at his watch. It was almost eight at night. Through his window, he saw it was dark and it appeared to be raining. The banging on his door continued forcing him to rub his eyes, shake himself fully awake and answer the door.

To the DCI's surprise, he opened his front door to find The Cap, Twiggy and Andy holding various bags and files. It didn't take much to realise that some of the white plastic bags contained take-away food, probably Chinese. Another bag looked like it held tins of beer, and Twiggy was clutching what looked like police files.

Steve invited the trio in.

"What are you doing here? It's not that I'm not glad to see you, it's just unexpected."

The Cap, as the senior interloper, spoke for his colleagues. "Well Steve, Twiggy and Andy had a meeting this afternoon and felt you should be brought up to speed. Plus, we three agreed we don't like what's going on and we want to help. Also, we knew you'd get home, fall asleep and not eat. We've come bearing food and beer and if you're annoyed, we're here and it's all Twiggy's fault. She still thinks you need mothering."

All four detectives laughed. Steve could see he was cornered, but he had had almost four hours of sleep and felt much better.

Twiggy took charge of the food. "Just leave everything in the containers. Steve, where are your plates?" Before he could answer Twiggy was opening cupboards in his kitchen looking for everything, she'd need to set up the feast.

They used Steve's coffee table and helped themselves. The food was good, and the beer washed it down a treat. Once everyone had had enough Twiggy cleared everything away and the four settled down finishing their beer and anticipating what was to come next. Twiggy was on water. It was part of her latest diet plan.

"Now then." Steve looked at his colleagues. "Why are you really here?"

"It was my idea, Steve." Twiggy had grabbed Steve's oversized sleeping chair so she was comfortably seated for once. "I've made progress with Eclipse's accounts and they're dodgy, to say the least. Also, I've got news on the credit card, but in truth, they are just excuses to be here. We're worried about you. We want to help but you have to trust us, just as you asked us to trust you."

Steve was touched by their concern but couldn't bring them in. Or could he? He decided to wait. He trusted these three with his life but the Syndicate, with its spread of unknown Disciples, wasn't something he wanted his friends involved in.

He looked at Twiggy comfortably taking up every inch of his large chair. "Tell me about the credit card."

Florance Rough, AKA Twiggy, gave a huge grin. She knew their decision to gate-crash the DCI's pad was correct. "You know it was being used in Bucharest by the embassy driver. Andy did some digging. It might be best if Andy explained first."

Steve thought this was a real cabaret act he was being given.

Andy as usual looked excited especially when he had information his boss would like. "This driver Constantine used to be attached to the Romanian Embassy in London. I spoke to someone in MI5 but didn't mention our case. It was just a routine enquiry so as not to raise any suspicions. It seems he was more than a driver. He was Romanian secret service. He didn't get up to anything here, so he was left alone and eventually returned to Romania." Andy drew breath.

"It appears he shouldn't have been given a job in our embassy. As his file was marked 'NO EMPLOYMENT STATUS' the embassy would have been aware of this when they vetted his background before giving him the job." Andy looked curiously at Steve. "Someone pulled strings big time to get him inside our embassy."

Twiggy picked up from there "The card was set up with AEB in Jersey as we know. The director, a man called Roger Lamb, was helpful but wouldn't divulge who opened the account, so Andy did more digging."

"Turns out the Director of AEB is the brother-in-law of Sir Timothy Head. He's Head of the Civil Service here in the UK. I checked with Somerset House and got bios on all the high-ranking people I'm aware have been mentioned or have been helpful. I know you talked to this Sir Timothy, so I put him on my list. We got lucky."

Twiggy was back. "Once Andy told me I called AEB back and threatened all sorts of trouble unless he told me who it was who set up the credit card arrangement. I asked him directly if it was Sir Timothy and he didn't say no." Twiggy luxuriated in her oversized chair. Maybe she'd ask Steve to sell it to her after his wedding.

"It was the Head of the Civil Service who opened the account and set everything up. I've checked on how the monthly bills are being paid and this Sir Timothy has access to a discretionary account for off the books payments. It's to pay people the government wouldn't want to be seen paying. All he has to do is sign off on a payment, code it to this account and it gets paid. No questions asked."

Steve sat up impressed by Twiggy and Andy. "You're saying there's a definite link to the credit card and Sir Timothy Head is involved?"

"Yes."

Steve thought back to his conversation with Sir Humphrey Campbell at the post-mortem in Chelmsford. He had been surprised that Sir Timothy had asked for a copy of his post-mortem report. Steve had given Sir Humphrey some details on the Syndicate and both men agreed Sir Humphrey would only produce one copy of his findings and that would go to the DCI. The whole incident had raised questions about Sir Timothy's potential involvement with the Syndicate as a Disciple. Perhaps Twiggy and Andy had just supplied the proof.

"Good work you two; what about the driver?"

"We don't know, it's a Foreign Office matter. The recruitment of locals in our overseas embassies is down to them, but I'm pretty certain everyone must be vetted before they're given a job. There's no way whoever employed this guy wouldn't have known about his background. Somebody must have pulled strings." Twiggy, being thorough, had looked up how foreign nationals were employed in UK overseas facilities.

"Tell me in simple language about the accounts for Eclipse Medical?" Steve could feel his visitors were disappointed. They clearly hoped that the data on the credit card would allow him to open up to them. By pursuing the accounts Steve was signalling he wasn't ready.

Twiggy gathered her papers. "You won't be surprised to learn that Eclipse banks with AEB. Over the years there have been a lot of unexplained international transfers to various parts of the world. More recently large amounts have been transferred to Romania. The money was directed to a company called The World Trading Company, WTC for short. It started over two months ago. Small amounts to start with but the last transfer was for over one hundred thousand pounds. I got this from the bank statements. Money appears in their bank account regularly but there's no corresponding entry in the accounts. No legitimate invoices for any work done. Nothing." Twiggy was almost indignant at the thought of rogue accounting.

"When I cross-referenced these payments to their accounts, I found they were simply creating false invoices to cover them and showing them as payments to UK suppliers. When I checked with Companies House, I found that the suppliers don't exist. This is one example, but I've followed a few transfers and each one is the same." Twiggy studied Steve. "Is that simple enough, boss?" She grinned.

"I think so. They are sending money to Romania and writing themselves fictitious invoices to disguise the transfers."

"Well not exactly. There are regular payments of thirty-five thousand pounds at a time. It's these payments that are being falsely accounted for. I've tried to split out the amounts and it looks like fifty percent of the amounts are being sent to WTC. The other half goes to another bank in Jersey, but I haven't tracked it down yet." Twiggy had a look about her that Steve knew held the promise of more revelations.

"That's about it. Any half-decent forensic accountant would spot it at one hundred paces."

Steve stroked his chin. This was the first time in several days he'd needed this comfort action. Twiggy had given him more connections to Romania and it was obvious Eclipse Medical were involved. But where was all this leading?

The Twiggy and Andy show went for their big finish. From her comfortable chair Twiggy carried on. "I spoke with Andy and showed him what I had."

Andy picked up the story. Steve thought when his DC was on a roll he really did look like a schoolboy. "Florance showed me the bank statements. Each individual payment of thirty-five thousand had to have come from somewhere."

Twiggy was back. "I found the codes and was able to give Andy details of the banks where these transfers originated."

Andy continued "With these codes, we can go back to the banks and get the names of the account holders. We'd have a list of people paying Eclipse Medical and be able to ask why." Andy thought he knew why but he didn't want to be seen as stealing his boss' thunder.

Steve considered this and yet again admired how well Twiggy and Andy had worked on this.

The DCI made a decision he hoped he'd not regret.

"Listen you lot. I'm deeply touched that you came over and I'm grateful for this information. It's a great team effort. Andy, get onto your pal Dimitri and ask him to get us intel on this World Trading Company. Twiggy, what can you do about AEB?"

"Nothing at the moment. They aren't breaking any UK or EU banking laws. We'd have to build a European case for money laundering but with Brussels these things take time."

In many ways, Steve was glad to hear this. It would buy him time with the Syndicate and Lars Jenson.

The Cap spoke up. "Come on now boss, are you going to trust us?"

It was a direct challenge. If he said no, then he'd lose forever, the working relationship with his team that he'd built up over the past year. If he said yes, he'd be breaking a confidence, the Official Secrets Act and potentially putting his friends in danger.

He tried to bluff. "Look fellows, I've been sworn to secrecy. I'd love to get you involved but this thing is way over all our heads and could get a bit hairy."

Andy surprised Steve by saying, "Steve we're all grown-ups here. We came to help and to be truthful I think you need our help." Andy's moment of bravery had passed. He sat back looking at the floor afraid he had spoken out of turn.

"Look Andy, you're absolutely right, but this is way beyond solving the two deaths. You know that these thirty-five-thousand-pound payments must be from people who've had an organ transplanted and that the donor probably came from Romania and sold their organ illegally. We can build a case and maybe even show that if an organ hadn't been removed then these girls would still be alive. That's where I want everyone to concentrate. Let's prove a murder was committed and pull this clinic in front of a court. Anything else is beyond our pay grades."

Steve knew he'd not convinced them. There was silence after his speech. He carried on and tried one last time to persuade these detectives to leave him alone with his self-imposed problems.

"I don't want any of you getting in the way of what's going down. You don't know but I'm up for a disciplinary soon. Because of certain circumstances, I've been reported to Professional Standards and I don't want any of you near them. So please." Steve put on his best pleading face. "Just do as I ask. Solve the two deaths in Essex and keep your noses clean. If at the same time you can just trust me, I promise to bring you in when I can."

The Cap had been silent throughout the exchanges. He knew he was a good thief taker but was not as good as his colleagues were at working out other things, but he had good common sense and knew his boss wasn't going to admit them into whatever was going on. As the next senior officer, he had to bring order to this get-together.

"We have to respect what Steve says. We've offered and that's all we can do. We've enough to be getting on with so maybe it's better if we crack on and allow Steve to do his thing. He knows we're behind him and we're here when he needs us. Come on, it's getting late and I'm knackered. Let's go!"

Everybody stood up on Abul's command. They all knew this wasn't over and that at some point their boss would need them. After the usual goodbyes and promises for Monday morning, Steve closed the door and phoned Alison Mills. He needed cheering up.

They spoke about their day, their wedding plans, Steve's lack of enthusiasm for selling his flat, their shopping list for tomorrow and the wedding itself. Alison reminded her fiancé they'd booked their own church and vicar. No matter what Steve had to agree to on Sunday she was not allowing Lars Jenson to organise her big day. They discussed Sunday at length and Alison agreed to maintain the lie about arrangements for their big day. They were expected at Lars Jenson's country estate in Buckinghamshire for eleven a.m. to attend a church service followed by Steve's admission into the Syndicate followed by lunch.

"We can sort everything out tomorrow." Alison was a very practical person. "Oh, and darling, I've a patient tomorrow first thing so you can have longer in bed. I should be done by around eleven. See you then."

Steve headed for bed with a feeling of dread, but he was comforted by his discussion with his fiancée.

Chapter Twenty-Five

Saturday the 16th of March dawned bright but cold. Not that Andrei Popa saw the dawn nor his drinking partner of the previous evening, Detective Inspector Dean Grantham. After the pair had more or less finished the duty-free whisky, Dean treated Andrei to a night at his favourite pub in Chelmsford. Dean, although well over the limit, drove but parked up in a spot where he could retrieve his car the next morning. The pair had quite a riotous night, one bar leading to another, and at each pub, the girls began to look better and better.

They finished up in the small hours in a strip club that offered more than ladies with no clothes on. Both Dean and Andrei took advantage of everything on the menu. As the owner knew Dean, he got what he jokingly called the 'two-for-one' rate. By two a.m., both men were well past caring about anything. The owner of the strip club knew how to deal with Dean. He had had to get him home many times. Andrei simply showed his room card for the Holiday Inn and for some reason had forgotten he could speak English. Taxis were ordered and both men left.

It was nine a.m. before Andrei Popa surfaced. He had the mother of all hangovers. He stumbled about feeling sorry for himself and eventually found the shower. He opened the valve and sat in the shower tray allowing cold water to spray over him. After ten minutes he felt well enough to shower properly and get dressed. There was an inch of whisky left in the duty-free bottle. The Romanian drank it down in one in the hope that the golden liquid might somehow stop the hammering inside his head.

Dean Grantham was in the same state, but he didn't have to make the journey to Buckinghamshire his drinking buddy was about to make.

Sir Patrick Bond received a full verbal report of Popa's and Dean's activities from the agent assigned to shadow Popa. Sir Patrick had deliberately chosen smart but junior agents to remove any fear that they might be Disciples. He was confident that, being junior, they were clean.

***

Steve arrived at Alison's house just before eleven. As he let himself in, he wasn't surprised to hear talking. Alison had said she was seeing a patient in the morning.

The strange thing was the voices were coming from her living quarters, not her surgery.

He walked in to find Alison and Twiggy enjoying a coffee and the pair seemed to be enjoying each other's company.

"Hello, darling." Alison stood and kissed Steve lightly on the lips. "Want a coffee?" Before Steve could answer she was in the kitchen pouring strong black coffee into a large mug.

Steve wasn't sure what was going on. He hadn't expected to see Twiggy, and she hadn't mentioned anything about seeing Alison today.

Twiggy saw her ex-boss' confusion. She quite enjoyed it but decided to put him out of his misery.

"Don't worry Steve, I'm not moving in. I've taken Alison up on her offer to help me with my weight. God knows I've tried everything, but Dr Mills says she can help. I'll be gone in a minute."

Alison handed Steve his coffee and everyone sat. "I've told Flo that if she loses a stone before the wedding, she can be a bridesmaid."

Steve almost choked on his coffee. Not that he didn't like Twiggy. He instantly formed a mental picture of the wedding photos with probably the largest bridesmaid ever to attend a wedding as part of their wedding day for all to see even years later.

Steve was quick to hide his thoughts. "Good idea," he said with no conviction. "What are the chances? It's only five weeks away. Fourteen pounds in five weeks seems a lot." He tried to sound concerned that maybe Twiggy wouldn't make it.

Alison, who was enjoying Steve's discomfort, said, "We can only give it a try. Flo's promised to stick with what I've prescribed. I'm sure she can do it."

Alison smiled at Twiggy and patted her hand noticing how puffy it was.

Twiggy finished her coffee and prised herself out of her chair. "Thank you, Alison, I promise to stick to it and keep you posted."

220

"Come and see me again next week, same time. I want to monitor your blood pressure and see how those tablets I've prescribed are working."

Before leaving Twiggy turned to Steve. "Are you all right after last night?"

"Yes, you and Andy work well together. We'll have a meeting on Monday and sort out an action plan."

Steve had a thought. "Twiggy, get Andy to list all the names, addresses and dates he gets from your bank statements from Eclipse. I'm curious to see when this started and how many operations they've done."

"No problem, Andy's in the office now and I'm just off there myself. That's exactly what we planned to do this morning." As she made for the door and with a cheeky grin, she looked over her shoulder. "You see we're also detectives. Enjoy the shopping." She was gone.

They finished their coffee and planned their day. Alison had insisted that if they were to live in what was her house then it should be redone to make it as much Steve's as hers. They'd employed an architect and an interior designer. The architect had drawn up plans for the complete remodelling of the living space which involved knocking down walls and building others. This was a greater upheaval than either of them initially envisaged but they agreed it was a good idea. They had commissioned the architect to oversee the works which were due to start in a week's time. Alison was going to move in with Steve until the wedding and the plan was that when they returned from their honeymoon the works would be finished.

The interior designer was a work in progress, and they were to visit her today. Alison, being more practical, had a list of other visits to be made, but they both agreed to have lunch at The Steps Restaurant, their favourite place for lunch.

After cleaning up the coffee cups, the pair set off hand in hand.

***

Andrei Popa had a metabolism that handled his excessive alcohol intake well. By ten a.m., he was ready to get his day underway. He wasn't sure how to approach the problem. A knock on his door delivered a package covered in brown paper. It was from London. His contact hadn't let him down. The package contained a Mauser automatic. With it came fifty pristine .38 calibre rounds that could fire through a wall. Now he felt complete and ready for action. If only the hammers in his head would stop pounding.

Andrei's boss, Luca Radu had told him to "sort it" but he wasn't sure what "it" was. He knew they had, over the past few months, been sending girls over to have some internal organs removed for transplants. He had even shadowed them on a few occasions. He hadn't been involved in setting it up, but he'd met the main players once. He had the names and addresses where they lived. He also knew the last two girls had been somehow intercepted, and that Luca Radu was out of pocket because of it. One particularly drunken evening when Luca put him in charge of this latest enterprise, he'd been told it would be worth millions and his commission would make him very rich.

Andrei liked the thought of being even richer than he was. He liked what money could buy but he didn't like the thought that some upstart policeman might rob him of his new wealth.

He formed a plan. He'd go to the clinic first and ask around. See who knew what. Maybe talk to the chief, a Dr Symonds. In Andrei's experience, professional people who turn rogue for money always know what's going on. They seemed to become very greedy, as though without their tax-free income, they couldn't survive. Andrei gave a small smile. Removing such people was his speciality.

After visiting the clinic, he would go and stake out the leader's place. He knew Lars Jenson lived in a grand country estate. He wasn't sure about questioning him. It might be better to hold off and see if the next shipment of girls arrived safely. If not, then he'd have words with this Jenson guy. Luca had said he was odd but very dangerous. Andrei would have to be careful.

His hire car had sat nav, so he keyed in the coordinates for Eclipse Hall. He saw it was close by, just outside of Harlow in Essex. He set off heading for the M11 motorway. He didn't see a grey Volvo slide in behind him nor did he see the passenger talking on his mobile reporting their target was on the move.

Steve and Alison had parked up in an underground car park close to their interior designer's studio. They passed what Alison described as a "sweet" little coffee shop so before visiting their designer they stopped for a coffee. When Steve saw the prices, he wasn't so sure that 'sweet' was the word he'd have used. Still, the coffee was good even at a pound a sip.

Alison was talking about the guest list when Steve's phone buzzed. He looked at his fiancée with an apologetic look and a shrug of his shoulders that said *sorry, but I'll have to take this*. He saw it was Jenny Fuller from Chelmsford.

"Hi Steve, look I'm really sorry to bother you but something strange is happening here."

"Oh, like what?"

"Like DI Dean Grantham has been reinstated and is now Detective Chief Inspector Dean Grantham. I know we had him until you let him go, but I can't get my head around what's going on. The guy's a prick, he's useless at his job and he's on police bail. Everything says he should be sacked, not promoted."

Steve was conscious that Alison was listening. He needed to buy some time to think.

"Jenny, do you know who was responsible for his promotion?"

"No." She sounded dejected. "I suppose if I dig around, I might find out. My father certainly could but he's not up to it, although he's a lot better."

"That's good news. Is he conscious?"

"Yes. He gets tired but he's awake and alert."

"Jenny, I asked you to trust me and I meant it. Believe me, I'm trying to be one of the good guys. Can you ask your father how to get the name of the officer responsible for the promotion, and follow it up? When you have it, let me know, but don't under any circumstance follow it up yourself. Is that clear?"

"Yes, it's clear but Steve, what the hell's going on?"

"Just get the name, and I promise I'll tell you everything when the time's right."

"Fair enough, I'll get back to you," replied an unhappy and not very convinced Jenny Fuller. They ended the call.

Alison looked at Steve. "I know, it's work. I suppose this will be my life to come."

She took his hand and lightly kissed it.

"I'm afraid so darling but this is exceptional. I'll never have to deal with anything like this ever again." He silently added, *I hope.*

Steve paid the bill without having to visit the ATM and they set off to meet their interior designer.

***

Andrei Popa pulled up outside the gates marked 'ECLIPSE HALL. MEDICAL AND SURGICAL CENTRE'.

The gates were open, but he sat just outside and surveyed the area. There was a high stone wall that fronted the drive and curved away from the gates, obviously leading to the building. The grounds were lightly wooded and mainly covered in grass. An old rusted, low iron fence ran up both sides of the drive. The area was countrified with the nearest habitation at least one mile away, from what Andrei could judge. He felt it was a bit sinister and potentially dangerous. He told himself he was a big Romanian gangster and felt the Mauser in his waistband.

He drove on up the drive which led to a large porticoed white building. It had three steps up to an imposing double door. The driveway was pebbled, and the sound of his hire car's tyres seemed loud. He thought this might be for extra security. Anyone driving up would be heard.

He parked in what he took to be a car park, although there were no other cars parked. Andrei assumed there must be a separate staff car park.

He tried the double doors but found them locked. There was an old-fashioned bell pull to the right of the doors. He pulled it twice and heard loud chimes from the other side of the double doors. He waited but no one answered. He impatiently pulled again, four times. After a further delay of several minutes, he heard footsteps approaching the other side of the double doors. He noted the doors were painted red and thought it an appropriate colour for the entrance to a hospital.

One side of the double doors was opened by a man dressed completely in white. He was tall, athletic and looked slightly feminine, but capable of looking after himself in any fight. His shirt was a size too small, obviously designed to show off his biceps, and his trousers were a very slim fit, designed to show off whatever attributes he thought he had. Andrei admitted this was a handsome devil who was slightly intimidating but also gentle. Andrei wondered if he might be a 'zana', a homosexual in Romania.

The man in white had a name badge pinned to his shirt. It said *Mathew Spink, Head of Security*.

Andrei didn't wait for an invitation. He simply barged past the security man into a magnificent entrance hallway that had a central staircase rising to the upper floors. There were doors around the hallway, and each had a printed sign saying what was behind each door. Andrei noticed one was called Haematology. He'd no idea what it meant but it sounded important

"Excuse me," the man in white spoke. "What do you want and who are you?" His voice didn't match his physique. It was an octave too high.

Andrei wasn't going to be junior in this conversation to a 'zana'. "You're not very busy. I see the car park's empty."

The man in white gave out an exaggerated sigh before addressing Andrei as though he were a schoolboy. "That's because that is not our car park. If you'd read the signs, you'd have seen the car park is at the back, as is our main entrance. This entrance isn't used. So again, who are you and what do you want?"

The head of security had taken a few paces towards Andrei and looked as though he was thinking about throwing this unwanted guest out.

"I'm here to see Dr Symonds, take me to him." In Romania, if you spoke down to the staff, they more readily understood your position in relation to theirs. Unfortunately, it didn't work in England.

"I'm sorry, Mr Symonds can't see anyone at the moment, he's busy. He works very hard and cannot possibly see anyone without an appointment." The man in white's voice was now even higher. "If you leave me a contact number, I'll see he gets it."

Andrei now decided to play the heavy. He took the three paces necessary to be square onto the man in white. Andrei was about an inch taller and certainly carried more bulk. He stopped inches from the head of security and could smell coffee on his breath. He placed his hands on the other man's shoulders. "Listen, I've come a long way so take me to your boss now."

Andrei, in this mood, wasn't something most people could withstand. Mathew Spink was no exception. He closed and locked the door before turning to Andrei. "I'll take you through but as I said he's busy. What's your name?"

"Just tell him I'm from Bucharest."

Andrei was shown into the grand office of Robbie Symonds. After polite but tense introductions, coffee was offered, and both men relaxed in comfortable armchairs positioned to look out over the manicured lawns of Eclipse Hall.

Andrei got straight down to business. "Look Doc, we've stopped the last two shipments because you lost the previous one. Luca's sent me over to find out what's going on. We're losing money and we've got a lot invested."

"Hang on. First off, it's not doctor, it's Mr Symonds. I'm a surgeon, not a quack. Second, I've got eight patients here now waiting for the next consignments so we can carry out their operations. You say you're losing money." Robbie was angry. "What do you think I'm losing?" He gulped his coffee hoping it might calm him down.

He didn't like this Romanian on sight but realised he'd have to humour him. "We set this clinic up around six months ago on the understanding your organisation could provide an unlimited supply of tissue matched donors. You've seen the numbers. We all stand to make a lot of money from our arrangement. So far, we've only scratched the surface. I could do five times the transplants if I had the donors so please, don't come here and think the problem is at my end."

Andrei didn't like this pompous medic especially as he was putting the blame on the Romanian side of the operation.

"Listen, Doc. We can get you all the donors you want, but we sent two over a few days ago and it appears they didn't arrive. That's a problem. We've not been paid, and you don't seem to know where they are. So, let's stop playing games. I need to find out where these last two donors are and sort out the problem so we can do some serious business."

Robbie acknowledged to himself that this Romanian gangster was probably correct. Something had gone wrong and it needed to be sorted. The Clinic was all geared up to increase the number of operations and hence the financial rewards.

Robbie himself was banking on a windfall payday. He'd already spent most of what he was expecting to receive from his illegal operations. He'd planned by now to be doing at least twenty transplants a week. They had the patients. All they needed were the donors.

Andrei finished his coffee. He was surfacing from his exploits of last night and was beginning to feel normal again. "I met with a cop from Chelmsford last night. Do you know him? He's the one who meets the donors and brings them here."

"No. I've never met him. The first I see of the donors is when I examine them."

"This cop told me he'd been arrested before he could pick the missing girls up."

Robbie was stunned. "Arrested, how, our organisation is supposed to make sure these things don't happen?"

"Yeah. Well, it did and the girls are out there somewhere, and you need to find them." Andrei's eyes narrowed. "Unless you got them here on the quiet and you're scamming us out of our cut?"

"Don't be silly. Hang on." Robbie walked to his desk and hit a few buttons on a complicated-looking machine. He returned and resumed his seat. Neither man spoke.

A few minutes later the office door opened, and Mathew Spink entered.

"Mathew, it seems two donors have gone walkabout. Do you know anything?"

"Why yes Robbie, remember I told you. I got a call from one of the last two to arrive asking what to do. I sent a taxi to pick them up from Stanstead, but the taxi never arrived here, and I never heard from the girl again."

"You've no idea what happened to them?"

"No. Nothing at all." Andrei noticed the 'zana' was sweating. He clearly didn't like upsetting his boss.

Andrei didn't like this. "Have you spoken to the taxi driver? Find out why he didn't complete his fare?"

"No. I just called the local company in Harlow. I've no idea who the driver was."

Andrei knew this sounded true, but he didn't like the incompetence. "Well, my friend," Andrei stood up, "I suggest you get in touch with the taxi company, ask them which driver was sent to the airport and get him here *now*!" He shouted the 'now'.

Mathew looked crestfallen and stared at Robbie for guidance.

"You'd better do it, Mathew," Robbie spoke gently to the head of security. "We need to know what happened to these two girls."

Andrei thought Mr Symonds was too gentle with Mathew. He wondered how close they might be.

The head of security left.

Both men were now seated, and a heavy silence descended until Andrei broke it.

"This cop who meets the donors. He told me another cop, someone called Burt, was behind his arrest. Seems he's been sticking his nose in. Do you know him?"

"Yes, I've met him. I think he's a straight policeman, but he's about to join our Syndicate, so I'm surprised if he's a problem now."

"Hang on. Are you saying this Burt was doing his job when he caused us to lose the two girls, but now he's on our side he's not a problem?"

"Yes, that's exactly what I'm saying."

"You mean. If this guy was the problem, then the problem's solved?"

"I suppose so."

Andrei weighed up this information. Could the loss of the two donors simply be bad timing? If Burt had joined the UK organisation earlier, he wouldn't have arrested Dean Grantham, and everything would have been normal? It sounded good but Andrei knew he'd have to be sure. He still needed to meet this cop and make his own mind up.

Robbie Symonds offered to show Andrei around his clinic whilst they waited for Mathew to get in touch with the taxi driver. The use of the word "his" wasn't lost on Andrei. The place was impressive. It seemed to be in two halves. The original manor housed specialist laboratories such as Haematology. Robbie explained to Andrei this was simply the study of blood. Robbie also explained that the upper floor was given over to bedrooms where the donors were kept when they arrived. The other half of the clinic was ultra-modern and built onto the rear of the original house. This part housed the operating theatres which to a layman like Andrei looked very impressive. It was explained that this part also housed staff quarters, a restaurant and recovery rooms together with luxurious bedrooms for the recipients of the organs.

Robbie explained that the other surgeons were from various parts of the world and were here just for the money. Some had lost their licence to practice in their own country but given what they were doing at the clinic medical ethics had to take a back seat to the money.

"Very impressive, Robbie, I can see you're ready to scale up."

Just as Robbie was about to answer, Mathew appeared. He explained that the taxi driver refused to come to the clinic but said he'd been arrested by a coloured female detective sergeant. He thought her name was Fuller. They asked him questions about the booking but let him go because he didn't know anything. He only knew the girls had been taken away.

"That's all he said; he doesn't know anything."

Andrei looked sadly at the head of security. "But it means the police might. The only good thing is the donors can't identify anybody." He went into what looked like a trance before asking. "You said the woman was called Fuller. Any idea where she would be based?"

Mathew was now eager to please in the hope this individual would leave. "No, but it must be Chelmsford."

"The same as Dean Grantham!" Andrei stood up ready to leave. "Good, good."

He turned to Mathew Spink. "Are you the person who arranged for the two dead donors to be disposed of?"

This sudden change of tack shook the man in white. In a croaky uncertain voice, he answered, "Yes."

"Mr Symonds..." Andrei looked at Robbie and emphasised the 'Mister'. "I suggest you get rid of this incompetent fool. If he had employed someone who knew how to dispose of a body, I wouldn't be here and we'd both be somewhat richer."

With that, Andrei left without a goodbye or a handshake.

***

Andrei sat in his car and keyed in the coordinates that would take him to Lars Jenson's country estate. He then phoned Luca Rada and told him what he'd found out. He said he thought it was under control because this cop Burt was now part of Lars Jenson's group, but he'd check it out for himself. In a rare moment of levity, Luca asked if Andrei had used his Mauser yet. With a laugh, Andrei answered no but it was early days.

The man from Romania drove his hire car through the gates and followed the directions being given to him by an educated but remote English voice. He'd find the estate and get a hotel room locally for the evening. He planned to see Lars Jenson in the morning.

A grey Volvo set off in the same direction. The passenger in the front seat used his mobile to call his chief and report in.

Chapter Twenty-Six

Steve and Alison arrived back at her house following a successful, if exhausting, day's shopping. They didn't have bags with them. Most of the shopping involved ordering items for the soon to be refurbished flat that was to become their home. Steve considered his credit card limit but consoled himself with the fact the projected profit from the sale of his flat would help meet all of the bills.

Alison prepared a simple meal of spaghetti and opened a bottle of red wine to wash it down. Afterwards, wrapped in each other's arms on the sofa they discussed the future and where they might be in twenty years. Steve reminded his fiancée he had a large case starting trial on Monday at the Old Bailey and with any luck, he'd be operating nine-to-five hours for some time.

Alison reminded him the builders were starting on the renovations in just over a week and he'd better be around to help her move her stuff into his place. They joked about the move and having finished the wine relaxed to watch a re-run of a re-run of an old movie. In truth, they didn't care what they watched. They were happy and content. Steve was able to forget his troubles for a few hours.

***

Sunday the 17th of March presented a grey dawn but with the promise of a brighter day to come. The couple got up early, showered and dressed in their best outfits.

After breakfast, they set off for Lars Jenson's Buckinghamshire estate. On the way, they discussed the coming hours. Alison had eavesdropped on Steve's conversation with Sir Patrick Bond and was aware of the role her fiancé must play. It was agreed they'd both play along with the notion that Lars was arranging their wedding and that the Syndicate would meet the bill. Alison seemed to revel in the subterfuge of it all. She said she felt like a modern-day spy, but she reminded Steve he had to be careful. They were on Lars' home turf.

They arrived just before 10.45 a.m. Lars had said his Sunday service would start at eleven. After parking their car, the couple was met by a uniformed butler and escorted to the church that was set on the grounds about one hundred yards from the main house. They spotted a vicar standing outside welcoming his congregation. To Steve's surprise, as they approached, he saw the vicar was Lars himself.

"Steve, Alison!" The vicar was gushing, seeing his latest recruit. "Welcome, welcome, I'm so glad you could come." Taking Steve's arm, he steered him away from Alison. "After our service, we'll have drinks and then we'll all meet in the library for your signing-in ceremony. After that, we'll have lunch and a bit of a party." Without waiting for confirmation Lars, now the vicar turned to greet more members of his congregation as they arrived, leaving Steve and Alison to make their own way inside the church.

As newcomers, they decided to sit near the back. Steve looked around but didn't recognise anyone, due mainly to the fact he was looking at the backs of their heads. By the time the organ music started, and the vicar took his place in front of his flock, Steve counted twenty-six couples, meaning twenty-six Disciples were present. He knew no women Disciples were allowed. He'd considered asking Patrick Bond for some form of spy camera to try and photograph the Disciples present. At least it would be a start to identifying some of them. However, he dismissed the idea because he'd no idea how tight security would be, and he didn't want to risk being caught with a secret camera.

When the background organ music stopped, Lars, dressed in his church robes, stood and welcomed his Disciples and their good ladies to yet another Syndicate family service. He followed the traditional service with hymns, Bible readings and the climax, a sermon delivered by the Master himself. Steve had to admit as entertainment it wasn't bad. Lars threw his arms around as he praised the Lord. He spoke softly one minute about the sins of the flesh and the next second he was raising the decibel level to maximum saying he was a servant of God and God was directing his every move. His performance was intersected by a good few

'Hallelujahs'. He implored his Disciples to look out for each other and gain good grace with the Lord. He spoke of Eclipse Medical's good works helping ex-soldiers injured in the service of their country and the rewards all would receive in Heaven. He thanked God for showing him the way to help people enjoy a better life through the skills of transplant surgeons. Lars was on a roll.

His grand finale was to praise the work of his Disciples again and implored them to continue believing in the justness of their cause. All governments were corrupt and stupid, but the Syndicate through its Disciples would soon be in a position to challenge the whole electoral system by undermining the stupid and lazy politicians the people of the country had been duped into electing.

Lars stood with his arms stretched wide. He asked his congregation of Disciples to pray. Everyone stood. Lars launched into another tirade of nonsense that he called prayer and that lasted another five minutes.

Eventually, Lars stopped, wiped his brow and thanked everyone for coming. The service was over.

Steve had looked sideways at Alison a few times during Lars' tirade. She'd given a small smile each time but continued to look straight ahead. If Steve thought Lars was a bit of a nutter before this performance, he was now convinced of it. He surveyed the congregation and to his surprise, everyone appeared to have hung on every word the Master had spoken. It was smiles all around as the congregation emptied out.

Everyone was directed to a lavish lounge where uniformed waiters circulated with trays of champagne and canapes. The mood was light and there was a lot of laughter. Steve, standing next to Alison, surveyed the room. He began to wish he'd asked for a spy camera. He recognised at least three high court judges, someone from the CBI he'd seen interviewed on TV, a Deputy Commissioner from the Met and of course, Commander Bowles. He also recognised certain celebrities he knew again from television and Alison became excited when she recognised a famous pop singer.

Robbie Symonds sought the couple out. They made small talk and Robbie told Steve about the visit of Andrei Popa. After all, Steve was about to become family. While Robbie and Alison spoke about her visit to the clinic on Tuesday, Steve mulled over the information concerning

Popa. He didn't like the implication of this turn of events. It could spell additional danger.

Robbie moved away and his place was taken by Commander Bowles. Given he'd shopped Steve to Professional Standards, the DCI thought he had some nerve.

Then he realised it was only because of Alfie Brooks' heads-up that Steve knew that this man was a self-serving treacherous animal. He wouldn't expect Steve to know until Monday at the earliest of his double-dealing. Steve played along, introducing Alison, saying how much they'd both enjoyed the Master's sermon and how he was looking forward to joining the fold as a Disciple.

As they spoke, Steve noticed a figure standing by the window talking to Lars. He recognised him as Sir Timothy Head, the number one civil servant in the land. Steve and Sir Patrick Bond had suspected this senior individual's involvement but here was proof.

Lars broke away from Sir Timothy and approached Steve and Alison. He courteously leant forward and kissed Alison's hand. "My dear, on these occasions, it is customary for the ladies to gather in the day room whilst we indoctrinate a new Disciple."

A woman in her early forties approached and sidled up to Lars. "Ah, my dear." He acknowledged the new arrival. "Let me introduce you to Steve and Alison. This is Lady Stephanie De Court, a very old friend. Stephanie will escort you," he indicated to Alison, "and introduce you to the other ladies."

Steve's initial opinion of Stephanie was favourable. She was elegantly tall at around five foot ten inches, her figure was slim, and he noticed her fingernails were highly manicured and polished.

The Master stood back to allow both ladies room to pass. As the room emptied of ladies Lars announced, "Will everyone now please enter the library for the signing in ceremony of our latest Disciple." Still dressed in his religious robes he took Steve's arm and guided him forward.

***

Andrei Popa hadn't been allowed access into the estate. When he arrived, he'd pressed the intercom button and announced his arrival. He was told to wait and five minutes later a Land Rover appeared with two large men and an ugly, vicious-looking Alsatian dog. He was told in words of one syllable he would not be allowed in without clearance. He should call the Master's office and arrange an appointment. No matter what Andrei said or threatened there was no way in.

With steam coming from his ears, he reluctantly backed away promising death and destruction on both men's houses. He didn't mention the dog. Andrei hadn't expected this form of reception. He now had to plan how best to approach Lars Jenson. He drove back to the pub he'd stayed at last night and booked in for another night. He took up a position at a table by the window, ordered a beer and sat thinking.

Sir Patrick Bond was informed of this development.

***

The library in Lars' house was huge. It was lined with books from floor to ceiling. Everywhere there weren't books you could see highly varnished dark wood. The whole appearance was one of quality.

In the centre of the room was a large ornate desk on which was a small sloping stand. Steve noticed to one side a false wall had been drawn back revealing a large safe obviously built into the wall. The door was open.

Lars guided Steve to the far side of the desk and both men stood facing their audience of Disciples. Steve looked at the lectern. On it was a large Bible. It was closed but a wide silk bookmark was jutting from the bottom of the good book.

"Disciples," the Master began, "the Lord has directed me to find our brother Disciple, Steven Burt. We are gathered here to induct Steven into the Syndicate and to acknowledge him as a Disciple. Disciple Steve has already proven his loyalty to our Syndicate by assisting a fellow Disciple to avoid a nasty situation with the law. By inducting him today we acknowledge him as a Disciple of the Syndicate." Lars lifted a small box from the desk and ceremonially lifted it above his head. "Disciples, note our new member is hereby given the Syndicate tool to sign his name. This

235

tool is a weapon. It is the most powerful weapon in the world. Wars have been started and finished by a signature with a pen. Contracts worth millions have been settled, and laws have been enshrined, all by signing with a pen."

The Master opened the box and lifted out a black Mont Blanc gold-tipped fountain pen. Steve noted it had the Syndicate logo on the side. With a theatrical flourish, Lars removed the top and handed it to Steve. He then lifted the bookmark that jutted out of the Bible and flung back the front pages to reveal the page Steve was to sign.

What Steve saw amazed him. On this page were his photograph, his warrant card number, address and a summary of his police career. He knew instantly that this data could only have come from his police personnel file.

Lars smiled at Steve and indicated he should sign. Steve did.

"Disciples, by me as Master countersigning page fifty-one of our good book, I am acknowledging that Steven Burt is now our fifty-first Senior Disciple."

The Master signed and the audience stood and applauded. Lars took Steve's pen and screwed the top on. He replaced it in its velvet-lined box and presented it to Steve.

Steve was now officially a Disciple of the Syndicate. But for how long?

There was a lot of hand shaking and back slapping before Lars called for everyone to proceed to lunch. Steve held back. He wanted to get as much information from Lars as he could. Lars was busy closing the Bible and placing it in a purpose-built leather box. Steve would have to be careful.

"Master, that's a magnificent Bible but the extra pages in front seem to be part of it."

Lars beamed. "Yes Steve, the Lord ordered me to buy this good book and to have it rebound to incorporate a hundred new pages at the front. Each page is of the highest quality paper. You see God instructed me to appoint one hundred Disciples. By keeping their details within this book, they will be nearer to God. Soon Steve you will feel the power of having your signature next to the words of the Lord."

Steve wasn't too sure. "Why a hundred Disciples?" Steve asked sounding as innocent as he could.

"You are our number fifty-one. When we have one hundred Senior Disciples, we will be ready to do what we know needs to be done. God will direct us come the day." Lars was off on another rant. "With a hundred Disciples, we can control any government. We will remove the so-called power they think they have and return total power to the people. But enough for now. Let me replace the book in the safe and we can go and enjoy our lunch and talk about your wedding."

Steve needed to know about the fifty-one pages. "Sorry, Master, I'm being a bit slow, but in the book do you have all the Disciples' details, so they are *all* next to God?"

The Master beamed. He felt that Steve and he were now soulmates. "Oh yes, when the one-hundredth page is signed, then my work is done. All one hundred Disciples will be next to God within His book. It will be a glorious day, Steve."

The Master continued to place the book in the safe, lock it and replace the false front of books that matched the other books in the library. No one would suspect there was a safe behind this wall. For good measure, Lars pulled a narrow table in front of the false front. Presumably to further disguise its existence.

Lunch was a buffet and when Steve walked into the dining room, he saw Alison talking with Lady Stephanie and another comelier woman Steve didn't know. Before he could make his way to his fiancée, he was intercepted by Sir Timothy Head. Sir Timothy had obviously enjoyed the free champagne and was holding another glass of alcoholic beverage. Steve thought whisky.

"Steve, congratulations on becoming one of us." He offered his hand and Steve shook it. "In future, if you need me for anything you'll be put straight through. Anything at all, just call."

"Thank you, Sir Timothy, that's very kind."

"Not at all. We help each other and come the day who knows who our supreme leader might be? You never know who you'll need once we reach the magic one hundred." Sir Timothy slapped Steve on the back and headed into the crowd gathered around the dessert table.

Steve joined Alison and her two companions. The third lady was introduced as Mrs Strummer. Her husband was Deputy Governor at The Bank of England. Steve was impressed and again wondered how high up the Syndicate had managed to get. He realised he needed a plan to either steal the book or photograph it. The problem was he couldn't open the safe and even if he could he didn't have a camera.

He joined the ladies in small talk and was informed by Lady Stephanie that the wedding was all arranged. Alison looked bemused and with uncharacteristic enthusiasm stated, "Oh! Yes, darling, Stephanie has taken care of everything. She's really super. Do you know she's related to one of the minor royals and says if you want, she can arrange for them to attend the wedding? Isn't that just super!" Alison was moving her arms as she spoke. Steve suspected this new home-counties Alison was a ruse. He suspected she was not being serious but felt her two companions weren't aware of it.

"So, is it all arranged?" Steve tried to sound sincere.

"Yes, darling. We'll have the church, a marquee on the grounds, even a famous group to play live music. Steph's going to do the menu, the flowers and the invitations." Alison was off again. "Isn't it super? It's our wedding and we don't have to do a thing. How lucky can one couple get?"

Steve saw this might not end well. He saw Alison was struggling to maintain her facade of politeness. She was bordering on sarcasm.

"Well, that's good. Look darling, I'm sorry, but I think we'll have to go. I've an important phone call to take. If we leave now, I'll just about make it." Taking Alison's arm, he apologised to the ladies and steered his fiancée towards the door.

As they made their way through the crowd, they made their apologies. Steve saw Lars and gave him the story of the phone call. They were both congratulated on a wonderful event and eventually, Steve and Alison reached their car.

No one said anything for the first five minutes of the journey. Suddenly Alison started laughing a wild almost hysterical laugh. She had tears in her eyes. "Those bloody people. They're so wrapped up in their own little world they've no idea when they're having the pee-pee taken out of them. That Stephanie really believed I wanted a punk band for the music." She continued to laugh uncontrollably. Steve joined in and they were soon both almost doubled up with laughter.

"You know," Alison was now more serious, "those bloody women really believed I was happy to let them run our wedding. If I'd said I needed a dress I'm sure they would have asked what size I took." She shook her head. "It's unbelievable."

Once things settled down and Steve could concentrate on his driving Alison told him of her time with the ladies and tried to remember who their husbands were. Steve told of his induction, his free fountain pen and that he knew where the list of Disciples was kept but he'd no way of getting it.

The drive to London was quicker than expected. Steve was staying at his own flat so after seeing Alison inside and enjoying a protracted good night kiss he set off for his own place and a good night's sleep.

Just as Steve was leaving with Alison, Andrei Popa phoned Lars Jenson. He'd found the number on his mobile. Lars wasn't pleased to hear from the Romanian and told him so. The Romanian wasn't pleased with his treatment by Lars' guards and he told him so. Both men argued over nothing in particular. Eventually, it was obvious Lars would have to meet Andrei. He told him to arrive at the house at seven p.m. Lars promised to feed him, and Andrei said he liked English steak.

The two men parted on more amicable terms.

***

Steve was sipping a beer in his oversize chair, thinking about everything that had happened. He considered calling Patrick Bond but thought he'd leave it till tomorrow. He thought about what he'd tell Professional Standards. They were bound to be on his case tomorrow. He thought about the case as a whole but didn't reach any conclusion. He finished his beer and went to bed.

***

At 06.17 a.m. his phone rang.

"Steve, it's Patrick Bond. Lars Jenson's been murdered."

Chapter Twenty-Seven

As Steve got the message about Lars Jenson's murder, Andrei Popa was sitting on his hotel bed. He was cleaning the Mauser pistol he'd acquired. He did this in times of stress. Not known as an early riser, he found the time difference between Romania and England difficult to accept. His body clock was out of sync and he felt slightly confused.

As he held the pistol's parts in his hands he thought back to his meeting with Lars Jenson. He thought Lars a decent but greedy man. He pretended to want to help his fellow man but deep down, his motivation was money. Andrei also felt he had an overwhelming desire for power. He recalled being given a ten-minute lecture on how corrupt and inefficient the West's democratic system was and how he was putting in place a team of people who would soon be in control not only of the UK but all of Europe. Andrei thought he was a mad man, but it was none of his business. Luca had to deal with this saviour of the world. All Andrei had to do was make sure they could start sending donors again and make sure Luca got his money.

Lars had been welcoming and friendly and after he settled down was reasonably good company. They were joined by the doctor Andrei had met the previous day at the clinic in Harlow. Lars said that Robbie was in charge of the transplant project and if Andrei had any questions, it was best Robbie answered them. The more the doctor spoke the less Andrei liked him. It was clear this surgeon was an arrogant fool whose only motive was money. He spoke of his investments, his get-rich-quick schemes and of how if you had lots of money you were certain to make more. He boasted about his multi-million-dollar investments, in Caribbean property. He explained he had bought into an entire development for only a deposit and how he would be a billionaire within three years.

When Andrei asked how he was to fund the rest of his Caribbean investment if he'd only paid a deposit, Robbie Symonds grinned. "Well, that's where your donors and my skill come in. I need the throughput to get the money. This delay is killing me financially."

Andrei remembered Lars Jenson's remarks to his surgeon along the lines of 'don't be too greedy and overstretch yourself'. Andrei was surprised that the two men were so different. He realised they really weren't friends at all. Just convenient bedfellows.

Once Andrei managed to get the conversation turned to the reason he was there, the meeting became pure business. The doctor admitted it started with the botched disposal of two bodies. These were donors who didn't recover from surgery. He'd instructed his head of security to dispose of them and he, in turn, had used Dean Grantham. Andrei got the full story and now understood where this guy Burt fitted in. He was again reassured this detective was no longer a problem.

They had a few drinks and parted on fairly friendly terms. As Andrei left the two Eclipse Medical Directors sitting drinking their whisky, he told them he had to report back to Romania before the supply of donors would start again. He could tell Robbie Symonds wasn't happy with this statement.

***

Andrei had called Dean Grantham once he had returned to his hotel bedroom yesterday. They'd discussed a few things and Dean told Andrei it was a Detective Sergeant called Fuller who had intercepted the girls at the airport. Dean told of his promotion despite mishandling the disposal of the bodies and that he could now control the detective sergeant. Andrei didn't think Dean was up to the job and regarded him as a bit of a liability.

"Listen, I want to meet this woman. I'll drive to your police station tomorrow. Arrange for her to be there. I need to know what the girls told her and how much she knows. Sometimes it isn't only the top man who has the knowledge and is the danger. Sometimes the foot soldiers can be just as dangerous."

It was agreed Andrei would be at Chelmsford HQ at ten on Monday morning.

This had set Andrei's plan for the day. Before doing anything else he phoned Luca Radu to update him on events so far. He told his boss of the various meetings he had had with the people he'd met and now thought the problem detective had been neutralised. He explained he was just off to meet the detective who'd arrested the missing girls and gave his opinion of Dean Grantham.

"Their personnel problems should not concern us unless you suspect they are working against us. Double-check that this senior policeman has been neutralised. I don't like the sound of it. It's too convenient, and this other police officer you're seeing today, find out what the girls told her."

Andrei agreed and the two talked about more domestic issues but always returned to their transplant business. Andrei shared his view with Luca that Lars Jenson was a mad man who in turn agreed.

"Last time I met him he sounded like a religious maniac. He's certainly an 'om nebun'. Both men laughed.

"To say he's a mad man in our language sounds even more frightening."

After a few more minutes the conversation stopped with Andrei promising to get things wrapped up and return to Bucharest within the next forty-eight hours.

After reassembling his Mauser, Andrei packed everything away and set off for Chelmsford. He'd stop on the way and have one of those filling English breakfasts.

As he set off, he again failed to notice a car following. This car was a green Seat and the two MI6 agents inside had relieved the agents with the Grey Volvo at midnight. The passenger reported they were on the move. It was six-thirty a.m.

***

Steve showered and dressed at lightning speed. He called The Cap and told him to get a pool car and they'd meet in the garage at New Scotland Yard.

He flew from his flat and en-route to the Yard he called Sir Patrick Bond. "I'm awake now. Fill me in."

"I don't know much. As promised, I've been shadowing all the main players of Eclipse Medical. That included Lars Jenson but obviously, my lads couldn't get inside the estate. They reported movements in and that included you. I got a call saying all hell had erupted this morning. Police cars and an ambulance arriving with sirens and blue lights on. My guys were smart enough to gate-crash the party to see what was going on. They found a DI Ian Shelly was in charge and once they found him and showed him their credentials, he took them seriously. He told them Lars Jenson had been found shot in his library by the early morning cleaner.

"I'd briefed them already, so they knew about the Met's interest in Lars Jenson. My boys took control, told this DI Shelly to clear his men away and that an officer from the Met would be arriving to take charge. I got the call, told them they'd done the right thing, told them to stay put and not to let any plod near the crime scene. I called you straight away thinking you'd want to get down there. My lads are waiting for you."

Steve was impressed by Sir Patrick's organisational skills. "Thanks, and yes, I'm on my way. Leave it with us and I'll keep you posted." Steve hung up.

He called Andy at home next. It was one of the few times he'd called Andy's home number. The DC always seemed to be in the office. A sleepy Andy answered but was instantly awake and ready for action. Steve explained what he could and asked Andy to call out the cavalry. Scene of crime, forensics, pathologist and a search team for good measure.

Steve felt the raw excitement coming from his detective even over the airwaves. Andy would be up and in the office in record time.

He met The Cap as arranged, but he didn't look at his best. He needed a shave, his hair hadn't been combed, and his suit was very creased. He explained his normal morning routine included his wife laying out his clothes for the day, but not at 06.20 in the morning. As they drove, Steve pulled his DI's leg about his domestic arrangements and Abul retorted by suggesting Steve should train Alison to do the same thing once they were married. Both men looked at each other and laughed. "You know that'll never happen."

***

Abul was driving with the blues and twos flashing. He was a competent driver and even at speeds approaching one hundred miles an hour Steve felt completely safe. As they drove Steve explained what had happened. He was tempted to let Abul in on his mission with Sir Patrick but decided against it. This would be treated as a straightforward murder until events dictated otherwise.

The two Yard detectives made the journey to Buckinghamshire in record time thanks to the power of flashing blue lights. As they parked in the same spot Alison and Steve had parked in the day before, they were accosted by a tall, slim man dressed in a shabby raincoat. Although it was not yet fully light there was enough illumination from the external house lighting to identify the newcomer as a policeman. People often said you could always tell a policeman in or out of uniform. Steve thought they were right.

The policeman powered up to the two detectives obviously in no mood for small talk. "I suppose you're the guys from Scotland Yard. I've spoken to my Governor and he's told me to tell you to push off. You've no jurisdiction here, no matter what these two spooks say."

Steve assumed a reasonable pose and a quiet tone of voice. He sympathised with this officer and surmised he'd be the same if the roles were reversed. He calmly explained the victim was a person of interest in a case he was involved in and the case concerned national security.

The Cap's eyes almost popped out of his head. He'd not heard anything about national security and wondered what Steve was up to. He decided to file this information away but vowed to have a serious word with his boss at the first opportunity.

"Well, sir," DI Shelly was calmer but not convinced, "I've called my Super and he's not pleased. He's getting onto somebody in the Met but he says because MI6 are here, I'm to go with the flow until he sorts this out. The body is in the library waiting for you."

"Excellent." Steve was being very friendly. "We'll go over to the library. Our own people will be dealing with everything at the scene so there's not a lot for you to do. Leave half a dozen uniforms and I'll make sure you're updated as we go."

With a broad smile and a wave of his hand, DCI Burt dismissed DI Shelly.

"That was neatly done. I bet his superintendent isn't too pleased though."

"No, Cap, but I bet we don't hear anything. With MI6 involved everybody's going to tread gently." As the pair walked towards the house, Steve raised his hand to indicate The Cap shouldn't talk. "And before you ask, no I can't tell you anything about MI6's involvement." Steve considered things for a moment. "At least not yet."

The local force had taped off an area around the entrance to the house, indicating the entire building was a crime scene.

A uniformed sergeant approached the two detectives. "Morning sir." He addressed Steve as the obvious senior man. "I've taped everything off as you can see, and I've got the witnesses and the house staff together in the hallway. I had a look in the library just to confirm our man is indeed dead. Looks like he's been shot. Then I closed the door. The crime scene is pretty much untouched."

Steve eyed this sergeant. At a guess, he was around the late twenties, tall and fairly good looking. His accent was home counties and given his overall assured attitude Steve pegged him as a fast-track graduate entrant. He'd have Steve's rank before he was thirty-five. Such was the modern police force.

"Thank you, Sergeant, well done. Do you know where the MI6 officers are?"

"No sir, I believe they left once they saw you arrive."

"Typical spooks, just disappearing into fresh air." The Cap wasn't impressed but Steve wasn't surprised. Patrick Bond wouldn't want his agents making statements to the police that would be kept on file.

As the two detectives entered the main hallway of the house, they saw three civilians seated being guarded by a uniformed constable. Steve nodded to the constable. "Take them into the day room." He pointed to a door off the hallway. "They'll be more comfortable in there. We'll interview them shortly."

Abul had yet another question for his boss. He thought *how the hell does he know so much about this place?* but as before, he decided to wait for the appropriate time to question his DCI.

Steve and Abul, their feet covered by blue plastic, entered the library. The body of Lars Jenson was lying on its back in front of the desk Steve had stood behind only yesterday. A chair was lying on the floor not far from the body and what looked like a rope was on the floor between the body and the chair.

"How come he's in his pyjamas?" The Cap was squatting down beside the body.

"Good question. I don't know." Steve was looking towards the safe. It was open and as far as he could see it was empty. The box containing the Bible was gone.

"Steve? Look at these marks on his wrists and these other marks on the soles of his feet. What do you make of it?"

Steve squatted beside The Cap. "I'd say he was tortured. Looks like he was tied to that chair by his wrists using that cord." Steve pointed to the upturned chair and the cord. "I'd bet the marks on the soles of his feet are cigarette burns and look at his face. Those bruises are nasty." Both men stood up.

"I'd say Lars Jenson was well and truly worked over to give up the combination to the safe." Again, Steve pointed. "Whoever did this, knew there was a safe hidden behind that false wall of books."

The Cap didn't disagree with his DCI's analysis but wondered again how he knew so much about this place and the false wall in particular. This was something else for later. His boss knew a lot more about this place than he'd so far admitted.

Steve stood and stroked his chin. A sure sign he was thinking. "He's been shot in the chest. Looks like a mid-calibre maybe a .38 or a .45. Cap, get the housekeeper and let's look at his bedroom."

As Steve was leaving the library the circus arrived from London. He briefed the senior forensic officer, told him what he'd observed and as usual asked for his findings ASAP.

The housekeeper opened Lars Jenson's bedroom and returned to the day room. Steve and Abul entered with caution, being careful not to disturb anything. The room looked as though it had been searched and there was what appeared to be blood on the bed cover and floor. The room itself was bigger than a normal bedroom and the attached bathroom would not have been out of place as the main convenience for the house.

"Cap, notice anything?"

Abul hated it when Steve played these games. He always felt inadequate. There was nothing obvious other than the blood and Abul said so.

Steve allowed himself a small smile. "Look at the bed. What do you see?"

Abul looked. "An old-fashioned heavy dressing gown."

"What else?"

The Cap was stumped. Steve carefully picked it up for Abul to study. Still, The Cap couldn't see what his boss was going on about. "Remember the rope downstairs?"

"Yes."

"I think you'll find it's from this dressing gown. The cord's missing. I think that whatever happened started here. That's why Lars Jenson was in his pyjamas. The killer must have removed the cord from the dressing gown and somehow persuaded his victim to go to the library."

"But why, Steve?"

"Because he wanted something that was in the safe."

The pair stood looking around. There was nothing obvious in either the bathroom or the bedroom except what was obvious. The crime scene and forensic teams would discover anything useful if it were to be found.

They went back downstairs and into the day room. As expected, the maid couldn't tell them anything. She'd come running when she heard the cleaner scream.

She'd looked into the library and rushed outside.

The cleaner could only say she'd arrived to start cleaning and had gone to the library first because it was the easiest room to clean. She'd found her employer on the ground, dead. She's panicked and screamed, rooted to the spot until Mr Timms the butler arrived and guided her out.

Mr Timms the butler confirmed the cleaner's story. "I saw she was in a terrible state, so I escorted her out into the fresh air. I returned and phoned 999, sir. I knew from yesterday that you were a policeman, but I didn't have a number for you. I'm sure the Master will be more comfortable now knowing you are in charge. This is a terrible thing, sir. Who'd do this?"

"We'll find out Mr Timms. When did you last see Mr Jenson?"

"It must have been around ten p.m. At around seven, I took drinks into the library for the Master. He was entertaining Mr Symonds and a foreign gentleman. I believe he said his name was Popa."

"Did you see them leave?"

"Yes sir. The Master rang through for Mr Popa's coat. He left a little after eight. Mr Symonds remained for a short while and he too left just before eight-thirty."

"Did you see Mr Jenson after both his guests had gone?"

"Yes. He asked me to take him hot milk around ten p.m. That was the last time I saw him alive."

"Did you get any sense as to what was being discussed?"

The ever-faithful servant was clearly conflicted. "Mr Timms, your Master is dead. Anything you tell me can't harm him now and might allow me to apprehend his killer." Steve had used this line before to good effect.

"Well... I did get a sense that Mr Symonds wasn't happy about money. I heard him say he needed his cut now or else. I didn't hear any more. I'm sorry, sir."

"That's very helpful Mr Timms. Why not take the ladies and have a nice cup of tea with them? An officer will be along to take your statements shortly." Steve had a sudden thought.

"Mr Timms, where were the security men?"

"They finish at ten in the evening sir. The two dogs are released to roam the grounds until the security detail comes on again at seven in the morning."

"I see, thank you, Mr Timms. Just one last thing. Where does the CCTV that covers the gate get recorded?"

"That'll be in the security hut just at the back of the house sir."

The three servants shuffled off to find a cup of tea.

The Cap was again curious. He now knew Steve was in this house yesterday. But why and why wasn't he sharing this with him? Abul was getting nervous. There was more to this than a straightforward murder. But what?

"Let's go look at the CCTV. You never know."

One of the uniformed security guards was in the hut and happily produced the CCTV images of the main gate. He confirmed no one could gain access unless they were buzzed in from this security hut. On exit, the gates opened automatically as a car approached them.

The images were surprisingly sharp. They knew Lars Jenson was alive at ten so Steve had the images played back from eight. They saw a car leave at eight-ten and another at eight thirty-five, presumably Lars Jenson's guests. There were no other movements, so Steve had the CD speeded up. As the image clicked forward to three thirty-five on Monday morning, a car was seen approaching the gates to leave. The security guard slowed the image to normal speed. They saw an old white Ford Cortina approach the gates. The driver had a cap on, and a scarf wrapped around his face. The registration number plates had been taped over with masking tape making it impossible to identify either car or driver. The tape was speeded up again until it showed the police cars and ambulance arriving at 06.31.

"Who was that leaving in the Cortina?" Steve asked the guard.

"I've no idea, sir. It's not a car I've seen before and if you'll excuse me, it's not the style of car we're used to seeing here."

"We've just seen it leave so it must have driven in. How could that be?"

The guard produced a log and handed it to Steve who handed it to The Cap.

"See, we record all vehicles entering. I saw you here yesterday sir, and you'll note your car was recorded as entering."

The Cap's ears pricked up and he found the registration number of Steve's car recorded as entering at 10.54 yesterday morning. Now Abul definitely knew his boss had been here but he still didn't know why.

"Give me all the discs for the past forty-eight hours. I'll have someone go through them."

The guard collected two discs and handed them to Steve.

Steve and Abul found the senior circus members to tell them they were going back to London and reminding them that anything however insignificant they were to contact either Steve or Abul at the Yard.

Steve found the pathologist. It was a woman Steve had worked with before and he knew she was a no-nonsense type of individual. She confirmed death was by gunshot, that the victim had indeed been tortured and the time of death was between one and five that morning.

"Thanks, Doc. Any chance of a speedy post-mortem?"

"As it's you, DCI Burt, I'll do it this afternoon. Say four p.m. if that suits?"

Steve looked at The Cap with a quizzical stare. The Cap recognised the invitation.

"Oh, I suppose so, I'll see you at four this afternoon, Doctor."

Both Steve and The Cap grinned at each other.

They sought out the fast-track sergeant and told him the same, plus he should keep two uniforms on-site twenty-four-seven until further notice. If he was given any grief by his superiors, he should tell them to contact Steve at the Yard.

Steve told Abul he needed a few minutes. Abul went to sit in the car as Steve hit speed dial on his mobile. Sir Patrick answered on the first ring.

"It's murder all right. He's been shot. Looks like a .38 or a .45. He was also tortured and the book with the Disciples' names is missing. I think whoever did this wanted the book but there's nothing to go on except an old white Ford Cortina was caught on CCTV leaving in the early hours. I think whoever was driving is our killer."

"And the book is gone?"

"Yes."

"I've had the Prime Minister on again. He's very concerned at our lack of progress. When I tell him the list of names is missing, he'll go ballistic. He told me to raid that estate and bust open the safe. I said we had it in hand but now… I wish I'd taken his advice." Sir Patrick was on a downer. He wasn't used to being in the direct line of fire. He was an administrator. Not an agent and didn't really know what to do next.

Steve could feel Sir Patrick's dilemma so spoke up. "Listen, Patrick, leave this with me. Can you ask your guys if they spotted this Cortina entering the estate sometime yesterday? Your lads were keeping watch so they must have seen it and maybe they got the registration number."

This positive spin cheered Sir Patrick up. "Good thinking Steve. I'll get right on it and I'm going to hold off telling the Prime Minister about

the book. I just hope to God you can perform a miracle and get it back."
The line went dead.

The detectives left with The Cap once again driving. He intended to use the journey to quiz his boss on what was going on. Or so he hoped.

Chapter Twenty-Eight

Andrei arrived at Chelmsford Police HQ at exactly ten a.m. He had stopped en route for his promised English breakfast. He couldn't believe that all Englishmen ate so much for breakfast every morning. It was delicious but too much food so early in the day.

After the usual checks, he was escorted to a meeting room on the first floor. He wasn't sure what to do with his Mauser. In the end, he took it with him and if questioned he decided to say he was handing it in for Dean Grantham. As luck would have it, the walk-through metal detector scanner was out of order so Andrei just walked straight through only answering a few questions. Needless to say, his answers were all invented.

The room he was shown to was basic and not very welcoming. Apart from an old table and six uncomfortable plain wooden chairs, there was no other furniture. The walls were painted off-white and there were no pictures on the walls. The floor was covered in industrial-grade linoleum. The whole room was depressing. This matched Andrei's mood. He was depressed and after talking to his boss earlier couldn't wait to get home.

***

Dean arrived followed by a tall, very beautiful coloured woman. Andrei was impressed. Women like this weren't common in Bucharest and this lady was shaped in all the right places. Andrei thought maybe his day was getting better.

After the necessary introductions Dean, as the new DCI, took the chair. "Jenny, Mr Popa is here to try to discover what happened to his two nieces. You remember, the two girls you picked up at Stanstead airport. The family are concerned for their safety and Andrei here has come over to find them."

Jenny thought as a cover story it wasn't bad, but she knew from Steve and the girls the real reason they were in the UK. She realised she'd have to be careful.

"I'm sorry Mr Popa but I can't help you. We found two girls wandering around Stanstead Airport, they didn't speak English and seemed to be lost. I didn't arrest them as I think you've been told. I merely handed them over to social services. I think you'd be better asking them." Jenny knew her reply was a bit weak, but it was the best she could do.

Dean sighed and opened his arms as though to say 'there you are'. Another interpretation could be "what did I tell you", directed to the Romanian. Jenny realised it was the latter.

Andrei smiled at Jenny thinking she really was a stunning woman. "My dear, I've come all this way to learn what happened to my nieces. Please don't tell me stories. You and your Mr Burt have caused me quite enough inconvenience already. I know you arrested them and brought them to this police station. Now please," he pleaded but it was too theatrical a gesture, "don't take me for a fool."

Jenny had been rumbled but she stood her ground. "Mr Popa, as I said, your relations are in the hands of our social services. I have no idea where they are or why they are in the UK."

The Romanian wasn't getting through and knew he was being lied to. He tried another approach. "Look, Jenny... I may call you Jenny?" He didn't wait for a reply. "Let's not fall out. I know you have the girls and you know they're not my nieces." Honesty or what passed for it was now the best policy but only up to a point. "They came to England looking for work. They were to be met by an agency who promised they could get them work in a factory for a month. The agency isn't operating legally and for some reason didn't turn up to meet them. That's why they looked lost when you saw them at the airport. Now I need to find them and take them home."

Jenny was impressed by this large frightening-looking man's storytelling abilities. She just hoped hers was as good as his. She pondered her reply. If she admitted knowing the truth, the whole investigation might be blown. Also, she didn't know who this Andrei Popa was. She made up her mind.

"Who are you, Mr Popa? You've admitted you lied about being the girls' uncle so what is your interest in these girls?"

Andrei didn't like being called a liar. He could see this beautiful, intelligent woman wasn't playing ball, so he tried a third and final approach. "Look Jenny, I think you know what's going on here. You're clearly a smart girl. Those girls are here for a purpose and I suspect you know the purpose. So, I must have these girls back. If you do that for me, a nice amount of American dollars will be yours, tax-free and no questions asked. Now let's be sensible. What do you say?"

Jenny wasn't surprised by the bribe but was shocked that it was made in front of the new DCI. Then she remembered who and what the new DCI was. She needed time to think. She couldn't hand these girls over. They were currently in protective custody as potential witnesses if Steve could put a murder case together against the transplant clinic.

She decided to play it straight. "Mr Popa you do realise in this country it is an offence to bribe a police officer. I could arrest you right now so please let's not be silly. I've told you all I can and I'm sure DCI Grantham…" she almost spat out Dean's name and new rank "… will be happy to show you off the premises."

Jenny sat with a straight back that emphasised her height. She hoped it made her appear inscrutable.

Andrei Popa wasn't worried. He'd been in situations like this before. He had one more card to play. He slowly pulled his Mauser from his waistband and laid it on the table. He sneered at Jenny as he stroked the weapon. He saw a mixture of fear and astonishment pass over her face.

"You see my dear, in my country life is cheap. That's why a nice amount of money in exchange for a favour is always the best way out of situations like this. If we can't reach an agreement, then we have to do things the hard way." He lifted the Mauser and moved it between his hands. "If I can't get what I want by being reasonable then there's only one thing left. You and your boss man Mr Burt might like to think about alternatives. Sometimes death is preferable to life in a wheelchair or being permanently hooked up to a machine." Andrei was in his element. This was the real Andrei Popa talking. "I enjoy my work and one or two more dead or disabled policemen isn't going to cause me any sleepless nights."

Even Dean Grantham couldn't stomach this. "Hold on Andrei! In this—"

He was shouted down by the Romanian. "I know! You don't kill or hurt people in this country to get what you want. Well grow up, this is real." He studied Jenny for a long moment. His gaze was fearsome, and the DS felt very scared. "I'm staying at the Holiday Inn beside the airport tonight. If you don't bring the girls to me by tomorrow morning, I'll come looking for you and our next meeting may not be as pleasant as this one."

Jenny tried to look professional and reacted as though being threatened by a Romanian gangster were an everyday occurrence. She tried to sound strong.

"Mr Popa, we have laws in this country and if my senior officer won't enforce the law then I will. I would like to remind you, DCI Grantham, I know you're out on police bail. Any mention of this conversation and you'll be right back in a cell." Jenny wasn't being very circumspect, but she was angry. She threw caution to the wind. "Mr Popa you're carrying what I presume is an unregistered firearm in the UK, you've threatened a police officer in front of another police officer and you've attempted to bribe a police officer — again, in front of another police officer, even though he's a waste of space. These are serious charges and I'm happy to arrest you right now." Jenny stood and looked down at Andrei safe in the knowledge he wouldn't shoot her here. Or so she hoped.

Dean also stood. "Hold on Sergeant, what you think you heard here today, you didn't. I've been here all through this meeting and I'm afraid my recollection of events doesn't match yours." Without any obvious embarrassment, Dean walked around the table to where Andrei sat. As Andrei stood, he returned his Mauser to the waistband of his trousers at his back. He looked at Jenny one last time. "Remember, tomorrow."

Both Andrei and Dean left.

Jenny sat down and trembled. She assumed it was delayed shock and she'd be OK after a few minutes. She didn't know how to react to these events. Dean Grantham was obviously corrupt and a waste of space. She'd have to think and speak to Steve.

The new DCI and the Romanian gangster arranged to meet in the early evening and have a repeat of their adventures from last Saturday night, although this time they would not be drinking copious amounts of whisky before they set out.

***

As The Cap drove, the atmosphere in the car was tense. Steve knew he'd opened up some questions that The Cap was smart enough to have picked up on, but he still couldn't bring him into the true investigation.

Steve called Andy.

"Steve I'm glad you called. A couple of blokes from Professional Standards are looking for you. You have to report to the eleventh floor as soon as you get in."

"What did you tell them?"

"I said you were out on a new murder case and I'd no idea when I'd hear from you."

"Good man. Now, Andy, pull up firearms certificates. See if anyone associated with Eclipse Medical owns a gun. Then put in a request to have Terry Harvey in Technical Support on standby. I've got a couple of CDs from a CCTV system. We need him to work his magic, but we need it worked today. We're looking for an old white Ford Cortina. Got that?"

"Yes. What else, apart from keeping Professional Standards off your back?"

Andy was growing up. Steve knew he would not have said that six months earlier. Despite his concerns, he smiled. "Andy, what was the name of that Romanian fellow you found used the credit card for his flight over here?"

Andy took a few seconds. "Andrei Popa. Why?"

"He was with the murder victim last night." Steve thought for a few seconds. "Get onto Bucharest. See what they know about this Popa."

Andy burst with a pride that Steve could almost feel through the airwaves. "No need, I've already got it. He's heavy muscle for a guy called Luca Radu. Radu runs something called The World Trading Company. It seems legit in Romania, but my contact Dimitri says they are into every crooked deal going. Andrei Popa has been suspected of several assassinations over the years, but nothing sticks to him. When they get evidence, this Luca Radu pays someone off and Popa walks.

256

Dimitri says if were dealing with Andrei Popa to be very careful. He kills for fun."

"Thanks, Andy. We'll be about an hour."

Steve was about to hang up when Andy was back on the line. "Steve, how old is this Cortina?"

"I've no idea, why?"

"Well, if it's old there may not be many registered around the home counties and the outlying areas. I could do a DVLA search for white Ford Cortinas. It's not a rare classic so a lot would have been scrapped over the years."

"Brilliant Andy, and just to show I'm not completely useless, it was an MK3, so you'll only have to look for Cortinas from 1970 onwards. My father had one, so I know they were only manufactured from 1970."

"Right, that'll help. I'll check it out and maybe have some good news when you get back." This time Andy did hang up.

The Cap had been biding his time. After Steve hung up, he let a few minutes pass before broaching the subject of Steve's obvious involvement with Lars Jenson.

"Look Abul, I know you have questions and yes, I was in Lars Jenson's house yesterday as his guest, but I still can't bring you in. Not yet, believe me, it's for your own good."

The Cap was about to press Steve to explain when Steve's phone buzzed. It was Jenny. She sounded strange. "Steve, we've got a problem. I've just met with Dean Grantham and a Romanian bloke called Popa. This Popa wants the two girls we picked up or he's threatening to kill both of us."

Steve sat back further in his seat. "Hold on Jenny, you don't sound yourself. Are you all right?"

"Yes, I'm just a bit shocked. He got a gun into the headquarters building and that idiot Grantham just sat there and said nothing."

"You saw Popa with a weapon?"

"Yes. Some sort of automatic."

Steve's mind was racing trying to tie this information to the killing of Lars Jenson. "Do you think he was serious?"

"Oh, yes. He said if I don't take the girls to him tomorrow, we will both be targets. He's definitely serious."

"Jenny, sign yourself out on annual leave. Go home and stay inside. If you're worried, go on a trip. I'm sure we'll have everything wrapped up including this Popa character in a few days, but until then make sure you stay safe. Do you understand?"

"Yes, Steve, and I appreciate the sentiment but this guy's a killer and he's out there."

"Jenny, I've got access to people who can take care of him. Just go on holiday for a few days."

"OK, I see your point."

"Good, now are the girls safe, and have you forwarded their statements to Andy?"

"Yes, they are safe and no, I haven't given Andy their statements yet."

"Do it now. I'm intending to arrest the people at the clinic tomorrow and we'll need those statements to make a murder charge stick."

"Fine. I'll do it this morning but keep me posted."

Jenny suddenly remembered the question she'd been asked previously. "You wanted to know who pushed for Dean Grantham's promotion. It was Deputy Chief Constable Spencer. That's the guy you said you met the day we arrested Dean."

"Interesting, thanks, Jenny. Now off you go. Keep your head down."

"Right." Jenny hung up.

***

Steve and The Cap continued their journey in silence. Although the atmosphere inside the car was strained it gave Steve time to think. Before he could organise his thoughts, his phone sounded again.

"Steve, it's Patrick. My boys didn't spot a white Cortina yesterday nor did they take any registration numbers of the cars going into the estate. Sorry."

"Yeah, me too." Steve didn't hide his frustration. He explained that if the MI6 officers had recorded the registration numbers of those attending his inauguration, then they could have tracked those Disciples and at least identified a fair few of the fifty-one who had been recruited.

Steve explained it was standard police operating procedure and suggested MI6 officers needed to go on a course.

Sir Patrick agreed he wasn't impressed and knew his organisation had slipped up. "When this is all over, I'll arrange for a complete retraining programme but let's put this to bed first before the Prime Minister has a heart attack. Everything else can wait. Keep me in the loop."

Steve decided to keep Andrei Popa's threats to himself for now. He needed time to think and figure out a way of avoiding Professional Standards and get his team back on his side and trusting him. He realised it would not be an easy task.

Chapter Twenty-Nine

When the two detectives walked into the office, Andy and Twiggy were deep in conversation. When Andy saw Steve, he broke off his discussion with Twiggy who in turn waved a welcome to Steve and Abul. Steve had no idea why Twiggy was here but knew he'd soon find out.

Andy went to his desk and fired up his laptop. "Steve, I checked firearms licences, and nobody connected to Eclipse Medical has a weapon, at least not a legal one."

"It was worth a try. What about the white Cortina?"

"I checked with DVLA. There are over three thousand MK3s still registered. I broke them down by post codes and taking in London, Kent, Berkshire, Buckinghamshire and Essex there are eleven hundred and two out there. I checked with the classic car club thinking their members' cars wouldn't be described as bangers so we could eliminate them. They have three hundred and sixty spread across the five areas. That leaves seven hundred and forty-two possible. Sorry Steve but without a registration number there's not a lot more we can do."

"Not to worry Andy. Did you tee up Tech Support?"

"Yes. Inspector Harvey said as soon as you're ready."

Steve gave the discs to Andy. "You crack on. We're looking for a white Cortina entering the Jenson estate anytime yesterday. We'll be along in a few minutes." Steve knew Twiggy was there for a reason.

The Cap, who was still in a mood because of Steve's apparent inability to trust him, left with Andy to review the CCTV images.

When Steve moved into his own office Twiggy joined him and took a seat on the visitor's side of the desk. They passed pleasantries until Twiggy worked up to the reason she was there.

"I've gone through the accounts and bank records for Eclipse Medical. I told you about the discrepancies and basic schoolboy attempts at covering up the false accounting. I got to wondering why a sophisticated operation like Eclipse would employ such obvious tactics."

Steve was all ears. Twiggy was here for something. "Go on."

"When I traced the payments from what we think are the recipients of the organs they all seem correct and go through AEB Bank. The amounts of course never appear within the payments section of Eclipse Medical accounts nor are there any corresponding invoices. Everything regarding these payments is false."

"OK, I understand so far, but didn't you already tell us this?"

"Yes and no. I hadn't looked at these specific payments until you asked me to find out who the recipients of the organs were. Andy's got the list by the way. There are thirty-seven names on it."

"Good."

"As I dug deeper and spotted these movements, I put pressure on that prick Roger Lamb at AEB. At first, he denied all knowledge, but eventually, he admitted to a secondary account. Of course, he was adamant a secondary account wasn't illegal, and Robbie Symonds was a signatory on both accounts." Twiggy tried to sit back to cherish the moment. The best she could do was shuffle from side to side.

"The secondary account is in the name of 'The Transplant Clinic' It's registered in Jersey and has one director."

"Go on." Steve was sitting forward.

"Robert Symonds set it up nine months ago and has been syphoning funds into this account regularly. So far, he's shifted over three hundred thousand pounds into his own account but that's not the whole story. The account has just under five hundred pounds in it as of this morning. It seems as fast as money goes in it goes out again and always to a bank in the Caribbean. The receiving account is a property developer." Twiggy smiled an all-knowing smile.

"I just thought, with the murder of Lars Jenson, whether this might be a motive. If Jenson found out Symonds was robbing him blind and confronted him... well, you know. He might have had to kill him to stop from being exposed." Twiggy was proud of her detective work and her analysis. She crossed her arms under her enormous chest but couldn't hold them there. She rested her hands on her lap.

"That's not bad Twiggy. You know, if I didn't know you were a pen pusher in the Treasury, I might recommend you for the Met as a detective." Steve smiled but was thinking of how this information might impact the murder of Lars Jenson.

With difficulty, Twiggy stood up. "I'll keep digging. I hear Professional Standards are after you. Anything I can do?"

"Afraid not. If I'm going to get out of this, I need to solve what I'm working on but thanks, you're a star."

"Yes, I am." Twiggy giggled. "Thanks to Alison I've lost three pounds in two days. If this keeps up, I may be the star at your wedding."

Steve had another vision but didn't share it with Twiggy. He filed away the analysis she had just given him. It made sense, but only if they could place Robbie Symonds at the scene after midnight. Maybe the CCTV would help.

***

When Steve arrived at Technical Support's lavish viewing room, the CCTV images were playing. Terry Harvey, the main man, was there stopping and starting the disc on command. Andy asked Inspector Harvey to stop the disc and asked Steve to sit. He then asked Terry Harvey to rewind so his boss could see what they'd found.

Steve sat back and watched. He saw the gate into Lars Jenson's estate was closed. The time tag was 15.07. The images moved forward until the time tag read 15.33. He saw the gates opening and a car leaving. He was surprised to note the gates didn't close because another car left two minutes later. Again a few minutes after the second car left a third and a fourth left. The gates remained open to facilitate a speedy exit for Lars' guests. Steve saw his own car leave at 15.41.

"Now watch this, Steve." Andy was in charge. "It's coming up now." A few seconds later. "There, see, a white Cortina drives in while the gates are open, and a load of cars are leaving at the same time."

Steve noted the Cortina arrived at 16.07.

Andy had Terry hold the frame.

"So that's how he got in! Everyone was too busy leaving to notice the odd car going the other way. Where were the security guards?"

The Cap spoke up. "I've already spoken to the one we saw earlier. It seems at four p.m. they have their break. No one monitors the gate between four and four-thirty and as he said, the guests were leaving, so any security threat was diminishing."

"Thanks, Cap, can we get the plate number or a visual on the driver?"

There was silence and an air of disappointment.

Andy took up the narrative. "Sorry, sir. Negative to both. All we've got is the car has been undercoated with black paint. Because it's white you can see where the painters missed the line and painted it too high up on the sill. But that's it."

"Carry on, Andy." The images resumed and sped forward until they saw the same white Cortina leaving. Steve and Abul had already seen this. They were no further forward except they knew how and when the Cortina, possibly driven by the killer, had arrived and left.

Steve thanked Inspector Terry Harvey for once again helping out. He called The Cap and Andy to him.

"Look, I've got to remain invisible for a while. Let's meet outside at the Costa down the road in ten minutes. We've got some planning to do but not here."

The three detectives found a corner table well away from prying eyes and ears.

"Look Steve, I appreciate you've got something going on, and potentially you're in a heap of trouble, but cutting us out doesn't help." The Cap had his opening speech prepared in advance.

Andy knew nothing of what was really going on but knew his boss had taken him into his confidence on a few matters, so he stayed silent.

Steve mused things over. "Look Abul, I keep telling you I won't bring you in until I know it's safe. All I can say is that we're dealing with something way above our level and it's important. I think, if we deal with the two cases, we have on the go now, everything will wash out, and I'll be able to bring you both in together with Twiggy. Please don't push it, OK?"

The Cap was disappointed and showed it. He didn't want to appear to be truculent, but he felt his boss was being unfair. He knew he had no choice but to go along with it, but he wasn't happy.

Steve got down to business. "First off, the murder of Lars Jenson. Here's what we've got, and I'll fill you in on some things you may or may not know." He looked at The Cap who shrugged but smiled. "Lars

Jenson was shot and tortured this morning between say one and five p.m."
The DCI broke off to remind Abul he was expected at the post-mortem
at four p.m.

"We believe whatever happened started in his bedroom and finished
in his library. Now, something you don't know." Both detectives sat up.
"I believe he was tortured for something that was in his safe. I think our
killer tortured him to get the combination of the safe. Once he had taken
what he wanted out of it I believe he killed Jenson to leave no witnesses."

"Go on then." The Cap was back. "What was in the safe?"

Steve realised he was opening up a little but still had to be a bit
circumspect.

"A book. A very important book that's key to our investigation.
Don't ask any more, that's all I'll tell you for now." Steve drew a deep
breath.

"We believe the killer arrived in a white Cortina and slipped in as
Jenson's lunch guests were leaving. We don't know, but I'm assuming
he hid up somewhere until the early hours." Steve looked directly at The
Cap. "Abul, check with Jenson's security detail. They must have seen
that car parked up on their rounds or saw a stranger moving around. I
don't believe any of the live-in staff are involved so let's find out how
someone hid a car and themselves for up to ten hours."

"Will do. Those security guys didn't seem top drawer." No one
replied.

"That's my working theory, but Twiggy's put another one forward.
It seems a guy who worked for Eclipse Medical was ripping them off and
embezzling money. Her thinking is Jenson found out and confronted him.
Things got out of hand and Jenson was killed. It makes some sense
because the guy is Robbie Symonds. He runs the clinic at Harlow, and he
was the last to leave Jenson's house last night. The torture bit doesn't
make sense, but there's a clear motive. Also, Symonds is short of money.
Andy, do a deep background on the guy. See what comes up."

"Got it."

So, there you have it. We're looking for a white Cortina and a stolen
book. Robbie Symonds might be in the frame but there's nothing to
suggest he did it. His car was seen on the CCTV leaving around eight-
thirty. Basically, we've nothing. Andy, keep looking for the Cortina. I

know it's a needle in a haystack but it's all we've got." Steve drank his coffee.

"Now tomorrow. Andy, has Jenny sent you the statements from the two girls we picked up at Stanstead?"

"Yes."

"Good. Remember Professor Campbell, the pathologist, said if we could prove the two dead girls from Essex had died because they'd had healthy organs removed for profit, then we might get a murder conviction? Well, with the two girls' statements we've got a crack at going for a murder charge." Steve paused for effect. "Tomorrow I'm going to arrest Robbie Symonds and his crew on murder charges, and we'll sort it out with the DPP later. We know what's going on at that clinic and at least we can stop what they are doing even if the murder charge doesn't stick."

"Well, about time Steve, I thought we'd have gone in a while ago."

"You're right Cap we should have, but the timing had to be right and I don't believe we've lost anything."

Steve felt the criticism but couldn't explain to his friend the real reason for the delay was the need to keep Lars Jenson believing Steve was a true Disciple.

"I've got an appointment at the clinic tomorrow courtesy of Alison. She's got a patient going there tomorrow, and I'm going with her supposedly just for the ride.

I'll check the place out as best I can and when I'm ready I'll call you and the cavalry in. We'll need a team and enough vans to cart off say, twenty people. Cap, you can set it up. Use as many uniforms as you think you'll need. We'll also need a search team to gather up any documents we find. I only want a maximum of five minutes from when I call you to come in so park up close by. I'm supposed to be there with Alison at ten-thirty, so allowing for pleasantries and so on, you should be in position by eleven. Any questions?"

Andy put his hand up. "Am I in on this, Steve?"

The DCI looked at Abul. "What do you think Cap? Can our boy be on the raid?" The Cap liked to tease Andy. "No, he's not big enough or ugly enough, but I suppose he could get the coffee when we're finished."

Andy looked at The Cap and laughed. He knew he was on the job. "Well sir," he addressed Detective Inspector Ishmal, "I'd check your coffee before you drink it."

The atmosphere between the three was almost back to normal.

"One last thing, Abul. Don't talk to anyone at Chelmsford HQ and don't ask them for manpower. I can't explain now but I will later. Clear?"

The Cap looked confused but nodded.

"What about the Hackney trial? That started today and we're all slated to give evidence."

"It usually takes the lawyers the first three or four days to get things moving. If they wanted us, we would have had a call. Let's keep going until we hear something." Steve knew how courtroom barristers worked.

As he sat drinking his coffee Abul suddenly said, "Oh, blast, I've got the post-mortem at four p.m." Nobody commented but his colleagues nodded in sympathy. Attending post-mortems wasn't the best job in the Metropolitan Police Force.

The three officers finished their coffee. To dodge Professional Standards, Steve declared he was leaving early, and he'd see his colleagues tomorrow at the clinic.

He headed for Alison's house. They'd decided to have dinner in a new Indian restaurant and Alison had booked. Steve didn't know whether or not to tell his fiancée about his plans for tomorrow. He knew she'd be angry if he didn't tell her, but he also knew he needed her to be her natural self to put Robbie Symonds at his ease. Steve decided to see how the evening's conversation developed.

***

From his car, Steve called Sir Patrick. "I'm going to arrest Robbie Symonds tomorrow and all of the clinic staff I can. We've come up with a theory that Robbie Symonds might be our man, but it doesn't sit right. Did your agents report anything unusual?"

"No. We've had eyes on him every hour since we agreed to monitor all the Eclipse people. Hold on." Sir Patrick was gone a minute and was back "He left Jenson's place last night after eight-thirty and went straight home. He has an apartment in the clinic. He didn't leave again last night and so far, today he's still there. I doubt he's your murderer."

"I think you're right. Can you leave your guys on him till lunchtime tomorrow? It should all be over and then we can start looking for that Bible with the names. So far all we've got is that Cortina, but we'll see. I'll keep you posted." Steve ended the call and was consciously relaxing. At least tomorrow he'd be doing some real police work and not playing at being a spy.

He'd only gone one hundred yards in slow London traffic when his phone buzzed. "It's Ian Fuller, Jenny's partner."

"Yes Ian, I know who you are. What can I do for you?"

"You can tell me why Jenny's frightened to leave the house. She's just called me and said she's taking a few days' leave and you advised her to take it."

Steve wasn't prepared for this. "That's true Ian, we're involved in a very delicate case and I think it's better if Jenny were away from the office for a few days."

There was silence on the line. The voice that returned was very quiet and concerned. "Steve, she's not in any danger, is she?"

"No Ian, I wouldn't let anything happen to her. Trust her and everything will be fine." As Steve said the words, he hoped he was right. Ian Fuller appeared satisfied and hung up.

They'd set events in motion and with luck two deaths would be solved. No one knew what would happen tomorrow, but nobody could have envisaged what was to come.

Chapter Thirty

The journey to Alison's was slow. For some reason, the traffic was heavier than it should have been in the middle of the afternoon. Eventually, he arrived and let himself in. Alison was in her consulting rooms below the living quarters. Steve knew she'd be up when she had seen her last patient.

He made a cup of coffee and sat. This was the first free time he'd had to consider the implications of recent events. He was tired and found the caffeine helped but he resisted the temptation to take notes.

He realised now that Lars Jenson wasn't around there might be a power struggle to replace him, or the whole syndicate might just fold. It was something he'd have to keep on top of if he was to retrieve the book. He thought about tomorrow. By arresting Symonds and his staff, he'd blow his cover with the syndicate. But did it matter? He agonised over whether to call off tomorrow's operation, but the policeman in him wouldn't allow it. Symonds was guilty of murder or at least manslaughter and had to be brought to justice. By closing the clinic down Steve wondered if he'd stop the supply of illegally harvested organs for transplant. On one level he could see that despite the illegal nature of the organ harvesting there was some good being done and that people were benefitting from this. On another level, it was wrong because it only helped those individuals who could pay. After a few minutes of mental gymnastics, he concluded this was a moral question and not best answered by a policeman. His job was to enforce the law.

As he drank his coffee, he decided that by tomorrow he would close the two suspicious Essex deaths case. His dilemma now was satisfying Sir Patrick Bond. He'd agreed with Sir Patrick to help and effectively spy on the Syndicate. Even the Prime Minister was involved so it was important. But what had he achieved apart from alienating his colleagues and landing himself in hot water by releasing Dean Grantham on bail, despite the evidence against him, and locking up Dean's brother who was only involved as an accessory? He remembered the threat to himself and Jenny. Before meeting Sir Patrick, none of this would have happened.

Steve would never have bent nor broken the rules. He now questioned if it were all worth it. Now the Master was dead and the list of Disciples missing.

Steve thought the whole Syndicate thing was disturbing, and the people concerned needed to be outed but how. Without the list it was impossible and now he had another murder and no real clues as to the killer. His brain was wandering and overloaded with information he couldn't process. Slowly his eyes became heavier and he fell into a deep sleep.

***

He woke to hear low music being played and the room lights dimmed. His shirt was wet and stained where he'd spilt his coffee as he'd drifted off to sleep. He rubbed his eyes and sat up. Alison was sitting opposite him on the sofa with a magazine in her hands. "You're back with me then?" Alison put her magazine down and looked fondly at her fiancé.

"What time is it?"

"Well, my darling, it's not quite Tuesday but in another hour it will be. You've been out for hours."

"What about the restaurant?"

Alison gave a loud chuckle. "As a detective, you'll have surmised that as you have been sleeping for hours we didn't go." She enjoyed teasing Steve. In a gentler voice, she said, "Don't worry, I rang and cancelled. It was obvious you were exhausted, so I let you sleep. Do you want anything before we go to bed?"

Steve wasn't sure if he had any sleep left in him, but he was still feeling a bit groggy. "No, I think I'll just let a medical lady I know soothe away my troubles and lull me to sleep."

They both stood up, Steve put his arm around Alison, and they moved into the bedroom. "Remember we should leave around eight-thirty tomorrow to get to Harlow." Steve hadn't told Alison of his plans for tomorrow.

***

The journey to Harlow was uneventful. Alison and Steve passed the time talking mainly about their wedding plans and the minute detail such events demanded.

Alison's patient was making her own way and would meet her there.

They pulled into the car park at the rear of the large Edwardian house at exactly 10.22. As Steve got out, he spotted a white Cortina MK3 with a black undercoat painted along the sills of the body. Trying not to show his excitement, he escorted Alison through the main entrance and made an excuse he'd left something in the car. He called Andy. "I've just spotted what I think is our Cortina." He gave the registration number. "Do a PNC check, and let's see who it's registered to. Call me back." The DCI hung up.

His mind was back where it was last night. If Robbie Symonds had access to this car, then was he the killer? Steve knew there were loopholes in this theory, but it needed examining. He joined Alison in the reception area where she was talking to her patient.

***

Just as Andy was asking for the PNC check on the Cortina, Andrei Popa was entering the drive up to the clinic. He drove to the rear as previously instructed by the 'zana', parked and sat thinking. His hangover this morning wasn't as bad, but he and Dean Grantham had enjoyed the company of several ladies last night and had spent a lot of money on cheap imitation champagne. As before, some kindly club proprietor had organised taxis and Andrei had woken fully clothed on top of his hotel bed.

Dean had called him at eight-thirty with the news Lars Jenson had been murdered. The pair discussed the implications, but Andrei thought it made no difference.

"Get that girl policeman. She knows where our two missing girls are." Andrei was in no mood for small talk. "Call me when you've got her."

He sat on his bed and thought the news about Jenson probably warranted a call to Bucharest.

"Boss it's me, Lars Jenson's been murdered. What do you want me to do?"

Luca Radu thought for a minute. "Have you found the girls?"

"No, not yet but that idiot Dean Grantham is chasing down the copper who knows where they are. I should have them today."

"Good, but I don't like this murder. It'll give the police a reason to crawl all over our operation." Silence. Andrei bided his time. "That doctor at the clinic. He's supposed to be second to Jenson. Go and see him and find out what he knows and remind him, as far as we're concerned, it's business as usual. I've got too much invested." Luca Radu abruptly hung up.

Andrei went down to his car and set the sat nav for Eclipse Hall once again. On arriving he left his car and made for the entrance but didn't ask to be shown to Robbie Symonds. He knew where his office was.

Chapter Thirty-One

Robbie had come out to greet Alison and her patient. He introduced them both to one of his colleagues. It was the American surgeon with no licence to practice in the States nor in fact anywhere in the world. The American took his patient off to be examined and Robbie volunteered to show Alison the clinic.

Steve stood to one side and listened to the exchanges. He wondered if Robbie had heard of Lars' demise or whether, as the killer, he already knew. His demeanour was outwardly calm and normal. He spotted Steve. "Steve, Alison said you might come along. Do you want the tour or are medical matters beyond you?"

In a different environment, Steve would have punched this pompous idiot on the jaw. He decided to ignore the insult by saying nothing. Out of the corner of his eye, he saw Alison draw a deep breath hoping Steve wouldn't retaliate.

"If you'd rather, you can wait in my office, we'll only be ten minutes or so." Robbie motioned with his arm and directed Steve to his office door. "Make yourself comfortable; we won't be long."

Steve saw the look on Alison's face. It said, 'be good and don't rock the boat'. Little did she know. That was exactly why Steve was here. The office was large by any standards and had an ornate desk positioned in the bay window looking out over the manicured gardens. Steve noted the old-style French doors opened out to give immediate access to the gardens, and a series of benches strategically placed to get the best of the sunshine. There were large oil paintings of various scenes on the walls and the pale blue carpet set the room off giving it a wealthy and luxurious feeling.

As Steve sat down on one of two long brown leather sofas that faced each other the office door opened, and a large burly man strode in as though he owned the place. He looked surprised to see Steve sitting on the large sofa and annoyed not to see Robbie Symonds. For a second the newcomer seemed not to be too sure what to do. Eventually, he closed the door and walked towards Steve.

Without any introductory small talk, Andrei asked if Steve knew where Robbie Symonds was.

"He's in the clinic but he should be back in a few minutes." Steve was being helpful. "Can I ask who you are?"

"You can ask, my friend, but I don't have to answer."

This wasn't the reply Steve had expected. The large newcomer took a seat on the same sofa as Steve but at the opposite end. Nonetheless, his arrival caused Steve to move further into his own corner of the sofa. The pair sat in silence.

Steve's phone buzzed. It was Andy with the name and address of the registered keeper of the Cortina.

Steve thought about engaging the stranger in conversation but his slightly accented English gave him pause. Could this be the Romanian that threatened Jenny? The DCI thought it was possible given the links to the clinic. He'd better be cautious with this man.

Almost ten minutes of silence passed before Robbie and Alison returned. As they entered, they were deep in an animated discussion about how wonderful the whole place was and how much it had cost to set it up. Alison really thought it was state of the art and was excitedly telling Robbie.

It took a few seconds for Robbie to realise he had another visitor. "I see you two have met." He wasn't sure he wanted these two to meet but here they were.

"No, we haven't; your guest didn't want to say who he was." Steve made light of it.

Andrei was in no mood for English manners. "I have to speak to you. Lars Jenson is dead; please have these people leave."

On cue, Alison sat on the same sofa between Steve and Andrei with Steve on her right. She was telling this rude man that she wasn't leaving. Robbie seemed not to know what to do.

Robbie sat on the sofa opposite the three who were now sitting equally spaced opposite him. "Let me introduce you all." He pointed to Alison and Steve and told Andrei who they were. He similarly introduced Andrei to the engaged couple as a business colleague from Romania.

Silence fell on the room and the atmosphere became more oppressive. Alison felt uncomfortable. Despite the obvious animosity caused by Robbie's introductions, Andrei needed to move things along. He was in the presence of the man who was responsible for his visit to England. The man he'd vowed to kill or harm if the girls were not returned. He was in the right place to keep his promise, but first, he needed Robbie's attention.

Similarly, Steve knew from Andy who Andrei was and his reputation. He'd also made the connection between the supply of donors, Lars and Robbie's clinic, the money and Romania. He was also aware of what this gangster had threatened.

Both men were in a dilemma. Neither wanted to call the other out but they both realised for different reasons they couldn't just sit there.

Alison felt the tension. She tried to lift it. "Well, Mr Popa, have you seen the facilities in the clinic? Aren't they're wonderful?"

"Lady, it was our money that built this place, but for us, it's purely business."

Robbie sprang to life. "Hold on, Andrei, it was Lars who put up the capital to build this clinic."

Steve thought it was interesting that Robbie was defending the dead man.

Steve was trying to work out how to get this Romanian thug into handcuffs. He assumed, based on Jenny's description, that he was armed. Steve couldn't risk getting Alison hurt.

Andrei scoffed. "Where do you think he got the money? When he brought his proposal to us, it was Luca Radu, who put up the money and that's why we need to talk in private."

"You can talk freely in front of Steve; he's one of our Disciples."

Alison almost choked not from fear but from humour. She knew Steve had been inducted but neither of them really believed grown men took such clubs seriously.

"Yes, he's right, I'm on your side, but Lars failed to tell me you were in the country. I had no idea." If Steve could engage Andrei in conversation, he might gain an advantage. He decided to play the 'I'm one of you' card.

274

Andrei ignored Steve's attempt to be friendly. He continued his conversation with Robbie. He spat out, "He's the cop that caused us all the problems," while twisting in his corner of the sofa to look at Steve. "He's got the two girls that I have come to take back. His other helper, that tall woman from Essex, knows where they are and Dean Grantham's with her now, so I don't need this guy's help." Andrei didn't know if this was true, but he hoped it was. Steve hoped it wasn't true.

Steve knew it was time to lie. Again. "Look Andrei if you needed the girls, you only had to ask. If Lars were here, he'd tell you, I'm a Disciple just like Robbie."

Andrei scoffed. He didn't believe this cop and he waved away his attempt at cooperation. He knew the detective wouldn't be armed so he had the upper hand. He considered shooting all of them. If he were his own country, he wouldn't have put up with this small talk. Romania was, in his opinion, a more straightforward place to work and get what you wanted. Nonetheless, he carried on in the English way. His conversation was still with Robbie. It was as though Steve were talking to himself.

Steve was about to become official, but Robbie spoke first. "That can't be right, Andrei." Robbie was almost pleading. "It was Steve who arranged to release Dean Grantham as a favour to Lars. No, no you're wrong."

"Listen, I know what I know, but enough of this small talk. You know why I'm here. We want things back to normal and we want our money. Just tell me who's taking over from Jenson so we can arrange things. Everybody's losing money and you need money more than most."

Steve needed to do something, but he wanted Alison out of here first. He nudged her right arm and indicated with a slight movement of his head that she should go. At the same time, he quietly and secretly took his mobile from his pocket and hid it between his hands. He couldn't afford for the Romanian to spot his actions. He intended to call in the troops but wanted Alison out of the room first.

Alison took the hint but had no idea what was going on, although she could put two and two together from the little detail Steve had discussed with her. She thought she'd stay a while longer.

Steve put his phone by his side ready for use. No one spotted him doing it. He decided the time had come to move things along and hoped

Alison would finally get up and go. He knew it was a risk, but he produced his warrant card and showed it to Andrei and Robbie.

In his most formal voice, he started. "I have reason to believe that one or both of you are implicated in the murder of Lars Jenson. Now I'm prepared to give you…"

Alison held her breath and squeezed Steve's left arm. She hadn't expected this and knew she shouldn't be here. She should have taken Steve's hint but didn't know how to leave now. She tried and interrupted Steve's speech. "Excuse me, it seems you gentlemen have things to discuss." She started to rise from the sofa. "I'll just leave you to it."

This ploy would have worked, and Alison would have been out of the room, except at that moment a figure, dressed totally in white, burst into the room through the French window. He was holding a revolver in his right hand and tucked under his left arm was a box that Steve recognised. It was the Bible box from Lars' safe.

Alison was on her feet and ignored the spectacular entrance of the man in white. She took a step towards the door but then stopped in her tracks.

"Sit down, lady." He pointed his gun at Alison who obeyed.

Robbie had spun round in his seat to look at his head of security who appeared to be crying.

"Robbie didn't kill that guy." He was pleading to the room as a whole. "I did, but I did it for *you*, Robbie."

Steve sat up looking for a way to disarm this man in white. The policeman in him asked, "Are you admitting to killing Lars Jenson?"

"Yes, so you see you can't arrest Robbie. I heard you when I was outside." The man in white was crying and screaming at the same time. "You said he was implicated, but he's not, he's innocent. You can't arrest him!"

It was clear this confessed murderer was close to a breakdown. Robbie Symonds looked shocked. "But Mathew, why did you do it?" Robbie spoke softly to this Mathew.

Steve had the name of the owner of the Cortina from Andy. The owner was a Mathew Spink, and Steve knew he was looking at the Cortina owner and he was holding a gun. Steve started to finger his mobile intending to open a line to The Cap. He couldn't chance speaking but if The Cap heard the conversation, he'd put it together and bring in the troops.

At the same time, Andrei started to slowly move his right hand to his back and felt for the grip of his Mauser. He was careful not to make obvious movements. Slowly would do. He hated these English 'zanas'.

Mathew placed the box on the desk but lifted the gun to cover all three people facing him sitting on the large sofa. "I knew you needed money and I knew Lars Jenson had it. You know I'd do anything for you. I love you and I didn't like seeing you having to go begging to that awful man." Mathew was still crying and wiping away his tears with the back of his spare hand. "I thought if I could get you the money, we might set up home together like you promised. You remember the way we talked about it?"

"Mathew, what have you done?"

Steve couldn't see his phone without lifting it. He knew this would be dangerous so decided to leave it. He was content to listen to this confession for now.

"I went to his house yesterday afternoon. I knew you'd be there, so I just drove in. The gates were open, and people were leaving. I hid the car under some trees. I stayed in the car and then just hung around. I saw you talking to this Lars character. I saw the three of you through a window and could hear what you were talking about." He pointed his gun at Andrei who instantly stopped his right hand's slow journey towards his Mauser. "I saw you there as well, but you weren't helping Robbie." Mathew almost spat at Andrei. "You're not his friend!"

Mathew was calmer. "After this fat one had gone," he pointed his weapon towards Andrei, "I heard you shouting at the Lars man. You said you needed money and the other guy wouldn't give it to you." Mathew was still crying although telling his story appeared to be keeping him calmer. "I saw the size of the house he lived in. It was obvious he had money, so I decided to give you a present." Mathew was like a small child telling a story to please his parents. He was actually smiling at the thought Robbie might be happy if he got him some money.

"I waited until he was in bed and there was nobody about. I remembered you'd told me he had a big safe in his library, so I took him there and made him open it." Mathew looked exhausted and slightly mad. He was sweating and his eyes were glazing over.

"There was no money, only that poxy old box with a Bible in it." He again used his revolver as a pointer. "He said not to take it, it was valuable. I offered to swap it for money, but he just laughed. He said it was worth more than money and told me to get out of his house."

Andrei had his right hand on the grip of his Mauser. Steve knew Andrei was armed and knew he'd try something, so he was keeping him in his peripheral vision while listening to Mathew's confession.

Mathew now looked longingly at his friend and lover, Robbie.

Steve stood and Mathew became agitated again.

"Look son, put the gun down. We can sort all this out. Robbie knows you only did it for him, but if you carry on, you'll be locked away and never see him again."

Steve was about to take a pace towards Mathew as his confession continued. It was as though he hadn't heard the DCI.

"I told this guy Lars if I didn't get money, I'd kill him. So…"

Mathew spotted Andrei bringing his gun out. Steve saw it a fraction of a second later and was set to try to stop him using his weapon but before he could react, Mathew fired. He wasn't firing at Steve but was aiming to his left, towards the Romanian. His first shot missed. Andrei's weapon was snagging on his jacket so he couldn't aim it properly. Mathew's second shot, fired immediately after his first, also appeared to miss but his third punched a hole in the dead centre of Andrei's chest.

Steve turned to look behind him to see what had happened. His gaze immediately went to Alison, and he saw a bright-red stain appearing on the front of her blouse. There was another shot, but he didn't take any notice. His whole focus was on Alison. He realised she'd been shot. He held her to him and saw her eyes were closed and her breathing shallow. He cried out. He wished he could turn the clock back. He wanted the love of his life in one piece. He knew something had to be done. He screamed for help. "Somebody, dial 999!" He felt the tears on his cheeks. He wouldn't let her die. He didn't care what was going on in the room. The man in white could kill him but please let Alison live.

Suddenly Robbie Symonds was lifting Alison out of Steve's grasp. "Leave her to me. We'll get her to the theatre."

"No, we need an ambulance, dial 999." Steve was screaming.

Robbie gently explained this was a hospital and he'd take good care of Alison. Then Robbie and another man raised her body and put it on a hospital-style trolley. Later Steve had no recollection of what had happened after he saw the red stain. All he saw was blood.

Alison would be operated on by a murderer. The man he'd come here to arrest. He sank his head in his hands and wept.

After a few minutes, his training kicked in. He *was* a policeman. The logical side of his brain told him Alison had been shot but she was still alive. Robbie Symonds, despite his faults, was reputed to be a fine surgeon and Alison had said the operating theatres in the clinic were state of the art. There was nothing he could do now except pray and clear up this mess.

He looked along the large sofa and saw Andrei Popa sprawled in the corner. His Mauser was in his right hand, but his finger wasn't on the trigger. Steve's brain, operating on a kind of auto pilot, processed Andrei had been shot in the chest and was dead. He stood up, lifted his phone and saw Mathew Spink lying on the floor and a familiar face applying a tourniquet to his left leg. In his detached state, Steve didn't immediately register that the angel of mercy was Jenny Fuller. His muddled brain just accepted her presence but didn't immediately question it.

Steve stumbled out the French door Mathew Spink had used. His brain had enough charge in it to remind him to lift his mobile, speed dial The Cap and call in the troops. He sat on one of the garden benches and stared into space. The Cap and Andy were there now beside him with Jenny Fuller. The squad that The Cap had brought with him were busy doing what they'd come to do, except Robbie Symonds hadn't been arrested. The Cap realising it was a murder scene had called a full scene-of-crime team.

Three hours after calling in the troops Robbie Symonds was still in surgery working on Alison. The team realised Steve was in shock, so no one pressed him on what happened. It would all be explained later. Jenny supplied hot sweet tea for no other reason other than she knew it was good for shock. Steve sat on the benches in the garden sipping his tea while The Cap and Andy set about organising the troops.

Someone, probably Jenny, told him Mathew Spink was in custody.

Steve told himself to snap out of this. He was worried about Alison, but also, he realised getting back to work was the best thing. He gave himself a good silent talking-to. He had to snap back and get things into focus. He was still the senior officer on site and realised he was almost at the end of his mission.

He walked briskly back to the office and there on the desk was the box. He stood for a moment contemplating what he had done to get this book. He slowly lifted the lid and was relieved to see the Bible. After reverently lifting it out he opened the cover using the wide silk bookmark. There was his entry. It seemed as though he'd signed it a long time ago and not less than twenty-four hours ago. He flicked through the other pages and was amazed at some of the entries. He re-boxed the Bible and carried it to his car. His head still wasn't in a good place, but he was making progress.

Steve called Sir Patrick and told him he had the book. Sir Patrick was deeply concerned as he'd heard about Alison and knew how much retrieving the book had cost Steve. He commiserated and hoped Alison would be OK. He had already arranged for a high dependency military ambulance and a full trauma crew to be at the clinic within the hour. He'd organised a private room in St. Thomas' and arranged for the head of surgery to be in attendance on Alison.

Steve was grateful and told Patrick the book was in the boot of his car. Patrick Bond said it would be collected within a few minutes by the MI6 agents who'd been shadowing Robbie Symonds.

There was nothing left to say. The government had the list of potential traitors. In the end, that's what this had all been about. But not the shooting of Dr Alison Mills.

Chapter Thirty-Two

Alison had been in an induced coma for forty-eight hours and was in a private room at St. Thomas'. She was now awake and, although heavily sedated, was going to live. Steve had been at her bedside since she had arrived.

The staff at St. Thomas's were full of praise for the skill shown by Robbie Symonds. It was agreed had he not acted and had the medical facilities not been on hand then Alison would surely have died.

Steve had taken compassionate leave for a few days but was now back at work, comfortable that Alison was going to be OK.

As he walked into his office The Cap, Andy, Jenny and Twiggy were all there. They'd visited Alison after she emerged from the coma and five-minute visits were allowed. They all shared Steve's good news and after the euphoria had subsided, Andy got back to work. "Steve, you've to go to the twelfth floor and see the new Commander. Bowles has gone."

Still a little shell shocked and knowing he wasn't one hundred percent yet the DCI exited the lift and headed for the commander's office. As he entered, the new man was seated behind his desk with his back to the room. Steve couldn't see him so he politely coughed. The chair spun around, and Steve's jaw almost dropped to the floor. The new Commander was Alfie Brooks.

Alfie gave a hearty laugh at seeing Steve's expression and Steve laughed along with him. It felt good to laugh again. "If you're surprised, imagine what *I* feel like, not to mention Mrs Brooks."

The newly appointed Commander stood and came to meet Steve. They shook hands vigorously, Alfie ordered coffee and the pair sat in the two comfortable chairs set off to one side.

"First things first, I've had a visit from a spook called Sir Patrick Bond. He explained everything, so you don't have to concern yourself with Professional Standards. Also, I've had your bagman, DI Ishmal undo the fiasco with Dean Grantham and his brother. I spoke with the CPS and the DPP. No action is being taken as you acted in the public interest. You've had a rough couple of weeks Steve, but you've performed magnificently. I've spoken to the Commissioner and once I knew the full story, I insisted you should be recognised for what you did. Don't tell anybody but there's an MBE on its way in the Queen's birthday list. Call it poetic justice. That scoundrel Bowles was getting it." Both men chuckled.

"Before you go on sir, I'm puzzled. You were retiring and here you are. I'm not knocking it, in fact, I'm really pleased you're here, but what happened?"

"Forget the 'sir'; it's still Alfie." The commander drank his coffee.

"When the spooks got that list there was an immediate council of war at Downing Street, all the top brass. They decided to keep things quiet. You understand, no fuss, no trials, just orchestrated resignations and loss of pensions, withdrawal of knighthoods, peerages and other honours. The only exceptions are those who perverted the course of justice. An appeals court judge is the main one there. We've also got two civil servants on corruption charges but mainly they'll disappear. The list of fifty insurgents — because that's how they're being viewed — is now locked away with a fifty-year gagging order on it but the fifty are now on the MI5 terrorist watchlist." Alfie smiled a satisfied smile.

"I was sent for by the Commissioner the same day as the Downing Street meeting and told I'd be taking over from Bowles; my retirement date had been extended by three years and I'd be briefed by someone from MI6. That was it. It all happened last Tuesday, the day you got the list."

Steve could see how quickly Sir Patrick had acted.

Alfie continued. "Because we know no MI5 people were on the list, trust has returned, and MI6 has handed over to them. They've rounded up most of the names and are putting them through the grinder. It's maybe just as well you don't know all the names on the list of Disciples, but it was very impressive. There was even a Royal." Alfie paused.

"We were all sorry to hear about your fiancée, wrong place wrong time. The surgeon Symonds is in custody, but I think he'll get a lenient sentence. The people at St. Thomas' say he saved Alison's life. He operated on her for just under five hours and by all accounts did a cracking job. It doesn't mean he's not guilty, but a good defence brief should get a decent result."

They finished their coffee. Alfie walked Steve to the door. "If I were you, I'd take your team into your confidence. You've got a couple of good lads there and the DS from Chelmsford is very impressive. I know her old man from way back. She'd make a good addition. Take my advice and tell them the full story. No harm can be done now by them knowing and it's better coming from you."

Steve was grateful to his old mentor and was pleased to have a real policeman in charge.

"Thank you, sir, I'll do that."

***

Outside the commander's office, Steve used his mobile to phone Andy. "Get everybody down to the interview rooms Andy. I've got something to say. See you there in five."

The whole team were waiting in interview room three including Twiggy and Jenny. The custody sergeant was amused that serving officers should use one of his rooms for a meeting but obliged Abul by providing extra chairs. Steve looked at them with pride. He'd trust his life to any one of them and probably just had.

Steve began. "I asked you all to trust me over the past few weeks. I know it's been difficult and confusing and at times I haven't been easy to live with."

The Cap interrupted. "Oh, really sir, I don't think any of us noticed a difference."

As usual, The Cap was making light to keep everyone's spirits up. He was good at it.

"Thank you, Abul. Anyway, I promised to tell you everything when I could, and the time is now." Steve looked at his hands. "I'm going to tell you everything because you deserve to know, but the reason we're here in the interview room is because with that door locked no one can hear us. I've got the key to the observation room before anyone asks. The reason I've been awkward with you all is this is top secret and I need your word not to mention any of it to anyone outside this room."

Everyone was fascinated by what was to come and readily agreed.

Steve started at the beginning with the initial case, the two bodies, the conspiracy of Commander Bowles, the obviously poorly performed post-mortems and how he called in Humphrey Campbell. The approach by Lars Jenson and how this led to his being recruited to help MI6. He told how Sir Patrick Bond had been chosen to unearth the members of the Syndicate purely because he was responsible for overseas operations and was less likely to be a member of the Syndicate. No one, no matter who, was above suspicion.

He went on to explain how the Syndicate and the Disciples worked, and how they intended to replace the democratically elected government. At the time it was impossible to trust anybody especially senior establishment figures. He admitted to having become a Disciple to get closer to the Syndicate on instructions from Sir Patrick. He explained how MI6 couldn't identify who was or wasn't a Disciple and how he was told there must be a list of names and he was best placed to get it.

None of his colleagues interrupted. They were fascinated.

Steve explained they knew about the connection to Romania and the illegal trade in human organs. He told them this was not part of the Syndicate but served to provide funds for it. He told how he'd been inducted and had become aware that the list of names he was looking for was contained within a Bible. When Lars was murdered it was MI6 who tipped him off. He realised when he saw the safe open that the Bible with the list was missing.

"The rest you know. Last Tuesday we went to arrest Symonds, but it all went wrong. I'm a bit vague after Spink fired his weapon…"

"It's OK, Steve." It was Jenny. "After you told me to keep my head down, I went to see my dad. He's much better and more like his old self. I explained about the Romanian and the threats. In typical old copper advice, he told me to get myself tooled up and shadow the Romanian. If I were following him, then he couldn't be a threat to me. I signed out a weapon and staked out his hotel, so that's how I came to be at the clinic."

"Smart bloke, your father." It was Twiggy.

Jenny carried on acknowledging this remark with pride. "I saw that guy in white go into the building with a pistol in his hand, so I followed and listened at the French doors. When the first shot went off, I went in, saw the guy was firing almost blindly so I shot him. I'll admit I wasn't aiming for his leg, but it worked. He dropped the gun and fell down. After that, it was a bit chaotic. I saw Alison was hurt; I heard Symonds shouting for help and a couple of guys came in. Then a trolley appeared, and I saw them take Alison away, and I looked after my wounded victim. I cuffed him, bound his leg and then followed you outside. That's it."

Steve was proud of this team. "Look, guys. I know you were concerned and I'm grateful. Everybody did more than anyone could have asked for. I'm not singling out any one person for praise. It was a team effort." Steve paused. "There I've said it. I'm not one to heap unnecessary praise but you guys are the best and I'm a bit emotional, so this meeting is now over." He looked around and smiled

Then he remembered he was still a DCI and things needed sorting.

"Cap, I understand you sorted out Dean Grantham and his brother?"

"Yes, the new commander briefed me. Dean's been charged with murder and other offences. The DPP think it'll stick. His brother was released with a caution."

Twiggy raised her hand. "Steve, it's only eleven-thirty. What say we all go and surprise Alison. Take her lots of flowers, chocolates, grapes. You name it, we'll go over the top." She looked around the table. "Of course, I'm on a diet so won't eat anything we buy."

The team laughed loudly, the sound echoing around the small room. They didn't care. Subject to Alison getting better all was once again good in their world. Until the next time.

***

Three weeks later, Detective Chief Inspector Steven Burt married Dr Alison Mills in a simple ceremony conducted in a private room within St. Thomas' hospital. The bride wore the only part of her original dress she could, her veil. She was still confined to bed and had to make do. A small party was present including the world's largest bridesmaid, even though she had lost over one stone in weight.

Steve had an appointment at 10 Downing Street the week after his wedding. The Prime Minister thanked him personally on behalf of the nation. Sir Patrick was present and after the meeting suggested Steve might have a future in MI6.

Both men looked at each other and laughed. They knew it would never happen. Steve Burt was a policeman.

THE END.